T0099369

GUMSHOE
ROCK

Also By Rob Leininger

The Mortimer Angel Series
Gumshoe on the Loose
Gumshoe for Two
Gumshoe

Other Novels
Richter Ten
Sunspot
Killing Suki Flood
Maxwell's Demon
January Cold Kill
Olongapo Liberty

GUMSHOE ROCK

A MORTIMER ANGEL NOVEL

ROB LEININGER

OCEANVIEW PUBLISHING
SARASOTA, FLORIDA

Copyright © 2019 Rob Leininger

All rights reserved. No part of this book may be reproduced in any form or by any electronic or mechanical means, including information storage and retrieval systems, without permission in writing from the publisher, except by a reviewer who may quote brief passages in a review.

This book is a work of fiction. Names, characters, businesses, organizations, places, and incidents either are the products of the author's imagination or are used fictitiously. Any resemblance to actual events, businesses, locales, or persons living or dead, is entirely coincidental.

ISBN 978-1-60809-392-2

Cover Design by Christian Fuenfhausen

Published in the United States of America by Oceanview Publishing

Sarasota, Florida

www.oceanviewpub.com

10 9 8 7 6 5 4 3 2

PRINTED IN THE UNITED STATES OF AMERICA

For Rana and Lorna, world-class sisters and friends

ACKNOWLEDGEMENTS

Thanks once again to the entire Oceanview Publishing team for their professionalism and dedication to excellence. And thanks to John Lescroart for his continuing friendship and support.

GUMSHOE ROCK

CHAPTER ONE

ON THE FIRST page of the Internal Revenue Service form for those seeking employment—right after name, address, phone number, social security number, and date of birth—there is a question followed by a yes/no checkbox:

Do you have a soul? Y☐ N☐

Before they look at anything else, they look at those two boxes. If you indicate "y" they quit reading and toss the form, go on to the next. It's a new form. If they'd had it when I started out, I never would have gotten a foot in the door. When I was twenty-five I suspected I had a soul, hadn't given it a lot of thought, but after sixteen years as a field agent for the IRS I knew it for certain, so I got out of the business of state-run thuggery and became a world-famous private investigator.

In training.

* * *

Eleven fourteen p.m. in the Green Room, a bar tucked into a remote corner of Reno's Golden Goose Casino.

As usual, the place was all but deserted, having not yet been discovered and ruined by hordes of raucous Millennials— "Echo boomers." The only other person in the room was a late-middle-aged guy on a stool at the far end of the bar—a gloomy silhouette hunched vulture-like over a drink. He'd been there when the three of us came in. If he hadn't ordered another martini ten minutes ago, I would have thought he'd expired and hadn't yet fallen off the barstool, he was that still.

I had the eerie feeling I knew the guy. He had a celery-stalk neck supporting a small head above bony shoulders. Maybe it was the faint nimbus of evil wafting off him. I'd known evil in the IRS, and afterward, as a PI. Evil was tracking me around like a Yeti hunting meat. I wondered what I'd done in a previous life to deserve it.

Virulent green track lighting above the bar put a faint ghoulish glow on our faces—Lucy, Ma, and me. It might have been the lighting that kept the Echos at bay. The three of us were used to it, but a lot of folks stopped at the entrance and did U-turns. It's hard to look cool and impress a potential pickup with luminous green skin.

Channel Four news was segueing into weather and sports without having run so much as one story about the ongoing and mysterious disappearance of anyone, which meant—

"Dodged a bullet there, boyo," Ma said to me, reading my mind. "No one's missing." She blew a plume of green smoke at the TV above the bar. Ma—Maude Clary—was sixty-two years old, five foot four, something of a fireplug, with a well-deserved reputation as the best private investigator in the state of Nevada. I, on the other hand, was recognized as the preeminent locator of famous missing persons in the entire country. People who, as luck would have it, were either dead but intact, or dead missing body parts, dead being the common denominator there.

"Whew," I said. Beside me, Lucy laughed quietly. She was thirty-one but looked like an eighteen-year-old cheerleader. Or seventeen, which was both frightening and useful, depending. A scar on her upper left arm had been made by a .38-caliber bullet that grazed her three months ago—same revolver that had clipped the top quarter inch off my right ear, blown a hole through my shoulder, and put me in the hospital for five days in Las Vegas.

"Wouldn't have time for anything like that anyway," Ma said, stubbing out the last inch of an unfiltered Camel in a glass ashtray with the Golden Goose logo on it. "We've got two cases, Galbraith and Joss. I had to turn down a guy who runs a motel on East Fourth wanting to find out who's getting into rooms and stealing stuff. Which would've been easy money."

She gave me a sidelong look. "Got that, boyo?"

"Yup. Easy money. No one is missing."

She shook her head, lit up another Camel.

I made her nervous. I was hell on wheels when it came to stumbling across missing people. Last August, fourteen months ago, I found Reno's mayor and district attorney, both missing for ten long days, and acquired the kind of national fame your basic run-of-the-mill PI's can only dream about since the two men had been decapitated and I found their heads. My notoriety was greatly enhanced in that the mayorly noggin had turned up in the trunk of my ex-wife's Mercedes.

Two months later, middle of October, I found the primary shaking part of Senator Harry Reinhart's presidential campaign—his right hand, severed and FedEx'd to me by his loving trophy wife, Julia—which eventually led to his bludgeoned body being discovered fifty feet down an abandoned mineshaft in northern Nevada.

Late June this year I'd come across a dead gangsta rapper by the name of Jonnie Xenon and annihilated the dreams of untold millions of fourteen- and fifteen-year-old girls throughout the country.

The first two capers earned me mixed reviews nationwide, but finding Jonnie-X, known in the tabloids and to teen girls as "Jo-X," sent my approval rating through the roof since he was dead and his lyrics had been as toxic as an upstream mercury-lead-arsenic dump in the Ohio River.

Ma Clary was seated to my left, Lucy Landry to my right. Lucy and I had turned Clary Investigations into a three-person operation. As was often the case, Patrick O'Roarke was tending bar. He wasn't on the team, but he was good for a bunch of free-drink coupons whenever any of us got wounded in the line of duty.

Ten thousand hours of training are required to become a licensed PI in Nevada, which is a bitch of a mandate that weeds out the wannabees by the truckload. Having topped fifteen hundred hours, I was on track to become a fully qualified investigator in another six years, two years shy of my fiftieth birthday.

Lucy was curvy and beautiful, breasts on the small side so she almost never wears a bra, and as flexible as your basic boa constrictor. She could stand on her hands, arch her back, and put the soles of her feet on top of her head. She claimed to be my assistant, which to my mind made her my assistant trainee. To the licensing board, however, she was a full-fledged trainee, not merely my assistant, with four hundred hours of sleuthing under her belt, which meant her degree in Art History was really coming in handy.

So—today's excitement on TV was as follows:

Weather: about what one expects in Reno the last week of September—no rain, patchy clouds, highs in the low to mid-eighties. Sports: the Dodgers were ahead in the National League West, Padres and Giants tied, only one game back, so it was a close one, still anyone's race.

About that time, the scrawny hunchback planted at the far end of the bar slid off his stool and came weaving toward us. He slowed as he got near, stopped behind me, a bit off to starboard.

"Mort? Mort Angel? Is that you?"

Aw, shit. I knew that voice. Pitched a quarter-octave high with a peculiar note in it like someone just starting to strangle a chicken. He was three feet away. I turned. He had on an ugly brown suit that looked as if he'd slept in it the past week.

"It's Mortimer to you, Warley."

My name is Mort Angel. I usually correct anyone who calls me Mortimer, a mistake that ended up on my birth certificate due to my mom's wicked sense of humor or faulty handwriting. But some people don't have the right to call me Mort, Warley being a prime example.

"That right? You changed your name?"

"Nope. It's always been Mortimer to you, Warley. But now I think 'Mr. Angel' is even more appropriate."

That slowed him down for two full seconds. Then: "Well, hell, Angel, this is a doggone nice surprise, running into you like this. First time I've been in the place."

"That's *Mr.* Angel, Warley. Try to remember that."

"Uh-huh. Anyway, it's good to see you. Been a while. We kinda miss you down at the office."

Proper manners and ordinary politeness dictated that I should return the pleasantry. Reality dictated otherwise. "Yeah," I grunted, hoping that would cause him to disappear in a cloud of sulfurous smoke. Of all the people to ruin the ambience of the Green Room, Warley Sullivan, IRS, a man truly lacking a soul, was the worst possible choice now that Manson was dead.

Long fibrous pencil-neck, a beak of a nose that looked like the blade of an ax, six foot two and rail-thin, slender fingers with lumpy knuckles. At the IRS, an organization with no discernible sense of humor, he was known as Ichabod. Two years ago, at an IRS Christmas party—*IRS party* being a world-class oxymoron—Warley bragged that he had forced a recent widow to sell off one of her children, a blond girl seven years old, to pay off eight hundred fifty-four dollars in back taxes along with the inevitable fine and interest. He waited five seconds too long then said, "Joke," slapped his knee, guffawed, and spilled his punch.

Ha, ha. Good one, Warl. Really had us going there. Watch out for lightning.

In fact, that might have been the moment when I realized I had a soul, so, sonofabitch, maybe I owed Warley one.

"And, hey, who might this be?" he said, giving Lucy a long look. "This your daughter? What's her name?"

And he wonders why women avoid him the way they avoid people foaming at the mouth and waving guns.

But Lucy doesn't take shit off anyone, including me. She once hit me in the chest with thirty-six thousand dollars' worth of gambling chips that had recently belonged to the Luxor in Las Vegas, then said something about ripping my heart out. Little bit irate at the time, she was, but she got over it.

She popped off the barstool and poked his pot gut, the size of an eight-pound ham below his sunken chest. "I'm his *wife*, Warley." Little lie there—okay, big—but I let it go because I like my heart right where it is.

"Hey, hey, Mort. Robbing the old cradle, eh?" Warley said, unaware of the proximity of death.

Lucy poked him again. "I'm old enough to be in this bar. He's forty-two. So what? Have you ever seen *Funny Face*?"

His mouth flopped open. "Funny Face? What's that?"

"A movie with Fred Astaire and Audrey Hepburn. They got married at the end, and when that movie was made, Astaire was fifty-eight, Hepburn was twenty-eight. You should try to keep up, even if you're developmentally challenged."

"Fred Astaire . . ."

"I never actually knew him since he died before I was born, but you and he could've been drinking buddies, depending on his tolerance for gloom and boredom. And," she went on, "I've heard you're the troll who delights in terrorizing widows and old people."

Warley smiled. Actually smiled. "Terrorizes, huh?"

"Ugh." Lucy turned away and got back on her barstool. "Totally ugh."

Warley's smile faltered slightly. Then he gave me a closer look and said, "Huh, your *ear*, Angel."

Ah jeez. "*Mr.* Angel. What about it?"

"It's . . . the top of it is missing, isn't it?"

"Is it? I hadn't noticed."

"It is, yeah. I mean, holy Toledo, Mort. That doesn't look like the kind of thing a guy would miss."

In the mirror behind the bar, Lucy mouthed "Holy Toledo?" I eased an arm around her waist just in case.

"So what's the story there, Mort?" Warley said.

"It's Mr. Angel to you. Try to remember that. You ever see those Bennihana commercials, Ginsu knife speed cutting? I was whacking Romaine lettuce, got a little carried away."

"You . . . really?"

In the mirror I saw Lucy's slow smile.

Then Warley noticed Ma, seated on the other side of me. "Well, hey, if it isn't Miz Clary of Clary Investigations. We met a few years back, remember? Fancy meeting you here. You with this

Mort character?" Unable to focus on anything for long, he turned to me again. "Been hearing about you in the news, Mort. Looks like your new job is treating you good, huh? Finding all those . . . well, all those dead people."

"They were suicides. Right after your audits."

"Ho, ho, ho, hee, hee." Warley let it all out in soprano. "Good one, Mort. I gotta use that down at the office."

"*Mr.* Angel to you, Warley. You still there at the IRS?" In fact, I could tell he was by the bad skin, the black light in his eyes, the halitosis, the conspicuous absence of a soul.

"*Hell,* yes." He puffed up, pulled his shoulders back an inch, neck size went up to twelve inches. "I'm the Man, now."

"Wow," Lucy breathed.

"The man?" I said to egg him on.

"Yep. When Soranden disappeared, I was next most senior person in the place. I ran it for a month, but Soranden never turned up so the IRS commissioner himself promoted me. That would be William V. Munson," he said with enough pride and hot air to re-inflate the Hindenburg.

"The Toad disappeared?" I said. To everyone in the office, Ronald Soranden was The Toad, just as Warley was Ichabod.

"Sure did. Second week in July. I filled in, then took over full-time starting August tenth."

I hadn't heard about that, which made sense. Second week of July, I was in the hospital with a drain in my shoulder and a catheter I'm still trying to forget. At the time, a missing cretin in Reno wasn't my first priority. But a missing cretin, especially a local cretin, was right up my alley. Soranden had gone in a puff of smoke? Probably the devil's work. I was sorry I'd missed it.

"Where'd he go? I mean, where'd he finally end up?"

Warley shrugged. "No one knows. Didn't end up anywhere anyone knows. But I've been the head honcho since the tenth of August." He grinned. "The Big Cheese, as it were."

Jesus. Warley was now the "honcho." And that Big Cheese thing was vintage Warley. It was always all about Warley. Ronald Soranden's disappearance was a minor side issue. Warley was one of those leeches who attach themselves to conversations and drain essential fluids.

"Got fifty-four people under me now." Warley put a hand on my shoulder. "It'd be fifty-five if you came back. I'd give you your old desk, old cubicle. Just like old times."

"You shouldn't touch me," I said. "Bat bit me a week ago and gave me rabies. I've still got two shots to go. Doc says I'm no longer contagious, but this afternoon when I coughed, he ran out of the office."

Warley removed his hand as if scalded and backed up a foot.

"So you're in charge of Terrorism R Us," I said.

"Ho, ho, ho, hee, hee. I gotta use that too."

"When Soranden went missing, was there any indication of how or why? No hint of where he might have gone? Suicide note or a ransom demand for ten bucks?"

"Nope. Lucky me, right?"

"Oh, yeah. Lucky you. Bet that made your day."

Warley Sullivan's smile was a show of yellow-green teeth under the lighting. "It made my entire *month*. Fact is, it's been a hell of a good year. As Head of Office I get an extra eighty-one hundred thirty-six dollars and forty-seven cents per annum."

"Crossing over the River Styx is gonna be a bitch, Warl. I hear it has a *hell* of a heat problem and the air-conditioning is always on the fritz."

He gave me a blank look. "Hah?" Then in typical Warley non-sequitur fashion he said, "Say, you find people, don'tcha?"

"As you've already noted, I've found my share. More than, if you must know."

"You oughta find . . . or, well, maybe not . . . I mean, if you did, maybe with some of these new tax laws, he wouldn't be up for taking back his old job . . ."

It was like conversing with a bottom feeder as it scavenges for decomposing meat. I'd been trying to enjoy a Pete's Wicked Ale, but it was starting to sit in my stomach like acid.

Warley turned back to Ma. "It's been a while, Miz Clary. I never forget an audit. What was it? July, five years ago?"

"That's right. Do you remember the results of those audits you never forget?"

"I sure do. You . . . well, you were . . . uh . . ."

"Overpaid my taxes. So busy I forgot to include a bunch of business expenses. You spent six hours scrambling all over my office, and the IRS ended up owing me four hundred fifty-three dollars and nineteen cents. Good job. *Warl.*"

He stared at her, numb.

Ma gave him a look that would kill gophers. "Maybe you can tell me why the IRS doesn't pay penalties and interest on the money they overcollect."

"We, well . . . we, uh, couldn't do that."

"Don't have the money or don't have the integrity? Which is it?"

He blinked. Twice. Then, "See you around, Mort, huh?"

"Mr. Angel. And not here, Sullivan."

He hesitated. "Huh?"

"This has been an IRS-free zone ever since an IRS guy out of Tucson was tracked down, shot, and killed in here by a guy who'd lost his house, job, wife, golden retriever. The IRS even took his white picket fence and sold it on eBay."

Warley's eyes lit up. "You mean a *tax dodger*. Sometimes they go off the rails like that."

"The IRS guy ended up with five bullets in his head, one of which, against all odds, actually hit his brain. I'm just saying, Warley, this might not be your kind of place. Bad luck tends to stick around places where violence has occurred."

"Well . . . you come here a lot?"

"First time ever. The three of us took a vote. We don't care for the green. I doubt we'll ever be back."

Warley looked up at the track lighting. "I hadn't noticed, but now that you mention it . . ."

"I prefer the Oasis, down at the Atlantis. IRS guys don't get bumped off there. We might see you there from time to time."

"Oasis, huh? Okay. Good to know."

He left, looking a little unsteady on his feet. Out the door. Gone. Good riddance.

"Oasis?" Lucy said. "Place we'll never go, right?"

"Yup. It's too busy, too bright, and I just gave it a dose of social strychnine."

* * *

"Oh, no," Lucy said. "No, no, noooo." She ran over to her car making sounds of anger and dismay.

We'd left Ma at the Green Room and gone up to the second floor, across the skyway to the Golden Goose parking garage. We had driven over earlier in Lucy's Mustang convertible. Now the top was slashed, big rip across the top over the driver's seat, a gash big enough to drop a basketball through.

"Aw, shit," I said. Goddamn vandals out getting their kicks on a Friday night. The damage would run seven hundred bucks to fix right or two dollars' worth of duct tape to fix wrong.

I had the keys since I had driven over. As it turned out, that was preordained, since *I,* not Lucy, opened the driver's-side door and was therefore the one who found the gleaming skull leering up at me from the driver's seat.

Me.

Finding parts of dead people again.

Really dead.

CHAPTER TWO

BUT IT TOOK a while for me to get there. A skull? Seriously? My first thought was it was glow-in-the-dark plastic. A joke. Ha, ha. Buy one at Walmart. A pre-Halloween gift, four weeks early. It was bone white, which sort of figured, but it looked too clean and white to be real, and no one expects a real skull. Ever.

I picked it up.

Whoa.

Heavy. So—not from Walmart since their stuff is cheap. It didn't have that slick plastic feel. It felt slightly grainy. I put it back on the seat.

"What'd you find?" Lucy asked from behind me.

"A skull."

"A *skull*?" She elbowed me to one side and stared in at it. "Seriously? Some dimwit lowlife slashed my roof to drop that stupid thing in my car?"

I picked it up and gave it to her. She hefted it, then handed it back, wiped her hands on her jeans. "Ick."

"Ick?" I hefted it again.

"It's . . . it feels . . . you know. Kinda real."

And, of course, it was. When I held it up and got more light on it, I even knew whose it was. Or whose it once was, now that the previous owner had entirely vacated the premises.

* * *

Depending on how bold or snarky editors had become, the lead paragraph in the *Reno Gazette-Journal* story might read that the head of the Head of Northern Nevada's IRS office had been found at last, literally. Maybe they wouldn't go that far since the rest of him was still missing—so, fifty-fifty odds on that.

Ronald Soranden hadn't smiled often, a basic requirement of IRS employment—not smiling, since it would give the wrong impression—but on those rare occasions when he had, his smile revealed a gap in his upper incisors big enough to hold a number two pencil. The late Terry Thomas had had nothing on our man Soranden. It was said that The Toad could flick his tongue out through that gap in his teeth. Also, Soranden's left incisor was badly chipped and the right incisor was discolored. The effect was similar to identification by fingerprints. Call it a skull print or tooth print. However that would go, this hunk of bone was once the very personal property of Ronald Soranden, missing, according to Warley, since the second week of July.

Having made that identification, I set Ron back where I'd found him and wiped my hands on my jeans, just as Lucy had.

"Soranden," I said.

"You know this guy? I mean . . . knew him?"

"Worked with him. He was my boss at the IRS. Top man in the office. More or less a satanic shithead. The guy Warley told us had disappeared."

"Oh, great. Now we're gonna get audited for sure."

* * *

Which might put us in contact with Warley Sullivan again. Just my luck. Soranden wasn't coming back, not that I would miss him, but Warley was *The Man* now, and the one glaring flaw of the Peter Principle was that those above him who had risen to the level of their incompetence would, as a result of that incompetence, promote Warley two or three levels beyond the level of *his* incompetence. Call it the enhanced Peter Principle.

In life, Ron Soranden had been five-six, two hundred fifty pounds, surly, given to favoritism to a select few of those below him as long as they regularly kissed his ass and didn't pose a threat, obsequious to those above when they happened to drop in from the West Coast Internal Revenue Center in San Francisco, or were one of the big guns in from D.C. Bald as an egg, with close-set squinty eyes behind Coke-bottle glasses, damp rosebud lips—now missing—Soranden was the quintessential IRS goon, which, unlike an FBI agent, was something that squatted behind a desk and had the power to grab property and ruin lives without a trial, lawyers, or a court system, none of the foolishness that might slow down or even terminate an overzealous and illegal government operation. In 1941, Soranden might have sat at a desk at Dachau, smiling to himself as he made out lists.

Okay, that's dark. But Dachau was a dark place, and Nazis found people willing to run it, and the IRS finds people willing to grab Uncle's reins and go, so there's that. I still have old IRS dreams that cause me to wake up in a cold sweat.

But now I had to give the good news to my buddy at Reno Police Department, Detective Russell Fairchild. I'd done a job for him earlier that year and wound up protecting his daughter, Danya, from what would have been a slam-dunk murder charge if all the facts had come to light. That had put Russ in my debt, and therefore in my pocket. In fact, we had the goods on each other, so our working relationship was a bit unusual for a homicide detective and a PI-in-training. According to him, my best qualities were that I was a maverick and unprofessional.

I pulled out my cell phone. Got him at home and sound asleep since it was now pushing midnight.

"Whozis?" he answered groggily.

"Your favorite PI, Russ."

"Aw, no. *Now* what?"

"Got a live one for you . . . well, not a *live* one, not in the sense civilians use it, but it's something you might want to get on soon, not that I think there's a big rush. An EMT would really be at sea with this one since chest compressions wouldn't be an option—"

"What the *hell*, Angel."

"Call me Mort, now that you're in my pocket. Lucy and I are in the parking garage at the Goose." I looked around. "Third floor, east side. You can't miss us."

"And I want to come all the way over there, why?"

"Got something that's right up your alley, Russ. You like talking into microphones on TV, answering reporters' questions, don't you?"

I hung up.

"Cool," Lucy said. "He'll be here in like half a minute."

"In his skivvies, or not even that?"

"Okay, maybe not. Hope not, anyway." She crouched down and looked Soranden in the eye or would have if he'd had eyes. "You sure this is that guy?"

"Take a closer look, kiddo. It's not *all* of him. Not even Weight Watchers is that good, but, yes, it used to be a critical part."

She looked up at me. "You're always like that, aren't you?"

"Pretty much. Can't help it."

"I would still marry you within two hours if you ask."

Same thing she'd told me earlier that summer in Tonopah, less than an hour after we met. That was the first of July, and it was only the twenty-eighth of September now.

"Even though you were recently buried alive and got hit by a bullet, for which I take full responsibility?" I said.

"The bullet only nicked me, and getting buried wasn't your fault, so, yeah, ask me to marry you and I'll drive us to a twenty-four-hour chapel, get us hitched up *mosso*."

Reno. Gotta love this place. "Mosso?" I asked.

"That's music-speak for fast."

Married to Lucy. I could think of worse things. In fact, I couldn't think of many better things. But this PI gig was nothing like what my nephew Greg had told me it was. When I first escaped the IRS and became a PI trainee at his firm he told me private investigation wasn't exciting, that it was dull, plodding work, plowing through records, phone embedded in an ear, nothing to make the heart race. Three days later, I found his decapitated head on his desk in his office. Third head in as many days. Since then, I've nearly been killed three times in the line of duty, and my fiancée, Jeri, was murdered by a psychotic lady we were tracking, so I was leery about Lucy getting into the business. I was having second thoughts about staying in it myself. I think it would be better all around if people would quit trying to kill us.

"What's *that*?" Lucy asked. She was crouched beside the Mustang looking in at Soranden's primary head bone.

"What's what?"

"This." She pointed to something dark on the driver's seat. Three somethings. I took a closer look.

Ants. Big sons of bitches, too. Dark brown, over an inch long.

"Ants," I said.

"*That* big? Where the hell'd they come from? They're not alive, are they?"

I poked one with a finger. "Not alive, and, best guess, they were rattling around inside Soranden's otherwise empty skull."

"Oh, great."

My thought exactly. I got a Kleenex and picked up the ants, wrapped them loosely, and said, "Open your purse, kiddo."

"What? Oh. O-o-oh, no. Not in *my* purse, Kimosabe."

"Yup. Open up."

She did, not happy about it, but I reminded her that she was a gumshoe-in-training and this was part of it.

"Part of it how?" she asked.

"Gathering evidence. Goin' with the flow."

"You mean tampering with evidence. Which means now I am. We might end up in San Quentin."

"Which is an all-boys institution, so you're out. Okay, we'll leave one for the fuzz." I put one back on the seat, kept two—one for us, one for Ma since she could use a proper paperweight. "You good now?"

"Not really. I've still got two giant ants in my purse."

"Don't let them out of your sight."

Finally, Russ showed up. He had the behemoth in tow, so the Force was out in force. The behemoth was Officer Clifford Day, Russ's ex-brother-in-law, all six feet six inches, three hundred thirty-five pounds of him. He'd gained another five pounds since mid-July, working his way toward four hundred.

"What's the story?" Russell asked as he and Cliff ambled toward us from where he'd parked his Ford Explorer, forty feet away. Day fired a finger-gun at me as they drew near, as if to remind me that he'd sat in the back of Russell's Explorer that summer and kept me from bleeding to death while Ma drove me to a hospital in Vegas at a hundred miles an hour. Which meant I owed him one. Not sure how to pay something like that back. Maybe chocolates or a decent bottle of wine.

"In the Mustang," I said. "Which is Lucy's car, not mine," I added. "Just sayin'."

"Gee, thanks." Lucy bounced an elbow off my ribs, then got up on tiptoe and brushed my lips with hers.

"Aw, jeez," Russ said, which is what he says around Lucy when she looks eighteen and kisses me.

He looked into her car, did a standard Looney-Tune double take, then looked up at me. "What the hell is that?"

"It might be a what, but I tend to think of it as a who. That is Ronald Soranden."

"Who's that?"

"Head IRS honcho in Northern Nevada who went missing sometime in July. Which, by the way, I just found out."

"You're kidding." He stared at me. "You're not kidding."

"Nope. Really, I just found out."

He gave me a police-look. "That ain't what I meant. This thing's real? It's a real skull?"

"Hell of a fake if it isn't, Russ. Pick it up."

"Jesus. And you think you know who it is?"

"Head of the head of the IRS. Local. Ronald Soranden."

He stared at me, then shook himself. "Sonofabitch. You didn't pick it up, did you?"

"Both of us did."

"Well, shit, Angel. Fingerprints?"

"We didn't think it was real. I mean, who would? It looks like it came from Toys "R" Us. I never picked up a skull before. It was dropped through the roof, like a joke or something. Which it still might be."

He stood up, checked the slashed roof. "You think it might be a joke?"

"Sort of. Not real funny, though. Like Senator Reinhart's hand being FedEx'd to me."

"Christ, let's hope not. That was a fuckin' circus. Hasn't been solved yet, and it's been almost a year."

"Language," Lucy said.

Russ looked at her. "Sorry." Then he turned to me. "What makes you think this is that guy, Soranden?"

"The teeth."

"The teeth?"

"I'm a forensics wonder, Russ. And this parking garage has a hell of an echo."

Day smiled, snorted a laugh that sounded as if it had come out of a barrel in a cave full of bats.

"Check the teeth," I said to Russ. "Upper incisors."

He looked. "How do you know this isn't Terry Thomas?"

"The gap's too wide. This is Soranden, no doubt."

"Guy had a butt ugly smile, huh?"

"It's an IRS qualification. With a friendly smile, you don't rise up in the ranks. You should see the head IRS guy in Reno now. So, are you gonna call this in, get a crew out here before sunrise?" I glanced at my watch. "You've got about five hours."

"Well . . . sonofabitch. I didn't want to get any more sleep tonight anyway."

* * *

So the circus returned to Reno, and I got more than another fifteen minutes of Warhol's fame, and Ma threatened to fire me again, which is what she does whenever I go behind her back and find stuff. Soranden had been news for a few days when he disappeared in July, but good news doesn't have the legs of bad news, and the local IRS mafia chieftain wasn't well known so he'd quickly fallen off the radar. I was the "heads guy," finding yet another head, so the media brought out the calliope and the cartwheeling clowns and once again I was a national sensation. As it should be.

Now that Soranden had turned up, it was time to prospect around for suspects. Warley had left the Green Room twenty minutes before Lucy and I found Soranden's skull, and Warley had taken Soranden's top spot at the IRS when Soranden went missing. All of which caused Russ's homicide antenna to twitch violently. As a result, at ten a.m. the next morning I ended up on the other side of the one-way mirror in the interrogation room at RPD, looking in on the room with the third-world ventilation system in which Russ and I had spent many hours last year getting to know one another. But on this side of the mirror the coffee was better and the chairs weren't bolted to the floor. Detective Don Kreuger was taking lead on the case, same as he did on the Jo-X thing three months ago—a case that still had Russ nervous, wondering if the FBI was still poking at it, hoping they wouldn't get lucky and take his kid down.

We looked in on Warley Sullivan. He was alone, staring at the walls like a Russian inside Lubyanka Prison fearing that the back of his head was about to stop a bullet. Sweat beaded his forehead.

"Think he did it?" Russ asked me.

"Nope."

"Nope? No back-and-forth here, no doubt?"

I shrugged. "Guy's a vampire, not a killer. His joy in life is bleeding you until you pass out, but if you die there's no more blood, no more all-important revenue, so there's no percentage in taking it all the way to murder."

"Except that he took Soranden's place, got his job. This might be an internal IRS malfunction."

"Okay, there's that, though Warley wouldn't call it a malfunction. More like a cause for celebration."

"Man, it sounds like you got out of there just in time."

"Soon as I realized I had a soul, I was gone."

Silence for ten seconds.

"Look at that bastard sweat," Russ said. "He did it."

"Probably not, but if he did, there's a sixty-one percent chance he wouldn't lose his job at the IRS."

Russ stared at me. "Say what?"

"Fact: sixty-one percent of IRS personnel who get caught cheating on their taxes do not lose their job. Tax cheats have a fair idea of how the system works, and knowing how the system works is job security in the IRS. Firing good employees isn't the best way to keep the revenue floodgates open."

"Jesus. But how good are they if they get caught?"

"Once they know *how* they got caught, they're even better at it. The knowledge circulates. It's called professionalism."

"Jesus H. Christ."

"Know how many people in the IRS pay mortgage interest and property taxes on a second home?"

"Do I want to know?"

"A lot more than own a second home, Russ."

"Shitfire."

Then Don Kreuger entered the room with Officer Day. Day was present to keep Warley Sullivan from going nuts and killing Kreuger—Warley weighing in at one-sixty-one, Kreuger at two-fourteen. They were both six-two—but one looked like a Roman gladiator, the other looked desiccated.

A transcript of the interview is available to personnel with a need to know at RPD, and the FBI has a copy, but the essence of it went like this:

Kreuger: You kill him?

Sullivan: No.

Kreuger: Okay, then. We'll be in touch.

There was more to it than that, but boring. Sullivan said he didn't put the skull in the convertible. Never saw the car. Didn't know Mortimer Angel was going to be at the Green Room. He didn't know there was a car, or a skull. He didn't know anything about anything. Yes, he'd spoken to Angel at the bar, got a good tip about a bar at the Atlantis Casino called the Oasis where IRS agents weren't assassinated, said hi to Ma, and that was that for the evening. He'd gone home, gone to bed, slept okay, woke up at six twenty that morning, had some coffee and a bagel, found out about Soranden after he got the crossword done.

"That about all?" Russ asked me as Kreuger was wrapping it up with Warley.

"Not sure about that bagel or the crossword."

Russ stared at me.

"Pretty much," I said. "He hit the relevant high points."

"Guy's a ball of fire, huh?"

"Not yet. Will be after he's turned away from the Pearly Gates though."

* * *

Fingerprints on Soranden's skull were all mine and Lucy's. No partials under either of ours, so it was determined that we hadn't destroyed evidence. It also made us suspects, especially me since I'd worked under Soranden, knew him as The Toad.

The skull was clean, inside and out. Not easy to get the interior of a skull that clean, said the coroner, Boyce Carroll. I got the story on the skull secondhand from Russ because he and I were buddies, but informally, not something known within the department at large. I was permitted in the viewing room as an observer who not only knew Sullivan from the past but might also detect inaccuracies and omissions in his account of what had taken place in the Green Room the night before.

But the skull was pristine, like few skulls are unless they'd been buried for fifty-plus years, and if they had there would be weather pitting, yellowing, other signs of age. Moreover, Ronald had been in full possession of his own skull at least up until July of this year. It was Boyce's considered opinion that Soranden's skull had been picked clean by hundreds of those huge ants that Lucy had found in the car, not that we mentioned we'd kept two of them, one for us and one for Ma, and that we might have ours bronzed. It might have taken less than a day for a big colony to strip every bit of flesh off the skull, inside and out. An LED light and a borescope through the eye sockets and the neck showed that the brain was entirely gone, cleaned out as neatly as all the external flesh. All that incomprehensible and contradictory IRS knowledge had been relocated into an anthill somewhere. With luck, it would stay there.

"Groovy," Lucy said when I told her. "So we're looking for someone with a bunch of giant ants."

"Nope," I said.

"Someone with a monster private anthill, like in their backyard?"

"Not sure how that's different, and nope again."

"Still nope?"

"It's not our case so we're not looking for any of that. It has nothing to do with us and how we put bread on the table."

"Except the skull was left in my car. So it's mine."

"Don't count on possession being nine-tenths of the law in this instance, kiddo."

"Okay, but it's sort of our case, isn't it? You said you used to work with Soranden, that you went on a few audits together before he became chief."

"True. Those were obviously high points in my career. But like I said, his death has nothing to do with us."

Ma seconded that. We were in her office, the one with the Feng shui–enhanced sideboard with its bullet hole, put there by a guy just released from prison who'd popped in with the intention of murdering Maude and was bounced around like a rag doll by my fiancée, Jeri, a year or two before she became my fiancée. He ended up in the hospital then back in lockup and will walk with a pronounced limp the rest of his life. So much for guns when you're a half-wit.

"We got clients," Ma reminded us. "Galbraith and Joss. We don't need this Soranden mess."

Galbraith and Joss, neither of whom were in the public eye. "Joss" was Evelyn Joss, a fifty-something CPA whose junior partner, Michael Volker, had, without Evelyn's knowledge or permission, removed $13,600 in June from Joss & Volker's business account. The other case, Karen Galbraith, was a small-business owner wanting to track down her daughter, Megan, age twenty.

Megan's last known address was somewhere in the San Fernando Valley, northwest of LA. Megan was missing, but not the least bit famous, so my unique skills didn't apply.

"I want you to take Joss," Ma said to me. "Lucy and I will have a go at Galbraith."

Which was boring but made sense. My so-called expertise was in accounting, and funds were missing. Spreadsheets, ledgers, bank accounts, a job not unlike stalking tax cheats for Uncle. $13,600 wasn't an ordinary accounting error. Volker had taken the money, left a trail a monkey could follow, and Evelyn Joss had learned of the embezzlement, if that's what it was, only last week.

If that's what it was . . . hah. Of *course* it was, although Volker was allowed to sign on the account so it might not meet the legal definition of embezzlement. But Joss was the senior partner and had, by unwritten agreement, asked Volker to let her know if he removed any significant funds from the account. By any reasonable measure, $13,600 was a significant amount. She hadn't accosted Volker with the knowledge because maybe he had a good reason for taking the money and she didn't want to pry or upset the partnership. The lady had a good heart but not a lot of sense. She'd asked around, found that Clary Investigations was the best in Reno, best in the state, and hired Ma to find out what was going on.

Ma and Lucy would handle the Galbraith deal, a missing-person case. Because Megan Galbraith's last-known address was in the San Fernando Valley—the "Valley"—Lucy and Ma were headed that way. Lucy could use the trip to brush up on her Valley Girl lingo so she could sound fifteen if we were stopped by the highway patrol and maybe get a video of me being put in handcuffs. She and I were going to be apart for a while, and she and Ma were going to talk about me behind my back. Great. Of course, they might just go shopping, in which case I wouldn't be a blip on the old estrogen radar.

"Do *not*," Ma said to me, "dink around with that goddamn Soranden thing."

Man, I take a lot of unwarranted flak.

"Dink around?" I said.

She gave me the evil eye, the one that executes gophers. "I don't care if you found the head. Do not so much as breathe in that direction. And watch out for that slippery damn Fairchild. He'll drag you into that cluster-whatever-it-is if you let him."

"Don't know what Russ could possibly want, but a cop in my pocket, Ma—you don't think that's worth something?"

"It's worth a lot, which is why I've got a shitload of cops, politicians, and lawyers owing me plenty, ready to jump the minute I say boo. But Fairchild's already in your pocket, and mine, and if you fool around with Soranden, you're fired."

"Okay, then. Glad we got that cleared up. But—" I turned to Lucy—"open your purse. Let's see that tissue."

She reached in, got out the Kleenex. I opened it and set an ant the size of a warthog on Ma's desk. Actually, we'd measured it and it was an inch and a quarter long. *Big.*

Ma scooted back in her chair. "Shit! What's that?"

"An ant. It fell out of Soranden's skull the night we got it."

She scooted closer, touched it gingerly with a pencil. "Jesus Hummingbird Christ, that's huge. Is it really an ant?"

"Yup. All yours if you want it. We kept one and left one for the cops to poke at with their pencils."

She considered that for a moment. "I might run this guy up to Paul Werner at the biology department at UNR. Never seen anything half this size around here." She carefully put the ant aside, then looked up at me. "What day of the week is it?"

"See, when you get to a certain age, that's the kind of thing you can no longer keep track—"

More evil eye. "It's *Saturday*, boyo. Guess what days of the week are especially good for tracking down missing persons?"

"In my case, any doggone day of the week. Of course, they have always ended up, you know . . . *dead*."

Lucy laughed. She could be dark too.

"Saturday and Sunday," Ma said. "People are home a lot in the daytime. And neighbors who might know where a person is, or where they might've gone if they're no longer there. So—"

"So you've already got plane tickets for you and Lucy, and you're headed out today, ready to hit it big tomorrow."

She tilted her head at me. "Okay, not bad, figuring out the tickets. We're on Southwest at three forty-five. Gotta get to the airport an hour early for the strip search, which I wouldn't miss for the world. We gotta be there—" she glanced at a clock on the wall—"in two and a half hours."

"And, don't tell me. I'm dropping you two off."

"That's right, boyo."

Lucy hugged my arm. "That's my gumshoe. Give him a few hints and facts and watch him go to town."

Ma's lips twisted. "If that's all it was, I wouldn't worry so much. It's what he does without hints and facts that gives me heartburn."

* * *

"I need my back scrubbed," Lucy said.

"Your back is dirty?"

"It's *filthy*. I can't get on a plane like this. I would totally gross out the other passengers. The pilot wouldn't take off with me like this." She kicked off her shoes, removed her shirt, then pursed her lips and gave me her Valley Girl voice: "Your clothes are gonna get like totally sopping, mister."

She sounded fifteen, looked seventeen. She was five-five, had a twenty-three-inch waist, thirty-three-inch hips. A shiver ran up my spine. We'd been together for almost three months, and I still hadn't gotten used to this.

"Mort?"

"Uh-huh, yup, sopping clothes."

"Only if you don't get naked. Naked works better."

"Right, right." Spade and Hammer were in a corner of the room, rolling their eyes. Sam and Mike, couple of clowns. We were in my house, in the big upstairs bedroom with a view of the backyard. Lucy had her own place, a studio apartment a mile away, but sleepovers were common.

So I scrubbed her back and a lot of the rest of her. Flexible as she is, she apparently can't reach her boobs, so I have to do those—which I do even though I complain a lot about the extra work. Then we had to take an afternoon nap, which never works out, napwise, then we had to pop back into the shower, then we had a quick bite to eat because afternoon naps use extra calories. I drove her over to Ma's, then drove them both to the airport.

No strip search. Ma made it through security unscathed, but Lucy got a second look, not because she looked like a terrorist, but . . . just because. Or because her ID said she was thirty-one and she doesn't look old enough to vote. When she really wants to push security buttons, she pitches her voice high and speaks in Valley Girl, looks and acts like a high school sophomore. I tell her it's not a good idea to push TSA buttons because their sense of humor is modeled after IRS humor, which is modeled after Gestapo humor circa 1940–42, but she pushes buttons just to push and see what'll happen.

Then the security vortex spit them out the other side and they were gone. I went to the parking garage and got into my car, sat there for a moment in the silence, found myself alone and in sole charge of the Joss investigation.

Hot damn. Three in the afternoon and Great Gumshoe was on the case.

Now what?

CHAPTER THREE

JUDO, OF COURSE. And street-fighting moves never seen in Olympic competition. Monday, Wednesday, and Saturdays were my regular judo days. Lucy's, too. We tried to miss as few lessons as possible.

Rufus Booth is the last guy you'd want to attack in a dark alley, if you were inclined to do that sort of thing, which I'm not. Rufus is black, an even six feet tall, two hundred ten pounds, so we're the same weight give or take two pounds, and any sort of similarity ends right there. Rufus could take on four of me and walk away whistling in six seconds. Okay, three of me would run away, and he would have to track them down, which would take time, but in the event those Mort clones decided to stick around and try their luck, Rufus would have them on the ground and in need of serious medical attention in six seconds.

All of which meant he was a hell of a teacher. When I got back from Australia, I thought a little training in self-defense was in order. A phone conversation with Jeri's brother, Ron, had put me onto Rufus Booth. Ron DiFrazzia was one of North America's finest judo and karate experts, but he lived over a hundred miles away. Booth was local, with a private dojo in his house on Plumas Street, not half a mile from Ma's house. Ron had trained under

Booth, who had taught him street-fighting moves you would never see in a regular dojo.

A decade before Ron DiFrazzia's first try at the Olympics, Booth was already a six-time North American judo champ. He'd eventually given up Olympic competition, but he taught take-down moves to RPD and Washoe County sheriff's deputies and gave private lessons to ex-IRS agents who'd turned gumshoe, so I qualified. Beautiful female art history majors training to be gum-shoes also qualified, so Lucy was learning judo too.

Judo is all about repetition. It would be hard to find a better workout. Judo works muscles you didn't know you had and a few that don't exist. In addition to being a potential killer, Rufus is also a third-degree sadist, so I knew I was going to get a workout that would leave me limp the rest of the day. I always am. But I didn't have anything else going on, so I called him up, asked if I could make it an hour early, he said c'mon over, and, like always, he damn near killed me.

"What up?" he said when I walked through the door. "And where's Lucy?" I had a duffel bag with a fresh gi in it, and a yellow belt Booth had given me when he determined I was no longer a rank-ass beginner. Booth was a ninth-dan judo master as recog-nized by the Kōdōkan. Not many of those in the United States. By comparison, Ron DiFrazzia was sixth-dan, and there's not many of those around, either.

"Lucy's headed for LA with Ma. What's up is I need the usual, and whatever else you want to show me."

He grinned like a wolf. Overhead light shined on his bald dome. He was dark black and a hell of a nice guy who played a sax in local clubs with four other brothers, two black, two white.

"Too bad about Lucy," he said. "Another couple weeks and she'll get her yellow. But get you outta them street clothes and I'll tune you up, bro."

Well, I'd asked for it, and I got it.

No point in enumerating the number of kicks, punches, and throws I made and defended against. Suffice it to say my legs were so weak when I left I could barely stand, and I might have trouble lifting a fork to my mouth. The love taps Rufus gave me made me feel fully tenderized, ready for the grill.

Repetition. Over and over, faster and faster, defense moves done slowly, then faster, trying for one smooth motion. Rufus was big into defense. In fact, Rufus was all about self-defense. He didn't teach kicks and punches so someone could go out and whip ass. The point was, his students went out and hopefully didn't get their asses whipped. That philosophy didn't work well in Olympic competition. Two guys circling each other like two bears, both in full defensive mode, could starve to death before anyone made contact.

"Punch through your target," Rufus said. "But not two feet through like you hear sometimes. Real shock and power is in that last few inches when your joints lock out. So hit four inches through a face, elbow, groin, knee, whatever. Now I want to *feel* your punch, not some wet-noodle love tap that's got no sting in it. Gimme a piston, and if you give me a dumb-ass windmilling roundhouse, I'll flatten you."

Okay, so no dumb-ass windmilling roundhouse punches. A hundred piston punches with each arm and leg. Then a hundred more. Then a hundred more. Shitfire. And that was after three useful self-defense moves done a hundred times each, to stop an attack by an asshole gangbanger—Rufus's non-PC description—who didn't go by Queensbury Rules. Defense against a knife, a club, and a windmilling brawler. Easiest was defending against a brawler, hardest was someone with a club, like a baseball bat or a length of iron pipe.

At the end of the session as I was changing back into street clothes with arms and legs that no longer felt connected to the rest of me, he asked, "What's your number one defensive tactic, Angel?"

"Avoid trouble, run if you can."

"Got that right. Remember it. All this punching and kicking shit is last resort. Ain't no dishonor in runnin', 'specially if you know you could probably kick ass."

As if I could kick the ass of a Barbie doll right then.

Rufus stopped me as I was about to go out the door. "Now gimme a Sun Tzu quote," he said. He'd given me fifty Sun Tzus in the past six months.

"If I do, do I get an orange belt?"

"You're gettin' there. Another month or two, you might get your *Rokkyu*. Now gimme a Sun Tzu."

"Appear weak when you are strong."

"That's a good one. Now get outta here."

I staggered out into the day, unaware that I was going to use that Sun Tzu in less than twenty-four hours.

* * *

"Nice goin', Spitfire," O'Roarke said. "Folks all over the Midwest are hauling out their Rand McNallys, finding Reno on the map, headed this way, wanting to catch sight of what we in Northern Nevada call the Great Gumshoe."

"Chamber of Commerce oughta give me a bonus."

The Green Room at five forty-five in the afternoon is a good place to sit and think. I thought about the missing $13,600 and how to approach the Joss investigation. Pete's Wicked Ale doesn't help with the thinking, so I sat there with a sarsaparilla in front of me. Sarsaparilla doesn't help either, but it doesn't hinder the process quite like Pete's.

"It's not six o'clock yet. What're you doing here?" I asked O'Roarke. "What'd you do with Ella? She's better lookin'."

"She called in sick. I'm pulling a double. Speaking of better looking, what'd you do with Lucy?"

"Who?"

He gave me a stare that could frost a mug. "Do not tell me you two are kaput or I'll poison you and dump you in the river."

"We are by no means kaput."

His shoulders sagged with relief. "Give up on that girl like you did on Holiday and you'll never be allowed in here again. I'd run you out with a fire hose."

"I didn't give up on Holiday."

"Says you. She doesn't come around anymore."

"You sort of like Lucy, huh?"

"Unlike you, she's a real ray of sunshine."

"Thanks."

He gave me a one-eyed squint. "A skull, for chrissake? You found a skull last night?"

I shrugged. "It's a knack. Don't ask me to explain it."

"I won't. I only hope it's not catching."

"You can't catch that kind of thing."

"What can't you catch?" Rosa plopped down beside me. Ripe cleavage, long legs, short black dress. She was a hooker, but cute as hell and extremely picky about clientele.

"Knacks."

"Oh, right. That'd be by definition. Either you got it or you don't. And, hey, Mort, you came through again. Good for you. How 'bout a pink panther mocktail, Pat?" she said to O'Roarke. She put a hand on my arm. "Mocktail. That's virgin, like me."

"Uh-huh. Good one, kiddo."

Pineapple juice, pureed strawberries, 7 Up, bit of whipped cream, shaken, not stirred. Little more whipped cream on top. If I caught Ella working, I might try one of those. Ella Glover was a good bartender and not as mouthy as some I know. O'Roarke would laugh at my mocktail, make some snide-ass comment.

"A skull this time?" Rosa said. "That's different. Sounds like you've upped your game."

"Speaking of games, how 'bout those Giants? They're only one game out."

Just in time, my phone rang, "Purple People Eater" fired up. Sheb Wooley, '58.

"What happened to 'Monster Mash'?" Rosa said.

"I've upped my game."

"Don't think so."

Russ was on the horn. I told him where I was. He said he'd be over in ten minutes and to save him a Bud. I hung up.

"Jiggers, the cops," I said to Rosa.

Rosa stared at me. "Seriously, Mort?" Her cheeks pulled in as she sucked on her straw, then she smiled at her drink. "This is pretty good, but I'll have to run an extra five miles tomorrow so that kinda sucks."

"You could return it, get a club soda."

"Not happenin'."

Ten minutes later, on the dot, there was Russ. He nodded toward a corner. I got up and followed him with my sarsaparilla and his Bud Heavy. We pulled out chairs and sat at a table.

"Thanks," he said, taking the beer. "I don't think Sullivan is the guy. We'll keep nosing around, keep him in sight, but if he did Soranden, he's one hell of an actor."

"Stay on him. IRS is full of two-faced characters."

"I thought you said it wasn't him."

"It isn't, but the IRS could use payback. Warley especially. Keep on him, and make sure he knows it. So, what's up?"

His smile looked a little gray. "I was wondering if you had any of your half-assed maverick ideas. Back in July and August the FBI was all over Soranden. Internal Revenue guy disappears, the Feds go bananas, terrified it might be the start of a civilian uprising. But that investigation didn't go anywhere."

"Couldn't come up with any suspects, huh?" The inanity of the thought made me smile.

"They came up with about eighteen hundred of 'em."

"That few? They must not've been trying. Of course, we *are* talking about the FBI."

"People with what looked like good-sized gripes with the local IRS in the past two years. List looked like a phone book. Nothing panned out, but it's impossible to go through that many people and not miss something. And whoever killed him took out the head guy, not some guy who got in their face. Soranden was a desk jockey, not a . . . what do you call 'em?"

"Field thug," I said.

"Yeah. One of those. So now that Soranden's skull showed up the feds are on it again, but it's in my ballpark too—I mean, RPD's. They made it a joint op, us and the fibbies, which means they'll blame us if we strike out, and they'll take all the credit if we catch some guy."

"Not your case, is it? I thought it was Kreuger's."

"It is, but, hey, a feather in my cap couldn't hurt. And you're a maverick, which I think is what we'll need here."

"That mean you're hiring me again?"

"Not per se. Especially not after you're the one who stirred up this hornet's nest. But . . . you know, if you happen to come up with an idea..." He wound down, stared for a moment at his beer, then took a gulp to re-pressurize his neurons.

Last few days of June, Russ hired me to try to locate his daughter, Danya, and find out who killed rapper Jonnie Xenon. Things got a bit complicated, but the upshot was that the FBI had missed a few critical details so Danya was still free. Now here I was, back on the FBI's radar having found Soranden's skull. This did not make Russ happy, if I was reading his body language correctly.

"The thing is, Russ, I don't catch 'em. All I do is find 'em. Well, mostly."

"I wouldn't be here if that's all you did. You caught those two crazy women who killed the mayor and the D.A."

"They caught me, Russ."

"That's sort of semantical—not sure if that's a word—kind of a chicken or the egg deal. Those two broads are dead, Victoria and, and..."

"Winter."

"Yeah, weird name. But they're dead and you were onto them, which is what counts."

"You check out Soranden's family? Most likely person to kill some guy is a disgruntled family member."

"Only disgruntled, huh?" He smiled. "We were all over that back when he went missing. 'We' being RPD and the feebs."

He pulled out a pocket-size spiral notebook. "Soranden was divorced, ex-wife Debbie Combs, living in Minneapolis, hasn't seen him in twelve years. Older sister in Carson City, Esther Soranden, never married. Another sister in Ogden, Utah, one year younger, Alice Ann Loomis. Two kids by the ex, a daughter in Maryland, Kate, dental hygienist, and a son in the Army, John, a major who hasn't been out of Korea in about six months, since his last leave. We checked 'em all eighteen ways from Sunday when you came up with that skull, but the trail's so cold we didn't come up with shit. So if you've got any ideas, or come up with anything that, you know, shines a light . . ."

"You'll be the first to know, my good friend."

Irony.

* * *

However . . .

Side trip, distraction, detour. The Green Room was a trove of well-traveled diversions. I knew that before I got there, knew it wouldn't get me one step closer to figuring out why Volker had boosted over thirteen grand from Joss & Volker's operating account. This was like putting off mowing the lawn until small children get lost in it, then you have to do something.

What better time, as Ma said, to hunt for missing persons than a Saturday or Sunday? Although Evelyn Joss was missing money, not a person. But it was Saturday evening, Lucy out of town, me with nothing to do but switch to Pete's Wicked Ale or work on the Joss thing. So—Joss. I finished the sarsaparilla and got out of there to go hunting. I didn't expect to do more than go through the usual unproductive motions since I'm a trainee, not a qualified investigator. But even wasted hours add up and I had eighty-five hundred to go, so . . . onward.

Six fifteen p.m. After hours. No one answered at Joss & Volker, Inc. in a little suite tucked away in a business park on a winding street in southwest Reno, but I wanted to see the place, get an idea of who these people were. The building was crescent shaped, one of four such semi-interlocking crescents in the park, home to accountants, chiropractors, therapists, insurance agents, others of that ilk. Concrete walkways looped through manicured lawns and plantings. Pleasant, but sterile pleasant. Joss & Volker was just one small business among sixty others.

One of Ma's special programs on an iPad got me home and cell numbers for Evelyn Joss and Michael Volker. Evelyn didn't answer. I didn't leave a message. I drove to her house in the northwest. Old frame house in good condition, yellow with off-white trim. I rang the bell, no one home.

I got an answering machine at Volker's, again left no message, but sleuthing hours added up so I drove over to his place near Damonte Ranch High School, southeast Reno, and parked on the street. His was a two-story house in pale desert stucco, about $400,000 worth even after the ongoing housing debacle, now in its second decade and finally crawling out of the doldrums. Three-car garage, two cars in the driveway, a five-year-old BMW 3, silver, and an old red Honda Civic sporting multiple dings and scars. It looked like people were home, so that answering machine was guarding the portal, keeping the riffraff out. Riffraff like me. I parked on the street, went up the driveway, through an arch into a courtyard with rose bushes and a dry four-foot waterfall, and rang the bell. Didn't hear anything, so I rang it again.

The door opened and there was a standard teenager, a girl of sixteen, twenty pounds overweight like a lot of them are these days, ugly nose ring that glistened below her nostrils like a little hunk of snot, eyebrows pierced, underdressed in a crop top that put too much emphasis on a lightly tanned Michelin Man jelly roll around her middle, vapid expression, entitled to everything life gave her and to things she hadn't yet acquired, so bored the moment she saw me that her eyes almost rolled up in her head. Except, wait . . . I caught a little flutter in her eyes, a brief instant of recognition, so she might have recently passed by a television at a time when the news was on. I figured she was six or seven weeks into her junior year with a D-minus average, F-minus in math, no upcoming high school diploma on the distant horizon, might acquire a GED about the time she hit thirty. But I could have been wrong about all that since I very often am.

She stared at me for half a second then turned and walked away, across a tiled foyer toward a hallway. Stairs led up to the second floor. Formal dining room to the left, part of the kitchen visible beyond that. "D-a-a-a-d! It's for you!" Voice that could loosen roofing tiles. I stood outside the open door, waiting.

"No need to yell, Precious," a man called out, not far away. "I'm right here."

"So why didn't *you* answer it then?" she hollered from the depths of the hallway. Precious indeed. I could already hear her when she was forty. She would sound like a chainsaw trying to cut through a galvanized garbage can.

Mike Volker emerged from a room to the right. He was in jeans and socks, shirt pulled out at the waist. Early forties, five-eight, carrying thirty extra pounds, balding. A question stayed in his eyes until he got a good look at me, then a flicker of interest and caution overlaid the question.

"Mr. Volker?" I asked.

"Yeah. You, you're the guy who found that skull yesterday, aren't you? Saw you in the news."

"I had that misfortune, yes."

His eyes grew wary. "And that rapper. You found him, too, earlier this year. And that senator's hand last year. Reinhart."

"What can I say? It's a knack."

"Well, uh, what can I do for you?" He looked past me, out at the street. Expecting squad cars with flashing lights?

"I wonder if we could talk for a few minutes." Behind him, at the hallway entrance, Precious stood watching us.

"What about?" Good-sized hint of paranoia in his voice.

"How about we talk inside, Mr. Volker?"

"This can't be about Soranden, that skull you found."

Interesting comment. "It isn't."

He looked at me a moment longer, then stood to one side. "C'mon in." He shut the door behind me, then directed me to the room he'd been in, a living room, two steps down. To one side, a steel ramp topped with rubber sloped into the room. A television was on, sound turned low. Gray carpet, couch and a love seat in rich black leather, La-Z-Boy recliner in dark green fabric, big bookshelf laden with trophies and pictures—bowling trophies and photos of the team—no books. "Be right back," he said. I heard him padding away up the stairs to the second floor.

A boy of ten with a moon face and glasses leaned his head past the doorway and gawked at me for several seconds, then turtled back out of sight. Precious came in, gave me a murky, empty smile, the kind of thing modern teenagers give strangers, straightened a maroon afghan on the back of the couch, plumped up two pillows, one on each end, then left.

And there I was on TV. Great timing. I saw myself going into the police station with Russell Fairchild and Officer Day. I was the "heads guy" again. They liked that phrase. Catchy. As I watched, it occurred to me that anyone with a need to dispose of a head or any other inconvenient body part might, after all this and previous publicity, be inclined to palm it off on me due to the confusion factor, and to be certain it got on TV so they could record it on TiVo and play it back later, chuckling as they rolled doobies and got high. I was getting too much attention. Ma was probably right about that. Soranden's skull had been dropped into Lucy's car, which was more or less ours and might therefore qualify as the "heads guy's car," a dumping ground of sorts. And it was a ragtop, convenient if you had a knife. Soranden ending up there could hardly be a coincidence, so maybe someone had followed me and Lucy to—

"Sorry 'bout that," Volker said. I was standing, looking at the bowling trophies and pictures, not really seeing them. Volker indicated the couch and took the love seat at a right angle to it in front of a glass-topped coffee table. He'd put on slippers and his shirt was tucked in.

A gaunt woman in her late forties, early fifties, rolled to the living room entrance in a wheelchair, small fleece blanket on her lap, and looked in on us. Volker looked over at her, then at me. "This is my sister, Marta Geer. Marta, this is Mr. Angel."

"Mort," I said.

"I know who you are," she said to me. Polite. Soft voice that held no judgment, one way or another.

"We should probably make this private," I told Volker.

"Anything you have to say, Marta can hear it. This is her home too."

"You might make that determination later. I'll leave that up to you. For the moment, however . . ."

He didn't like that, but Marta turned the wheelchair around. "I'll be in my room." She left.

"I hope that was worth it," Volker said tersely.

"We'll see." I waved a hand at the bookshelf. "Looks like you bowl better than I do. Been at it long?"

He didn't like me, but he liked to bowl. I wanted to get him talking. "Fifteen years. We're the Alley Cats. Team had two-oh-two average this year. Best in the league by eight points."

"I once bowled a one seventy-three. That was ten or twelve years ago. Got two strikes in a row that game, first time ever. And I had only two open frames. I've still got the sheet. I had it laminated."

A faint smile broke through, sort of a grimace. I figured he wasn't going to invite me onto the team anytime soon to suck them down into last place.

"That BMW get around okay in the snow? I was thinking about getting that same model myself and winter's coming."

He gave me a look. "It's okay. Studded tires help."

"Wife drive the Honda?"

"I'm divorced. I bought it for my daughter in June, soon as she turned sixteen. Gotta say it's been nice, not having to drive her everywhere."

"Great kids," I said. Maybe the boy, but the girl appeared to be anything but precious. "Girl's name is Precious?"

"No. Sometimes I call her that. Probably shouldn't when someone's at the door. I'll hear about it later. That's Kimmi. If you saw my boy, that's Derek."

"Saw him. We didn't bond."

No smile. "He's curious, kinda skittish though. Straight-A student, fifth grade. How about we get to the point, Mr. Angel? What can I do for you that Marta can't hear?"

"Just wondering what you did with that thirteen thousand six hundred dollars, Mike."

Hit 'em right between the eyes. See if they break. We did that at the IRS. It made eyes jitter and sweat break out, skin go pale and clammy. Best reaction was when they fainted dead away and didn't come to for over five minutes. Five minutes was worth bonus points back at the office.

Mike stared at me. His mouth opened, then closed, but no sound came out. Finally, "What? What thirteen thousand?"

"And six hundred. You tell me."

"I . . . I don't know what the hell you're talkin' about."

I raised an eyebrow. Got that at the mandatory in-service training at the IRS. We had to repeat the training and pass a test every two years or lose our jobs. Twenty-four ways to register disbelief, ranging from subtle to the last method: a brief yelp of involuntary laughter and tears in the eyes. We would gather in a conference room and raise eyebrows at each other, look amused, tilt heads, smirk, purse lips, roll eyes, squint, shake our heads, and snort. Fun day—*and* we got paid for it. Almost makes me wish I were still back with Uncle's Stormtroopers.

Raising a single eyebrow took practice. I was glad to see I still had it. After indicating disbelief, the procedure was to wait, give the suspect time to self-incriminate. So I waited.

"You . . . I think you'd better leave," he said.

Incriminating.

"Does Marta know about it? You confide in her about stuff like that?" I asked, glancing toward the hallway. "We could get her back in here if you want."

"She . . . you need to leave. Now."

"No problem. But talking with me could mean the police don't have to get involved. If I leave, next person to bring it up might not be so understanding."

That spun him around. Now it could go either way.

He stared at me. Licked his lips. Glanced at the entrance to the room to see if anyone was listening in. Looked back at me. Made his decision.

Guilty as a sonofabitch, and what he said was, "I don't know anything about thirteen thousand dollars. I mean, where the hell did you get a crazy goddamn idea like that?"

"Good enough." I stood up. "Expect company."

He got to his feet. "Seriously, man. Whatever this is, you're on the wrong track. I mean, I don't know what your game is, but it's . . . it's . . ."

I smiled benignly, a benign smile being an affectation also on the agenda at those IRS trainings. "But it's what?"

"It's . . . nothing. Please go."

"I'll show myself out."

I left him there and went into the foyer. Precious Kimmi was ten feet down the hallway, staring at me. No sign of Marta. Near the top of the stairs, Derek was sitting on a carpeted step, hugging a baluster, watching me. "Bye, you guys," I said. No change of expression on either face.

I went outside. Maybe that was a normal household. Other than Kimmi's foghorn voice, I had the feeling it wasn't unusual. Teenagerwise I felt out of touch. It had been six years since my daughter, Nicole, was Kimmi's age, and there hadn't been any destructive in-your-face piercings. Those damn snot-nose rings are something else, though. The statement is as simple and clear as ringing a Chinese gong: Fuck You.

Dad could put a string through it and give it a yank, really get her attention. It might save her life, but, of course, that would be child abuse and land him in jail for ninety days and prove to her, once and for all, that she was in the driver's seat.

* * *

I got in the Toyota and took off. Went two blocks, turned around and came back, parked a block away where I could see the front of Volker's house and the cars in the driveway. Maybe my visit would spark some sort of result.

Seven twenty-five. The sun had gone behind the Sierras, temperature into the seventies. I killed the engine and tuned in an oldies station, got a Buddie Holly tune: "Peggy Sue." Before my time, before gangsta rappers, before heavy metal, acid rock, antiwar songs, shock lyrics.

I turned it low and watched the house, adding to my hours of training.

Eight o'clock. Eight ten. Eight twelve. Time crawling like a sloth trying to drag itself out of the suction of a tar pit.

A pickup went by, covered in dried mud, color uncertain. It stopped, blocking Volker's driveway. A horn honked. Precious skipped out of the house, circled the truck, and piled in.

Follow Precious Kimmi or stay put? Watch the guy who lied and told me to get out, or see what his kid was up to? Go with the action or let my butt fall asleep staring at a house?

Not much choice there.

I fired up the engine. The pickup hung a U-turn in the street and came my way. I ducked down as it approached and went by. I gave it fifteen seconds, then U-turned and went after it.

Saturday evening, kids going out as kids do. I probably should've stayed on Volker, but tailing is good training.

It wasn't hard to keep after the pickup. One taillight was brighter than the other. We circled around, got onto 395 north, headed toward downtown Reno. Through the Spaghetti Bowl where 395 does a square dance with Interstate 80, still the ugliest freeway interchange in the western hemisphere, and got off at Sierra Street, went south, then into a parking garage on First Street. I went up after them, parked on the top floor, the fifth, nothing but stars above, Venus bright over the Sierras. I found a slot forty feet from Precious and her date, who turned out to be a six-foot-one skinny guy who might run about a hundred fifty-five pounds, shoulder-length greasy hair, black jeans, oily-looking denim jacket, hand up under Kimmi's shirt for a good long feel and a sloppy kiss beneath a lamp. It ended with a girlish giggle, probably hers but you never know, then off they went toward the stairs.

By then I'd put on a blond hairpiece, an unkempt thing that partly covered my ears, Giants ball cap, nonprescription glasses with heavy black rims, an L.L. Bean field coat in saddle brown, and took off after them, stuffing my wallet in an inside pocket of the field coat. I Velcroed the pocket shut, put a second wallet in a back pocket. It held five one-dollar bills and no ID. This was, after all, downtown Reno.

Down four flights of stairs to ground level. I hurried to catch up on the last flight, looked both ways on the sidewalk, saw them headed west on First, forty feet away.

All of which counted when it came to accumulating hours as a world-famous private investigator, but I was probably right on the outer rim of those hours, following a high school girl with the apparent intelligence of a box of dead batteries.

I could still be wrong about that, but who wears a nose ring that glistens moistly below their nostrils if they don't have to? Kimmi was essentially parentless, on her own. Volker had lost all control, but that wasn't unusual these days. Given our "nanny state" court system, controlling the toughest kids was no longer possible. Touch them and you end up in front of a judge, then in mandatory counseling, social workers dropping by to ensure that you don't parent your precious kids the way your grandparents parented your parents, then everyone wonders how society's youth got so feral. And, of course, if your kids turn out bad, it's all your fault, not that of the courts or the System. The nanny state is all-wise, all-powerful, and is never at fault.

Kimmi and the denim jacket turned right at the corner, walked up a block to Second Street, turned right again, then disappeared into a nightclub second door down. Cacophonous noise that no one in their right mind would call music rumbled out into the street. "Wildcat" was inscribed in bright yellow neon above a door painted flat black. The sign was yellow, but small, just fifteen inches wide, which is one reason I hadn't noticed it before, the other being that Millennial and iGen clubs on Second Street had a tendency to change names every few months.

I went in cautiously, not wanting Kimmi to see me, see through the disguise, then consider the coincidence that here I was in disguise less than an hour after I'd spoken with her father eleven miles and a universe away.

The interior of the room was painted black, packed with the kind of human crush found at English soccer games where they riot if the team loses and a dozen or so end up trampled to death. The music, if that's what it was, was loud enough to whip brain cells into a froth, prohibiting all thought. This was "compressed" sound, one continuous blast of atonal crap that was like sticking your head in a jet engine. A month in there and a teenager would be stone deaf, wondering how it had gotten so quiet, why all the screeching had faded into a faint white-noise hum. A sign on the front door read: *No persons under 21 allowed.* In my naiveté I expected Kimmi to be rousted and hustled out the door, in which case I might not be deaf before I turned forty-three. No such luck. A bouncer gave her ID a perfunctory glance and handed it back. Fake ID might've cost her twenty bucks. She was good to go, sixteen going on forty, gaining the kind of life experience that might prepare her for a career as a common streetwalker. Thank you, Nanny State.

I sidled up to the skinny guy she was with, put him between her and me. I had three inches and fifty-plus pounds on him, but what he lacked in bulk, he might make up in weapons. I was still in Borroloola shape after digging holes for fence posts with a sixteen-pound iron bar for nearly a mile in Australia, one hole every eight feet in ground that felt like cured concrete. I figured I could arm wrestle this guy and toss him across the room, but he didn't look like the "let's-arm-wrestle" type.

I put him at twenty-four or -five, perfectly reasonable age for a girl of sixteen. Sallow complexion, thin face, cheekbones that looked like misplaced shoulder blades, dark, deep-set eyes, face pierced in a dozen places; earlobes gauged—stretched—out to hold black onyx rings an inch and a half in diameter—the kind of antisocial, in-your-face disfigurement that would prevent him from getting any sort of a job that might require him to look more intelligent than a low-grade meatball.

But I could be wrong about that too. The world is changing, and not for the better. I have the awful feeling that I'll run into a bank vice president one day with a Harvard degree and earlobes gauged out to hold silver dollars. His reassuring speech will be enhanced by a tongue pierced by a stainless-steel bar. My only remaining hope was that he wouldn't be sporting a snot-ring.

Kimmi's guy, Max—had to call him something—was turned away from me, shouting in her ear to be heard. A kind of buzz came from his mouth, but I couldn't catch a single word of it. If they used sign language they could communicate better, and in fact, American Sign Language, ASL, would probably be their primary mode of communication in the coming years, once their hearing loss was up around ninety decibels, a loss that, of course, would never, ever happen to them. Hearing loss was for old people, *really* old, like . . . forty-two.

Already my ears felt as if they'd been packed with cotton. The place was giving me a headache. We were there for three minutes when a guy tapped Max on the shoulder. Something passed between them. The guy was in his late twenties, early thirties. Jet-black hair, moustache, four-day beard stubble, inch-long soul patch, the kind of whippet-thin guy who would carry a switchblade and know how to use it. The exchange wasn't particularly subtle, not up to CIA standards. I saw a flash of bills at waist level, the glint of a baggie, and the switchblade guy, dressed all in black, melted into the crowd like a puff of smoke after giving me a fleeting look that would compare favorably to that of an airport scanner.

I gave it another minute. When I turned to leave, I felt a tug at my back pocket, like a bass taking bait, right side. I clapped a hand on my pocket, trapping a hand, got my left hand around a wrist, didn't look to see what species I'd caught, and bulled my way through the crowd, dragging someone or something behind me like a poodle on a leash.

Outside on the sidewalk I discovered I had a girl with short purple hair in tow, and she wasn't happy. Five-seven, a hundred five pounds, black eye shadow applied with a spray can, more fucking piercings, black lipstick, eyes that spoke of a life in total disarray. Beneath all that Gothic crap, she was pretty. Thin but very pretty, and probably not over twenty years old.

She tugged her arm, trying to free herself. When that didn't work, she kicked my left shin, staggered a little when she missed, so I wrapped her in a bear hug, gave her a Borroloola squeeze that emptied her lungs and kept them empty. Into her ear I said, "You don't have to be like this. You're not a pickpocket. You can do better, honey."

But I'm not a social worker so I had nowhere to go from there. She wasn't my problem. I turned her loose. She coughed once, got her lungs working again, then said, "Can . . . can I borrow a dollar, mister?"

Crazy.

Kimmi and Max came out the door. I turned away from them and backed the girl against a wall as they went by. I pulled out the spare wallet and gave her two bucks, let Kimmi and Max get to the corner, then went after them.

They turned left at the corner, went south on West Street. I followed. Halfway down the block, they jaywalked across West to the other sidewalk. I crossed the street after them. Heard light footsteps behind me, turned, and, of course, it was the girl from Wildcat, following me like a stray puppy.

"You goin' after Dooley and that girl?" she asked.

"Shush."

"I mean, if you are, what for?"

I got her by the arm and kept going. "So the guy's name is Dooley, huh? What's yours?"

"Mira. If you don't know him, why are you following him? You're not gonna, like, try to take his drugs or anything, are you? That wouldn't be smart."

"Keep your voice down, Mira."

Ahead of us, Kimmi and Max—now identified as Dooley—turned right at the corner and disappeared around a building. I hurried to catch up. Mira followed.

"If you are," she said, "you should know he's real mean even if you are kinda big . . ."

"Quiet."

We reached the corner and turned right. The sidewalk was empty. Only a hundred feet back and I'd lost them.

Great Gumshoe.

CHAPTER FOUR

MY PHONE RANG as I was gazing at the empty sidewalk. At the ringtone—"Purple People Eater"—Mira took a step back and gave me a wary look. I dragged the phone out of an inside coat pocket. Traffic was sporadic on the street. A streetlight halfway down the block made the shadows deep and dark around us.

"Hey, Ma," I said. "What's up?"

"I called four minutes ago. Where were you?"

"In Wildcat getting my ears hammered."

Silence for a few seconds. "I'm gonna let you talk to Lucy since she apparently understands you."

More silence, voices, then, "Ma says your speech is slurred and she can't make it out. Why is that?"

"It's her ears. She's losing high frequencies."

"I'll let her know. Where are you?"

"First and West, down by the river looking west."

"At?"

"An empty sidewalk."

"Groovy. Why?"

"I was following Kimmi and Dooley, but they vanished into thin air. Like smoke."

"Okay, maybe Ma was right."

Mira tugged my sleeve. "They went in there." She aimed a finger at a building that took up half the block.

"What's in there?" I asked her.

She shrugged. "Just a bunch of apartments."

"Who's that?" Lucy asked.

"Mira."

"Uh-huh. Mira who?"

"Dunno." I looked at Mira. "What's your last name?"

"Tanaka."

"Mira Tanaka," I said to Lucy.

"Groovy redux. Sounds Japanese. Who is she?"

"Sort of a long story, but the short version is I'm on a case and you've got nothing to worry about, kiddo."

"I never worry unless someone's trying to kill you. Or us."

"That sounds more or less Zen, but no one's trying to kill me at the moment."

"Me either," she said.

"So we're good." Mira was listening, waiting with infinite patience, as if this slice of reality was as good as any other slice.

"You sure they went in there?" I asked her. The building was nineteen-fifties brick, four stories tall, yellow light glowing behind a few windows that faced the street. I'd seen the place a hundred times in passing, never paid it much attention.

"Of course. I live there. Well, sort of."

I didn't know how anyone "sort of" lived anywhere, but now was not the time. "So have you caught up with Megan yet?" I asked Lucy. Galbraith's missing kid.

"Well, jeez, Mort. We barely got here. I mean, in all the traffic from the airport in a rental car and checked into the hotel and everything. We'll start looking tomorrow. Right now, we're in a restaurant down the street. Chinese."

"Which reminds me. I haven't eaten for eight hours. I'll get something after I look into this Kimmi and Dooley thing."

"Who the heck are they?"

"Volker's sixteen-year-old daughter and her boyfriend who looks mid-twenties and might have a few years of prison under his belt. If he doesn't, I'd say he's due."

"None of that sounds good."

"It's our country in this great new millennium. It might not be much of anything, either. Mostly I'm piling up investigation hours. I'll fill you in later."

"About Mira, too."

"Will do, but it's nothing. She's a pickpocket."

Mira stared at me, face suddenly tragic, then turned to walk away. I caught her arm, kept her from leaving while I ended the call.

"I'm nothing," she said. "Just a pickpocket." Her voice was flat, more empty than mad.

"Everyone is what they've decided to be." Well, shit. Right then I decided not to pursue a career in politics or work a crisis call line.

"Yeah, right." More mad than empty this time, but low-key mad, as if she didn't have the energy to really get into it.

I'd exhausted my social worker skills and had nothing to fall back on except IRS banter, which only works if you're trying to intimidate. "You think they went in there?" I looked up at the building. "This place got a name?"

"Truckee River Apartments. He lives there."

"And you?"

"Not *with* him, no. Just, I've seen him there. I stay in like four different places with people. Robin and Gayle let me crash on their couch. They share an apartment. I don't like to stay with them too much in case they end up thinking I'm in the way and tell me no more. So I try to sort of circulate."

Circulate. What a way to live. "Okay. Any idea where this Dooley lives?"

"Sure. Same floor as Robin and Gayle. Across the hall and down a little."

Iffy. But in a blond wig, Giants ball cap, glasses, maybe not. And they'd had plenty of time to get into the apartment and out of sight, unpack the baggie, get the drugs going.

"Show me?" I said.

"Like . . . for ten dollars maybe?" she said hopefully.

"Sounds fair."

I followed her to a door facing First Street. She opened it with a key and we went inside. A wall in the foyer held a long row of mailboxes with names on the front. Four rows of sixteen, so sixty-four apartments. Best guess, five hundred a month, so the place could take in almost four hundred thousand a year. The headaches of having to deal with sixty minimum-wage tenants in an old building would make it barely worthwhile, if at all.

"Which floor do you live on?" I asked.

"Second and third, mostly."

Jesus. "Okay, what about this Dooley?"

"Third floor."

"Is Dooley his first name or last?"

"I don't know. Everyone just calls him Dooley."

I scanned the third-floor mailboxes. No Dooley on any of them. "Let's go have a look," I said.

We went up a stairwell. "You . . . you could stay a while," she said. "Like, for maybe an hour."

I shivered. This was a different proposition than what I got from Rosa in the Green Room. Rosa wasn't serious. This was. I felt so far out of my element it was like the walls were closing in. Some gumshoe I was. Spade and Hammer were somewhere up ahead, looking back at us, yukking it up, poking each other in the ribs. Twenty-five feet off the street and here was an entirely different world. An odor of urine lifted from threadbare carpet covering the stairs. I lived in a world generally untainted by urine, where educated people owned their homes, held jobs that supported those homes, paid into 401(k)s, made enough to hate the IRS, had term life, owned mutual funds or had enough saved up to weather a three- or four-month bad spell, had a backyard, lawn to mow, fence to keep it reasonably private.

I didn't answer her. I didn't feel fully in my own skin. We reached the third floor, went through a fire door, and walked down a dimly lit hallway. Another fire door with a red glowing exit sign was at the far end.

"This's my place," Mira said, stopping at number 304. "I mean, Robin's and Gayle's."

"Not so loud," I said softly. "Which one is Dooley's?"

"Over here." She went another twenty feet and pointed to number 307, other side of the hall from 304.

Good enough. End of the line. Time to get out. Or I could knock on the door and ask Dooley and Precious what kind of drugs they'd scored at Wildcat, see if they were in the mood to share. Probably not. I heard the mutter of a television coming through the door. Could've been any one of three dozen reality shows, none of which were as true to life as *Hogan's Heroes*.

We returned to 304. I gave her ten dollars and kept going.

"You could stay," she said.

I looked back. She was by the door, looking at me. I went back, gave her another ten. "Thanks for the tour."

"You could. Like—for a while. It's Saturday. They won't be back for at least until midnight."

"You should get some real food in you," I said, using the dregs of my social worker repertoire. I went to the stairwell and looked back. She stood outside the door, watching me without expression. I went down to the first floor.

In the foyer I found the name on the mailbox for apartment 307: G. Orwell.

Great.

Either George was still kicking, or Dooley was an English major. Neither of which seemed likely.

* * *

Two names were on the box for 304: Riggs/Jarecki.

Out the door, east on First to the parking garage, up the stairwell to the fifth floor past laughing young people on their way down, over to the Toyota. I got in, fired up the engine, put it in reverse, hit the brakes to avoid running over a dark shape standing almost behind the car.

Mira.

Swell.

I powered down the window and she came closer. "What?" I asked.

"Are you . . . gonna get something to eat?"

"That's the plan."

"Can I come?"

Now what? No? Buzz off? You look about half-starved, but you're on your own, kid, I can't be bothered. I've got a job, a real home, a half-assed car, a freakin' 401(k), and I don't want your dim and messy world to touch any part of mine?

Her affect was flat. If I said no, she would look at me for a moment, processing the no, but her expression wouldn't change. She had been turned down a thousand times in a thousand ways, expected it. She would leave without a word.

Sonofabitch. And to show what a nice guy I am, it took me six seconds to open the passenger door and say, "Hop in." Six seconds to do for her what I would do in half a second for a hungry dog. This is the world of noninvolvement, of safety and paranoia, which isn't an unreasonable way to operate given the way things are turning out.

She got in beside me, shut the door, didn't say a word. Was this getting me closer to Joss's $13,600 problem? If so, I didn't see how. This was a side trip, a little complication to work out along the way. It took me a while to decide to back the car out and head for the exit ramp. Down and around, down and around, four levels to the street. I gave the attendant two bucks for the thirty-two minutes I'd been there, nosed the Toyota onto First, and headed west, past the Truckee River Apartments. We got to Arlington before I finally said, "What kind of food you like?"

"Whatever. Anything."

Tells a story. When you're hungry, it's just food. You can be picky when you're rich. And I was spoiled. Most of us are. Hit the switch and the light is supposed to come on. I like having the light come on. If it doesn't, the world isn't right, it's damned inconvenient. So, spoiled. We expect things to run smoothly. We hate power outages. We turn the faucet and there's water. Open cupboards or the refrigerator and, hey, there's food. My guess is it isn't like that in much of Somalia.

"When did you last eat?"

"I don't know. I think maybe yesterday."

Barely a hundred pounds. Skinny arms and legs, almost no chest on her, thin face. Faded blue jeans with a designer rip or two in them, except the jeans looked old and the rips looked real.

Low-rent sneakers that might've cost two bucks at Goodwill. Thin short-sleeve pale yellow shirt, no coat.

But piercings, too much makeup, and she'd offered to take me into room 304 for an hour. None of this was my problem. I had what I had, and she had what she had, and I didn't have any reasonable way to share. That's not how the world works. With all their billions, Warren Buffett and Bill Gates weren't at her side, giving her a hefty wad of hundred-dollar bills, enough to change her life. Her being hungry wasn't my fault, or Warren's or Bill's. I could feed her, but I couldn't fix her.

I took her to Gold Dust West, a casino west of downtown that had a brightly lit coffee shop with cheap but reliable food. They served a twenty-four-hour breakfast, so I suggested something along those lines. She shrugged, happy enough to be sitting in a booth with the prospect of food sometime in the next half hour. So I ordered for both of us, same thing—three scrambled eggs, link sausage, toast, side order of pancakes, milk. Protein and carbs. Survival food. No fettuccini alfredo, no lobster thermidor.

The food arrived. She tucked into it like a Marine in boot camp, but with quiet intensity and no snarling "back-off" wolf sounds like you get with Marines. From time to time she gazed up into my eyes. No words, but she looked grateful. Took her a while, but finally the pancakes slowed her down.

"I'm sorry," she said. "I guess I'm sort of a pig."

"Pigs just eat to eat. Hungry is different."

She leaned back, looked down at her hands, then back up at me. "At that club, outside when you grabbed me, and I couldn't breathe for a moment, you said I could do better."

"Not just you. We all can, trust me."

"No one ever told me that before." She gave me a funny look. "I, uh . . . I don't even know your name."

"Mort."

"Mort? That's funny."

"Funny how?"

"I don't know. Just funny. It sounds funny."

"I guess it does at that. You should hear it with the 'imer' my misguided mother tacked on the end of it."

"I'm not a hooker."

I blinked. "I didn't think you were."

"I mean, it's not like I do that kind of thing all the time. Like when I asked if you wanted to, you know, stay for a while."

"You don't have to explain."

"I just don't want you to think that I, that I . . ."

"I don't. Mira Tanaka."

She smiled, then fell silent.

"How old are you?" I asked.

"Twenty-two."

"If you don't mind my asking, what's with the goth look? The black lipstick and makeup? I never understood that."

"Think it's kinda, like, creepy?"

"A little. I just don't see how it helps."

"Helps what?"

"You."

She thought about that for a moment. "Guess it doesn't."

"So, why?"

She shrugged. "It's, I don't know. Just a way to be. I don't always. I was at Lori's this morning. She let me put this on, so why not?"

"Lori?"

"Girl in 211 on the second floor. Where I stayed last night."

"Circulating."

"Uh-huh."

"So tell me about this Dooley guy."

"What do you want to know?"

"You see him at that place a lot, Wildcat?"

"Sometimes. When I go there. Sometimes he hangs out for a while and sometimes he just buys from Ramon and splits."

"Have you seen that girl with Dooley before? The one he was with tonight."

She shrugged. "She's been around."

"Okay. Now back up. Who's Ramon?"

"Just this guy. Sort of older." She hesitated. "He . . ."

"He what?"

"He told me to try to get your wallet."

Cold fingers walked up my spine. "Black hair? Thin? Has a soul patch about this long?" I held a thumb and index finger an inch apart.

"Uh-huh."

"He told you to get my wallet?"

"Uh-huh. I think he wanted to know who you were. Like if you were a narc or something."

So I'd caught the exchange and put a faint glowing spot on his radar. Little switchblade whippet fucker was not the kind of guy whose radar I wanted to be on.

"You do what this guy Ramon tells you to do?"

"If you don't, you can get hurt."

"And you go to his club?"

"It's not his, but . . . yeah. I mean, there's other places I can go but they're all pretty much the same. He goes there, too."

"What's Ramon's last name?"

"I don't know. I never heard it."

"Do you know what Dooley bought? What kind of drugs?"

"Most likely meth. Ramon doesn't deal a lot of coke these days. I think he has some angel dust, but not much and only if you ask for it and he knows you."

Jesus. "Mind if I say something from the heart, Mira?"

She pursed her lips. "I know, but go ahead."

"What do you know?"

"I know what you're gonna say."

"How about, get cleaned up, lose the black makeup and the eyebrow piercings, smile, get a job, eat more, keep away from Ramon and anyone like him."

"Knew it. How'm I supposed to do all that?"

"Just do it. Make a decision. You're young. Start with the makeup and the piercings. You can fix that in half an hour. The purple hair should probably go too, but I'm not sure about that. Depends on the job. Then go out and ask around. Keep at it and eventually someone will hire you. And no one is forcing you to go to Wildcat or those other places."

"Sure." She said it with very little force. Life comes and it goes, doesn't leave much residue along the way.

I left a few bills on the table. We got up, went outside, and I drove her back to the apartments, dropped her off at the curb.

She got out, bent down, and looked in at me. "Thanks. You know, for the food and the advice."

"You're welcome. See you around."

"Yeah, I guess." She shut the door.

I checked for traffic in my side mirror and pulled out. She stood on the sidewalk and watched me go until I finally turned a corner and she was gone.

* * *

I drove home. I felt disoriented, back in my safe world with Mira's world still clinging to my thoughts, giving me a case of the megrims.

I shook it off. It was 10:05, Saturday night. I could maybe sleep, but it felt too early for that. I could spend an hour or two in the Green Room at the Golden Goose, but . . . why? The thought of beer didn't have much appeal. Nor did sarsaparilla or O'Roarke's grousing about my using free-drink coupons.

But the house was empty. Too empty, too quiet. I missed Lucy. I wandered the rooms, finally decided to leave because the place had too many ghosts gliding around. Jeri was gone and the house used to be hers. Lucy was out of town. Quiet was a kind of unearthly vapor, seeping out of the walls.

So, Mort, go sleuth something.

Evelyn Joss hired us to find out why her partner, Michael Volker, had taken almost fourteen thousand dollars from their operating account without letting her know. That was the job, not Mira, not Ramon, not Dooley and Kimmi, and definitely not Soranden's skull.

The night was young. I could accumulate another few hours by staking out Volker's house. I might get lucky and he would go somewhere relevant, like to a casino Sports Book where he might drop a few hundred dollars on the horses or on basketball games— or off to see a new girlfriend who was bleeding him as long as his blood stayed green. I didn't know what I was doing, but I was lucky. And unprofessional. And a maverick.

Good enough.

I left the Toyota at home and drove Lucy's Mustang back to Volker's. I parked eighty feet up the street facing the house. Lights were glowing on both floors. The BMW was no longer in the driveway, but the beat-up Honda was there. So add it up, big guy. Kimmi partying with Dooley. The Beemer might be in the garage. If not—and you won't know one way or the other—then Volker was out running around, in which case the sister, Marta, was in charge of Derek, and you won't know that either unless you go ring the bell, which you're not gonna do.

Which is as far as I got, and it added up to nothing.

Wish Ma were here.

Nearest streetlight was a hundred yards away. It was dark where I was sitting, opposite a house with not one light showing. I tuned the radio to that oldies station, started off with Ricky Nelson, then got Simon and Garfunkel, sixties anti-war stuff, Elvis, Chuck Berry, Sam Cooke, Beach Boys.

Gumshoe rock.

Then, in the midst of boredom and music turned down low, with a belly full of food, I drifted off to sleep.

* * *

And jerked awake when a cop rapped on the window with a nightstick. The flashlight was blinding. "Proud Mary" was on the radio. I shielded my eyes, powered the window down, and got John Fogerty and Creedence under control.

"How you doin' there, bud?" the cop said. He was fortysomething, heavy, in a black RPD uniform with patches on both shoulders, web belt loaded down and creaking, patrol car behind me with the bubblegum lights sending red and blue lights across houses on both sides of the street.

"Fine," I said. "Doin' real fine."

"Been drinking?"

"Had a few beers three or four days ago."

"Smart ass, huh. Let's see a license and registration."

I fumbled out my wallet and, of course, got the wrong one, the one with a single lousy dollar left in it and no ID. Perfect.

"Oop," I said. "Wrong wallet."

And sure, everyone carries two wallets. Isn't that de rigueur these days?

Guess not.

"Please step out of the car, sir."

Polite, these guys, unless you start waving a gun. It's all that political correctness training. We didn't do PC in the IRS. We did IYF—*In Your Face*. So I got out of the car. Maybe that two-wallet thing wasn't de rigueur after all. Or maybe it was the big guy sleeping in an expensive neighborhood in a ragtop Mustang with a roof patched with duct tape, a car registered to a girl by the name of Lucy Landry. That might do it. He would have run the plate before rapping on the window.

"We can clear this up real fast, Officer," I said.

"That would be a first this week. And not very likely."

"Can we give it a try, save you some work? Paperwork's a bitch these days, isn't it? All those i's to dot and t's—"

"You need to keep your hands where I can see them, sir."

"A phone call? Just one, then we'll both laugh at this."

"I seriously doubt that. Some girl called it in. Said a guy was in a car, asleep, looked like he might be drunk or casing the neighborhood."

"Casing while asleep? You see a lot of that?"

His eyes narrowed unappreciatively at the logic.

"What girl?" I asked.

"We don't give out that kind of information, sir."

"One call, Officer? It won't take long."

He shrugged. Maybe he didn't like paperwork. He looked more like the kind of guy who liked patting people down then running them in, but that also involved paperwork, so . . .

I called Russell Fairchild.

"Jesus, now what?" he answered sleepily.

"Got a little problem, Russ."

"Can it wait till tomorrow? I was in the middle of a dream that was working out okay."

"It's hard to get those restarted."

"I'd sure like to try. Maybe if I go right back to sleep—"

"What time is it, anyway?"

"Sonofabitch, Angel. It's two-freakin'-thirty in the a.m."

"It's only a little problem. Shouldn't take long."

He sighed. "Okay, what?"

"Got a guy here wants to talk to you. Name on his uniform says Reynolds. I think he's thinking about hauling me in because I don't look like Lucy."

"You don't. She's a hell of a lot better looking." He sighed. "Okay, put 'im on."

I handed the phone to Officer Reynolds. He took it warily. "Yeah? Who's this?"

He watched me as he listened. Then he said, "Angel? *That* guy? You sure? This guy's got two wallets. And I've seen Angel on TV lots of times. This one's got long blond hair—"

I whipped off the wig, the ball cap, black-frame glasses. Forgot I had all that on. I was getting too used to disguises.

Reynolds goggled at me. "Aw, dirty son of a bitch. You gotta be shittin' me. No, not *you*, sir. Guy's running around with two wallets and wearing some sort of a disguise, but, yeah, it's him all right." He listened again. "Okay, *hell* yeah, I'll read him his rights. Happy to." He grinned at me, which tightened the skin around his skull bones. "Okay, will do."

"Seriously? You're gonna read me my rights?"

"Damn right. Back up against your car and face me."

Well, shit. I leaned against Lucy's Mustang.

"You have the right to sit in your fuckin' car looking drunk and stupid. You have the right to have two fuckin' wallets and wear a fuckin' wig and a dress if you want to. You have the right to phone a detective to bail your sorry ass out, and you have the right to kiss my ass, *sir*." He shoved my phone into my hands. "Have a nice fuckin' night." He marched back to his car.

I put the phone to my ear. "You still there, Russ? Police sure do say 'fuckin' a lot when they get worked up."

"It's a useful word. I use it, too. Two wallets and a disguise? What was that all about?"

"I was undercover. Sort of."

"Sounds illegal. Don't tell me another word. Night."

I shut the phone down. The cop left. Volker's house was dark, Honda in the driveway, BMW gone. I fired up the Mustang and drove home. I didn't know I had the right to wear a dress. Good to know. I'll have to ask Lucy what size to buy, get her opinion about colors and fabrics.

*   *   *

So I got in another five hours' surveillance and had a good time. When I got home, the quiet didn't have that weltschmerz quality so I was okay with it this time. I went to bed and fell asleep with a smile on my face. I had a detective in my pocket and Ma was gonna love the cop-stop story because it might've taught me a lesson in surveillance and had nothing at all to do with finding body parts or Soranden's ever-lovin' skull.

CHAPTER FIVE

EVELYN JOSS WAS six feet tall, fifty-five years old, carrying a few extra pounds, narrow shoulders, a bit stooped, with graying blond hair, an easygoing manner, soft voice, a great smile. We were in her office at Joss & Volker, CPAs, seated in cream-colored leather chairs around a small cherrywood conference table polished to a mirror finish. We had a view out a picture window of a somnolent afternoon, no traffic on the street, no one outside on the pedestrian walkways. It was Sunday and this was Evelyn's day off. But Volker's purported embezzlement was the order of business, and it couldn't be done with Volker in the next room, wondering why the Mortimer Angel of Saturday night who had mentioned something about $13,600 was in the next room chatting with his business partner of twelve years.

"Twelve years," I repeated what she'd told me. A glance at a clock on the wall told me it was 12:35.

"Yes. He had six years' experience with Wells Fargo when I hired him. I had more than I could handle back then. Now he's a full partner. It's been a good relationship."

"Up until now."

"Well," she said hesitantly, "I don't know. It depends on why he took the money, doesn't it? I wish he'd told me about it, but it's not as if he took it and ran. And thirteen thousand and a bit? That seems like an awfully gray area, doesn't it? Not the kind of money people generally take off with."

In my experience, no, but I didn't want to tell her that my experience in embezzlement as a gumshoe was exactly zero. On the other hand, as an IRS agent I had seen people unload bank accounts and abscond with wads of cash, but it was then up to the enforcement arm of the IRS to track them down and beat them with rubber hoses on the way back from Mexico or Brazil. I was never on the rubber hose team, but I'd heard it was a plum assignment, a wonderful stress reliever, better than antioxidants and yoga.

"How long have you known about the missing money?" I asked. I knew, but I wanted to hear it from her.

"Since Thursday before last, about ten days."

"You haven't said anything to him about it?"

"No. I would like to know why first. It isn't like Mike to do something like this, Mr. Angel."

"Mort."

"Mort, then. And, please, call me Eve. Like I said, Mike and I have had a good partnership for years. Something like this could change that, and I'm not willing to do that at this point, to mention it to him, not for that relatively small amount of money. He took the money in June. The account had thirty thousand in it. He took less than fourteen thousand, so it wasn't as if he was going to run, then got cold feet. If he were going to run, it seems he would have taken all of it—then if he decided *not* to run, he would put it all back. But that's not what happened. And, well, there's something I didn't tell Mrs. Clary when we spoke. I was going to, but as we were speaking it went right out of my mind. I wish that wouldn't happen so often, but . . ."

"What didn't you tell her?"

"That starting in July, toward the end of the month, Mike has been putting a thousand a month back into the account. Of course, I didn't know that either, until ten days ago."

Okay, that was more than a little significant. Enough that it made me wonder what I was doing here.

"So he's making restitution," I said.

"So it seems. But quietly. He never said a word, but I have the feeling he needed it for something and always intended to pay it back."

"So this investigation is for your peace of mind?" Which would make it border on a noninvestigation, but not quite.

"Something like that. I mean, it was so out of character for Mike. I would like to know why in case it's important or might happen again, possibly on a larger scale. It might have been sort of a trial run, although that doesn't seem right since it's not like we have enough in the account to make it worthwhile to take it all and run."

"He needed a short-term loan. Didn't want to announce it or explain it."

"That would be my guess, yes."

"But that was in June, and you didn't notice."

She smiled wryly. "The thrash doesn't end in April. It just rolls into amended returns, working on getting all the extensions out of the way in time, then keeping up with the usual tax stuff that keeps us busy all year long. So, no, I didn't notice. We don't touch that account, don't use it on an ongoing basis for anything. It's a reserve, rainy-day fund. Mike keeps track of it, not me. I handle a few of the bigger corporate accounts. I've had no time to worry about it. No reason to, either."

"A no-worry fund? I could use one of those."

She smiled.

I leaned closer. "So you want me to find out why he did it? Is that all?"

"Pretty much."

"And do it quietly?"

"If at all possible, yes."

"Too bad. I think that horse has already left the barn."

"Oh?"

"I went to his house yesterday evening and asked him to tell me about the thirteen thousand six hundred dollars. I didn't mention you or the fund, but I named the money figure."

Her shoulders sagged. "Oh, Lord."

"Sorry. This is not the kind of thing people want kept quiet, as a general observation. Anyway, it was an old IRS trick."

"IRS?"

"Don't know if Mrs. Clary mentioned it, but I was a field agent with the IRS until I discovered I had a soul. Mike would know where I came up with the knowledge that thirteen six had become an issue in any context."

"He would, yes."

"I might be able to smooth it over a bit, but investigating this thing quietly is no longer an option. I'm sorry about that."

She leaned back. "I imagine things will be . . . awkward, tomorrow. And now that he knows I know, I'm not a hundred percent certain I want to know why he took it. I mean, since he's been paying it back. This is getting so . . . well, messy."

"Does that mean Clary Investigations is off the case?" Ma would be pissed. If I'd quashed this, she wouldn't pick up the tab in the Green Room for the next three months.

Eve lowered her head, closed her eyes, and thought for half a minute. "No," she said at last. "I would still like to know why, but

I really don't want to ask him, especially if it's something he would prefer to keep private, which seems quite likely given the circumstances. I'm not a confrontational person, Mr. Angel—Mort. A little nothing quarrel can tie me up in knots for days." She sighed. "But I'd still like to know why, even if it seems so much like . . . well, like prying."

"He borrowed almost fourteen thousand dollars without a word to you. I wouldn't categorize your interest as 'prying.'"

"Perhaps not. One thing you should probably understand: our relationship is more professional than personal. That might seem strange since it's just the two of us here, but we don't have a lot in common outside of work. I'm quite a bit older than Mike. I know he bowls, of course. He must be quite good at it since his office here is full of trophies. I can't remember having been in a bowling alley in my life. I belong to a reading group. There's nine of us. We read the same novels then get together and share our thoughts about them. And I knit sweaters and do needlepoint. There's not much crossover between Mike and me, other than we're both divorced. But mine was twenty-five years ago so even that isn't much of a connection.

"I won't say anything to him when he comes in tomorrow. I just couldn't. And knowing Mike, he won't mention it either. If he does, I guess we'll deal with it, and I'll let you know. I hope he doesn't. It would make me sick all day. As it is . . . I really don't want to think about it right now."

"In the meantime, are you certain you want me to keep looking into it?"

"Only if you can do it quietly. Now. I mean, from this point forward. If you have a way to do that." She was silent for a few seconds, then said, "It makes me feel so darn sneaky, though."

"Private investigation is often like that."

She sighed again. "I suppose."

"If we need to meet, we can do it after hours, here or at your home. And I'll need to see the balance sheets of that fund."

"Of course." She looked down at her hands. "This has been so upsetting. I haven't slept well in a week. Some people seem to thrive on confrontation, but I hate it. I wish all of this would just go away, but . . . but I still want to *know*."

* * *

So I wasn't off the case, as exciting as it was. And I had Xerox copies of the rainy-day-fund balance sheets in a leather briefcase that made me look more like an accountant than a PI, but as a world-famous PI, I still didn't have any clear idea as to how to proceed. Which was great and made Ma's phone call as I was traveling north at forty miles an hour on Kietzke Lane a matter of good timing.

I pulled to the curb. "Hola, Ma. You find Megan yet?"

"Found out she moved to Albuquerque."

"Bummer."

"Huh. You been drinking?"

"Evelyn Joss gave me a bottled water. Does that count?"

"Jesus. Okay, Lucy and me are headed to LAX right now. She's driving. I wouldn't drive these freeways to escape a tidal wave. I'd take my chances with the water. We got a flight out in an hour and a half."

"To Albuquerque."

"Nothing gets by you, does it?"

Man, I hate irony.

I said, "You're not going to farm the investigation out to an outfit in Albuquerque?"

"I don't do that if I don't have to."

"My nephew Greg did it all the time."

"Maybe that worked for him. It don't for me. When I ask questions, I like to see body language along with answers. And if I find Megan, I want to talk to her, hear her story. I spoke to Mrs. Galbraith, Karen. She said not to worry about expenses like a flight to New Mexico. She just wants us to find Megan. *Hey!* Watch where you're goin', you road-hog retard! Sorry 'bout that. How'd it go with Evelyn?"

I gave her a rundown of our conversation, including the fact that Michael Volker was putting a thousand a month back into their joint account—which Eve had characterized as a rainy-day fund, not an operating account.

"Sort of changes things," Ma said, "but since she still wants answers, keep digging."

"Suggestions, Ma?"

Silence for ten seconds, then, "You might keep an eye on Volker a while longer, see where he goes, what he does. If that doesn't get you anywhere in a day or two, we'll see if we can get into his bank records, try to figure out what he was doing with the money that way."

"Bank records? No court order? Is that legal?"

"I never got a court order in my life, Mort. We'd get stalled into forever if I had to, and I'd never get one if I asked anyway. Private investigation isn't about court orders."

"Let me guess. It's about end runs."

"Yep."

"Illegally, Ma?"

"How 'bout we use the expression 'extra-legally'?"

"Harder to pronounce, but you got it."

"Jesus. Okay, Lucy got us off that fuckin' interstate alive and we're almost to car rental at LAX. Who's Mira?"

"Not to worry, Ma."

"That's not what I asked, boyo. You're a step ahead of me and two ahead of Lucy."

I parsed that for a moment, still didn't know what Ma had asked or implied, so I said, "This girl, Mira, tried to pick my pocket so I bought her dinner, which was breakfast."

"I'll have Lucy talk to you later. You're breaking up. Hope so, anyway."

She disconnected.

*   *   *

I drove back to Volker's house. No BMW in the driveway. The red Honda was gone. Two lawn mowers were in use on that block alone, and a woman was walking a golden retriever and an Irish setter, getting their leashes tangled. And two boys were tossing a Frisbee across the street from yard to yard. An old guy sitting in his car watching a house wasn't an option, so I kept on going.

Mira.

Maybe she needed feeding again. Some people eat more than every other day, which has long been my preference. And if I went up in that parking garage again, would I see a beat-up red Honda? Only one way to find out.

I went all the way to the top floor. No Honda. I didn't know what I would've done if I'd seen it. I didn't know what I was doing anyway, so what did it matter?

I locked the Toyota after putting on a shaggy blond wig, black frame glasses, and a navy-blue porkpie hat. Got forty feet from the car then went back and traded the porkpie for a ball cap with the improbable inscription *World's Greatest Grampa* above the bill. Ma's trick. Give 'em something to remember. I went down and hiked west on First Street, stood on the sidewalk in front of Truckee River Apartments, caught the door two inches before it shut when a young guy in a goatee, buzz cut, and a dirty green army jacket came out.

Up the stairs to the third floor, down the hallway. I stood in front of 304 for thirty seconds, trying to figure out what I would say if Mira answered, what I would say if it was someone else, what I would do if Dooley and/or Kimmi popped out of 307 down the hall. I couldn't come up with anything, so I knocked.

A chubby girl four foot ten answered. Brown hair down to her butt, huge breasts, wearing a plain white tight T-shirt, black panties, bare feet, not the slightest hint of embarrassment. "Yeah?"

"Is Mira in?"

"She don't live here."

"Except sometimes?"

"She stays here sometimes, yeah, but she don't live here."

"Know where she is?"

"Nope." She smiled and poked her chest out another inch, which was impressive and entirely unnecessary. "Hey, you want to come in, have a beer? I'm Robin."

"Can't stay. Sorry."

"Too bad. You're really big."

"Uh, yeah. Bye."

She watched me all the way to the fire door. I opened the door and looked back. She was still there. Must be a dearth of males in the building, or maybe in this part of Reno. I walked the hallway on the second floor. What was that other apartment number Mira mentioned? Two something. Two eleven.

I knocked on 211's door. Heard nothing, gave it one more try, heard a scuffling sound, and Mira opened the door an inch and peeked out. "Oh, hey. Hi," she said quietly.

"You hungry, kiddo?"

"I . . . um, no."

Good enough. I was about to leave when I got a closer look at the eye peering out at me. It was half shut, looked dark, so I eased the door open a bit further against almost no resistance.

Black eye, and not due to makeup since she wasn't wearing any. Makeup doesn't result in swelling. Or a split lip.

"What happened to you?"

"I, you know. Like walked into a door."

Uh-huh. Lot of that going on in these United States. Doors are a conundrum. Proper usage should be taught in high school. "Was the door's name Ramon?"

"What?"

"Ramon do that to you?"

Five seconds of silence. "Um, no."

She shut the door. I stood there for a moment, wondering if I should knock again or leave. Finally, I left.

I couldn't adequately explain why I went up West Street to Second, turned the corner and went into Wildcat. Every time I was about to leave Rufus Booth's in-home dojo he asked the same question: "What's your number one defensive tactic?" And the answer was always the same: "Avoid trouble or run."

Got that right.

So there I was inside Wildcat. Smart. As if I hadn't learned anything in the fifteen months I'd been a gumshoe. Maybe it was because I was still in training, hadn't picked up the finer points yet. But it was Sunday, two fifteen in the afternoon, not four people in the place, and the music was at a reasonable volume. "Graceland" by Paul Simon. Hard to imagine anything tamer than that. Well, "Garden Party" by Ricky Nelson, "Love Me Tender" by Elvis. So I sat at the bar, no one else nearby, and ordered a sarsaparilla.

"You kidding?" said the barkeep, a woman I put just shy of thirty. Pretty, no makeup, five-two, wearing a Wildcat T-shirt.

"I never kid about sarsaparilla."

"That's funny. We don't carry it. You're probably the first person to ask. Ever. Puts you in a class all your own."

I smiled. "How about an ice-cold Mountain Dew?"

She planted her elbows on the bar. "You're a riot, hon."

"Milk?"

"That I can do. How about an Adam Bomb Two? Colorado Bulldog? Or I can do milk, neat."

"Ugh, actually."

"Thought so, Gramps. You look like the sarsaparilla type. Big, but sorta mild. Sorry I can't accommodate."

Gramps? I lifted my eyes to the underside of the ball cap's bill, had second thoughts about that *World's Greatest Grampa* thing. "Mild. That's me. How about Pete's Wicked Ale?"

"That I can do. Glass or bottle?"

"Bottle's fine."

She popped the cap, set it in front of me, looked toward the door, then wandered off toward the far end of the bar. She lifted a section of bar and went through, then disappeared into a back room.

As I took a sip of Pete's, shadowy movement in the mirror behind the bar caught my eye. I turned, and Ramon—last night's whippet—was coming up on my right side.

Well, shit.

But he didn't know me, didn't know I knew who he was, so I turned away and kept an eye on him in the mirror. Baggy cargo pants, black T-shirt, three heavy gold chains around his neck.

"Back again?" he said.

I turned slowly and faced him. "Huh? Are you talking to me?"

"See anyone else in here, dude?"

I looked around. The place had emptied out. Which wasn't a big trick since there'd only been a few guys nursing beers near the front entrance at a table beneath a TV with the sound off. They'd gone, left their beers on the table.

This was Ramon's turf. I was just some old guy sitting on a barstool. Rufus had impressed upon me several pieces of advice in the way of self-defense. Avoid trouble if you can, run if you can, never panic, don't let the thought of pain paralyze you, but if confrontation is likely or inevitable try to show fear because that particular Sun Tzu puts assholes off their best game. Ramon was looking like an asshole at the moment, so I tried to pacify him.

"Buy you a beer?" I said in a friendly voice.

"Like you bought Mira dinner last night? Like that?"

"Mira?"

He pulled out a butterfly knife, gave it a smooth whip-whap that revealed a gleaming four-inch blade.

I got off the stool and backed away. "Hey, hey, hey. Whoa, friend. What's with the knife?"

Okay, that bit about not panicking isn't easy, Rufus, in case you didn't know. I took a deep breath, which helped. Rufus said to breathe, smacked my head every time I didn't breathe enough. So I remembered to breathe.

"Friend?" Ramon said with an eerie smile. "You want to be friends? Maybe buy me dinner too? Then maybe you and me, we go see a movie, eat some popcorn?"

"Look, I'll just leave if that's what you want."

"You were in here last night."

"Well, yeah. It was loud so I left. Look, no trouble, okay? All I want is to get out of here."

He held the knife underhand, pointed at me, ready. "How 'bout we talk first?"

"C'mon, sir. Really, you don't need that knife . . ."

He grinned. "Sir?"

Actually, I thought that was a great touch. If Ramon didn't kill me, I would tell Rufus about it—seeing that killer's look in Ramon's eyes dim slightly. But this business with the knife also made me mad, to put it lightly. I hadn't expected that. I was tired of people trying to kill me. The world is filling up with vermin, psychotic trash, and I was getting damn sick of it.

I edged sideways. "I'll just go, okay?"

He lifted the knife another inch. "Stay where you are, dude. I ain't done with you yet."

"What? What do you mean?" Weak. Afraid. This guy was a scary little weasel, but he was beginning to really piss me off.

"What're you doin' here? You a cop? Narc?"

And if I was, *then* what? If he thought he'd just pulled a knife on a cop, where did he think this was going to end up?

"Nothing like that. I came in for a drink, thought I'd check the place out when it was a lot quieter."

"Sure you did."

I took a step back. "Don't . . . don't do this. Please."

He smiled.

Truth is in the eyes. This guy's eyes were rabid wolverine, nothing human inside, glowing with anticipation. Even if it has never happened to you before, you know when someone has crossed a mental boundary and made the irrevocable decision to hurt you. Ramon was seconds away from cutting.

"Look, if it's the hat you want, I'll just leave it on the bar." I took off the ball cap with my left hand and tossed it three feet to the bar, used the quarter-second distraction to grab his right wrist in my right hand, palm up like Rufus had made me do a few thousand times in the past six months. This time I did it faster.

"Anything you do for real, do it with speed and power," he told me over and over. "If someone threatens your life, don't hold back. It's not a game. Give it a hundred and ten percent."

So I didn't hold back. I twisted his wrist counterclockwise, which he would see as clockwise. He was wiry, not strong. I cranked his arm in a half-turn that locked his elbow out and took all the leverage out of his arm. The knife was suddenly useless in his hand. I pulled his arm toward me then down and across my body as I spun hard to my left and slammed my right hip into his elbow. I felt the joint go. *Felt* it. He screamed. Probably hurt when tendons tore loose. Or ligaments. The knife clattered to the floor as I grabbed his wrist in both hands, lifted his arm, ducked under it as I twisted it further and cranked his arm above his head, kept turning to my left, felt the shoulder joint go the way Rufus said it would, then I slammed him back against the bar. The entire sequence was one continuous movement that didn't take three seconds.

He bounced off the bar and dropped like a rag doll, giving off a high-pitched squeal that was mostly an airless scream, as if he couldn't breathe. I made sure he had no more fight left, then I picked up his knife, kept an eye on him.

"Thanks," I said, putting it in a pocket. "I always wanted one of these." Which was of course a lie. I'd never given knives as weapons a moment of thought.

He stared at me with eyes so full of pain he might not be seeing or hearing much of anything. He was on the floor with his head on a brass foot rail, right arm twisted unnaturally. It would take surgery to put it back together and physical therapy before he would be tying his shoes again.

I crouched in front of him and looked into his eyes. "Arm hurts a little, don't it?"

He stared at me through a glaze of pain, but balefully. An animal disguised as human.

I poked his forehead with a stiff finger. "Next time, I won't stop until you're dead." Pretty fuckin' macho since I was so full of adrenaline I was about to puke. The words rolled out of me without thought. My voice was shaky, a quarter octave high. A knife? In a Second Street Reno bar on a lazy Sunday afternoon? What kind of a world was this, anyway? This subhuman had made the decision to slash me, watch me bleed, maybe kill me? What did he think gave him that right? What kind of a person could stick a knife into another person?

I grabbed him by the ears and bounced his head off the brass rail. Hard. It made a short hollow ringing sound. His eyes rolled up in his head. Out. Then I gave him another bounce for good measure and because I didn't like him.

The bar was empty. Miss Barkeep still gone, no one else in the place. Guess everyone there had known Ramon, had a good idea of what was up, didn't want to get mixed up in anything. He might have said something to the guys at the table near the front door as he came in. They might be out on the sidewalk right now, keeping anyone from coming in until Ramon took care of business and strolled out, grinning. It might be taking longer than expected. One of them might have a peek inside soon to see how it was going. Or someone might've already called 911.

So, time to leave. I got my hat off the bar, took the bottle of Wicked Ale and its fingerprints with me, went out a back exit and found myself in an alley with garbage cans and plastic bins full of empty bottles. I made it to the end of the alley and around the south side of Wildcat before an out-of-body feeling hit me with so much force I felt like a helium balloon, as if I'd become untethered from the world. A bar fight? A *knife* fight? Me? Had that actually happened? I floated along in a haze, no thought about where I was going, no memory of reaching the West Street sidewalk and walking south, no idea how I got to Virginia Street or having crossed the bridge over the Truckee River, or when or where I got rid of the bottle of Wicked Ale.

CHAPTER SIX

THREE TWENTY P.M., I rang the bell outside Booth's dojo.

He opened the door and stared at me, gave me a quick up and down look. His eyes narrowed. "What up, brother?"

"Need to talk."

Having walked over a mile to his place from Wildcat, I was partly back inside myself. And disturbed by what I'd done, that I had put myself in that situation. I was not my favorite person at that moment.

"You okay?"

"I've been better, Ruf."

Rufus took me into the dojo and sat me in a wooden chair. He looked into my eyes. "You didn't run."

"How'd you know?"

"You still got that spiky adrenaline thing going. Your eyes aren't right. How you feel?"

"Not good."

"Are you hurt?"

"No."

"You need water." He went through a door, came back with a plastic bottle, uncapped it, gave it to me. "Drink it slow."

I took a sip, then leaned forward, put my head between my knees. Held that position for half a minute, then looked up at him. "I'm an idiot."

"We all are, to one degree or another, but you mighta had a special moment. How 'bout you take ten or fifteen minutes and come down a little more? Get some air in you. Shut your eyes. Breathe. I'll be back."

He went out, left me there. I closed my eyes and got air. It helped. I downed more water. That helped too.

When I opened my eyes, he was crouched in front of me. I hadn't heard him come in, not a whisper.

"Tell me about it," he said.

I got the knife out of my pocket, handed it to him. He took it, flicked it open, flicked it shut. "Benchmade Morpho," he said. "A fifty-one BK. Worth about three hundred bucks." He handed it back.

"Good to know."

He smiled. "That knife takedown worked, huh?"

"Just like you showed me."

His smile went out like a blown light. "You got any idea how lucky you are? You mighta practiced it a thousand times in here the past half year. Maybe two. Sounds like a lot, don't it? I wouldn't want to try anything out there I hadn't run through at least *fifty* thousand times. If it isn't pure muscle memory, hard and fast, no thought involved, then it ain't worth spit, ace. You had no backup move. What I oughta do, I oughta cut you loose. There's a world out there where dangerous people crawl around in the gutters. If you think this judo shit makes you invincible, you're not gonna last long."

"It wasn't like that."

"Says you. It's almost always like that. Now tell me about it from the beginning, and I'll tell you where you fucked up."

So I told him, as much of it as I could remember. Already it was getting fuzzy in my mind.

He slapped me upside the head, just hard enough to make it hurt some. Not many people could do that, but Rufus could do it anytime he wanted and I couldn't stop him if I tried. A ninth-dan judo master isn't like other humans.

"You fucked up the moment you took your first step in the direction of that Wildcat place."

"I know."

"Don't go back." He popped my head again. "Ever."

I nodded. I deserved this. I'd brought it on myself. After I'd seen Mira's face, I had been on a kind of automatic pilot, which is the exact opposite of thinking rationally.

"I don't fit in my own skin, Ruf."

"You won't. It'll take about three days to get it out of your head. It'll go a little faster if you do familiar easy things. Best is if you take a long slow run, take the edge off that adrenaline."

"Sounds like a plan."

He stared at me for a while. "Guy pulls a knife on you, you took it away and tore him up pretty good."

"That's the short version."

"Good for you. Better than gettin' cut." He thumped my head one last time. "Next time, ace, *run*. I'm gonna rethink that orange belt of yours."

* * *

According to Lewis Thomas, everyone has a desire to be useful, which is nonsense, patently untrue. Ramon had no desire to be useful to anyone, including himself. At best, he had a little shit's desire to be admired by other little shits.

Enough.

* * *

One of the better things about my buying Jeri's house from Ron DiFrazzia after Jeri was murdered is that it's on Washington Street between First and Second, only four hundred feet from the Truckee River and the bike path that stretches from East Sparks all the way to Verdi, a distance of some twenty miles. I could pop out the door and go. I went west to Mayberry Park and back, total distance of about ten miles, at ten minutes a mile, an easy lope, trying to get Ramon out of my head.

Which worked, sort of. Then I showered, dressed, and my phone rang. It was Lucy.

"How's Albuquerque, kiddo?" I said.

"Hot. How's Reno?"

"Got in a knife fight and took a ten-mile run."

"Wow, that's so not funny."

"You find Megan yet?"

"We're maybe tracking her down. She was at one place and it looks like she probably changed her name. I'm learning a lot of cool stuff with Ma."

"She's like that."

"You figure out that embezzlement thing yet?"

"Workin' on it."

"Miss me?"

"Like crazy, Luce."

"Well, good. Maybe we should get hitched."

"It's on my radar."

"Okay, good. But no pressure, Mort. Gotta go. We're about to go into a restaurant here. I'm starving."

We ended the call. So knife fights weren't funny. I thought that myself. Lucy would give me hell for it later, especially the way I'd said it but hadn't said it. She would probably slap me upside the head too, harder than Rufus had.

I walked over to the Golden Goose in yet another disguise. Disguises were getting to be routine. This time it was a golfer's hat, long white hair, white moustache, sunglasses, a cane, fake limp, and a foam and polyester pad under my shirt that rounded me out at about three hundred pounds. Television had turned me into something of a celebrity, made me more recognizable than the vice president, not a difficult trick. I kept off Second Street and stayed well away from Wildcat—not that Ramon would be there. Odds were, he would be in surgery another hour or two. I could still hear that chicken-bone sound of his elbow joint going.

You proud of that, Mort?

Nope.

Well, sort of, to be honest. The son of a bitch pulled a knife on me. Far out there on my mental horizon was the smoky haze of a long-ago gunfight at the O.K. Corral.

I got to the Green Room at 5:57. O'Roarke was just coming on duty and Rosa was at the bar in a sunflower-yellow cleavage-rich dress that revealed lovely legs up to mid-thigh. It felt good to be among friends in a familiar place. Rosa was twenty-four, slender, pretty, and, last I'd heard, she was charging fifteen hundred a night. I'd told her how to avoid a big tax liability. Tax forms have a long list of codes for occupation, but none for hooker or call girl, so we had her down as an artist, claiming an income of about $48,000 a year, which covered the usual living expenses. All the rest, something north of $120,000, was getting packed into a safe deposit box. It was earning zero percent interest, but out of Uncle's sight.

I sat beside her, leaned my cane against the bar, put my hat, wig, and moustache on the seat to my left, glasses on the bar.

"A cane?" she said. "Since when?"

"Think of it as insurance. You never know when you'll pull up lame."

She laughed, showing a pink tongue, even white teeth. Her eyes had a healthy sparkle to them.

"What'll it be, Spitfire?" O'Roarke asked. "It used to be Pete's, but you've been all over the place the last few months. Got a new shipment of sarsaparilla in, just for you."

"Wild Turkey, barkeep. A double, straight up."

"Whoa," Rosa said. "Been one of *those* days, huh?"

"One of those, yeah."

She patted my arm. "Well, if you need comforting, just let me know."

"Will do. Have to ask Lucy first."

"I'm sure that'll go well." Rosa looked around. "Where is that gorgeous little minx of yours, anyway?"

"Albuquerque." The double whisky landed in front of me. I knocked back a third of it to get it started. One more reason to dislike Ramon. Now the bastard had me drinking hard stuff.

"What's in Albuquerque?" Rosa asked.

"Gila monsters, dust, armadillos."

"You're the hardest person to talk to I know."

"It's a knack. And I work at it."

Then RPD Detective Russell Fairchild walked in. "I was driving up Fourth Street, saw some guy, thought it might be you headed this way. You got a cane, put on weight?"

"Hey, look," Rosa said, pointing at the television.

We looked. There I was, six o'clock news, telephoto shot of me entering the police station with Russell and Officer Day. Ronald Soranden's skull was still above the fold, so to speak. The fact that he was the top IRS man in Northern Nevada before he went missing kept the story on a front burner. People really liked that IRS part. A lot of folks believe in karma.

"Over here, Mort," Russ said, nodding toward a table in a far corner where the green lighting didn't penetrate.

I grabbed my disguise paraphernalia and we sat at the table, facing the bar and the entrance.

"What do you know about Soranden?" Russ asked me.

"He was a shithead, that help?"

"Not much. He was IRS, so that was a given. You know anything personal or private that might help me figure out who killed him?"

"Other than being a shithead and having eighteen hundred enemies? Isn't that enough?"

"You'd think. So far it hasn't been."

I closed my eyes. Couldn't see Soranden, but Ramon was still there. His butterfly knife made that evil *snick-snack* sound as he whipped it open. "Give me a while. The knife fight I got into this afternoon still has me a little loopy."

He gave me a classic double take. "Say what?"

So I told the story again. Most stories improve with age, but this one still sucked. After what happened earlier that year, Russ and I had few secrets we couldn't share. Ours was a mutually-assured-destruction relationship, but it felt as if a real friendship was starting to bubble up out of this summer's initial murk when I'd found that dead rapper in his daughter's garage.

"Can't let you out of my sight for a minute," he said when I was finished.

"I've already had my head slapped thrice about it, so unless you pull a gun your softball opprobrium isn't worth a shit."

"Opprobrium. That's a big word. Ripped the guy's arm out of his shoulder and tossed it on the bar, huh?"

"That's not what I said, but it's a meaty image. I might use it when I write my memoirs."

"That hint of pride in your voice gave you away. Hold on." He got out a phone, hit the screen a few times, asked someone on the desk at RPD if he ought to know about anything going on that afternoon downtown. He listened, had to ask a few leading questions, finally hung up after four or five minutes.

"One Ramon Rafael Surry, age thirty-two, is still in surgery at Renown Medical getting his arm reattached. Someone about beat him to death with it."

"Must've happened after I left. His arm was still connected to the rest of him when I went out the back way."

"Kidding. But Surry's in bad shape. Considering he's done time and has a record of robbery, assault, and dealing means you deserve a medal, not that you'll get one since they don't know who tore him up, just some guy in his forties or fifties, six-six, maybe six-seven, blond hair, heavy black frame glasses, blue jeans, polo shirt, blue ball cap with something about *Grampa* above the bill. I've heard worse descriptions, but I think they're not gonna get anywhere with that one."

"Six-seven, huh? Man, that's big. Arness was six-seven. It could've been him, except he's deceased."

"Who the hell is Arness?"

"*Gunsmoke*, Russ. James Arness. Before our time. *Way* before, but you can still watch it on DVD."

He shook his head. "Lady bartender was the only one they found who saw the guy. If she's short, then six-four or six-seven is about the same. Anyway, eyewitnesses are unreliable as hell. Still got that knife on you?"

I dug it out of a pocket. "It's a souvenir. My first and last knife fight. Booth said it's worth about three hundred bucks so I think I'll have it bronzed." Wasn't a cop in the city who didn't know Rufus Booth.

Russ fumbled the blade out, tested it with a finger. "Sharp sonofabitch. Bronze would take the edge off, so I wouldn't. We could book Surry for assault with a deadly weapon. Record like his, he might get ten years."

"The room emptied. No one actually saw the fight. And it would drag me into it, Reno's 'heads' guy. If you want a circus, there it is."

"Not sure we need to put a rush on it. Surry'll keep." He handed the knife back. "What're you gonna do with that if you don't have it bronzed?"

"I might use it in the kitchen. Hate to throw out a three-hundred-dollar knife."

"Slicing mushrooms, apples, stuff like that?"

"It's like you're a mind reader, Russ."

He got up, stretched his back. "About Soranden. Anything you think of that might help, call me anytime."

"Three in the morning?"

"*Any* time—if you get something. I'd love to stick it to the fuckin' FBI. Bunch of prima donna hotshots."

He took off on short bandy legs. I went back to the bar and sat beside Rosa again. "Sarsaparilla," I said to O'Roarke.

"That's more like it, Spitfire. Hard stuff doesn't suit you. Welcome back."

CHAPTER SEVEN

Nine forty-five p.m. I was sitting in my Toyota three doors down from Volker's house, other side of the street, ruminating on how stupid one private eye could be when "Purple People Eater" made me jump. Might be time to change the ringtone to chirping birds, or maybe a snoring hamster.

It was Lucy. "Hola, kiddo," I said.

"That knife fight joke thing, whatever it was, it got me thinking about it all evening. That wasn't like you."

They are so much smarter than we are. I ran that "joke" past O'Roarke before I left, and he smiled and said, "Good one, Mort," and went fifteen feet down the bar to serve two ladies of advanced middle age who had come in desperate for mai tais, asking if they could get those little paper parasols in them.

I said, "I should tell you about my day, Luce."

"Uh-oh. Seriously?"

There wasn't anything I could do except tell her what had happened. That brought it all the way home for me, how stupid I had been. I didn't want any part of Ramon's world, but I had let it touch me. Well, never again. This gumshoe thing had nearly killed me four times before Ramon pulled that knife on me. I'd had a sword run through my chest, a gun blasting away at me in the desert night, been buried alive in the trunk of a Cadillac and shot high in the shoulder with a .38, lost a quarter-inch off the top of my right ear that I had to hide with long wigs that didn't always suit me. Add it up like that and this gumshoe business was a bitch. Last thing I needed was to put myself in the sights of a lowlife scumbag like Ramon. I smacked myself upside the head, made it sting.

"What was *that*?" Lucy said.

"Proxy Rufus slap."

"Rufus is there?"

"Nope. I'll explain the word 'proxy' when you get back to Reno. Maybe even give you a demo."

Silence. Then, "I'm coming home."

"You find Megan?"

"Ma can handle it—as long as she stays off the freeways around here. You need me."

"No argument there since the bed has been so empty lately it actually echoes, but I'm okay—*and* I've got this Rambo thing under control, so if Ma still needs you . . ."

"Rambo. Right." Then she sort of snickered, which was a nice sound. "I'm the one who chopped down Buddie, not you, in case you don't remember."

"Makes you Ramboette," I said, "but with a merit badge."

Lucy had stuck a tree saw with razor teeth nearly an inch long right between the legs of a naked three-hundred-fifty-pound maniac who was, at the time, charging around trying to kill me, and had popped a nut out of his scrotum and opened a femoral artery, all while I was looking like a fat kid in a dodgeball game.

"At least you didn't get hurt," she said. "Did you? I mean, not at all, right?"

"Just my self-respect, Sugar Plum. I thought the neurons in my head worked better than that. But this was a onetime deal, never to be repeated."

"Good. And I like the Sugar Plum. So, did the experience teach you anything?"

She sounded like my mother when I was nine, so I said, "Avoid iffy situations, don't go into bars inhabited by the kind of scum who carry concealed weapons, don't smoke in bed, and don't accept rides or candy from strangers."

"Okay, then. That candy thing in particular. And I'm still gonna come home. I'll let you know when my flight gets in since I don't actually have one yet."

"I'll be waiting at the gate, whatever time it is."

The call ended. I gave up watching Volker's place at eleven ten when all the lights went out, drove home, went to bed, dreamt much of the night about fishing of all things, something I hadn't done since I was sixteen years old, but the fish were big and had needle teeth, dead eyes, thick blubbery green lips, the water was dark and deep, and I was scared to death I might actually catch one of them or fall in and get dragged under and eaten.

* * *

Monday morning. Lucy phoned at eight, told me she would arrive at 7:44 that evening on Southwest. I told her she would probably need a good cleaning after a long flight, cooped up in a tight space like that, and she said she probably would and she might need help with that. I told her it sounded like a lot of work for me, and she said, tough, I had chores to do just like she did, and complaining was childish.

Good 'nuf.

So I had nearly twelve hours to kill. I thought about how far I'd gotten in the Joss investigation and decided I was truly a neophyte. In a dark corner of the kitchen, Hammer and Spade were nudging each other, agreeing that, yes, I ranked somewhere below a greenhorn amateur and putting *PI* after my name on a business card was hubris of the first order.

As I saw it, the immediate problem was a lack of coffee. I brewed it strong and dark, not bloodless caffeine-free shit either, but the real thing that makes your heart palpitate.

When the drugs reached my brain, I tried again to come up with an approach to the Joss-Volker situation. And it occurred to me that if Volker had needed money back in June, he might've tapped his own resources first. If so, then the situation, whatever it had been, was desperate.

Worth looking into.

Which meant I needed a way to peek at Volker's checking and saving accounts, and maybe other things, like mutual funds and precious metals. So I gave Fairchild a call.

"You'll need a court order," he said in the kind of hollow voice that meant he was cupping a hand over the mouthpiece.

"Thanks." I hung up.

We weren't going to get a court order. I called Ma on her cell phone. She answered on the first ring. "Hey, Ma, I need to get a look at Volker's banking accounts."

"It's nice of you to tell me that on what amounts to an open line," she said.

Well, shit. I would have to rephrase. And dump this call in case the NSA was on the party line.

"Call me back, Ma. On my cell." Ma was big into burner phones, which were cheap, untraceable, and kept us out of prison.

I disconnected. My burner rang ten seconds later. "Yeah?" I said. "Who is this? If you're sellin' I ain't buyin'."

"What was that nonsense about a goddamn knife fight?"

Well, shit again.

"That'll be the last time I wander into Wildcat, Ma. Place has marginal folks with emotional problems."

"*Wildcat?* What the hell were you doin' in there?"

"Trying to get a sarsaparilla. Had to settle for a Pete's." If I could spin her around a little, maybe she would forget about the other thing.

"What was that about a goddamn *knife* fight, boyo?"

Nope.

"Guy called Ramon got feisty. I had to take his knife away. He didn't like that, but it's hard to call it a knife fight since it lasted three seconds and no one got nicked or cut."

"Jesus. Testosterone's a bitch, huh? You okay?"

"Never better."

"So what about that Joss-Volker thing and banks?"

"You got a way to check accounts, past and present? Back as far as May or June."

"I can. You can't."

"Let me parse that. Suppose I could use some information in that direction. Is it your contention that I'm like a kid outside a locked candy store and you could be of some assistance, like with a set of keys or a brick or some such?"

"Jesus H. Christ. Here's Lucy."

"Hi, Mort!"

"Ma in a snit?"

"No, she's in a coffee shop. Well, so am I in case that's not obvious. Also, she's in dark slacks and a dark green shirt, if that helps, not sure why it would."

"You sound a lot like me when I want to be annoying."

"It's catching. Kinda like dengue fever, which is also called breakbone fever."

"Wow, sure hope *that's* not catchin'. Put Ma back on."

Moments later, Ma said, "Got a pen, pencil, something to write on?"

"Gimme a sec. Okay, go."

"5YG23P1B8AD4. Just the way I taught you. All caps on the letters. Now read it back."

I did.

"Okay," Ma said. "And send it through Finland."

"Gotcha."

Then she gave me instructions, which I had to write down in detail because they were specific and fairly complicated.

I ended the call, happy that Lucy was coming back, not so happy that she and Ma thought it was necessary, then I went to work on the code she'd given me.

It wasn't meant to fool anyone more sophisticated than an insurance agent working a newspaper Jumble while his secretary did all the work, which is the routine at every State Farm agency I've ever been in, but "the way she taught me" meant dump the first two characters, which got me to G23P1B8AD4. Then start at the back, then bounce to the front, then second from the back, second from the front, and so on until you've gone through all the characters. Simple enough. This resulted in 4GD2A38PB1, an anagram of what she'd told me, minus the 5Y.

Three point six million permutations, which would take the NSA about point zero six seconds to run through, if they knew they had to drop the first two characters, and had been on the burner line, and had any idea who was on the burners, and where and how and when the code was going to be used.

Routing numbers are open-source data on the internet. I found all the bank routing numbers for Nevada and printed out the pages.

I got on the laptop, logged onto a proxy server in Sweden—
Finland was just verbal misdirection—and the bottom line according to Ma was that 4GD2A38PB1 would get me into an
encrypted program created by a hacker in Reno where I could
input a bank's routing number, type in a name, and access the account for that name, if it existed.

Man, how illegal was *that*?

But I was going to do it through a server in Sweden, so maybe
no one would break down the door and haul me away. Still, it
made me nervous, so I tried to work quickly.

I went through the biggest banks in Northern Nevada first,
typing in routing numbers and the name "Volker." I found a few
Volkers in the first bunch of banks I tried, but none of them were
Michael. Finally, I got a hit on Fidelity National, fifth bank on the
list. The home address also matched.

For the past four years, Michael and his sister, Marta Geer, were
joint tenants with rights of survivorship. Michael was the primary. His sister could only access the account in the event of
Michael's incapacitation or death.

Account activity showed a checking balance of $2,883.27 on
June tenth, unchanged on the eleventh. But a savings balance of
$3,201.88 had dropped to a hundred dollars in that same time
frame, just enough left in the account to keep it open. But the
amount removed wasn't huge, didn't have a crisis feel to it.

Now what?

People often had money in both banks and credit unions. So I
hunted through the local credit unions and came up with a
Michael Volker in Washoe Sierra Federal Credit Union.

Two accounts: $33,496.40 in savings on June 10, stripped down
to $200 on June 11. And an IRA of $95,288.05 that hadn't been
touched, most likely due to the ten-percent penalty and tax

implications that meant Uncle Sam would give Volker a pittance of his own money and use the rest to send a passel of senators to Tahiti for ten days on a fact-finding mission. Volker had taken $33,296.40 from savings—which had that crisis feeling I was looking for.

I got out of the program, got out of Sweden, turned off the computer, glanced out the windows to be certain federal agents and a SWAT team weren't setting up outside, not entirely sure what I would've done if they had.

Now—drop the pennies and add it up.

$33,296 plus $3,100 plus the $13,600 he'd taken out of the business account came to $49,996, which was remarkably close to $50,000. He could find another four dollars in a pile of loose change on his dresser top.

Inescapable conclusion: Sometime around June 10, Volker had needed to come up with $50,000 on an emergency basis.

* * *

I began to feel better about this gumshoe business. Ma would be so proud. Even more proud if I could find out what Volker had needed the fifty thousand for, so that was next on my bucket list— which, according to Lucy, was not something to strive for, at least not in this instance. A "bucket list" should be called a "kick the bucket list" since it's a list of things to do before you kick the bucket, and I hoped to find out why Volker wanted those fifty Gs a good many years before I bucketed.

I had a little trouble with the next part—trying to think up a way to find out why he'd needed $50,000 almost overnight.

I could go ask Volker, which felt unprofessional, especially since Evelyn Joss had hoped I could do this quietly. But Russell had hired me in July this year because I was unprofessional *and* a maverick, so there was that. I had a track record. To get the job done, you sometimes have to kick down doors. And I'd already kicked Volker's door half off its hinges by mentioning that $13,600 the other evening so this wasn't going to be a nice quiet investigation. It was going to get untidy.

My forte.

But going straight at Volker felt premature at this point, so what else might I try?

Could I find out where he put the money? I gave that some thought, didn't come up with anything except some "what-ifs" that demonstrated the probable futility of discovering what he'd done with the money. What if he'd purchased some real estate in Idaho or California or Montana, a never-to-be-seen-again deal too good to pass up? How could I get a lead on anything like that? What if he'd given it to someone for some reason and there was no record of the transaction? What if his sister had needed it for some obscure reason, such as paying off medical bills in another state, like Kentucky? What if he was the victim of some sort of a scam? What if he'd purchased $50,000 worth of gold bars after listening to the scare tactics of folks who sell gold?

Too many *what-ifs* into which money could disappear as if into a black hole.

What if the only way to get going here was to kick down a door? Well, I already had Volker's hanging on by a single hinge. Did it matter if I gave it one more kick with a size-twelve boot?

Time to think about that.

There were a number of ways to approach it. What I finally came up with was, of course, sheer genius.

Bowling night.

CHAPTER EIGHT

WHICH WOULD'VE BEEN genius if a pair of IRS goons out of Washington D.C. hadn't rung the front doorbell at ten fifteen that morning.

Goons wasn't correct, but I have long been susceptible to over-simplifications, like when I once called Ronald Soranden a turd to his face when in fact he was an overzealous bureaucratic backstabbing pile of horse extract. Turd worked, however, in the heat of the moment, and had the advantage of fewer syllables. Then again, that particular simplification had left out a number of pertinent details.

But back to the goons. My first thought, naturally, was that they were FBI, sent by the NSA to round up the clown who had hacked into a bunch of banks in Reno in the past hour. And, of course, I was still in a bathrobe and slippers, perfect for greeting guys in suits with beady eyes and government-issue haircuts.

"Mortimer Burris Angel?" said the shorter and balder of the two. Relative to me, they were both short and hair-challenged, so right away I had a huge advantage.

"I don't use Burris much on a daily basis," I said.

"Which isn't what I asked, but for identification purposes I think it'll do. But if you're *not* Mortimer Angel, though you look a lot like the guy in his picture, you might want to say so now to save us all time, aggravation, and unnecessary paperwork."

Smooth. I might like this guy.

"Let me see the picture," I said. "Just to make sure, help you guys out if I can."

Amused, he brought it up on his cell phone, held it out.

"Sure enough," I said. "That does look like me. You might have the right guy."

He went silent, gave me a few seconds to think the situation over, then said, "I'm Agent Renner and this is Agent Bledsoe. IRS, D.C." He whipped out a shiny badge. Bledsoe stood behind Renner. He held up his badge in a no-nonsense black leather case. His badge was shiny, too. Nice.

"You both have the same first name. Agent. That's unusual. Probably a source of confusion at parties and such."

Renner sighed. "I'm George Renner, this's Dennis Bledsoe. My boss's boss, IRS Commissioner Munson, told us you might be like this."

Munson. Great. "I might be like what?"

"Hard to talk to. Which, I've gotta say, you have been and it's only been two minutes."

"Uh-huh. How's Slick Willie doing? He got that Hostess cupcake addiction under control yet?"

Renner smiled. Man had a sense of humor. Which meant he couldn't be IRS, no way. "Slick Willie?" he said. "Clinton?"

"William Munson. We called him Slick when he was the head guy at the IRS here in Northern Nevada. Then he was made commissioner—with Senator Reinhart's help. Something of a slipshod Nevada nepotism deal."

"Then last year you found Reinhart's severed right hand," he said, either showing off or making a point.

"I wouldn't exactly call it a hat trick since it was FedEx'd to me. All I did was open the package."

"Right, right. You don't kill people, you just find 'em. I heard something about that."

I shrugged. "That's how it's been. Not sure why I've been chosen for the honor, and I should mention that I don't actually see it as an honor. Anyway, I didn't have a bit of trouble filling out my 1040 earlier this year, guys. But it was nice of Slick—I mean, the commish—to show how much he cares by sending out his finest. Give him my best, okay?" I started to close the door to see how that would go.

Renner put a gentle hand on it. "This isn't about your 1040, Angel. This is about you finding that skull. Dennis and I are in Investigative Services. You'd be familiar with that. How about we come in and talk? Would that be okay?"

Investigative Services? I shrugged, opened the door wider since they were going to come in and talk one way or another. They didn't come all the way out from D.C. to say hi and leave.

"I'll be right back. Make yourselves at home. There's milk in the fridge, blankets and pillows in the hall closet."

I left them in what had once been Jeri's office, now a living room with the usual—area rugs, couch, love seat, coffee table, bookshelves, rainbows flitting around like butterflies. I'd left the prisms hanging in the windows. Jeri would've liked that.

I put on dark slacks and an off-white Guayabera shirt, black loafers without tassels, returned to the living room.

Renner was five-nine, Bledsoe was five-eleven. Shrimps. I detected slight bulges in their suits in the vicinity of their left armpits. These were big guns in the IRS, with the unannounced but real authority to suggest to higher-ups that people's lives be changed without a trial, so I decided it might behoove me to play nice. Not my style, but a little practice wouldn't hurt.

"What's up, guys?" I said.

Renner looked around the room. "Rainbows. Very pretty."

"Glad you like them. Shows unusual sensitivity. You must be new at the IRS."

Renner grinned. "Commissioner Munson asked us to ask if you would be willing to give him an hour or so of your time. He's at the airport in a Gulfstream."

"Ask, huh?"

"More or less. It's entirely up to you, but I would suggest that taking him up on it would be a nice gesture on your part."

"What model Gulfstream?"

"It's a two-eighty."

"Yeah? What's one of those babies cost?"

"I think right around twenty-five mil."

"Our tax dollars at work."

Renner grinned again, then shrugged. "Yours and ours. It's a way to get around."

"So's a Volkswagen beetle."

"Beetles almost never get up to five hundred miles an hour. And they don't have wet bars and bathrooms."

"Willie Munson's slumming here in Reno?"

"We stayed the night at the Grand Sierra Resort. Munson got a suite, we didn't."

"Isn't that always the way? And he wants to chat with me? Such a nice man. What's it about?"

"I'm sure he'll let you know. By the way, that must've been a nice move you pulled on Surry yesterday in that bar, Wildcat. You'll have to show it to me sometime. Although," he went on, "you ducking out the back way afterward might not've been strictly kosher."

"Okay then. How about we go see what Willie wants?"

"Thought you'd get around to that. We should take our car, save you a gallon or two of gas."

"If you insist."

"I wouldn't put it that way. It's convenient, though. We're parked right out front and the engine's warm."

"Let's go."

We went outside and I locked up. The car was a basic blue-gray Chrysler 300 sedan. Bledsoe drove. I sat in the back with Renner, at his suggestion. I had the feeling I was about eighty-five percent under arrest, but the Internal Revenue Service treats everyone that way, so I tried to relax.

The Gulfstream was parked at Reno Charter Services, well out of the way of prying eyes. It didn't say IRS on the fuselage anywhere because a few folks might have black market Stinger missiles. I had a vision of climbing aboard, the stairway folding up into the body, plane heading into the wild blue, east, toward Washington D.C. and the unknown.

Bledsoe, Renner, and I went up the steps, not in that order, but the stairs stayed put. William Munson didn't get to his feet when I went back and found all two hundred ninety pounds of him nestled into a chair of some nubbly blue fabric that looked more comfortable than anything you could buy at R.C. Willey. To call him plump would be a kindness. He folded a newspaper and set it aside when he saw me. On a tray beside him was what looked like a martini, though it could've been bottled water with an olive in it.

"Mortimer," he said. "Been a while. You look good." His throat wattled as he spoke. He was only in his late fifties, but he looked closer to seventy, little wisp of gray-blond hair in a nasty comb-over, potato nose, unhealthy sallow skin.

"Hey, Will. You got out of here just in time. Guess what? Your replacement, Ronald Soranden, lost his head."

He stared at me. "That supposed to be funny?"

I took a seat wide enough for two, facing him. Love seat on an airplane? You don't often see those on Southwest or United. Renner and Bledsoe took seats closer to the open doorway. I'd glanced at the cockpit as we came in. It was empty, so this might be a social call, not a hijacking.

"I forgot," I said. "IRS doesn't hire anyone with a sense of humor."

He chuckled—no doubt trying to prove me wrong, which might have worked if the chuckle had reached his eyes. Munson would laugh when told he had no sense of humor just to prove, inadvertently, that, in fact, he had no sense of humor.

"What can I do for you, Commissioner?"

"What is it with you finding . . . finding . . ."

I sighed. People often found it hard to say what had made me a world-class, world-famous PI. "Finding body parts of dead missing people. And entire dead missing people."

"And now . . . skulls."

"Just one."

"Ronald Soranden. Your former boss here at the IRS. After I left, that is."

"Yep. Boss and former thug-mate."

"Don't you find that a little strange?" Munson asked, the "thug-mate" comment not causing so much as a ripple.

"Strange how?"

He raised an eyebrow. "Strange as in coincidental."

I appeared to give that some serious thought. "Wow, Will, that never occurred to me, but now that you mention it . . ."

Another dry chuckle. Eyes still beady with the blink rate of a monitor lizard. "The decapitated head of Reno's mayor, found in the trunk of your ex-wife's car."

Show-off. "That's old news. And it was a Mercedes S550. She sold it not long after."

Another stare. "Decapitated head of the district attorney, found in the dead mayor's house. Then your nephew's head, on his desk in his office. Not long after he hired you."

"You make it sound like I was having fun. But it turned out to be two crazy women who happened not only to be mother and daughter, but half sisters as well."

"I read the file. Crazy doesn't begin to cover it. *Then*, you end up with Senator Reinhart's right hand. Via UPS."

"FedEx. I got the principal shaking part of his presidential campaign. FBI still hasn't solved that one yet."

That comment got a nod. "I'll come back to that in a while. *Then* you find that nauseating rapper guy, Xenon, strung up in the garage of two girls married to each other, one of whom is the daughter of a senior Reno detective."

"You've memorized my entire dossier. Good job."

"I have. You find missing people."

"Who end up dead. It's a knack. I would give classes but it can't be taught."

"What it sounds like—it's either the weirdest case of serial murder in U.S. history, or . . . dumb luck. Which, according to all the files, is exactly what it is."

"Luck. That's a knack too."

"Strangely enough, I believe that. Some people are lucky in weird ways. Or unlucky. Park Ranger Roy Cleveland Sullivan was hit by lightning seven times, survived them all. But *seven*. Figure one chance in fifty thousand of getting hit once in your lifetime,

Sullivan beat odds of about a billion trillion trillion to one. Lotteries don't have odds like that. Not even close. If they did, no one would win. Ever."

"I prefer my brand of luck."

"I would too."

"Although that's how my dad died. Lightning."

"Interesting." He took a sip of his martini, smacked his lips froglike as he looked at it, and set it down. "But let's talk about luck. This business about Soranden disappearing and his skull being dumped in your car months later—"

"Lucy Landry's car."

"Ah, yes. Miss Landry's convertible. Through the roof into the front seat, I understand. But you were the one who first saw it and picked it up, so let's say it was meant for you, maybe even in a spiritual, preordained sense."

"Yes, let's. That oughta be a riot."

Dry chuckle. "Investigationwise it's early yet, I know, but I've been in close contact with the FBI and I can't say that I'm hearing a Niagara outpouring of optimism."

First sign of a hollow feeling went through my stomach.

Munson went on: "These things tend to make waves when they get in the news. IRS in particular. You heard about Victor Buchholz over in Toledo?"

"No. Who's that?"

"Local head of the IRS out there, like Soranden was here. He's been missing since Saturday, eight days ago."

"Eight days? He might still be in a bathroom somewhere."

"Probably not. And he missed getting an award at a Lion's club meeting. I doubt you've ever met him, but Victor wouldn't miss an award for anything. Not for *any*thing. Buchholz gone, now Soranden's skull turns up. This isn't the kind of thing we'd care to see escalate. Which it could."

"We?"

"We at the IRS, of course. Polls suggest that we are not the country's favorite institution. Kidnappings, murders, bombings— once that kind of stuff gets in the news it tends to percolate among people who aren't tightly wrapped."

"It riles people when agents bust open piggy banks of six-year-old children to pay daddy's taxes."

"We haven't done that lately."

"Things like that tend to stick in the mind."

"Before my time, Angel. I've ordered agents not to do that sort of thing. Not only is it counterproductive, it's insignificant when it comes to filling the nation's coffers."

"Uh-huh." I looked around the cabin. "Spiffy ride, Will. Better than what you get on Allegiant Air. All of this has been interesting, but are we coming to a point here?"

"We are. I'd like to get ahead of the curve on this. But very quietly. Like I said, the FBI isn't optimistic about putting this Soranden murder to bed anytime soon, just like that Reinhart deal, which is still unsolved and it's been nearly a year. But *luck*. Luck sounds like just what we need."

Splendid. Add lucky to maverick and unprofessional and guess whose name pops up?

"Well, shit," I said into a few seconds' silence.

"I wouldn't put it that way, but . . . what I *would* like to do, now that you've become a private investigator, lucky one too, is I would like the IRS to employ your services."

Perfect. Workin' for the IRS again.

* * *

"And you want it done quietly," I said. "Not that I accept, you understand."

"Not quietly," Munson responded. "*Invisibly.* Last thing the IRS needs is for something like that to get out."

"You mean, it's the last thing *you* need."

For a moment he didn't say anything, then he gave a curt nod. "That's putting a mighty fine point on it, but yes."

"Something like this finding its way into the media is the last thing I need too."

He smiled. "Then we agree."

"Nope."

"No?" He lifted a single eyebrow, which meant his former IRS field training was still operational. Good to know.

"We haven't talked money yet. And we need to back up to that business about luck. You're hiring luck, is that right?"

"I suppose I am. Yours seems . . . exceptional."

"As if I can conjure it up."

"You have a hell of a track record."

"Still, there's no guarantee of anything. *At all.* Luck isn't like that."

"It's something of a long shot. I will stipulate to that."

"I forgot, you have a law degree. 'Stipulate' is one of those words I oughta use more often."

He smiled. "I wouldn't if I were you."

"Okay then, I won't."

"I think luck is underrated. I think it exists. But to give it a bit of a push, I will offer a . . . call it a finder's fee, if that's the right term, of, oh, how about ten thousand if you're successful within, say, a month? And, of course, before the FBI catches up with the perpetrator—Soranden's killer, that is—at which point all this would become moot."

Great. Suddenly I was competing with the FBI at the secret and very likely deniable behest of the IRS. I couldn't imagine anything more likely to get me into the deepest possible shit. Say, Leavenworth deep.

"Fifteen thousand," I said. "After all, it's taxpayers' money. And I'll have to pay taxes on it or Renner and Bledsoe will be back and I haven't bonded with those two yet. Unless, of course, they accept bribes."

More eyebrows. Then a nod. "Done. Fifteen it is."

"Actually, it isn't. It's a very long shot that isn't likely to amount to anything. I'm going to need a retainer. But I've got an idea that appeals to me better than money."

"Not sure I like the sound of that since, when it comes down to it, there isn't anything better than money."

"That's the IRS I've come to know and love. Where's the pilot and copilot for this thing?"

He nodded somewhere outside the plane. "Charter Service lounge. They didn't need to hear anything we had to say in here. What have they got to do with anything?"

"Ask the pilot how long it'd take to get to Albuquerque."

"Albuquerque? What's over there?"

"My assistant. Lucy."

His eyes bulged. "Lucy Landry? Your *assistant*? I missed that. She out of high school yet? I saw a picture of her after that serial killer thing you were involved in around Vegas a couple of months ago, thought she was your kid or possibly your niece or something."

"We're sort of engaged."

"No . . . foolin'. I might be in the wrong business here."

"I've heard *that* before. That involves an entirely different kind of luck. So, Albuquerque?"

"Bledsoe!" Munson yelled. "Get the pilot and copilot back here. Tell 'em we got kind of a whistle-stop run to make."

* * *

Whistle-stop in a Gulfstream. I might not have given Slick Willie enough credit way back when. Bledsoe came back with a good-looking redhead, the pilot, and a bad-looking guy, copilot. The redhead, Brenda Dawson, gave me an amused look as she fed me flight information. Then Brenda and Bob went up front and minutes later the turbines started to spool up.

I punched Lucy's number into my cell phone. "How's it goin' there, Sugar Plum?"

"Wonderful. We're stuck in downtown traffic since about all the businesses let everyone out for lunch at the same time."

"They do that intentionally, hoping it'll keep folks at their desks."

"Are you okay, Mort?"

"Never better."

"Groovy. So . . . what's up?"

"Got you an earlier flight if that's okay with Ma. What you need to do is get over to Cutter Aviation. That's on Clark Carr Loop, little bit south of the main terminal there."

"Why? I've already got a flight."

"Mine's better."

"Like an old biplane and I have to walk the wing all the way back to Reno?"

"Wow, what a terrific guess. Can you be there in about two hours?"

Half a minute of silence while the two women talked it over. Then: "Yes. If I can get out of this dumb rotten traffic and Ma and I don't die because we're behind a city bus gassing us with something like World War II blister agent or phosgene."

"Sounds great. Wish I were there."

"Got room for Ma on your rental biplane or whatever it is? Turns out we're done here."

"I think she'll strap to the left wing okay. The goggles are free."

"I'll let her know. So, was that Chopper Aviation?"

"Cutter. Off Clark Carr Loop."

"Okay. I'll call if we have any trouble finding it."

"See you." I ended the call.

Minutes later, the G280 lifted off, headed south. By then, I had a beer in hand, Renner and Bledsoe had Diet Pepsis, Munson had a fresh martini and was reading his newspaper.

A Gulfstream. Man, I oughta get one of these. Probably have to buy it used, though.

* * *

I walked across the tarmac and into Cutter Aviation and looked around. Lucy gave a little squeal of delight, broke away from Ma, and ran over to me, wrapped me up in a hug like an octopus. Hundred fourteen pounds of live-wire woman-child.

We drew stares, not that there were many people in the place. It wasn't like the terminal of a major airport.

Ma walked over to us. "You two."

"Hey, Ma. Got your man, huh?"

"Girl. Megan changed her name to Mary, kept Galbraith, so it was a no-brainer."

"Sounds like my kind of investigation." I looked around. "So where is the wayward Galbraith? You got her in leg irons?"

"I was only told to find her, not to bring her back. I phoned her mother, told her where she could find her kid."

Lucy pulled my head down, gave me a hard stare. "Knife fight? Seriously?"

"Turns out, it was just one of those things, more like a judo mixup than a knife fight."

"A *judo* mixup?"

"Yup."

She punched my belly. "Don't ever do it again."

"Got it off my bucket list, Cupcake. Next up is a running leap off El Capitan in a self-packed parachute."

"How about we just get married? Get you calmed down and semi-domesticated. No knife fights, no parachuting off cliffs."

"You can see me happily domesticated? Even semi?"

"Well . . . not exactly."

Ma broke in. "Let's get a move on. Where's this so-called plane of yours, boyo?"

"It's being refueled. They said it'll be ready in half an hour, but your wing's ready. You can strap in now."

"They? Who's they?"

"Brenda and Bob. Who else?"

She shook her head. "Forget I asked."

* * *

Lucy's eyes went wide when she saw we were headed for the Gulfstream. "No way. You gotta be kidding."

"I never kid."

"Yeah, *right*."

Ma stopped fifty feet away and stared at it. "If you got it as a charter and put it on the business account, I have no words for how unbelievably fired you are."

"I got it as a retainer."

Her eyes squinted down to the kind of narrow slits you find in university physics labs where they do advanced laser research. "A retainer?"

"I was hired to do a little job."

"A little job gets you the use of a Gulfstream? I don't like the sound of that. *At all.*"

"C'mon, Ma. Buck up. You should see the client."

"Jeez. There's something *so* not right about this."

Nothing gets by her.

Bledsoe was standing by the stairs. He followed us up and into the plane. Pilot Brenda hit a button that hauled the steps up, then went into the front where they keep the levers and dials and the gas pedal.

Ma stopped when she saw Munson sitting froglike in his seat, martini within reach on a small fold-out table.

"Oh, no." She turned to me. "Tell me you didn't make a pact with the devil."

"Not so much a pact as an arrangement, Ma."

She plopped down in the seat facing Munson. "Will," she said. "I see you have managed to corrupt my partner."

"Corrupt is an ugly word, Ms. Clary, and so very inaccurate when all I've done is to hire him. But do have a martini, will you? This is my second. Or maybe my third. I tend to lose count. They're quite good. Mr. Renner? If you would be so kind as to get Ms. Clary one of these? Shaken, not stirred."

Ma surprised me. She took it. Took a sip. "Very good, yes. And do you remember, Will, the last time you and I had a bit of a go-around? I believe it involved a woman named Kimberly. By now she might be thirty years old."

His eyes jittered momentarily. "No need to bring that up."

"And you hired my partner in spite of that?"

"I was hoping you and I could put that behind us. It's been ten years." About then, the turbines started to spool up. "A while ago Mortimer and I were discussing luck. That you and he have joined forces is the kind of coincidence—luck—that I hope to have employed."

"I see." Ma smiled, leaned back. "Good luck with that. You have no idea what you're doing. That's good."

* * *

We buckled in and took off. When we reached cruising altitude, Lucy disappeared into the restroom with her carry-on, came out a few minutes later wearing white jogging shorts and the light-weight pink cotton tank top she'd been wearing when I first saw her in McGinty's Café in Tonopah, complete, as usual, with slight bumps in the fabric. Perfect. Bright pink toe socks on her feet added a new dimension to the outfit. Long legs, perfect skin, she looked seventeen.

George Renner stared. Dennis Bledsoe tried not to but was unsuccessful. Munson about lost his eyes. "Good Lord," he said, unaware that he'd said it until it was out.

"Nice outfit, kiddo," I said to Lucy.

"I've been cooped up in other stuff for two days, except in motel rooms. This feels so good."

"Looks good, too."

Her eyes sparkled. "Thanks. Oh, and I'm not responsible for what other people think, say, or do. They are."

"That's a philosophy. What do you think, Ma?"

"This martini borders on excellent. I may have another."

Good enough.

* * *

We held a little powwow somewhere over the southwest corner of Utah and into Nevada. I was surprised when Munson waved Renner and Bledsoe over to join in. The middle section of the plane became a conversation pit. A bench seat along one side faced Munson and Ma. I sat on it beside Lucy. Agents Renner and Bledsoe sat on either side of us to keep us from escaping.

Before we got started, I said to Lucy, "How about I set the record straight here? The standard misconception is obviously running wild and free."

She knew what I meant. "Go ahead." She examined her fingernails, which were painted a dark shade of pink that would have come out of a little bottle with a name like *sunrise sienna* or *coral dream* or some such thing.

I looked at each of the men in turn, then said, "Lucy looks eighteen, if that, but she is thirty-one years old, so whatever you might be thinking about her has a good chance of being wrong."

Three pairs of eyes got wider. "Not possible," Renner said under his breath.

"Okay," I said to Munson. "*Now* we're ready."

Munson smiled at Lucy. "Mortimer was always something of a kidder. We never knew what he was going to say next. You can't be old enough to step foot inside a casino, hon."

Lucy's eyes narrowed. "His name is Mort, and Huns were basically barbarians, so don't call me *Hun*. How about that?"

Munson's eyes bugged out. Finally, he said, "I see you have your hands full, Mort."

"Hands full," Lucy said. "That's a good way to put it." She flexed her toes in her toe socks. "Now how about you get on with it since it's starting to get boring in here?"

Munson coughed, possibly to get the minutiae in his brain re-started, then he told Lucy and Ma what he'd told me earlier.

When he finished, Ma said, "Luck? That's it? You're hiring Mort because he's lucky about finding people—which also means you're hiring Clary Investigations so you might want to give that a little more thought."

Munson nodded. "I'm a great believer in luck."

"So am I," Lucy said, and all eyes went to her except Ma's, not because of what she said, but because she said something, any-thing—which gave those in the vicinity whose testosterone levels were redlining permission to get another three- or four-second freebie look at her. Okay, a scan, not a look.

"*Are* you?" Munson said, half smiling.

"She is," I said. "Like you wouldn't believe, but I think it would be a good idea for us to move on." This, after all, was the head honcho of the nation's IRS, and though Lucy and I had paid esti-mated taxes on the fifty-odd thousand Lucy had won in Vegas in July, this was not the venue in which to bring it up and draw the slightest bit of attention to Stephen Brewer, the false identity I had used when we were there.

Munson said, "Luck is akin to . . . unseen forces." He gave Renner and Bledsoe a look. "Which statement shall not find its way anywhere beyond the six of us without dire consequences."

"Of course not," Renner murmured. Bledsoe nodded his head an eighth of an inch.

In brief, Munson told Ma and Lucy the story of Ranger Roy Sullivan being struck by lightning seven times. "Moreover, there have been several multiple lottery winners. A woman, I forget her name, won four lotteries of over two million each. *Four*. The odds against that are simply staggering. It hints at unseen hands guid-ing events. Back in my Reno days, a man hit three royal straight flushes in four days on a poker slot machine, beating astronomical odds. Some people are . . . lucky, there's no other way to account for it. And that's all the explanation I'm prepared to give," Munson said with a note of finality.

But . . . unseen forces, unseen hands. It gave me the vague impression—probably false, but you never know—that Munson had a little soul in there, humming away down deep inside.

And the admission put him in our pockets, Ma's and mine.

Our nation's IRS commissioner.

Talk about luck.

CHAPTER NINE

BEFORE WE LANDED, Slick Willie told me that Renner and Bledsoe would be my shadow until the Soranden thing was cleared up. I told Slick that if he was hiring my luck, they would *not* be my shadow because those two looked like luck vacuums. We went back and forth for a while on that and ended up with the kind of stalemate that meant Renner and Bledsoe might be around, or might not, and that I would shake them loose or cause them grief at every available opportunity.

I got Munson's private cell number. Turns out it was also a burner, untraceable. Slick Willie of the IRS would be a target for all sorts of hackers, including the National Security Agency and probably a bevy of professional backstabbers high up in his own agency—therefore he'd opted for a drug dealer's end run around any sort of eavesdropping. He told me to pick up a burner and get back to him with its number so we could talk without undue governmental interference if the need arose.

Can you say conspiracy? But then, who has more power, the FBI or the IRS? A question with an answer so obvious as to be laughable. One of those agencies more or less obeys the law while the other makes up its own.

* * *

Lucy needed a shower when we arrived back at my place on Washington Street. Due to the inflexible nature of her arms, I had to help with the soaping down of the girl. Then I got tired, so she had to help with the soaping down of the Mort. It's a good thing she and I are helpful types, willing to pitch in when the going gets tough.

Then dinner. Then sleep. Which is when I finally had time to think about Renner and Bledsoe and where they had to have been when I left Wildcat through the back door and down that alley. They hadn't seen the altercation—sounds more civilized than knife fight—but they had watched me go in, knew how I'd left, had a good idea of what had taken place in there, even knew Surry's name, so I had been under surveillance for at least two days and hadn't known it. They were Munson's men, which meant Munson had been a presence in the background for longer than he'd let on.

And luck. IRS Commissioner Munson was hiring luck? Did I believe that? Then again, he'd mentioned unseen forces in the universe, and I found it hard to believe he could come up with anything so mystical if it didn't have some sort of a grip on him. Mystical Munson. Something like that getting out could end an IRS career like a cherry bomb in a toilet, an image so accurate it was eerie.

* * *

Tuesday morning, back in Ma's office on Liberty Street. It was good to be back with my people in familiar surroundings. Even the bullet hole in the sideboard was a comforting touch in the room, put there by a loser named Isaac Biggs half a second before Jeri bounced him around the room like a rag doll.

By the time Lucy and I got to Ma's, she already had a new case lined up—massively boring, as PI work often is. A lawyer for an insurance company wanted her to find evidence that one Oscar Vinton was not in fact suffering debilitating back pain due to a supposed accident at a loading dock in a Sparks warehouse. No one witnessed the accident. Oscar claimed that a Husqvarna roto-tiller had tipped off a pallet and landed on him. Oscar had yelled. Two guys had come running and lifted the tiller off poor Oscar. X-rays showed no sign of damage. It looked like a setup to the insurance company, not that I'm in love with insurance companies. Everything always looks like a setup to them. Do not allow your house to burn down. First thought is that you set it on fire yourself for any number of reasons. You will march through hell and back trying to convince them to give you so much as a nickel until finally, at last, maybe, with a great deal of luck and weeks of anguish and anger management therapy, you might be able to rebuild—but don't count on it. Their bottom line depends on their ability to delay and deny claims, which is where they put ninety-five percent of their resources—well, that and cashing those checks you send to them like clockwork.

But that was Ma's case. I still had Evelyn Joss and the Volker deal on my plate. And once again I had a beautiful young assistant to help out with surveillance and coffee runs. I got an elbow in the ribs when that inspired comment left my lips.

"Volker freed up fifty thousand dollars?" Ma said.

"Emptied his bank and credit union savings, then removed nearly fourteen thousand from the rainy-day fund. Total it up and you get fifty thousand in a twenty-four-hour period."

"Sounds like a payoff," Ma said.

"Or a red-hot real estate opportunity, too good to pass up."

She gave me a narrow look. "Quietly remove funds from the business instead of taking out a perfectly reasonable credit union loan for a perfectly reasonable real estate purchase? We should make a side bet on that, boyo."

"No, we shouldn't."

"And what about this deal with Willie Munson?"

"What about it?"

"Feels iffy, probably a waste of time and energy, although that Gulfstream hop was nice and I can still taste that martini. Not thinking about pursuing it, are you?"

"What, the martini?"

"Watch it, sonny boy . . ."

"You probably meant the Soranden skull thing. Not really. I've got no handle on it, no kind of lever. I can't get a fingernail under any tiny crack of it."

"Papers," Lucy said.

"Huh?" Ma and I said together.

"Soranden's got to have a ton of papers, like bank accounts, property, mortgage, loans, address book, notes, tax documents, car registration. And a gazillion computer files."

"Good luck gettin' any of that," Ma said.

"RPD is probably already rooting through it. And Mort has a defective detective in his pocket. How about that?"

I smiled. "Don't let Russ hear you use that adjective."

"I already did, two months ago. He just laughed."

He would. Lucy had him wrapped around her little finger. I looked at her, then at Ma. "Yeah, how about that, Ma?"

She shrugged. "That would be a hell of a paper chase. RPD *and* the FBI will be all over it already. You would go blind. You don't even know what you'd be looking for. But if you've got nothing else to do and get bored, have at it. Lucy could work on it, then both of you could spin your wheels, see what real private investigation is all about."

Lucy and I looked at each other.

I said, "I've never been blind."

Lucy said, "I've never actually spun my wheels."

"I have," I said. "Last time was on ice on Virginia Street. That badass winter of '17."

Lucy said, "I'll call Russell. Ever since I pretty much got his daughter off the hook for murder, he likes me. A lot."

"Have a ball," I said. "I'm still all over Joss-Volker."

* * *

Turns out, the Soranden affair looked like a real dog. All the FBI had was a missing IRS chief, eighteen hundred suspects, a hyper-clean gap-toothed skull, and a very large ant. Therefore, they were more than willing—okay, *eager*—to share the blame once the investigation hit what they saw as an inevitable bridge abutment. RPD was the upcoming fall guy. Russ said the Reno Police Department would be happy to supply Lucy with Xerox copies of everything the FBI had given them as long as no one at the FBI or RPD found out. Such was the benefit of having a homicide detective tucked in your pocket, or wrapped around an aforementioned little finger.

"But why do you want all that?" he asked Lucy.

"To collect a fifteen-thousand-dollar bonus."

"Okay, I don't want to know. But good luck with that. I've been through it and it looks like a lot of nothing. At least nothing that has anything to do with his murder. I'll bring it to the Green Room at six this evening. Tell Mort to buy me a Bud."

I'd been listening with my ear two inches from Lucy's. She smelled good, and everyone was offering us good luck in subtly ironic tones, which was interesting. I took the phone from Lucy. "Make it ten o'clock, Russ," I said. "Bud Heavy included."

"I'll be asleep at ten."

"No you won't. You'll be at the Green Room with bells on. Turns out, I've got you in my pocket."

"Fuck you, Angel. You're in my pocket too."

"Mutually Assured Destruction. Look how well it worked for the U.S. and Russia. Decades without an actual nuclear war. The Cuban Missile Crisis in '62 was a close call, but Nikita blinked, no one got hurt. So, Green Room at ten. I'm buying."

"Yeah, yeah." He ended the call.

Ma swiveled around in her office chair. "You got any sort of a handle on Volker and what he did with that fifty grand? If not, we oughta shut that turkey down."

"Bowling night," I told her. "I'm gonna knock a door off its hinges in the interests of investigative professionalism."

Lucy smiled. "Groovy. I'm learning stuff like crazy."

* * *

"Where to?" Lucy said. We were in a miniscule parking lot behind Ma's office on Liberty Street. Lucy was at the wheel of her ragtop Mustang. The slash was still covered with duct tape.

"South. After we lose our shadows."

"Meaning George and Dennis?"

I stared at her. "You're on a first-name basis with those two monkeys?"

"Keep your friends close. Keep your monkeys closer."

"I may have underestimated you, Sun Tzu."

"That's a given." She backed out, nosed out into Liberty Street, and waited for a break in the traffic.

"There's Bledsoe," I said, pointing.

"Where?"

"Homeless-lookin' guy across the street, half a block down with a phone to his ear. He was coming this way, did a U-turn when he saw us. Which means they've probably bugged this car. Not a *bug* bug, but a tracker."

"How do you know?"

"They're IRS—I used to be IRS. It's a family thing, sort of like Queens mafia. Also, take note: Bledsoe's not in a car so he's not worried about losing us. Hence—a tracker."

"Great. Now what?"

"Now we debug the car." I pointed left. "Up that way to the light at Arlington, hang a left and gun it."

She did. We went half a dozen blocks south, turned right, and pulled over. We hopped out and checked under the car. Fifteen seconds later, Lucy stood up. "Is this it?"

She held up a small black plastic box. No dumb-ass light on it blinking away like you see in dumb-ass movies. That would do nothing but drain the battery and make it easier to find, two things you don't want if you're more intelligent than a radish— but a plain black box doesn't film well so directors grit their teeth and bite that bullet. The box had no on/off switch. Insert a battery and it's on, good to go. A ceramic magnet on the case kept it stuck to the frame.

"That's it. Keep looking. You found that one pretty easy so there's probably another."

I found it hidden farther up under the right rear wheel well. "That's it. Let's go," I said. "Fast. Back up to California Street, then west and over to Keystone."

I pulled the battery on one of the units, let the other one do its thing. Lucy reached Keystone Avenue. I told her to go right on Fourth Street. By now, Renner and Bledsoe would be circling around, trying to catch up. I spotted a Citifare bus ahead.

"Get behind the bus," I told Lucy. "When it pulls over, stop right behind it."

Didn't take long. Two blocks, then the bus pulled over to pick up an elderly lady with a handbag big enough to lug around a Great Dane. I got out, jogged to the rear of the bus, put the bug up as high as I could with a modest jump. Renner would have to get on Bledsoe's shoulders to reach it.

Back in the Mustang I said, "Go."

She went. I pocketed the inactive bug. Might find a use for it later. I wanted a video of Renner and Bledsoe tracking down the bug and hopping around like elves trying to debug the bus. That would go viral on Twitter, especially with a voice-over to let the world know they were IRS elves.

South a few miles on Virginia Street, Lucy and I ended up at High Sierra Lanes. We went in. That time of day, only a third of the lanes were in use. I'd always liked the smell of rental shoes and the hollow rumble of balls headed toward pins, the clatter of pins flying around, even the thunk of the ball as it went into a gutter followed by a muttered four-letter word.

"I once rolled a one seventy-three," I bragged.

"I rolled a two eighteen when I was down in Phoenix, and what're we doin' here?"

"Not bowling, Cupcake. Not if you're not kidding about that two eighteen."

"That's a lot of nots. What're we doin' here? And where's that door you're gonna knock off its hinges?"

"We're checking out a league. Actually, a bowling team in a league. And don't worry, that door thing will come later."

"Okay, good. Don't want to miss that."

A bored girl in her early twenties was at the rental counter. I asked her if they had league bowling.

"Yah, sure." She snapped her gum, gave Lucy a look then chewed, giving me a bovine stare.

"Teams have names?" I asked.

"'Course."

"Got a team called the Gutter Bugs? They're a bunch of photographers. As in, shutter bugs?" I've found starting off with misdirection is best. Old IRS trick.

"Might. Dumb name, though." She stared at me.

I pulled an old badge, set it on the counter. "IRS, hon."

"Yeah?" Snapped her gum again. "What's an IRS?"

Well, shit. Our educational system in action. And we're supposed to compete with Russia, the Chinese, Guatemalans? I took the badge back. Impersonating an IRS agent can hang you up at the Pearly Gates. "IRS is Internal Revenue Service," I said. "That's income taxes. You get paid here, right?" I looked at her name tag. "Brittany."

Her shoulders straightened and her eyes got wider.

"Gutter Bugs?" I asked again.

She looked at a sheet behind the counter. "Uh, no team by that name."

"How about the Alley Cats?"

She looked again, brightened. "Yeah, they're here. I mean, they're here on Wednesdays."

"What time?"

"Like, seven's when they start. In the evening."

"Last one. How about Reno Outfitters?"

"Um, no. Don't see that one."

"Okay. Thanks." I leaned closer and looked her in the eye. "Who does your taxes?" Leave 'em with a reason to lunge for a worry stone when you're gone. IRS Field Directive 1998-17a.

"My . . . my boyfriend. Um. Why?"

"Just curious."

I nodded to Lucy and we left.

Outside, she said, "She'll be headed for the bathroom about now, probably at a sprightly jog."

"Bathroom. That's sort of like a worry stone, isn't it?"

"Huh?"

"We'll be back tomorrow at seven, have a chat with Volker away from his house and family, away from where he works. He's got some explaining to do. Right now, the sun is bright, it's almost ninety degrees, won't be many more days like this this year, so how about we take a drive on a lonely desert road, like up to Gerlach and back?"

"In my car?"

"Yup."

"With the top down?"

"Yup."

"I mean . . . both tops down." Which is what she'd done in Southern Nevada in July when I first met her. Something I could get used to, given a little more practice.

I said, "What I like about you, you catch on fast."

"Groovy. Let's go."

* * *

I've found that it's best not to overplan things. Spur-of-the-moment decisions keep you loose. We made a quick stop at her apartment, another one at a Walmart to pick up a burner phone to keep in touch with Munson, then went out to Fernley on I-80, north on 447. I slid a Chuck Berry CD into the player. First up was "Maybellene." Perfect.

Once we were through Wadsworth, one of us removed her shirt and sat up on the back of the seat in the last blast of hot air we were going to see until June next year. On the other hand, I wore khaki cargo shorts and a blue Guayabera shirt. Starting to like those Guayaberas.

"Remember to steer," Lucy said. "Keep your eyes mostly on the road, okay?"

"Mostly?"

"You might glance over here from time to time to be sure I'm still here, didn't get blown out."

"I'll do that, Sugar Plum."

So I did. After every bump and dip in the road, I made sure she hadn't been tossed out, and there were a lot of bumps and dips. We passed five big rigs on the way up. All five gave her a hearty blast of horn as we went by. The longest was by a woman in her fifties.

* * *

Lucy had her top back on by the time we reached Empire, but she got fifty miles of sun and wind. Then it was five more miles to Gerlach. Waldo's Texaco was still there. And Corti's Motel and Casino. This was Lucy's first visit.

I filled the gas tank at Waldo's. I remembered that Hank Waldo shut the place down at eight and got stinking drunk, so this was a necessary stop. Then we went on to Corti's Casino.

"Well, if isn't Chandelier Man," said Cheryl, Dave's wife, six seconds after we came through the door.

What a memory. Dave was the nighttime bartender. He and I had bumped pig knuckles last year, something of an unspoken male solidarity gesture celebrating the outfit Holiday was wearing when she and I were up there trying to find her missing sister.

Lucy had an arm around my waist. "Chandelier Man?" she said.

Cheryl gave her a look, then gave me a thumbs-up. "Sure can pick 'em." She smiled at Lucy. "One more sarsaparilla and he was gonna do bare-ass trapeze tricks on old Bucky there." She nodded at a six-foot western chandelier made of deer antlers in the middle of the room.

Lucy raised an eyebrow. "Bare-ass, huh?"

"That was the deal. He didn't follow through."

"I'm shocked." Lucy looked at me. "Why didn't you?"

"I was going to after my third sarsaparilla, which I didn't get, and, hey, look—that's the table where I opened that FedEx package with Reinhart's hand in it."

"Uh-huh. Don't change the subject."

"Yeah," Cheryl said. "Don't. Here you go." She shoved a sarsaparilla toward me. "Drink up, strip and swing."

Well, shit. I was going to have to hurt one or both of them if they didn't calm down. Instead, I said, "What's new?" which is the kind of sophisticated conversational feint a person learns in one of the better frat houses and nowhere else.

Cheryl shrugged. "FBI still comes nosing around."

Damn. I should've known the investigation into Reinhart's murder was still ongoing. Bump off a presidential candidate and the feds get their panties in a wad. "That right?" said Mr. Casual.

"Yup. In fact, two of 'em are here now. Well, not *here* here. They drove up north, probably to that old abandoned mine shaft where they found that senator and those others. Bureau of Land

Management got funding to fill it in so there's probably not much to see up there anymore."

"It's been a year," I said. "Trail's probably pretty cold by now." I took a sip of sarsaparilla. Casually.

"For sure. *Real* cold. And I'm not convinced either one of those guys could find his pecker in a mirror."

I almost sprayed sarsaparilla.

"Too small a pecker?" Lucy said. "Or too dumb to figure out how to use the mirror?"

Cheryl laughed. "Got yourself a live one there, Mort."

*　*　*

We stayed the night. I hadn't planned on it when we left Reno, but Lucy decided she liked Gerlach and wanted to stay. I had two reasons. I didn't want to give the FBI guys the idea I'd left because of them—and Cheryl might very well tell them that the investigative genius who'd found Reinhart's hand was in town and wasn't *that* somethin'—and I thought our being gone would give Renner and Bledsoe fits. So given that twofer, we got room eleven. Cheryl checked us in, told us it was right next door to one of the FBI guys. Great.

"Russ," Lucy reminded me.

"Huh?"

"He's supposed to meet us in the Green Room at ten."

"Oh, right." I gave him a call, told him we were out of town and to make it tomorrow night at ten. He said a word that would slow him down when he arrived at the Pearly Gates.

I remembered Munson and the burner phone. I figured out what my burner number was then phoned Slick Willie and gave it to him. He wanted to know how far I'd gotten with Soranden's

investigation and I told him patience was a virtue that would be
rewarded differently in the afterlife than heading up the IRS, and
he should rack up points while the racking was good. He hung up.
Then I called Ma, gave her the burner number too, told her I was
going to dump the previous burner I'd been using since we had
used it enough. She said she'd dump hers too and buy a new one,
get back to me with the number. Paranoia R Us.

Later I introduced Lucy to Dave. He'd taken over bartender
duties from Cheryl at six. We walked up to the bar, and I said,
"Dave, this is Lucy." He didn't say a word, just gave her a long look,
didn't know his jaw had gone slack, then slowly held up a fist and
we bumped pig knuckles again.

When he found his voice, he said, "Each one better than the
last. Don't know how you do it, man."

Lucy was wearing white hip-hugger jeans and a tight white
tank top that might've been silk. She had a twenty-three-inch
waist, three inches of flat tummy showing, one inch of which included the sweet flare of her hips. And, of course, no bra so that
top was getting more than its fair share of attention.

About then, the two FBI guys came in. You can tell FBI at anything under a hundred yards due to the stick-up-the-butt gait.
This time the walk was subtle, but their eyes gave them away, that
three-quarter squint as they took in faces and scanned the room
for hostiles. I made them two seconds after they came through the
door, even though they had on flannel shirts, jeans, dusty boots.

Lucy still didn't know that Ma, Holiday, and I had traveled to
Paris and sent Julia Reinhart on her way to whatever reward she
had earned after she'd murdered Jeri, *and* her husband, *and* her
lover, Leland Bye, *and* Holiday's sister, Allie, *and* another of her
lovers, Jayson Wexel. Julia was what is commonly known as a
Murderous Bitch. I didn't want Lucy to have to deal with that

knowledge. I didn't want to deal with it either, but it would take a lobotomy to get rid of it and I didn't want that even more than I didn't want the knowledge, so I lived with it.

Having dispatched Julia made me wary of these two FBI drones, but I didn't seek them out and didn't avoid them. I just accepted them as part of the scenery.

Until, that is, one of them came up to me and said, "You're Mortimer Angel, right?"

I turned. "Close. That'd be worth a point or two if we were chucking horseshoes."

He gave me a steely FBI look. "Say what?"

I'm not sure the question "say what?" can be found in the FBI field interrogation manual. That flannel shirt might have sucked up his entire reservoir of gravitas.

"The name is Mort. Mortimer is my CNN name. They get it wrong a hundred percent of the time."

Lucy nosed into things. "And who're *you*, butting in?" she asked him.

Smooth. But that was Lucy. Didn't take shit from anyone, including me.

"Nance, FBI."

"Weirdest name ever," she said. "Like totally."

His eyes jittered. Lucy had that effect on people. "Hah?"

"But a diminutive form would be *Nancy*," she said. "Which is actually pretty cool and it fits. Okay if I call you that?"

"*Darwin* Nance," he said.

"Wow, seriously, *Darwin*? That isn't much better. You're FBI? An anagram of that is FIB, which is really something, like maybe someone didn't think that through. Got a badge? No, please don't show it to me. Just nod your head. I don't want you to pull out anything and show it to me. Anyway, what Mort and I were doing here, we were having a pleasant conversation with Dave—that's the bartender and he's funny and real nice—then omigod *you* came along and barged unannounced into the flow and what we were saying sort of jumped the rails, so now it's gonna take us like a minute or two to figure out where we were so we can keep on with it, but FIB, that's really something, sort of like Eliot Ness, practically almost groovy, except not terribly, so if you're done here, Nancy, I'd like to get back to what we were doing before this interruption. Bye."

Ho-ly shit. And she said all that in one breath.

Nance turned and went back to his partner.

"Great lungs," I said to Lucy.

"Thanks. That's why I don't need a bra."

Dave choked on his club soda with a twist of lime. "Jesus, I wish I had a video of all that, start to finish."

Lucy smiled at him and leaned closer. "It sorta dried me out. How 'bout another mojito, light on the mint?"

"You got it."

"And a dinner menu."

"Got that too." He handed her a laminated sheet.

She ended up with a Caesar salad. I had grilled salmon on a bed of brown rice. We sat at a table. Twenty feet away, Nance and his sidekick glowered at us from time to time. Darwin was another shrimp, only five-ten. Sidekick was even shorter, five-seven, a shrimpette and ten or fifteen years younger than Nance, which put him somewhere around thirty. Their eyes looked like laser implants. Lucy had put us on their radar—but in a way that was actually decent camouflage, so I didn't worry about them.

Much.

When our plates were taken away, Nance and his shadow drifted over and sat at an empty table five feet away.

"Sorry for butting in," Nance said, then he waited.

Lucy stirred her drink with a finger, then put her finger in her mouth, pulled it out slowly. "Uh-huh. So, Nancy, who's your bud?"

"You can call me Nance. Or Darwin. This's Don Becker." He hesitated for a moment, then said to me, "You found that IRS guy. Sorenson. I mean his skull. In Reno."

"Soranden. And yes, I did."

"Last year, right here in this room, you found Reinhart's severed hand."

"It's a modest skill but it serves me well. It's not teachable because it involves FexEx and obviously psychotic people, so if you're looking for pointers, you're out of luck."

Back to laser eyes. "Makes me wonder what you're doing back here in Gerlach, Sport."

Uh-oh. Bad move, calling me "Sport."

Lucy spun her chair ninety degrees to face him. "*I* wanted to come, Nancy. In my car, topless sitting up in the wind since it's a convertible and there's not much nice weather left. You should third-degree me like with rubber hoses since it's my fault we're up here and because I've got a lot of totally cool stuff I could tell you, like how to identify a Grant Wood painting at fifty paces—not that Grant Wood of those two comatose farm-looking people with the thousand-yard stare, like they were in the trenches in the first World War—and who, in case you didn't know, look so freakin' humorless they could almost be FBI in farmer drag."

Farmer drag. How cool is that?

Two pairs of FBI eyes jittered.

"But first let's back up," she went on. "Suppose Mort had opened that FedEx package in, let's say, the public library on Center Street in Reno. Given that, would you then wonder what Mort was doing back in the library a year later?" Her eyes bored into Nance's. She could do that laser thing too.

He stared back, then looked away.

But Lucy is relentless. She doesn't give up. "Don't quit on me now, Nancy. Stay with me. What if he'd opened that package and found Reinhart's hand in the library. Then, *wow*, hold the presses, a year later, he's back in the library. Do you come over and 'wonder' to his face what he's doing there?"

"Well, no."

"Exactly. So you might revisit the logic that made you say you wonder what he's doing back *here*, when what he's *going* to do pretty soon, right here in Gerlach, is bed down with me after we shower together. But if you have any more questions, now's the time to spit 'em out and get 'em answered."

Wow. What a girl.

"Are you at least eighteen?" Becker asked, stepping right into it. "If not—" He gave me a hard look—not easy with a little residual baby fat still plumping his cheeks—thinking he might be about to make an arrest and get on *Good Morning America*.

In a soft voice, Lucy said, "How old are you, sweet pea?"

Sweet pea? I couldn't wait for the rest of it.

"Twenty-nine. Thirty next month," he added defensively.

Lucy smiled. "Show me a driver's license?"

He pulled it out, set it on the table in front of her. She slid hers out of a pocket—ID for the bartender just in case—put it in front of him. "I'm thirty-one. You're *way* out of your depth, sweetie. You might've been a cute baby, but now, not so much. You shouldn't mess with either of us until that magic moment when your IQ picks up another twenty points. Don't expect it to happen anytime soon. Now go away."

The feds got up and left.

Lucy. Perfect freakin' camouflage.

But later that night, after another few drinks at the bar with Dave pouring—and with Dave soaking up the sight of her—and after sleeping with each other—a euphemism for not sleeping with each other—she slept and I stayed awake another hour because I'd run into a truth that had eluded me for almost three months. An hour after Lucy and I first met, she told me she would marry me if I asked, that we could be hitched within two hours of my popping the question because we were in Nevada.

I'd thought that hadn't happened yet because I had known her less than three months even though I could tell she would be the catch of a lifetime—no disrespect whatsoever to Jeri who would also have been the catch of a lifetime. And I told myself it was too soon after Jeri's death, though that was coming up on a year ago. Was one year long enough?

It was partly those two things—not knowing Lucy quite long enough, and because of Jeri—but now, after coming across Nance and Becker, I knew it was more than that that had held me back. Lucy knew none of the details surrounding Jeri's murder, including the alibi Ma had cooked up for me that night with Holiday. She didn't know Ma and I had rid the world of Julia Reinhart because the authorities would never get her.

And I couldn't marry Lucy until she knew all that because I couldn't live that sort of a double life wrapped in a lie.

Which meant I couldn't marry her without Ma's okay. And Holiday's. And even if the two of them okayed it, could I drop a bomb like that on Lucy? Could she handle it?

I just didn't know.

CHAPTER TEN

"WELL, THAT WAS fun," Lucy said, breaking ten minutes of silence. She was driving, I was copilot. It was one twenty, Wednesday afternoon, eighty-one degrees, convertible top down, Lucy's top up. We were sixty miles south of Gerlach, approaching the town of Nixon, south end of Pyramid Lake. Nixon was a Paiute Indian reservation. A Buddy Holly CD was playing. "Peggy Sue."

"Yup," I replied.

"So articulate."

"Unlike you, I'm able to get the job done with a minimum of words. But I like your style, kiddo. Thing is, you're on the FBI watch list now. Your picture might end up in post offices."

She smiled. "I don't think they still do that, but it would be totally cool if they did. I would tell my mom. And I would get one and have it framed. So, are we going back to that bowling alley this evening?"

"Yup. Not bowling though, since you're a ringer and I'm a sore loser."

"Uh-huh. This is bitchin' music by the way."

"Fifties gumshoe rock."

She smiled. "We'll be in Reno in about an hour. We should see if we can get a look at that Ramon Surry guy. If he's still in the hospital, that is."

"No, we shouldn't."

"What I *mean* is, we could peek into the room and just see if he's there, Mort."

"That would be like twisting the tiger's tail. Not something I'd care to do."

"But we could."

I looked at her. "You're serious."

"Yes. Not to go into his room and like play canasta and get selfies and stuff. Just a peek, so I would know what he looks like. Which only makes sense. Think he's still there?"

"No idea."

"Bet Ma could find out. From what you said, you hurt him pretty bad."

"As a grammar Nazi, that'll get your knuckles rapped."

"I'm practicing my colloquial English in case I have to go undercover."

"Good job."

"So, Ramon?"

"Only if I dress up as a matronly old battle-ax nurse with an extra heavy-duty catheter and a bad attitude."

"Okay, then. We'll work on that."

* * *

Ramon was still there. Ma told us he was in room 335, due to get out tomorrow, Thursday. He'd had surgery on his elbow and shoulder on Monday after a bunch of X-rays and an MRI. Docs had to go in, put stuff back together. He had bolts and screws holding him together like Frankenstein's monster, so he might clank when he walks.

"Wow," Lucy said. "Judo rocks."

"Yeah," I said without enthusiasm.

"Hey, the jerk pulled a knife on you. I saw it too, the knife I mean. In the kitchen. It's nasty looking but great on tomatoes."

"You should see it when he's holding it. I was lucky, kiddo. I don't want to push my luck, have to try it again."

"Still . . . let's figure out how to get you matronly and find out if catheters come in triple-extra-large, like for horses."

"A six-foot-four matronly nurse they've never seen before. I don't think that's gonna happen. Sorry to disappoint."

She thought about that for a moment. "Okay. I'll see if his door is open, try to take a quick flyby video with my phone."

None of this was a good idea, but maybe not terrible, either. Ramon didn't know Lucy. She wasn't going to talk to him, not going to go marching into his room like an NBC crew and get an interview. Still, this was not a ripping idea.

"Or," I said. "We could hit the bowling alley early, get in a few games. I'll even throw a few in the gutter to make sure you kick my butt."

"Nope. I want to see what this guy looks like in case he shows up again anywhere."

Perfect.

So I drove us over to Renown Medical. I went up to the third floor with her, stayed at the nurses' station while she went down a hallway to room 335 with her cell phone ready, and there I was, watching, willing her to hurry up, when Surry came up behind me pushing an IV stand with his left hand, not looking much like the Saturday night hero whippet he once was, wearing a loose baby blue hospital gown and a body cast that encased his entire right shoulder and arm.

He glanced at me, kept going. Twenty feet down the hall, he stopped and looked back, looked into my eyes, held it for a few seconds, then kept going.

I wasn't wearing any sort of a disguise. I was recognizable all over the civilized world as Mortimer Angel, finder of stray body parts. Maybe that's what got his attention. Then, of course, Lucy came back down the hallway toward him. Ramon stared at her as she went by. I didn't know if he'd made me as the old guy who'd put him in this place, but I couldn't take a chance that he had, and that he might connect Lucy to me, so I shook her off with a little head shake, ducked into a stairwell, stayed by the door in case she came through and I'd have to push her back into the hallway. She didn't. Good. Smart girl.

But still . . .

Man plans, God laughs.

Perfect, just like I'd thought.

* * *

Michael Volker showed up at High Sierra Lanes at six forty-five that evening. I'd broken a hundred, rolled 104. Lucy had bowled 166. The house ball I'd used had a big chip in it that *thunk-thunk-thunked* down the alley. Lucy's ball was smooth as freakin' silk, which was why I lost. She laughed when I told her. I take enough flak that Kevlar underwear and a helmet makes sense.

"Hola, Mike," I said. He had on a green bowling shirt with a sporty-looking, cross-eyed, half-drunk Alley Cat on the back. Mike's name was on the front above a pocket. He had a bowling bag in one hand, ready to go get 'em.

He stared at me, then at Lucy who had an arm tucked through mine. "I don't have anything to say to you, Mr. Angel."

"Then just listen. Won't take long. I know you rounded up fifty thousand dollars in June this year, how about that?"

"That . . . nothing like that happened."

I gave him the IRS Medusa stare. "Yes, it did. We need to talk about it."

"Aw, Jesus." He looked all around, made sure no one was close enough to listen in. "How'd you come up with that?"

"I do more than find people. I also track money. Oh, and my assistant here—her name is Lucy—is hell on wheels when it comes to talking to the FBI. You should hear her sometime."

His face went white.

"Not to worry," I said, smiling. "I didn't mean to imply that the FBI actually likes what she has to say."

I'm such a liar. I meant to imply exactly that, see what kind of a reaction it got. The white face was a winner.

Then, to keep him spinning around, I said, "But when she *does* talk to the FBI, she's really something."

"Don't," he said. "Please . . . don't."

"Don't what?"

"Talk to the feds. If you haven't already. You haven't, have you?"

"Let's let that sit there as a possibility for a moment. Why shouldn't I talk to the feds about a boatload of money—that is, if I haven't already?"

His mouth opened, closed, opened again. "If you have, then I have nothing more to say to you."

I gave it a few seconds. "Okay, let's say I haven't, but that it could happen if the urge strikes."

"Then . . . then I can't talk here. This is a bad time. And my sister needs to be in on it when we do."

"Marta."

"Yes." He thought for a moment, then said, "Come by the house at eleven tomorrow. The kids will be in school. We can talk then." He looked at Lucy, then at me. "Will your . . . your assistant be attending?"

Attending. How very tight-assed. Volker might have been born with a prissy gene, although people sometimes pick it up writing essays in grad school and can't shake it off.

"She will," Lucy said.

His brow wrinkled. "If you don't mind my asking, how old are you?"

Lucy smiled. "You usually ask women their age?"

"This . . . tomorrow . . . it isn't for . . ."

I said, "We get this all the time. *All* the time. Add at least ten years to whatever you're thinking. At *least*. Maybe twelve. She's old enough, trust me. So, yes, she'll be there."

A white-haired man with a little pot gut clapped a hand on Volker's shoulder. His shirt was just like Volker's except for the name. "You're missing warmups, Mike."

"Be there in a second, Ralph."

Ralph's eyes lingered on Lucy. She gets that, I don't—even from women, which isn't fair. Finally, Ralph left.

"Tomorrow at eleven, my house," Volker said. "Okay?"

"It's a date," Lucy said.

He stared at her for a second, then went down into the pit with his team, looked over at us without expression, then got his shoes out of his bag, started to put them on.

"We should stay and watch," Lucy said.

"He would bowl a ninety-four and have to commit suicide, or his team buddies would kill him, then we wouldn't get to talk to him tomorrow. At eleven. That would put the kibosh on the investigation and Ma would fire us and we'd end up homeless or living in a trailer park somewhere in Iowa."

"You're so logical, I can hardly stand it."

"Many are the numbers of criminal tax-dodgers who have fallen beneath the razor's edge of my logic."

"Now they'll have to steam-clean the carpets in this place. Especially since you used the word 'kibosh.'"

"I know why, but go ahead and say it. It'll make you feel better."

"To get the bullshit out, of course."

"That's my girl."

* * *

Renner and Bledsoe were at the snack bar when we turned and were about to leave. Lucy saw them the same time I did.

"Go get 'em, pit bull," I said.

Lucy led the way over. I stood beside her as she sat at their table. "Hey, guys, we should have dinner sometime, get to know each other better. Got any pictures of the kids?"

Well, hell. My pit bull had become a Chihuahua.

"How about San Francisco?" she added. "Dinner at the Top of the Mark? Good eats. We'll see you there tomorrow afternoon at five. You buy. You can tell a bunch of IRS jokes."

Maybe a Doberman.

"We should all go in one car," Renner said. "Save gas."

Lucy tilted her head. "Makes you sound skeptical about us meeting you there, George. A little hint of paranoia there?"

Renner looked up at me. He had a yellow dab of mustard at the corner of his mouth. "You've got some property belongs to the IRS, Angel. Or you can cough up a hundred forty dollars."

"Possession being nine-tenths of the law, I might owe you fourteen bucks. But a hundred forty? You guys get ripped off every time you turn around. IRS would pay thirty dollars for a box of Cap'n Crunch. I could buy whatever you're talking about for twenty-nine ninety-five on Wells Avenue."

"Where is it? The tracker. I want it, *now*."

"In my bra," Lucy said. "I'm keeping it safe. And warm, if you must know. If you want it right now, you'll have to go in and get it." She pushed her chest out half an inch.

What a liar. She never wears a bra. But I didn't think they would peel her shirt off to get at their misplaced tracker.

Two sets of IRS eyes jittered. I'd seen a lot of jittering eyes lately. I tried to keep a straight face, had to turn around and look at the bowlers. I turned back. "I wonder how Mike's doin'."

"We should go see."

Lucy got up. We headed back to the lanes, stood behind the Alley Cats. They were three frames in. Mike had a spare and two open frames. Pretty soon his teammates were going to either set him up as a bowling pin or light him on fire.

* * *

Twilight. Purple-red glow above the dark Sierras, a sliver of moon headed west. We stood in the bowling alley parking lot, looking up at the first stars to appear.

"Neon will be getting bright," Lucy said. "Downtown."

"Yes, it will."

"You said Wildcat's sign was yellow. But small."

"Oh, no."

"You could drive by. I could get a look at it as we go past."

"Oh, no."

"Otherwise, I could be like walking around downtown at night and practically like stumble into it by accident."

"Not if you stick with me, kiddo, since I'm not going near that place again, but your Valley Girl is terrific."

"Mira might be there."

"Oh, no."

"According to you, she hangs out there sometimes."

"What I *might* have to do, I might have to give you one of those in-home chopstick lobotomies."

She turned and faced me, held me around the waist. "Kiss me."

I did. It went French, lasted a while.

"Damn," I said. "You sure are a tasty little wench."

"Wildcat. You drive so I can look."

So I drove.

We went west on Second Street, took a gander at the little bit of yellow neon, not much activity outside on a Wednesday evening, not yet seven thirty, turned around at Ralston and came back, closer now that we were headed east, same side of the street as Wildcat, and there was Mira, just coming out the door.

Great. Life is all about timing. Don't look, big guy. Don't say anything—

"Hey," Lucy said. "Is that that girl, Mira?"

"My name isn't Mira."

She slugged my shoulder, kinda hard, too. "She turned the corner. She's going down West Street, toward the river. Go around the block, let's see."

It wasn't like I had anything to hide. I just didn't want any of this to get us closer to Ramon, but Lucy yanked the wheel and to keep from expensively sideswiping a Jaguar XF I kept turning to the right and we went south on Sierra Street.

I looked over at her. "I should drive, Sugar Plum, since I'm over here and you're over there."

"Okay. But hang a right at the next corner."

"Who's drivin' this Uber, you or me?"

"Turn right. That was her, wasn't it?"

"Her, not she? Nice use of colloquial semi-English, kiddo. You're gettin' to be a real whiz—"

"Turn right or die. How's that?"

So I turned right. I was only forty-two. That seemed a bit young to end this trip.

No Mira at the corner.

"Turn right," Lucy said.

Onto West Street, headed north. Mira was on the west side of the street, walking slowly south.

"Is that her?" Lucy asked.

"Yes, it is, Miss Colloquial USA. And we're going to leave her alone."

"Because?"

"Because she's a pipeline to Ramon who happens to be not only crazy as a bedbug, but schizo and mad to boot."

"To boot, huh?" Lucy chewed her lower lip for a moment. "Okay. Let's go home. Then . . . we're supposed to meet Russell at the Green Room at, what? Ten?"

"That's right. So what'll we do in the meantime?"

"I'll think of something."

*   *   *

Man, that girl sure could think. Her brain was on steroids. We didn't get to the Green Room until ten after ten.

"You're late," Russ said. He had a beer in front of him and had commandeered a jar of beer nuts, going through them like a squirrel after a hard winter.

"Something came up," Lucy said.

"*And*," I jumped in before she could expand on that theme, "it took us a few extra minutes to find a parking space."

"Actually, we walked over," Lucy said.

I squeezed her waist. "Hush, little darling." I gave Russ's beer a nod. "You paid for that yet?"

"Nope."

"Got it covered, since you had to wait." I thumbed out a free-drink coupon from my shirt pocket and shoved it toward O'Roarke who was listening to all this.

He threw a rag on top of the bar, hard. "Next time you get wounded or even killed, do not count on a bunch of coupons."

"Gotcha. Thanks for the heads-up." To Russ, I said, "Did you get that paperwork I asked for?"

He kicked a cheap nylon bag at his feet. It was bright pink with yellow daisies and bumble bees on it, probably belonged to Danya when she was in the fourth grade. "Right here."

"That's not a Gucci bag, is it? Sure you want to let that out of your sight? It's a beauty."

He drained his beer and stood up. "If you can't tell, then, yeah, it's Gucci."

Man, I hate smart-asses. And irony.

"And," he went on, "I didn't give you nothin'. Don't know where you got that stuff."

"What stuff? And I haven't seen you for three days."

He gave my shoulder a buddy punch, softer than I had any right to expect, almost like we were friends, then he walked out.

*   *   *

My burner phone rang when I was halfway through a Pete's Wicked Ale. Lucy was sipping a half-sized vodka martini that O'Roarke had given her on the house. I used to get drinks on the house, but that has tapered off significantly.

I answered the phone: "You should get more sleep." The burner didn't cost twenty bucks, didn't come with caller ID, but Munson, Ma, and Russ were the only ones who had the number. Either way, sleep was good.

"That you, Mort?" Willie Munson was on the horn.

"Got it on the first try," I said. "Are you in D.C. right now? What is it over there? Must be way past midnight."

"It's one twenty."

"IRS never sleeps, huh?"

"You gettin' anywhere with the Soranden murder?"

"Is the FBI absolutely certain it's murder, not some bizarre accident involving ants?"

Silence so long I thought he'd hung up. Then, in a voice of finely measured beats, he said, "You gettin' anywhere with it?"

"Not so you'd notice. But I'm working on it like a son of a gun, Commissioner."

"If you find anything at all, let me know."

"That's a two-way street."

A moment of silence. "Yeah, whatever." He hung up after delivering that bit of IRS ambiguity, something they teach at the mandatory bi-annual hunter-killer trainings. Ambiguity is good. Sink people up to the armpits in verbal traps, then go for the kill.

At 11:02, I was on Channel Four finding that damn skull of Soranden's again. Slow news day. It'd help if Charlie Manson broke out of Corcoran State prison and headed east leaving a trail of corpses. Which is dark, I know, but true, or would be if Charlie hadn't died two or three years ago. Lucy and I took off as an FBI spokesman was delivering the news that nothing new had come up in the investigation in the past three days, but that they were following up several promising leads and an arrest was likely in the near future.

Everyone lies.

CHAPTER ELEVEN

"THIS'LL TAKE LIKE forever," Lucy said the next morning. We were in my home office. She had the paper crap of Soranden's that Russell had given us spread out on a four-by-eight library table against the south wall beneath a window with wooden blinds. She'd sorted the crud into piles: bank statements, car insurance, mortgage documents and payments, Edward Jones, printouts of email correspondence with sisters Esther and Alice, his children, Kate and John, and several others. Xerox copies of an address book, tax returns for the past four years, IRS pay stubs, car titles, health insurance, receipts for major purchases, car maintenance. He'd had an old dinosaur Rolodex. The FBI had hired a seventy-four-year-old woman by the name of Leneta Prato to go through it and put it all on Excel. She'd signed and dated her work. Lucky us, we had both the Excel file on flash drive *and* a printout. They'd included a Xerox of phone numbers and doodles on a desk pad, and a sheet listing all the magazines and periodicals they'd impounded.

"Go get 'em, Sugar Plum," I said. "You said you'd grapple with it so I could work on the Joss-Volker mystery."

I believe she produced a nasty little wolverine snarl. Then, "It's ten thirty-eight. We're supposed to be at Volker's house at eleven, Mort. And for the record, I don't grapple."

"Right you are. Let's go."

She turned at the doorway to the office and looked back at the fire hazard on the table. "Go get 'em. Ri-i-i-ight. I may have misspoken when I said I'd go through that crud."

"No takebacks, Sunshine."

Got me another snarl.

We took the Toyota over to Volker's house, hit sixty miles an hour on the freeway south, which made the mirror yodel like a Swiss goatherder.

"You should go faster or slower. That wail hurts my ears," Lucy said. "Or you could buy another car."

"Another car? You kidding? This baby's got another fifty thousand miles left in it. Maybe a hundred."

"Seriously? This thing is a wreck on wheels."

"Gets twenty-nine miles per gallon. What's your Mustang get?"

"Doesn't matter what it gets. It isn't a wreck on wheels. It just has a slashed top."

"This is better for surveillance."

"Got me there. No one would look at this piece of crap on purpose if they didn't have to."

"There you go."

"Yeah. Learnin' stuff like crazy."

We got to Volker's at ten fifty-nine. He answered the door. Marta was in the living room, in her wheelchair with an afghan on her lap, waiting for us. Kids in school. We had the place to ourselves.

"Something to drink?" Mike asked. "Water, coffee, tea? I have lemonade in the fridge, fresh made."

"Nothing for me," I said. Lucy had the same.

She and I took the couch. Mike settled into the love seat. Marta held a cup of tea on a saucer and watched us warily.

Small talk didn't look like an option, so I turned to Marta and said, "Whatever happened, you know about it?"

"Yes," she said. Nothing else.

I nodded at Volker. "You're up, then. Operating account at Joss & Volker is light by thirteen thousand six hundred bucks."

"I'm trying to make it good. I've been paying a thousand a month back into it."

"Which is a good sign, but I was hired to find out why, which is a reasonable thing for your partner to know. So let's get to it. Or," I added, "you can explain it directly to Evelyn, which would amount to the same thing and keep me out of it."

"No," Marta said.

I looked at her in surprise.

"We talked about this, Mike," she said to her brother. Her voice was mild, yet firm.

He was silent for a moment, then he took a deep breath, looked first at Lucy then at me. "This was never supposed to get out."

"Lots of things like that," I said amiably. "Like what really happened at Benghazi."

"I should do this," Marta said. "Since it's my fault."

"It's *not* your fault," Mike said. "Not at all."

Marta looked at me. "Mike wouldn't put the blame on me. He's not like that, but he's wrong. If it weren't for me, none of this would have happened." She gazed down at her hands, then up at me. "It's a bit complicated and the details don't matter, but four years ago I ended up owing the Internal Revenue Service thirty-seven thousand dollars. My ex-husband incurred the debt while we were still married. It had to do with his business, of which I knew nothing. Not that that makes any difference to the IRS. Ray and I stayed friends after the divorce, as many people do. We were on his motorcycle when a woman who was texting ran a red light and broadsided us. Ray was killed instantly, and I . . . I lost a leg from mid-thigh down. But that tax situation. Ray was trying to clear it up, but it wasn't going well, especially with the penalties and interest and his business struggling after a few setbacks. The debt became mine when he died and, of course, the IRS came after me once they got everything they could from Ray's estate, such as it was. That's when I found myself on the hook for that thirty-seven thousand. I was living in New Bern, North Carolina. I was in the hospital, then physical therapy, not doing well with crutches. I was going to lose the house. The IRS doesn't care what's right or fair or anything else, they only want their money. As if it's *theirs*." She glared at me. "Mike said you used to be with the IRS."

"Until I discovered I had a soul," I clarified.

She almost smiled. "Good for you. There wasn't a lot of equity in the house, but there was enough that the IRS wanted what they could get. After the real estate commission, I only had ten thousand I could give to the IRS. They were going to take the rest out of my IRA, which wasn't very big, and with that ten percent penalty, and then income taxes on top of that—"

"Which I couldn't let her do," Mike interrupted.

"I still wish you had," Marta replied. "After what happened later."

"We did what was right at the time, Marta." He turned to me. "I took out a loan and paid off the IRS. And got Marta out of New Bern. She couldn't stay there after . . . after . . ."

"After this," Marta said, indicating her wheelchair.

"Which isn't your fault," Mike said again. "Life happens. We are family. You would've done the same for me."

He faced me and Lucy. "That loan stretched me pretty thin. Actually, it was the loan on top of the car outside, that BMW I never should have bought, and the mortgage on this place, car insurance, property taxes, all the usual expenses everyone has. After all that, the loan made things pretty tight—"

"Which it wouldn't have if you'd let me use my IRA to pay the IRS," Marta said.

Mike shook his head. "Made no sense in the long run to do that. So I moonlighted. Did some 'off-the-books' accounting for cash. My partner, Evelyn, didn't know about it. Or the IRS. That wasn't kosher, but it was the only way I could think of to keep us going here. All I know is accounting, and I could do it here at home. But I guess when you start down that road, things happen and it just gets worse and worse."

"That was four years ago," I said. "And I'm sorry to hear it, but it doesn't account for the money you took from the operating fund earlier this year."

He stared at his hands for a moment. "No, it doesn't. This tax year it all fell apart. I was audited. Auditor was good at her job. She found the moonlighting. There was a discrepancy in my income from Joss & Volker and my expenses and the in and out of my bank accounts. I didn't think the IRS got that far down in the weeds. Also, the businesses I did accounting for claimed my work as a business expense, which of course they would. I know what I did wasn't right, but . . ." He spread his hands, palms up.

"But life happens," I said.

"Boy, does it ever. Like a ton of bricks."

"So . . . more penalties, interest, years of back taxes?"

"You'd think," Volker said. "But, no, that wasn't it. I mean, that wasn't what put me over the edge this year."

I lifted an eyebrow. "No?"

Mike looked me in the eye. "What must have happened is that the auditor passed all that up to that Soranden guy. I don't know exactly, and it doesn't matter. One way or another it ended up on his desk and he took over."

Maybe I flinched, I'm not sure. But . . . *Soranden*? I hadn't expected his name to come up during this confessional. This luck thing of mine was like the Loch Ness Monster, surfacing when I least expected it.

"So Soranden got into it?" I prompted him.

"He did. He called me up, told me to meet him at the IRS office here in Reno. At that point I didn't know what was up. The auditor hadn't said a word to me, just went over my books, income, bank statements, mortgage payments, car payments, the usual, then left. A week later I got the phone call from Soranden, went over the next day, and he took me into his office, just the two of us, told someone to hold his calls, closed the door, and he laid it all out, the money I couldn't account for, the underground accounting I'd done for local businesses, and he said all of it was indictable, that I was facing prison for tax evasion."

"Which is true," I said. "But very unlikely."

"Unlikely wasn't in my head. He made it sound like a slam dunk, that this was headed that way. Four *years* of tax evasion. Back taxes, penalties, and interest came to a hundred thirty-six thousand dollars, not to mention the illegality of it all. He told me I was looking at three to five years in a federal penitentiary. Then he paused and said, 'If it got out.'"

"Uh-oh," I said. "Big if there."

"That's right. *If* it got out. He dismissed me then, told me to come back in two days. Told me not to mention any of this to anyone, that he might be able to do something to help me out, but if I ran my mouth and it got out, his hands would be tied."

I saw where this was going. I knew Ronald Soranden had it in him to use this for personal gain. Soranden had always struck me as a man with hidden larcenies running rampant in his little IRS heart. His secret in-house name at the IRS was "The Toad" because of how he looked, and because he might, in the privacy of his office, flick his tongue out and snag flies. Now, hearing all this, nothing he did in the way of intimidation or blackmail felt unlikely or out of character for him.

"He blackmailed you," I said.

"Did he ever," Volker replied. "It was always just the two of us. No witnesses. He told me that for a hundred thousand dollars he could make it all go away. He acted as if he was doing me a big favor, that for a hundred grand, he could actually save me money and keep me out of prison, that it was his head on the chopping block if any of this got out, not that I would ever have any sort of proof of what he'd done. I could either pay him or go to prison, up to me. He gave me two weeks to think about it but suggested that I might start rounding up cash if I wanted to work with him and keep out of prison. He said all this as if he were doing me a favor, that he was, in fact, my friend."

"Solid IRS technique, but used somewhat differently," I said. "Believe it or not, blackmail isn't in the IRS field manual. At least not by that name."

"Couldn't prove it by me," Volker said. "In the end we had to raid Marta's IRA after all, pay the ten percent, and she'll have to pay income taxes on it this year. We cleared fifty thousand, left a pittance in the account to keep it open. And I stripped my savings accounts at the bank and credit union, and after all that we still came up short."

"By thirteen thousand, six hundred," I said.

"You got it."

"And you gave it all to Soranden."

"In cash. Untraceable. His word against mine if any of it got out."

"When was that?"

"Toward the end of June. The twenty-second."

"And then he went missing and ended up dead."

Mike shook his head. "That was . . . horrible. Unbelievable. I didn't have a thing to do with it, but . . . what would the police think if they got wind of him blackmailing me like that?"

"If he blackmailed you, he probably blackmailed others."

"Wouldn't really have helped me, would it?"

I shrugged. "It might have. If the police found out he was blackmailing others, you'd be in the pool, but that's all."

"Which I didn't want to be. I didn't want any of this to get out. I'm still at risk for tax evasion, don't you think?"

"No question about that. But prison's unlikely."

"Still."

"Yeah. You're out a hundred grand and you'd still owe the IRS that hundred thirty-six thousand. More now. I don't suppose you'd care to go to the IRS, tell them the entire story, see if what Soranden did would get you off the hook, put this behind you?"

"No way. I just want it to go away. I mean, it seems as if I've, well . . . that I've suffered enough. More than enough. This has been pure hell, these past months. I just wanted to put the money back into our business account and be done with it, try to replace everything we'd lost, which will take time, years. I don't know what Soranden did to bury what I'd done—four years of unreported income—but it appears to have gone away like he said it would. I haven't heard anything about it since."

"But then . . ." Marta said.

"Not sure about that," Mike said. "It might stir things up that we should just let lie. It'll take a while, but we'll get through this."

The two of them had been talking things over before Lucy and I got there. "Not sure about what?" I asked.

Marta looked at her brother. "Now that we've gone this far, I think we should at least ask."

I didn't know where all that was going, but they were going to figure it out themselves, didn't need me asking "what?" every few seconds.

"I don't know," Mike said.

"Last night you said something about a finder's fee."

"I think the money's gone, Marta."

"We don't know that. We should at least ask."

Mike stared at his shoes for a full minute. Finally, he looked up at me. "You're kinda high profile, Mr. Angel."

"Not by choice, but yeah."

"You're the one who found Soranden's head. I mean, his skull."

"Which is an important part of a head. It was something of an accident, me finding it five seconds before Lucy did."

"Last thing I want is high profile. But you . . . you've got ways to, I don't know, keep things quiet?"

"Some of what I've done this past year has been about as quiet as anything the National Security Agency has done. Just don't ask me to tell you about it."

He offered up a tentative smile. "National Security Agency. I sorta like the sound of that."

"It's a skill I've been developing."

Volker looked at his sister. "Marta?"

"*Ask* him, Mike. It can't hurt. Not *now*, for heaven's sake, after all you've told him. And Lucy."

"I suppose not." He gave me an inquiring look. "If you're accepting new clients, Mr. Angel, I think I'd like to hire you."

CHAPTER TWELVE

WHEN YOU'RE ON a roll, everyone wants to hire you.

"Mort," I said. "Hire me to do what?"

"Us," Lucy said. "Hire *us*. Let us not forget your assistant who is quite a bit more than your basic little gofer."

Volker had a question in his eyes. Same question he had at the bowling alley. Time to clear that up.

"She's thirty-one years old," I said. "Normally we wouldn't hand out ages like business cards, but she has been an exception for . . . well, for obvious reasons."

Volker stared at Lucy. "Are you sure?" he said to me.

"A while ago we cut off an arm and counted rings—" An elbow in the ribs brought that to an abrupt halt. I continued with, "It has been verified a hundred ways from Sunday, up one side and down the other."

Marta laughed softly. "It's okay, Mike."

"Hire us to do what?" Lucy asked.

"To . . . to try to get some or all of that hundred thousand back," Mike said. "While keeping all of this quiet, of course."

"Are you still moonlighting?" I asked.

"Some. Yes."

"Gotta cut that out. At least get Evelyn's permission to go outside the business, which I think she would okay as long as it doesn't cut into the bottom line. And you need to start reporting it as income to get all of this under control."

He lowered his head. "Yeah, okay. I've been doing it after hours, putting in fourteen- and sixteen-hour days, but . . . okay."

"You need to pay quarterly estimated taxes. Try to get that done today, tomorrow at the latest."

He looked up. "That mean you're taking me on?"

"Not yet. Evelyn's still my client. She asked me to find out what was going on. I'm going to tell her. No choice, Mike."

"I want to be there when you do."

"Don't see any conflict there. How about today at five? I'll give her a call, tell her I've got an answer regarding that money that went south."

He blew out a breath. "Yeah, okay. I'll be there. I mean, I'll *stay* there. I took a long lunch to be here, but I've got a couple of clients coming in this afternoon. Any chance you can give me an answer now, about seeing if you can get my money back? Some of it anyway?"

"Not yet. I'll have to ask my partner, Ms. Clary. I have an idea she'll be thrilled with the idea, Soranden being in the news as he is, *and* the subject of a red-hot FBI investigation."

"Not much hope there, huh?"

"Don't give up yet," I said. "My powers of persuasion are . . . legion."

* * *

"Yeah, right," said my assistant when we were back in the howling Toyota. "Legion."

"Ma hangs on my every word, kiddo. You've seen her."

"Hangs. Great metaphor, Mort."

"We can't all be English whizzes, but stick with me, kid. Pick up what you can."

"Bullshit is useful? Since when?"

"Since Congress made it their de facto modus operandi. Now how 'bout lunch?"

"Fabulous segue, and you used a bunch of Latin too. But, okay. Where?"

"Drive-thru at Taco Bell?"

"Anything but."

"Let's go talk to Ma first."

* * *

As I'd thought, Ma was thrilled at the prospect of trying to get Volker's money back from Soranden, who was about as dead as people normally get and unlikely to cough up so much as a wooden nickel.

"No," she said. "We're layin' off Soranden."

"I thought we were after Munson's bonus. We might have a pretty good fingernail under that case now."

"We were, now we're not. The case is still a dog and the FBI's all over it and square dancin' with that bunch is a loser."

"But—"

"No."

"Mike is—"

"No."

"And—"

"No."

"Okay, then. We'll talk later."

"No, we won't."

* * *

She's such a kidder.

"Legion," Lucy said as we left the Peppermill Casino and walked over to the car.

"Shut up."

"But thanks for the buffet. The salad was good."

"Not enough calories to support life. You lost more calories going through the line twice than you got by going through the line twice."

"Unlike you, Mr. Prime Rib and chicken, shrimp, egg rolls, mashed potatoes, pecan pie, ice cream, and a whole lot of other unhealthy stuff."

"Stop. You're making me hungry again."

"It's two forty. What'll we do between now and five, when we've gotta be at Joss & Volker's?"

"Not sure about me, but *you* are about to get all over that pile of Soranden crud since we got it. Especially now that we might be hitting it from two directions."

"Ma told us to keep away from Soranden. And I think that would be from *either* direction, Cowboy."

"She'll come around. I have powers of persuasion I haven't tapped yet."

"Yeah, right. We should put money on that."

"Fifty bucks, same as last time when you lost that bet this summer about where Shanna was headed."

"You're on."

* * *

Lucy leaned over the table, thumbing through Soranden's paper debris. "What're you gonna do?" she asked me.

"Supervise my assistant, of course." I pushed off and spun a complete circle in the office chair, great bearings, then wagged a finger at her. "Get on it. Check his car maintenance."

"Like car maintenance is the key to what killed him. Look at this stuff. FBI went bonkers with it. I'm surprised they didn't include his elementary school report cards. And you supervise like chimpanzees do ballet."

"That's an image."

"You could help. This is a mess. And don't tell me to start with car maintenance or I'll wallop you."

"Mmm, testy." I came over, put an arm around her waist, pulled her close, and said, "You smell good."

"Back off. It's just balsamic vinaigrette."

I picked up a sheet that listed magazines and periodicals found in Soranden's office at the IRS. Most were puzzle mags: crosswords, Sudoku, logic puzzles. "I never figured The Toad for this kind of thing," I said, discounting issues of *IRS Weekly* and a well-thumbed copy of *Accounting for Psychos.*

"Probably did it in his office with the door closed. He was really quite a crook, wasn't he?"

"We all were."

She bumped me with a hip. "*You* weren't. But he was in his office, planning blackmails and doing puzzles, getting paid how much per hour, ripping off Uncle Sam?"

"Oodles."

"Oodles, huh?"

"Right. Speaking of which, how 'bout this doodle sheet?" I picked up a copy of Soranden's meanderings, the kind of thing people do when they're put on hold, brain spinning in circles, listening to bad Muzak. Circles, spirals, dollar signs, a few stars, junk squiggles. It also had reminders: "5:00 A.J., E's B-day!, RM

& PL@TJ's." And a lot of odd phrases like, "about three u-boat there," "astute statue," and "si, a horse is ashore." I finally recognized much of it as a curious mix of anagrams, anagram-like nonsense, and half-assed palindromes.

After a while Lucy said, "Really weird stuff, but I guess he was a puzzle freak, bordering on half smart."

"I never thought he was short on brains, only integrity."

She picked up the sheet. "'Live evil, vile Levi.' That's over the top. 'Doom mood,' 'rat tar', 'toot, otto.' And 'OCD, Doc?' Okay, I like that one. 'Honest? Not she.' That's good too. 'Bob's boobs bob.' That's a palindrome. 'Drool, O'Lord.' Wow. Like I said, kinda smart, but on a scale of one to ten, I give him a creep rating of nine point five with leaking corpses being a ten."

"Leaking corpses, speaking of creepy."

We phoned the numbers on the doodle sheet. Numbers in area code 916 got us a body shop and an extended care facility, both in California, neither of which had heard of Ronald Soranden. The 917 number was an overlay to the 212 area code. The phone was answered by a guy in a bored voice, heavy Brooklyn accent, in the maintenance facility of the Port Authority in Manhattan. He'd never heard of Soranden either.

"Port Authority?" Lucy said.

"Buses. Young girls from Kansas with no talent get off in the Big Apple thinking they'll be the next Paris Hilton—okay, talent-wise how hard could *that* be—and end up walking Eighth Avenue."

"Yeah, that sounds like fun."

* * *

Four fifty-seven p.m. Lucy and I were back at Joss & Volker. Evelyn and Michael were there, as expected. Evelyn was just finishing up with a client, a middle-aged woman in Christian Louboutins, according to Lucy—heels like a giraffe, damned ugly, looking as comfortable as Marine footwear at Guadalcanal.

"How do you know that sh . . . stuff?" I whispered.

"My mom has a few pairs of Louboutins. Very expensive. Hers don't have heels like that, though. She's not that dumb."

"Yeah? How expensive? More than forty bucks?"

She grabbed my arm and hustled me toward a water cooler in the waiting room, got me a drink, which was kind of her. I glanced back at the Louboutins, created by visionary podiatrists to enhance their already terrific retirements. "How much would those run for real?" I persisted.

"About a hundred yards. Two if you were lucky, then the heels would break."

Man, I hate smart-asses. But her response made me think the price of women's shoes is a gender secret. If one of them spills the beans, the rest are obligated to stone her to death. If you see some dame hobbling around in shoes you don't think she could give away on Craigslist, do not ask her how much they cost. Some of those dippy broads carry guns and their feet hurt.

Eve's client left, working on her club feet, black toenails beneath a veneer of polish, and the four of us gathered in Eve's office around her conference table. She glanced at Mike, then gave me a darting look with a question in it.

"Got an answer for you," I said to get the ball rolling.

Mike was gazing intently at his hands. Eve turned to him. "I'm so sorry, Mike. I didn't know what else to do."

"It's okay," he said. He looked at me. "Now what?"

"It's your story," I told him. "You should tell it."

He went through it. He wasn't happy. He started off slow, then picked up a little speed. I didn't interrupt, didn't need to. I listened to make sure it was the same story. And it was. All of it, including Soranden's blackmail.

When he finished, Eve said, "Oh, I wish you'd come to me back when you needed that extra income."

He hung his head. All the abject signs you get from a kid who tried to raid a cookie jar, pulled it off the counter, broke it into a thousand pieces. Four years ago, he'd needed the job and hadn't trusted her enough to get permission to moonlight. It had finally come back on him and he looked sick.

"I wish I knew what to say," he said. "I managed to screw everything up. Everything. Even with the IRS."

She put a gentle hand on his arm. "We'll get through it, you and I." She turned to me. "But what *about* the IRS, Mort? Can they come back on Mike after all this?"

"The IRS can come back on Jimmy Hoffa, so, yeah, they can come back on you," I said to Mike. "But maybe Soranden fixed it. He would have access, passwords, ways to do that, and you probably weren't his first victim, so maybe he made it go away. Which means I'm not sure I'd walk into the IRS office with a rousing mea culpa right now and put myself back on the hook for a hundred fifty grand and a possible but very unlikely indictment. All of that could still happen, so you're going to be living on a tightrope for a long time."

"How long? What's the statute of limitations?"

"There's no statute of limitations on tax fraud, which yours was. They could come after you when you're ninety. Of course, by then the penalties and interest would be about the same as the national debt so they would have trouble collecting."

"Oh, Jesus."

"And," Eve said delicately, "Mr. Soranden is dead. How is that likely to . . . to affect Mike?"

"No idea. Now we wait and see what happens. Of course, it would be nice to get the money back, but we've got no way of knowing what The Toad did with it."

Eve looked startled. "The Toad?"

"His in-house moniker. Never to his face, of course, but I offer it up as insight into what his underlings thought of him."

"The Toad. My goodness."

I smiled at what my grandmother might've said. My mother would've said, "The Toad? Does he eat flies?" in which case I would've had to say, "That's the working theory. We had a few flies in the place, but no one ever saw a fly in his office."

But I didn't go into any of that.

Instead, I spread my hands. "So, we done here?"

"I think so," Eve said. "But if you would stay for a while, Mike? We need to talk. It won't take long."

"Of course."

Eve motioned me over to her desk. In a low voice she asked how much she owed me. I named a figure and she wrote out a check, handed it to me.

Lucy and I left. We were two steps out the door when Mike stuck his head out and said, "Could we meet someplace, Mort? In, say, half an hour, forty minutes?"

"Snack bar at the bowling alley?" We were at that end of town. Noise in a bowling alley would mask conversation, which might be a good idea.

He smiled. Tried to, anyway, managed to work up a modest half-grimace. "I'll be there."

About to leave, I hesitated, so he did too. For a few seconds I wondered if I ought to tell him about his sixteen-year-old kid hanging out with dope-buying Dooley, eight or nine years older than her. And apartment 307. It wasn't my business, but I was a father too. And Mike might become a client, depending on what Ma had to say about that.

Better to wait, I finally decided. If Volker became a client, I might be more or less obligated to give him that information since I got it in connection with the case, such as it was at the time. So I gently punched his shoulder, said, "Hang tough," and enhanced that buddie-bump with a "buck-up" smile.

"Sure." He ducked back inside.

"What was *that*?" Lucy asked.

"Just wondered if I ought to tattle on Kimmi, otherwise known as Precious."

She wrinkled her nose. "Tough call, huh?"

"Little bit. I'll have to think about it."

Lucy's Mustang was at the curb. Duct tape on the roof was starting to get a bit rough. We either had to redo it, or . . . I said, "Tomorrow's Friday. How about we get this thing in for a new top?" I waved Eve's check on which the ink wasn't yet dry. "I'm buying, since the person who dropped Soranden's skull in there probably thought it was my set of wheels."

Lucy gave me a good female hug. "A very nice gesture, but that check is at least half Ma's."

"True. But I'm still buying."

"In case you didn't know, I can pretty much afford it."

"You make it hard to be chivalrous, girlie."

"Okay, then. You pay. I'll try to think of some way to make it up to you."

"You do that. Surprise me."

"I might do that. So, bowling alley? Maybe we could get in a game or two before Mike shows up."

"Doubt it. My thumb's still acting up from the last time you kicked my ass in there. Don't think I can hold a ball, kiddo."

"Uh-huh. Lamest excuse ever."

* * *

Mike showed up at six twenty-five. Lucy and I were nursing a paper plate of French fries. Well, she was nursing, I was scarfing.

"I really shouldn't stay long," Mike said. "But, now, after seeing Evelyn, what do you think about my hiring you to try to get back some of that money?"

"Odds are you'd be wasting even more money," I said.

"You think there's no hope?"

"Not much."

His face fell. "I was hoping you had an in with the IRS." He shook his head. "Aw, jeez, I don't mean like that. This has been a lousy week. I'm not thinking clearly. What I was *hoping* is that you have some idea what Soranden might have done with the money since he was with the IRS."

"The IRS doesn't have a designated blackmail fund, Mike. Though that might be in the works as a secondary self-serve pension for employees."

He almost smiled. "So, no hope, you think?"

"Not much," I said again.

"But . . . any? I mean, if the IRS comes back at me like you said they could, I sure could use that money."

"Best guess—less than ten percent that I can track it down and get any part of it. There's no telling how much he might've already spent, or how."

"Still . . ." He gave me a hopeful look. "You've got a hell of a track record."

"Finding missing people. Who, by the way, end up dead. Can't say I'm a whiz at finding money, though I tracked down truck-loads when I was with the IRS."

"So you've got . . . techniques."

I thought about that. "The IRS had ways," I said slowly, think-ing that Ma had ways too. Illegal ways. The IRS had the same ways, but they were legal because Internal Revenue makes up its own laws, which makes them legal by definition—sort of a reverse Catch-22 deal with taxpayers on the losing end.

Speaking of things beyond the law, IRS thugs Renner and Bledsoe wandered in and took seats nearby. Perfect. If I pointed them out to Volker, he would've had a coronary.

Lucy got up and had a word with them. Don't know what she said, but their eyes jittered and they moved to a table farther away. She came back, sat down smiling to herself.

"I'd sure like you to try," Mike said, staring at the guys Lucy chased off. He looked at me. "At least it's worth a try. Uh, I sup-pose you'd need some sort of a retainer."

"How about a little pro bono?" Lucy said to me.

"Not right now, kiddo," I said, patting my stomach. "Those fries pretty much did the trick."

She slugged my shoulder, then rubbed it to take the hurt out. She looked at Mike. "We have a—shall we say, sort of a client who should remain nameless, but who is, shall we say, interested in roughly the same sort of thing as you."

"Nicely put, Ms. Circumlocution," I told her.

"Well, it's not as if this person wants to see their name on the front page of the *New York Times*, Mort. So, maybe we could keep Mike in mind while we stumble along with that other thing."

"Stumble. Ain't that the truth? Which Ma said we weren't going to do, if you remember."

"Except you haven't yet used your powers of persuasion on her, which I've heard are legion. *If* you remember."

"Forgot about that."

"I'd sure appreciate anything you could do," Mike said, eyes pinballing between us. "I don't know what this other thing is, but, hell, if . . . if you could at least keep me in mind."

Lucy hugged my arm, looked at Mike. "Mort's shy about his sleuthing powers, they're so incredible. He doesn't like to brag because it's like having a superpower, so I'll brag for him. He's . . . sort of not too awful at investigating stuff."

"Wow," I said.

"Well, you're not."

Mike smiled. "You two are something else." He stood up and shook my hand. "If it turns out that you need a retainer, I'll try to come up with it."

"Pro bono," Lucy said firmly.

* * *

"Incredible sleuthing powers," I said as Mike went out the door. "You should expand on that theme."

"That was like advertising."

"Advertising is all about lying without lying. Or bald-faced, sociopathic lying without flinching. Spinning a layered web of deceit around an ordinary stinky pile of horse pucky."

"Yup. Advertising is all of that."

"Okay, great. What would you like to do now that doesn't involve bowling or me trying to touch my toes?"

"Let's go home. I have an idea."

"Yowzer."

I got up, waved to Renner and Bledsoe, got a little stink-eye from Bledsoe, took Lucy by the arm, and we went outside.

* * *

But the "yowser" notwithstanding, all we did at home was change into going-out duds, me in brown slacks, loafers, white shirt and a sports coat, Lucy in a yowser two-piece black outfit, short skirt, short top with tummy showing, black lipstick, black eye shadow, gold hoop earrings.

"Ho-ly smoke, woman!"

She spun. "Like it?"

"Not on my daughter, no." And it reminded me of Mira, but I didn't tell her that.

"It's not *on* your daughter, Daddy."

Daddy. Last time she called me that we took the Luxor in Vegas for over fifty thousand dollars.

"Is that décolletage or cleavage?" I asked.

"Cleavage here. Décolletage in France and maybe Quebec. And, uh, hot tits in San Bernardino or Bakersfield."

"Gotcha. What's on your mind, Sugar Plum?"

"A suite. One with a Jacuzzi. And a great big bed, like a third of an acre."

"Free?"

"Probably not. But I might win enough to pay for one, you never know. Who's driving?"

"I'll Uber, you keep your legs together. That skirt looks too short for you to get out of the car without . . . without . . ."

"Don't say it. And, you need to put on your white wig and those amber-tinted glasses. And some kind of old fogey hat."

"As if I have a bunch of old fogey hats lying around."

"As if you don't."

The white wig had longish hair. This July, the top quarter inch of my right ear had been blown off by a .38-caliber bullet. All my wigs were long enough now to cover that identifying mark.

We went to the Grand Sierra Resort. They were big. They had suites and looked as if they could afford to cough up enough dough to cover the cost of a good one near the top floor.

They ought to check birthdays at the door. Lucy was born when four planets were lined up, not including Mars. That had a warping effect on her personal universe, and/or the universe at large. As she told me earlier that year, if you take the "k" out of Lucky, what's left? Lucy.

She slipped me five bills, hundred dollars each. "You need to give 'em to me when I ask for them," she said.

"Where'd you get these?"

"Gotta keep a little seed money lying around."

"Seed money. Right. I knew that."

Roulette was her game. One look at her and they wanted to see some ID. She had a fake ID that said she was twenty-three and her name was Britany Taggart. First I'd heard of it.

"I don't want to use my real name," she whispered. "And twenty-three fits the outfit better."

"Yes, it does. How many IDs you got?"

"Three. One legit. Two others. Now hush."

Three?

She settled in at a high-roller roulette table where two other people were playing—a woman in her fifties with diamonds here and there, a guy in his forties in old jeans and a T-shirt. And a Rolex. And a show-off two-carat diamond pinky ring. All I had was a Target Timex. Oh, and Lucy, so in the bigger scheme of things, I was the clear winner.

Lucy looked up at me. "Sugar-baby needs a hit, Daddy." Then she tittered like a girl I once knew in the seventh grade.

Great. *Sugar-baby?* No way. I couldn't call her that.

The other players and the girl running the wheel stared at Sugar, then at me as I got five hundreds out of my wallet.

"Go get 'em, Sugar Plum."

She popped out of her chair and thumped me on the chest. "You *know* I don't win when you call me that."

"I take it back."

"You better. *Right now.*"

She glared at me, hands on a baby-doll flare of truly great hips. "Say it," she said. "Sugar-*baby*."

"Sugar-baby," said the girl-whipped old guy.

"Okay, then." The glare lingered, then faded.

Sugar-baby sat down, got five chips, hundred dollars each. The ball was in play, whirling one way around the outside track, wheel spinning the other way, and Sugar put a chip on red and said, "Black, black, black," and the ball clattered, stopped, and the girl said, "Two, black," and Sugar stared at the table. "Did I say black?" She let out that high-pitched birdlike titter and said, "Oopsie-doodle. I put a chip on red, didn't I? Well . . . poop."

The chip went away. Sugar looked at the table, then put a chip on number two, black, same number that had just come up. "Doublesies, Daddy." Titter.

"Yup," said Daddy.

The girl sent the ball rolling, wheel turning, and Sugar said, "Doublesies, doublesies," and the guy in the pinky ring raised his eyebrows at me and I raised my eyebrows at him, and the ball clattered and, "Two, black," the girl said.

"Lookie, Daddy. I got the double-di-do."

Jesus.

"Mighty fine, Sugar-baby."

The girl set thirty-five chips in front of Sugar, who stashed all but one in a sparkly black purse then popped out of her chair like a gymnast. "Let's go *spend* it, Daddy!" She handed the chip to the girl running the table. "For you, since you've been so sweet," Lucy said, then she tittered.

"Uh, thanks," the girl said as we walked away.

And that's how Lucy paid for the suite. Which, I found out later, wasn't necessary, but it was a beautiful demonstration of how little I knew about my girl.

CHAPTER THIRTEEN

MORE BUBBLE BATH. So, of course, Hammer and Spade were off in a corner, snorting at all that unmanly sudsy iridescence.

But *let* them. *I* was in the tub with Lucy, not them. Bunch of sour-grape wannabes.

Lucy glided over like a seal and more or less stretched out on top of me. Buoyed by water, she weighed about five pounds. Then she started in with the kissing. Man, I hate that. But to keep her happy, I returned it, French style. She'd lost the black lipstick and the vampire eye shadow, looked like a high school cheerleader again, a junior, which gave me the willies.

"How is this getting us closer to whoever killed Soranden or where the money went?" I asked when we came up for air.

"Shut up. And by the way, that tickles."

"What?"

"This."

"Oh."

* * *

"You should touch your toes," she said.

"Would if I could."

"Could if you'd keep trying."

So I gave it a shot, managed to get my fingertips a little over halfway between knees and ankles. "Don't laugh," I said. "And, look, my legs are straight."

"Keep at it."

This was "stretchie" time, which was more or less a sequel to the Spanish Inquisition when folks were torn limb from limb. Twice a day, morning and evening, Lucy demonstrated what it was like to have been born without a backbone. At the moment she was standing on her hands in the middle of the room in black silk panties that were about half thong. Her back was bent almost double and she had both feet on top of her head, breasts stretched as tight as snare drums.

"I'll probably have to work up to that," I told her.

"Good luck."

Then she lowered her feet even further, put them flat on the floor by her hands, then slowly stood up. This was like a slow-motion front flip, which was technically impossible if you were human. Then she did it nine more times, all in perfect control. Then she did it backward, hands over her head, bent backward at the waist until her hands were on the floor behind her, then her legs went up, one at a time, until she was in another handstand, then her feet continued over until they were on the floor again, two inches behind her hands, then she stood up. This was like a slow-motion backflip. Again, not humanly possible. Then nine more times, always in control.

I got my fingertips down another half inch, which hurt.

"Don't bounce," Lucy said. "Bouncing can pull something loose."

"Like a backbone," I agreed. "It might come flying out and bust a lamp."

"Probably not an entire backbone."

"You don't know me."

Then, of course, basic splits—side to side, then front and back. Lucy, not me. She held each for thirty seconds, alternated them, did that for another six or eight minutes.

"That's gotta hurt like a son of a bitch," I said.

"Doesn't. It feels wonderful." She stood up. "There's one more thing that feels wonderful that we haven't done yet."

"We?"

"Yeah. I'll need you for this part."

Oh, great. More work. But I try to be a good sport when it comes to things like this, so I went along with it.

* * *

Later, looking up at a dark ceiling, I gave more thought to everything associated with Soranden, including me, since it was likely Soranden's skull was dropped in what had been mistaken for my car. Lucy was asleep, tucked in beside me with an arm across my chest as usual, but it generally takes me a while to let the day wind down. Especially after . . . Lucy.

About Soranden, we didn't know much, though it's likely we were ahead of the FBI with that blackmail thing. But IRS Commissioner Willie Munson didn't have any idea Soranden had blackmailed anyone, so other than counting on my supposed luck, I didn't know how he thought I could stay ahead of the FBI or solve that crime if they couldn't.

Soranden's skull had been dropped into Lucy's car, and I was with Lucy. Supposedly that tied me into it, or her, but I still had the feeling it was due to my being in the news so much this past year, starting with my first three hours as a private eye when I found Mayor Sjorgen's head in the trunk of my ex-wife's Mercedes.

Which was entirely bogus if we were talking about competence. All levity and feigned hubris aside, I wasn't a gumshoe, I was a patsy for the gods. I was Joe Blow who could walk through a forty-acre park in the dark and step on the one and only pile of dogshit in all that acreage.

Lucy was lucky. So was I, but in a different way. I preferred hers. Mine had put me on the national scene, in the national consciousness. That may have made me a kind of convenient dumping ground. Wonder what to do with an awkward body or body part? No problem. Just leave it with Mortimer Angel. And how do you locate this guy, Angel? Why, just watch the news. There's his house. It's on Washington Street, half a mile west of downtown. You can't miss it. Then once you've dumped that body or body part, you can catch the circus on Channel Four at eleven, narrated by Ginger Haley who is one foxy lady. Invite your friends over for buffalo wings and beer.

Earlier I'd told Ma I didn't have a crack of any kind in the case that I could get a fingernail under, no thread I could pull to unravel it. But now there was blackmail. In effect, Soranden had blackmailed Mike Volker for a hundred thousand dollars. It was unlikely, but possible, that Mike was the first. It would take a certain kind of tax evasion, and a certain kind of tax evader, for Soranden to pull it off, but chances were he had blackmailed others. From what Volker had said, Soranden was pretty smooth about it. He would have a blackmailee over a barrel. It would be someone with a lot to lose, someone the IRS could go after like a pack of bloodthirsty weasels.

Blackmail. If the FBI had a hint of that, Volker would be the first to know. It sounded like the kind of information the FBI might be able to do something with, but how could I push them in that direction without putting Mike back in that whirlwind?

We'd taken his case, such as it was—or we would once I convinced Ma we should. She loves pro bono. Therefore, we couldn't tell the FBI that Soranden had blackmailed citizens without exposing Volker or violating client confidentiality. I didn't know if that was good enough, but it was what it was, so I gently rested a hand on one of the finest female bottoms in all of North America and dropped off to sleep.

* * *

My phone rang at 7:25 a.m. It wasn't the burner, which Lucy and I had taken to calling the Munson Burner—a reminder that neither of us had found high school chemistry to be a hoot, but we'd at least picked up the part where you set things on fire in the lab and maybe, with luck, set off an alarm and everyone beats it out of the building and gets the next hour off as firemen drag a hose or two through the hallways.

"Hey, it's you, Ma. And it's not even seven thirty yet."

"Both things I already knew."

"Must mean you're caffeinated, ready to go."

"I am. Sounds like you aren't."

"Lucy either. But if you were to call back at, oh, say, ten o'clock, I think we could—"

"Funny you should say ten, since that's when you and me and Lucy are meeting Paul Werner at UNR."

"Well, sure, of course. I was kidding about that ten o'clock crack. Just hit me with a quick little reminder—who the hell is Paul Werner?"

"Biology professor. Entomology. That's bugs in case you didn't know. Ag building, room 222. Don't be late."

"Bugs. Meaning ants?"

"Right. Ants is bugs."

"And Ag building? Parse that for me."

"Agriculture, boyo. Southeast part of campus."

"My gumshoe training tells me this has something to do with Soranden's skull. I thought you'd given up on him."

"Willie reminded me we already got a retainer—that flight from Albuquerque. He sounded unhappy, said something about it costing around twelve thousand bucks. We couldn't give the flight back so I renegotiated the bonus, got him up to twenty-five grand, and told him we—you, mostly—would keep him in mind if anything came up."

"So we're back in the game."

"We are. But if the FBI gets anywhere near us and it's your fault, you'll be fired so fast you won't hear about it until you're standing in an unemployment line, disoriented and reeling."

"Wow, Ma. That's fast."

"Ag building, room 222 at ten." She hung up.

Lucy propped herself on an elbow. "Ants, and we're back in the game. Sounds like your powers of persuasion really *are* legion. And what was fast?"

"How fast I could be at the unemployment office if the FBI gets onto us. It was so fast the arrow of time got reversed. Even Einstein would've been impressed."

"Groovy."

"So, Cupcake, no calls to the FBI."

"Okay, I'll take them off speed dial."

* * *

A bunch of classes got out at 9:50, about the time Lucy and I arrived on campus at the agriculture building. I'd forgotten what it was like to be caught in the rush of students headed off to another class, or to the student union for caffeine and calories. Texting while speed-walking was new since I'd been in college. Lucy and I headed upstream against the flow, lucky not to have been swept across campus and into a chemistry class.

Ma met us in the corridor outside the room. She had on tan slacks, a pale orange shirt, and new Nike jogging shoes, puce on black.

"Nice shoes, Ma," I said.

Her eyes narrowed suspiciously. Man, I take a lot of flak, or implied flak.

"I think he means it, Ma," Lucy said. "They *are* nice."

"At least you two're on time."

Room 222 was a biology lab, complete with lab tables with gouged but essentially indestructible black tops, Bunsen burner outlets, ten or twelve aquariums that held tarantulas, scorpions, beetles, toads, and other low-maintenance critters.

Paul Werner was in his mid-forties, five-five, thirty pounds overweight, balding, small features in a round face, blue eyes. When he saw Ma, he rubbed his hands together in anticipation of what she'd brought him. Never in my life have I done that, even when I was eight years old and it was time to open Christmas presents. I'm not sure where the gesture came from, but it looks damn silly so I'm not going to add it to my repertoire.

"Whatcha got for me, Maude? You were a bit cryptic on the phone."

"I need you to identify a bug. And keep it quiet."

He flinched at the word "bug." "Quiet, huh?"

"That's right. Just between us."

"I must say that sounds deliciously ominous." He craned his neck to look up at me, then took in Lucy. "Well, hello, there, miss. What's your name?"

"Lucy."

They stood eye to eye. He shook her hand. "Charmed."

Charmed. I've never said that when meeting someone for the first time. I could try it out, see if it got a laugh.

"And you are . . .?" Paul said to me.

We shook hands. "Mort. Charmed."

He laughed.

Yep, it worked. I would have to try it on O'Roarke.

Then he gave me a closer inspection. "You look familiar. Have we met before?"

"It's possible. But not in person."

"Cryptic." He turned to Ma. "Wonderful. A day of mystery, and it's not even noon." He gave me the kind of look he might give a bug he hadn't expected to find. "Mort. I've heard that name recently. Don't tell me, though. I'll see if I can place you."

Ma took his arm. "When you do, *if* you do, none of us were here, Paul."

He hesitated. "How . . . mysterious. Well, then, what can I do for you?"

"Tell us whatever you can about this." She got a plastic container out of her purse, opened it, got out a bit of tissue and opened it, showed him the ant.

His face fell. "Another one. That's all?"

"What do you mean 'another one'?" Ma asked. "And it's freakin' gigantic, so what do you mean, 'that's all'?"

"Well, it's a Maricopa Harvester Ant, common as sin. Not around here, though. And the police showed me one a few days ago. Someone from the FBI was with them. They asked pretty much the same thing."

Feds and police. Werner was the local expert. Of course they'd haul that ant over here, get the skinny on it.

"It's huge," Ma said. "I've never seen anything like it."

"Some harvester ants are. Huge, I mean. This one's a good size." He pulled a small steel ruler out of his nerd pocket and held it up to the ant. "Three point two centimeters. She's a big girl. You'd never see anything like her around here, but you'd see plenty in Arizona."

"Arizona."

He shrugged. "Harvester ant population in Arizona would outweigh the entire human population of the state. By a good margin, too."

"Ten of those puppies would weigh as much as a person," Lucy said.

Paul looked startled. "Oh, no, it would take a lot more—"

"Kidding," she said.

He gave her a goofy grin and slapped his head. "Oh, yes. Silly me. Of course, you were kidding."

"But they *are* big," Lucy said.

"Yes they are. They also have the distinction of being the most venomous insect on the planet."

"Venomous, huh?" Ma said.

"Very. They don't bite, though. They sting like a bee, but with venom about twelve times more toxic. You wouldn't want to find yourself in the middle of them. If one ant stings you, it releases a pheromone that attracts the rest of the colony. If you get stung once, it's time to run."

"Or before you get stung," Lucy said. "But they're mostly in Arizona?"

"More than any other state. There are twenty-two species of harvester ant, but *pogonomrymex badius,* the Florida harvester, is the only one found east of the Mississippi." He indicated Ma's ant. "This one is *pogonomrymex maricopa,* found only in arid chaparral habitats, in the Southwest. Not much of that in Nevada.

This one came from Arizona, no doubt about it. Best guess, east of Phoenix and maybe Gold Canyon, or around there, possibly up in the hills."

"Will they eat flesh?" Ma asked.

"They're seed gatherers, but, yeah, they'll eat just about anything they find." He gave Ma a look. "This's about that skull the police found, isn't it? That IRS fellow."

Then he turned to me. "Angel. *Mortimer* Angel. Of course. *You're* the one who found it. I've seen you on television a time or two. Thought I'd heard the name."

I nodded, and Ma said, "None of us were here."

Werner turned to her. "Hush-hush deal, huh? I don't get much of that. As in, *ever.*"

"Not so much hush-hush as personal," she said. "Private. Let's keep it that way."

"If you want, sure. So, anything else I can tell you?"

Ma thought for a moment, didn't come up with anything, then I said, "How long would it take a colony of those ants to eat a pound of hamburger?"

His eyebrows went up. "Interesting question. Not sure I'd find it in the literature. Might be something to add to my list of summer projects."

I liked this guy. "Best guess?"

He shrugged. "They're voracious. It's nature. Get what you can as fast as you can. A pound of hamburger, huh? Might take a good-sized colony half an hour to tuck that away if it was spread out some so they could all get at it."

"Half an hour? That's all?"

"It's a guess. They don't fool around. But they wouldn't eat it on the spot. First order of business would be to nip it into bits and hustle it down into the nest."

Which is what happened to Soranden. It seemed too dark to ask Werner for an estimate about how long that took, so I didn't, but I had the feeling Soranden's skull was empty and clean as a whistle in a few hours, no more than a short afternoon.

Oh, and when someone says, I want to pick your brain, that isn't what they mean. Usually.

Jeffrey Dahmer might be an exception.

Okay, *that's* dark.

CHAPTER FOURTEEN

SOUTH SIDE OF the UNR campus was a mile and a quarter from Ma's house. She told us she'd walked over, hence the new shoes. In fact, Ma was on an exercise kick, walking two or three miles a day when the mood suited her. It still suited her, since she walked the mile from the biology building to my house on Washington Street. She let herself in the front door, found Lucy and me in the office, going through the Soranden contraband.

"That the stuff Fairchild gave you?" she asked. "The crud they gathered up in Soranden's house?"

"Uh-huh. And his office," I said. "We were going through his car maintenance records. Oil changes, tire rotation."

Ma stared at me. "Je-sus H. Christ, talk about glomming onto the least likely thing first."

"He's kidding, Ma," Lucy said.

"With Mort, there's no way to tell. Although he said 'we,' which includes you, and you wouldn't do that, so—" she gave me a look that would decompose rubber—"good one, Mort."

"Thanks, Ma."

More evil eye, then she took in the paper pile. Finally, she said, "I'd look at bank statements and any other financials first. And—" she picked up the doodle pad—"what the hell is this?"

"Guy was a doodler," I said. "Probably on the phone."

"That's sometimes good." She studied the sheet for a while. "Area codes 916 and 917. Huh. Sacramento area and New York City." She looked first at me, then at Lucy. "You tried phoning these yet?"

"First thing," Lucy said. "916 numbers were for an auto body shop and a nursing home. 917 got us the Port Authority in Manhattan."

Ma grunted. "Sacramento stuff'll be easy to check, if we want to. Port Authority is . . . weird." She looked over the pile a moment longer then picked up a Xerox sheet of addresses and phone numbers.

"This looks good," she said. "You checked these names or phoned any of these numbers yet?"

"Haven't had time, Ma," I said.

"You can go over Soranden's oil changes while Lucy and I have a look at this."

Well, shit. Guess I'd asked for that.

"Or," Ma said, "go through his bank statements. And this Edward Jones stuff. Follow the money."

That was more like it.

Ma settled on a couch beside Lucy. They checked out Soranden's one-page address book, which ought to take two or three minutes. I went through banking crud. Ronald Soranden had the usual bills, payments, deposits. Money in, money out. It looked like his average checking balance was about $3,500, give or take. Nothing there. Savings account went up slowly and was at about $9,400 when he went missing, but deposits were small, more or less evenly spaced. Nothing like a hundred thousand dollars lying around. At semi-regular intervals, eight or nine thousand dollars were taken out, leaving two or three thousand in the account. Suspicious. I liked that. We might end up doing to Soranden what we'd done with Volker—go on a fishing trip, see if he had accounts for which we didn't have statements.

Then on to the Edward Jones stack. Soranden had a run-of-the-mill IRA with monthly direct deposits from the IRS, and a Roth IRA. I was able to match withdrawals from savings to mutual fund and bond fund purchases in his Roth which meant it was out in the open and my previous suspicions turned to vapor. His bank accounts gave me nothing. His mutual funds in both IRAs were balanced funds, a steady, fairly low-risk buildup over a twenty-seven-year period that now amounted to $412,800. No unexplained deposits or jumps in the total. It was a nice total, but reasonable over such a long period of time. I didn't see the hundred thousand Volker had given him.

Supposedly given him. All I had was Volker's and Marta's word that Soranden had blackmailed him. Volker's money had gone somewhere, but if he'd purchased gold that he could stash in a safe deposit box and then claim blackmail if he got caught, I doubted I would ever find it. Thing is, that didn't add up. At all. If he'd cheated on taxes for four years then got caught, claiming blackmail wouldn't save him. And he'd been paying a thousand a month back into Joss & Volker's operating account.

Spinning my wheels . . .

Soranden's finances was boring stuff. I was coming up with a lot of nothing. At some point I might try to match his monthly expenses—mortgage, car payments, the usual household bills, and a few others, *and* what he was socking away into IRAs—to his income. Basic IRS technique. But not now.

I looked over at Ma and Lucy. "How're you two doing?"

"Names and numbers," Ma said. "Actually, it's a mess."

"It's one page. I thought you'd be done half an hour ago."

"It's not like a real address book," Lucy said. "It was the kind of book with blank lined pages you'd write in, sort of like a diary. It's not alphabetical. Sometimes there's an address, some names only have phone numbers. Here, take a look."

I sat beside Lucy and took the sheet from her.

AAA Cal 916-382-4750

Esther Soranden 2250 Penrose Dr. CC 775-059-1003

Alice Ann Loomis 41 W. 6th Ogden UT 385-151-2017

Janet Kay Anderson 916-421-3391 491-128-1782 ext 30

Arnold Anderson 115-242-1803 288-101-0134 ext 322

Michael Gunderson 775-112-0704 385-401-8823 ext 33

Eric Sandolon 632-912-8873 917-528-2297 ext 21

Donna Del Sarron 314-162-1441 311-002-7511 ext 122

Becky Sue Sarron 314-162-1441 917-404-2921 ext 17

John George Soranden Eighth Army G6 APO SF

Debbie R. Nielsen 505-315-9448 883-212-4050 ext 32

Darren Sandolon 632-202-1571 917-200-1035 ext 121

Kate Williams 3056 Walnut Rd. Crofton Md 410-077-9491

Jerry David Reynolds 816-397-4464 816-991-8801 ext 6

Ian Norse Danlord 916-052-1307 201-300-4084 ext 122

Nancy Gayle Elders 972-588-2091 972-194-3303 ext 44

Lara Rose Donndin 412-490-0807 720-019-1837 ext. 104

Bob Newell 915-009-1118 488-350-9922 ext 7501

"What do you think?" Lucy asked me after I'd given it five minutes.

"It's a mess."

"Great, thanks for the update. Anything else?"

"Okay, John George Soranden is Soranden's son. He's in Korea. Looks here like he's in the Eighth Army. Kate Williams is his daughter, dental hygienist in Maryland. Esther Soranden is his sister, lives thirty miles away, in Carson City. Alice Ann is another sister. All the rest of it is a mishmash of names and numbers I don't recognize."

Ma was on the other side of Lucy on the couch. "It's worse than that. I've been checking these phone numbers. Look at Bob Newell. Area code 915 is El Paso, Texas. But that next number, area code 488, isn't anything. It doesn't exist and yet it has an extension. The area code for Ian Danlord's first number is in Northern California, but 201 is in New Jersey."

"Call him, Ma."

She dialed the California 916 number, listened for a while, then disconnected. "Computer says there's no such number."

She poked at her cell phone a while longer. "Area code 115 for Arnold Anderson is in Davachi, according to Google." More cell phone tapping. "And Davachi is, get this, in Azerbaijan, and Davachi is its former name. Now it's called Sabran."

"Azerbaijan," Lucy said. "Cool. I bet not one high school senior in five could tell you which continent that's on."

I said, "Not one high school senior in five could name six of the seven continents, so no bet."

More tapping. "Both Sarron girls are in St. Louis," Ma said. "Same phone number, so they probably live together."

"Lot of extensions," I offered. "All these people are in big office buildings or corporations? Does that seem right to you?"

"Nope."

Ma dialed the number for Donna Sarron. She pulled the phone away from her ear. "Got an old fax whistle." She stared at the address book listing again. "This ain't right."

"I wonder if the FBI got anywhere with it," I said.

Ma shrugged. "You could try asking Fairchild, but my guess is they got squat. Just like us."

"Anyone up for a little bowling?" I asked.

* * *

Guess not.

Ma left. She said she'd walk. It was only half a mile to her office. Next up, she would be walking half marathons, losing weight, changing her personality, giving weight-loss seminars.

"We should ask Mike Volker if he recognizes any of these names," Lucy said.

"Anything to get us out of here, huh?"

"That's right. And we've got to get my car over to Valley Automotive for my new top at one thirty, or did you forget?"

"Nope. Let's go."

It was only twelve fifteen. We had time to go by Joss & Volker Inc. on the way to Valley Automotive.

Volker was with a client, but he hurried out when he saw Lucy and me hovering in the waiting room.

"What's up, guys?"

I showed him Soranden's address book, such as it was. I've seen longer shopping lists, mostly for Costco.

"Recognize any names on this?" I asked him.

He went down the list slowly. "Couple of Sorandens. I don't know any of 'em, though. This belong to that blackmailing shithead?"

"Language," Lucy said mildly.

"Sorry."

"It does," I told him.

He shrugged. "Just those two names. You think maybe he was blackmailing some of these people?"

"That's a thought." Which hadn't occurred to me. Or to Ma, unless she was hiding it from the staff.

"At least I'm not on the list," Volker said.

"If you were, you'd know it. You would've already been contacted by the FBI."

"Hell. Hope I'm not on any lists they find. Look, I gotta get back with my client. Do you need anything else?"

"Not right now."

"Okay, then. Let me know if you find anything."

He left. Evelyn Joss was busy. Lucy and I went out to her Mustang and she drove us over to Valley Automotive where a woman in her fifties in the office took the car keys and told us the car would probably be ready at four. She would call if there was any sort of a holdup.

Valley Automotive was on Valley Road, three blocks north of Fourth Street. Lucy and I walked down to Fourth, then west to the Golden Goose Casino, half a mile away. We couldn't let Ma outwalk us. If Ma started speed-walking, I might never hear the end of it. We went up to the mezzanine and into Miguel's Taqueria. I had the Enchiladas Plazeras and Lucy had Ceviche Baja style. After we ate, I pulled out the address sheet and we stared at it a while longer. Staring being all we accomplished.

"He knew people from all over the place," Lucy said.

"Including Azerbaijan."

"I doubt it. That's too weird."

"I don't think these are addresses or phone numbers. I think it's code. And I don't mean area codes or zip codes."

"The phone numbers all have area codes," Lucy said.

"Which don't seem to work. Like Becky Sue Sarron who is or isn't in St. Louis with sister or wife Donna."

"Shame on you."

"What'd I say?"

We puzzled over it a while longer, then gave up. I paid the check and we went down an escalator to the first floor, then into the Green Room to get something to make us smarter. Twenty years ago, that would've been a ginkgo biloba cocktail with a little umbrella on the rim. If I'd used ginkgo back then, and if it had worked as advertised, I would've remembered Dallas's and my third anniversary when I was twenty-two and not ended up sleeping on the couch.

Ella Glover was behind the bar. O'Roarke wouldn't come on until six. "Pete's?" she said when I told her what I wanted. "Kinda early for that, isn't it, Mort?"

"It's never too early for Pete's Wicked Ale, kiddo. I put it on Cheerios right after that first cup of coffee."

"Ugh." She turned to Lucy, narrowed her eyes. "I still don't believe you're older than me." I thought my English Nazi might jump all over that grammar lapse, but she didn't.

"Mort makes me feel young," Lucy said. "Works wonders on my arthritis."

"Huh." Ella stared at her, then sent a bottle of Pete's to me like a shuffleboard puck, whipped up a tonic and lime for Lucy. Under the bar's green track lighting, Lucy and I went over that damn address sheet one more time. I took out my cell phone and dialed AAA Cal's number, got an "out of service" message.

"Another dead end," I said. "Phone that Triple-A and you'd end up pushing your car or walking home."

"Got two Sandolons," Lucy said. "Eric and Darren. Same area codes, but the phone numbers are different."

"Yup. Maybe they're married, living apart."

"You're a jerk. Where's area code 632?"

I looked it up on my cell phone. "It's not a United States area code. Google has it for Manila, the Philippines. But only as a maybe. Didn't know Google did maybes."

"Sandolon. That sounds kinda Filipino. Not sure about Eric or Darren, though, but I guess it could happen."

"Yup. GIs were plentiful there in the nineteen forties and during Vietnam."

"So if this isn't some sort of coded stuff, Soranden knows people all over the world. And don't say 'yup' or I'll hit you."

"Yes'm."

She punched my shoulder anyway. "Testy," I said.

"Yup."

* * *

We walked back to Valley Automotive, got there fifteen minutes early, and the Mustang was waiting, ready to go, nice new black top on it. Lucy put her cheek on it, like it was a black lab looking for love.

She drove us home. We dressed in running gear and hit the River Walk, jogged five miles west to Mayberry Park and back, ten miles. Good training run, getting us ready for our judo lesson with Rufus tomorrow morning since, as usual, he would do his best to kill us. I figured I was in for an especially ugly workout after that bar fight in Wildcat. Maybe I shouldn't have fessed up to Rufus.

Six p.m. I turned on the news, saw no sign of Mortimer Angel or any mention of Soranden's skull, so I turned it off.

"Now what?" my assistant asked.

"We're not always on the job, sweetheart."

"Good to know. Now what?"

"We could see if Ma wants to go out to dinner."

"I like that. I think maybe she's lonely a lot."

I wasn't so sure about that. Last summer when we were up in Gerlach and Bend, I got a bunch of mixed messages. And this summer in southern Nevada when Ma showed up at Arlene's Diner just in time to get me shot while trying to save her—long story—she was with Officer Day, who ended up saving my life. But the point is, Ma had . . . boyfriends. Here and there. But then she sometimes gave off lonely vibes.

I phoned Ma. "What?" she answered. Lot of noise in the background.

"Hell of a way to answer the phone, Ma."

"It's loud as Hades in here. Talk fast or hang up."

"Where's here?"

"What's it to ya?"

Okay, that wasn't right, though Ma didn't sound as if she was in trouble. But it wasn't like her to go stealth on me, either.

"Sounds like you're in a freakin' disco," I said.

"Disco's been dead since I was thirty-five and you were in diapers."

"I was fifteen when you were thirty-five so that diapers circumlocution thing didn't cut it."

"Where the hell did you learn a word with twelve fuckin' syllables?"

"Ma?"

"Gotta go, Mort. Catch you later."

She hung up. I stared at my cell phone in disbelief.

"Disco and diapers?" Lucy said.

I shook my head. "Forget that diapers thing. And it wasn't disco. She's in Wildcat." Then I expanded on that by saying, "Dirty sonofabitch."

* * *

Now what? Wildcat wasn't a good place for me. Or Lucy. Or Ma, but Ma was just an elderly lady who could walk from here to Colorado and back in a day or two and put down more booze than your average college football team. It wasn't likely that anyone would recognize her or connect her to me.

I hoped.

But what the fuck? *Wildcat?* What did she think she was doing?

"Wildcat?" Lucy said. "Why?"

"With Ma, one never knows."

"Should we go and, I don't know, *help* her?"

"Not sure she needs help." Then again, I wasn't sure she didn't, or wouldn't in the next half hour. Precious Kimmi and Dooley could be there. They wouldn't know Ma from an alien just in from Jupiter. Mira might be there, but she wouldn't know Ma either. Would Ramon Surry be at Wildcat showing off his shoulder cast? That didn't seem likely, but who knows?

"We should go," Lucy said.

"I agree. But in disguises. I don't want anyone there having any idea who we are."

In the back of my mind a little voice softly whispered that someone had put Soranden's skull in Lucy's car, which might've been *my* car. So someone somewhere knew more than I wanted them to know; therefore the disguises had better be damn good.

Lucy looked different in a long black wig and a tight black top with a good amount of cleavage showing. The top had huge decorative safety pins down the front, designed to look as if they were holding it together. A short black skirt, black knee-length boots. Not the same outfit she wore when she took the Grand Sierra Resort for over three thousand bucks, but the face was the same with its black makeup. Might be perfect for Wildcat.

I was old and gray in an ancient duffer's outfit, white shirt, blue and gray Goodwill sports coat left unbuttoned, white hair in disarray over my ears, a salt-and-pepper moustache, glasses with gold wire rims. Under the shirt I wore the foam-filled polyester barrel gut that got me up to three hundred pounds.

"Totally bitchin' outfit," Lucy said, staring at me.

"You too. One thing did occur to me though."

She tilted her head. "What?"

"If I ever grow my hair out like this except longer and you see it up in a man bun, don't ask questions, just shoot me. And don't laugh until after you pull the trigger."

"Got it. No man bun, no laughter, just *bang*."

A man bun. What a world. Why would a guy want to look like Aunt Bee?

We drove over in the Toyota, parked it three blocks away, walked over to Wildcat, and went in.

The music—hard to call it that because it was like fifty garbage cans full of car parts rolling downhill in a thunderstorm—wasn't quite as loud as the night I was there tracking Kimmi, maybe because it wasn't yet seven p.m. But it was Friday so the place was a third full and the crowd was thick around the bar. I got a few strange looks—three-hundred-pound antique geezer in a Millennials bar with a Goth chick on his arm who looked hot,

hot, hot. Maybe attracting that much attention hadn't been the way to go. Too late now.

Ma was on a stool at the bar, big surprise.

We headed that way, but before we reached her, Mira put a hand on my arm and said, "Is it you?"

Well, shit. So much for weighing as much as an average NFL tackle. It might have been because I was the tallest person in the place. "I'm me, yes. Always have been. Who're you?"

"Mira. Don't you remember? You bought me dinner."

I wasn't going to bluff her away, so I got Lucy beside me and the two Goth girls checked each other out. Finally, I said to Lucy in a half-shout, "This is Mira."

"Figured." Then Lucy gave Mira a hug. Damn, that's what happens when girls who know me meet each other.

Lucy half shouted to Mira, "Hi, I'm Lucy."

Further conversation appeared to be all but impossible. A person could go hoarse and/or deaf in five minutes. Time to get out of there. I deftly bulled my way in to where Ma was trying to order another drink.

"How ya doin', Ma?"

She turned. "Trying to get this bozo's attention and what the hell are *you* doin' here?"

"That's what I was wondering about you."

"I'm undercover. Sorta. Checking the place out. You and that girl all in black beside you should leave. I'll be fine if I can get another freakin' drink anytime this week."

Which is when I felt a tap on the shoulder. I turned and Ramon Surry stuck a short knife in my belly and ripped upward. Sonofabitch. He had a long black coat over his cast, right sleeve flapping loose, nasty little three-inch blade in his left hand, surprised look on his face when I didn't appear to be fazed about the knife. We were inches apart so a standard punch was out of the question. I twisted and shot an elbow into his face, caught him on the left cheek hard enough to spin his head a full quarter turn. He went down, so I went down too, put a knee in his groin, got the knife out of his hand. We were on the floor in a forest of legs. Surry was out cold. I made sure of that by slamming the back of his head against the floor. It made a nice hollow *wok* sound, like his skull was empty. I did it again, *hard*, because I liked the sound and this was the second time the sonofabitch had tried to kill me, then I stood up. None of this appeared to have been noticed by those around us. The music was too loud, the crowd too close, and drunks passing out was probably the norm, but Ma had seen what I'd done.

"Let's go, Ma," I said.

"Nope. I'll stay, see what happens, if anything. Scoot."

No time to argue or haul her off the stool. I got Lucy by an arm, led the way through the press of people and out the door, and, of course, Mira was right behind her when we reached the sidewalk. I thought Lucy had seen some of what had happened in there. Probably not Surry's knife since he was right up against me when he'd struck, left-handed, but it was likely she'd seen me putting an elbow in his face and him going down. Mira had been behind Lucy, so she might not have seen anything.

"How about a movie?" I said in what I hoped was a jovial way. Mr. Cool, after his second knife fight in under a week.

Which was when I saw Renner and Bledsoe at the corner, Munson's goons. Great. First chance I got, I would have to call Slick Willie, tell him to get them away from me or the deal was off and he could piss up a rope.

I hustled Lucy and Mira away. The sun was down, but it wasn't dark yet. I had palmed Surry's knife. I stuck it in a pocket and glanced down at my stomach. The knife had torn the shirt, buried itself in the foam padding. Sometimes disguises are worth their weight in gold, but I'd lost a perfectly good shirt.

CHAPTER FIFTEEN

I FASTENED TWO buttons on the coat to hide the torn shirt.

"Don't tell Rufus," I whispered to Lucy as we headed west toward the car. Old duffer with two young Goth babes in tow. I might've been able to attract more attention with a portable siren and flashing lights, but maybe not.

"Why not?" Lucy said. "He would be impressed." She had an arm through mine. Mira was beside her, trailing along, silent.

"No, he wouldn't. He'd kick my butt. Except maybe for this." I showed her the knife, making sure Mira didn't see it.

Lucy's eyes widened and she stopped dead on the sidewalk. "Where'd you get that?"

"Guess." I pocketed the knife and got her moving again.

"Wow. You took that away from him? Okay, let's go eat since that's what we planned earlier."

"Nice segue. But it's hard to eat with a pint of adrenaline in your system."

"Why? All you did was deck him, right?"

Mira was in her own world, not taking any of this in, so I showed Lucy the torn shirt. "I decked him 'cause of this."

She stopped again. "He did that? With that knife?"

I got her moving again. "Guy's got a one-track mind. And let's keep motoring here. The blade didn't get through this fat-pad I'm wearing. I'm fine. But he's starting to piss me off."

We walked a block in silence, then Lucy turned to Mira. "We're gonna get something to eat. Want to come along?"

"Okay." Again, no force behind the words. She was a leaf on the river of life.

We piled into the Toyota and ended up at the Peppermill. Ever popular was the buffet. We could get prime rib, crab legs, stuff like that, or zero-calorie salad with beets and sprouts and other yummy roughage, so I paid for three and in we went.

Lucy helped Mira figure out the buffet. It appeared that she hadn't been through a buffet since Bush Two was president, if that. I ended up with real food and they ended up with . . . okay, surprise, a mix of stuff you could find on a riverbank, but also egg rolls and two kinds of fish and even some chicken.

"Um, thanks," Mira said. "For this."

"De nada."

For a while, we ate without a lot of talking. I went back for seconds, and, surprise, so did Lucy and Mira.

Finally, we slowed down enough that talk was possible.

"Your father's really nice to do this," Mira said. "I mean, if he's your father and not . . . well, you know."

Lucy coughed, then covered it up with another little cough that helped to stifle laughter. "He's a dear. We had so much fun in Disneyland when I was eight."

"He bought me dinner last week."

"Dad's a sweetie pie, for sure."

Aw, shit.

"You're not a real Goth," Mira said to Lucy.

"I'm not?"

"No tats, no metal. You're a pretender. But that's cool."

No metal. Meaning no random piercings, like a safety pin through her eyelids or a spike through the roof of her mouth into her brain. I never got that piercings thing. Seems like it probably started out with kids saying "screw you" to their parents and to the entire world, but then it became the thing to do to be cool and unique like everyone else around you. But what do I know? What I *do* know is if someone accidentally bumped the switch on a nearby MRI machine it would pull the entire face off some of these kids leaving a mask of torn, bloody flesh.

I hoped this comment wouldn't go where I didn't want it to go, but I said, "I saw Ramon in Wildcat tonight, Mira. It looked like he was in a cast or something."

She shrugged. "He is. Some guy in the bar like a week ago beat Ramon up real bad for no reason."

"No reason, huh? That's cold."

"Uh-huh. Ramon was just getting a drink and this guy went off on him like unreal."

"Ramon ever go off on anyone?" I asked.

"Well . . . he sort of can. Sometimes. Like if someone gets in his face."

"Do people get in his face very often?"

"A little. Sometimes." She looked at me. "You look older now. Um, I don't mean like, like *bad*, but . . . kinda older than you did."

"It's been almost a week. People age."

She thought about that for a moment. "I guess."

"So, did Ramon have anything interesting to say?"

She shrugged. "Nothing special. Just that his arm hurts like a son of a bitch if he doesn't take his pills . . . um, sorry about the language. It's just, that's what he said."

"It's okay."

Lucy said, "So, what about this guy he had a fight with? Did he say who it was?"

"No. Just some big guy who went nuts. It was afternoon so the place was about empty. No one saw it, not even the bartender girl 'cause she was in the back getting something."

Lucy reached out and gently touched Mira's lower lip. It had been split, but it was healing. "How'd this happen?"

Mira backed away. She touched her lip and looked at me. "I told you, didn't I?"

"Did you?"

"Don't you remember? That day you knocked on Lori's door. She's in 211 at the apartments."

"Oh, yeah."

"I was . . . I sort of tripped and fell, hit my mouth on the back of a chair."

Different story. Neither one was what had happened, but I saw no point in pursing it.

Lucy said, "Will Ramon be okay with you going away with us like this?"

Mira shrugged. "I don't know. Ramon is, well, he's up and down a lot."

"If he's not okay with you leaving, what will he do?"

"Do?"

"To you," Lucy said.

"Well . . . um, maybe sorta yell at me."

"Are you two like involved?"

Mira looked down at her hands. "Sometimes. Sorta. Not like all the time."

"He knows other girls?"

"Well, sure. Lots."

Quietly, Lucy said, "Do you ever think you should . . . get away? From him."

Mira wouldn't look at her. Or at me. "I dunno." Then she looked up. "But then, go where? Do what?"

"Just . . . get away from him, and from Wildcat and the bar scene. Find a new place to live. Never go back."

Mira hunched her shoulders. "I don't know."

And that's where we left it. I drove Mira back to Second Street, let her off a block west of Wildcat. She could go back to Wildcat or to the apartment building where she could circulate in the rooms, find a place to stay the night. But it was still early, not long after nine, dark outside, neon flashing, people laughing, cars rolling by. Friday night, party time. When I looked in the rearview mirror, she was headed back to Wildcat.

Sometimes it doesn't take, no matter what you say.

* * *

I lay awake for a while, eyes wide open, staring up at the ceiling. What could I have done differently? Nothing, except not go into Wildcat. And leave Ma in that place? Which I had, once Surry was on the floor and out of it. Best I could do now was never go back for any reason.

I tried to put Surry out of my mind.

Then there was the Soranden investigation, such as it was. Soranden. Were we spinning our wheels?

"Yes," Lucy said sleepily.

"Yes, what?" I asked.

"Yes, we're kinda spinning our wheels."

"You read minds now?"

She lifted her head, stared at me. "You said, 'Soranden.' Then you said, 'Were we spinning our wheels?' so I said yes even though what you said was past tense, which, if you think about it, is kinda weird."

"I said it out loud?"

"How else would you say it?"

"To myself."

"Well, you didn't."

Jesus. "Sorry 'bout that, kiddo."

"Not to worry. Perfectly natural. I've got a grandfather who does that. Except he's in a nursing home and doesn't remember who I am."

Yeah, great.

* * *

Saturday morning, staring at Soranden's detritus.

"This sucks," Lucy said. "Now what?"

"Your favorite question."

"I'm just looking for direction from my leader so we can head out and take on the world."

"I've got some Prozac around here somewhere. I think it's expired, but it might still kick in."

"You took Prozac? When? Why?"

"Kidding, kiddo."

"Too bad. I could use a hit, lookin' at this stuff."

We were in my office and the investigative fever wasn't exactly swelling in my breast. Or Lucy's. "How 'bout we give it a break?" I said. "Hit it again later when we're fresh."

"Suits me. Now what?"

"Let's phone Rufus, blow off the workout and head out of town."

"Groovy. Got someplace in mind?"

"Yep. How about I meet your parents?"

Her eyes narrowed to slits momentarily, then a big smile broke through. "Guys often meet the parents when they're about to pop the question. Or . . . we could be married in less than two hours, and *then* we could go see my parents, give them the good news. How 'bout that?"

This was a topic that came up every week or two. I still wasn't sure how to handle it.

But I didn't have to. She gave me a big hug and a kiss that weakened my knees. "No pressure," she said. "One day you'll be ready and you'll ask me and when you do we'll be married inside two hours—*if* we're in Reno or Vegas when you ask. If we're in like Barbados or Fiji or Bangladesh—which would be really something, and I'm not thinking Bangladesh would be at the top of the list—then probably not. So right now, you don't have to say 'no' or say anything at all. But visiting my parents is . . . um, maybe not such a super wonderful terrific idea."

"Why not?"

"They're sorta strange. Well, my mother anyway."

"Who, if you remember, I spoke to about an hour after we met in order to verify your age since you looked seventeen. Or less. Which you still do much of the time."

"I *do* remember. It's only been three months and my mind is still sharp."

"That wasn't a dig, was it, Cupcake?"

"Would I?"

"Yes, you would. But back up. Your mother didn't sound at all strange to me. She sounded nice. And sophisticated."

"Strange might not've been the best adjective. I should've said my family isn't . . . well, entirely normal."

"I can handle abnormal as long as it doesn't involve guns or exotic poisons or relatives chained in basements. Or hangings. I hate family hangings."

She didn't laugh. "It's not abnormal like any of those."

"Then . . . let's go."

"Only if you promise you won't . . . judge me by them. Or by their situation."

I stared at her. "That sounds ominous."

"I don't mean it to be ominous. Just a kind of warning."

"Warnings are ominous."

"Just don't judge, okay? Please?"

Whew.

*　*　*

The drive to San Francisco was pleasant. Fewer people were going to work on a Saturday, and the summer vacation crowd had thinned out. Lucy didn't say anything more about her parents. We kept it light, talking about knife fights, voracious ants carting brain cells out of skulls, things like that.

Before we left, I phoned Ma, made sure she'd made it out of Wildcat alive. She had. She said Surry was slid onto a gurney and hauled away in an ambulance after being dragged out from under people's feet at the bar. An ambulance. How 'bout that? I might've bounced his head off the floor a little too hard. Or not. That knife business had me more than a trifle riled. Last person I ever wanted to see again was Ramon Surry, though Soranden would probably be pretty ugly by now so I didn't want the rest of him to turn up.

"Luce and I are headed to San Fran," I told Ma.

"Gonna visit the parents, huh?"

Nothing gets by her.

"Yep."

"Good luck," Ma said.

"What the hell does that mean?"

"Good luck means good luck. Google it." She hung up.

Sonofabitch.

So we headed out in Lucy's Mustang, nice new top on it, day in the seventies. West on I-80, into California, past Truckee, over Donner Summit, past Sacramento, Davis, Berkeley, and Oakland, across the Bay Bridge, and into the city.

I was driving. "Where to now?"

She pointed. "Straight for a little while. I'll let you know."

We took I-80 past Eighth Street, curved right onto 434A, then north on Van Ness Avenue past Geary Boulevard.

"Geary," I said. "That's where you did that . . . that . . ."

"Off-off-Broadway Vagina Monologues play."

"Yeah. That."

She gave me a little smile. "What a memory." Her voice had a nervous tremor in it.

We kept going, then she said, "Take the next left."

We went west on Broadway, up into the hills. The houses got bigger, fancier, with marble and columns. Four blocks before we hit Divisadero, she said, "Slow down. Take a right at the next driveway."

I swung right, stopped facing a wrought-iron gate. Lucy got a remote out of her purse and hit a button. The gate rolled back.

"Whoa," I said.

"Just don't jump to any conclusions. At all."

"Right. No conclusions."

I drove past the gate. It closed behind us. The house was three stories of timbers and granite with a blue-black slate tile roof, a million windows, a deep porch with steps and four Doric columns facing a turnaround. A five-car garage was off to one side with a yellow Hummer and a black Bentley parked outside.

"Rich girl," I said.

"Don't." Her voice had a hint of gravel in it.

So I didn't.

"Park here," she said.

I did, and we got out. I looked up at the house. Okay, it wasn't a house, though there was a vague resemblance. It was a mansion, and this was Pacific Heights.

A woman opened the front door, which was nine feet tall, and came out, wrapped Lucy up in a hug. More women hugging while I stood around. Story of my life.

Nope. My turn. First the hug, then names.

"I'm so pleased to meet you at last, Mr. Angel. I'm Lucy's mother, Val. Valerie, but no one calls me that."

"Mort. Mortimer, but only my mother calls me that because she screwed up on my birth certificate and won't admit it."

Val laughed. Musically. Same voice I'd heard on the phone when Lucy called her to have her verify Lucy's age. Val was, according to Lucy, going on fifty-four—a fact I thought I should keep to myself—but, as advertised, she looked thirty-five. She was Lucy's height—five-five, and about a hundred twenty-five pounds. Short dark brown hair, no sign of gray.

"My, you're tall," Val said, hooking an arm through mine.

"Makes it easier to watch parades, ma'am."

"Ma'am." She gently punched my shoulder. "If you don't call me Val, I *will* call you Mortimer."

Women are always punching me. I don't get it.

"Val it is, then," I said.

Lucy took my other arm and the two of them escorted me into the house. Couldn't have broken free if I'd wanted to. Into a glossy marble foyer, up a half flight of stairs into a living room the size of a soccer stadium. Floor-to-ceiling windows offered a stunning view of the bay, the Golden Gate, Angel Island—a fine name for an island, by the way—Sausalito, the bay north, part of the Richmond–San Rafael Bridge, sailboats on the bay.

"Can I get you something to drink, Mort?" Val asked. "Water, beer, wine, something with a bit more kick to it?"

"Pete's Wicked Ale, if you've got it."

She gave me an amused moue. "Ale. Is that—what you said—light or dark?"

"Sort of a medium dark."

She and Lucy headed off to a kitchen somewhere else in the hemisphere while I stood at a window taking in the view. It wasn't merely stunning. It was staggering. I wondered what the house was worth. Thirty mil would be a ballpark figure. Off the foyer I'd seen an elevator. An *elevator*. At the moment I figured I was on the mezzanine. First time I'd been in an eight-figure shack. I couldn't pay the interest on the property taxes on a place like this.

Val and Lucy returned. Val handed me a darkish beer in a chilled glass. She and Lucy had white wines. Lucy rarely drank alcohol, but this was clearly an exception, possibly because she hadn't taken the Prozac I'd offered earlier. This was what she'd meant by abnormal. Elevators in houses—not normal, check.

I took a sip. "This is . . . really great. What is it?"

"Tutankhamen Ale. From the U.K."

"So it's been aged, what? Three thousand years?"

Val smiled. "Somewhat less than that, I imagine."

Later I discovered it ran seventy-five dollars a bottle. Good as it was, I wasn't going to order up a case.

* * *

The day turned into pleasant chatter. And a tour of the house since Val offered. Lucy's bedroom was on the third floor. It faced north, with a view of the Golden Gate, Angel Island, and beyond. Given the size of the mansion, it wasn't a huge room, but it had a walk-in closet roomy enough for a poker table with seating for eight.

Lucy didn't say much. She stared out a window as I took in the teak furniture and the queen-size four-poster, also teak. And a glance into a private bathroom with a shower stall and a bright red Jacuzzi, gold plumbing fixtures that gleamed.

The tour only disclosed three bedrooms, so I figured four or five of them had been omitted. The library was impressive with its four thousand volumes, a nice mix of fiction and nonfiction. One room held a $30,000 pool table.

Later her father showed up. Perfectly normal guy in jeans and a blue work shirt. No ascot, no maroon silk housecoat. He didn't twirl a moustache, didn't affect a British accent. Five-ten, hundred sixty-five pounds, still had all his hair, neatly trimmed, dark brown with gray at the temples. Edward Landry, but call him Ed. So, Ed and Val, just your typical neighborhood folksy folks. Not the least bit strange.

Another fifteen or twenty minutes of small talk, then Ed, with a bourbon and water in hand, took me down in the elevator to a wine cellar. The womenfolk stayed topside. Nothing was said so I figured they communicate telepathically. That might be what Lucy meant by not entirely normal.

"Thought we might want to talk privately," Ed said as we exited the elevator into a cool stone dungeon.

Uh-oh. This is when dad asks the purported beau what his intentions are.

"Don't worry," Ed said. "I have no intention of asking you about your intentions regarding Lucy."

Excellent work, Mort. Wrong again, so I was still in my comfort zone—except for Ed's obvious telepathic ability.

"That'd be too 1920s," he added. "But the gals don't have to hear everything we say. That's a two-way street. They're probably talking about us. Well, about you."

"I'm used to it."

"I bet. You got the whole world talking about you last year. And this summer when you found that rapper guy. I don't know why you haven't made the cover of *People* magazine yet. Latest thing is that IRS guy."

"Ronald Soranden. Government-sanctioned criminal."

He chuckled. "That sounds about right."

"Full disclosure: His skull was dumped into Lucy's car. In case that didn't make the news."

His drink was almost to his lips. He lowered it. "It didn't. At least this is the first I've heard of it."

"Someone slashed the top of her Mustang and dropped it onto the front seat, driver's side."

"Well, hell. Just his skull, is that right?"

"Just the headbone. Cleaned out by harvester ants, but you shouldn't repeat that. I think they're keeping it from the public."

"Man, you do get into some weird shinola."

"That's been my *modus operandi* ever since I started in PI work. I can't explain it. It's not like I go looking for it. More like it comes looking for me. I think it's punishment for working for the IRS for sixteen years, until I discovered I had a soul. I'm hoping I've about paid off the debt and it'll taper off soon."

He ran fingers through his hair, then looked around. "Okay, enough of that. We're down here. Got a decent selection of wine too. If you see anything you like, it's yours."

The wine cellar was smaller than I'd anticipated. Maybe a hundred fifty bottles. Wine isn't my thing, but I tried to look interested. It also had beer, much of it exotic. And there was a big gun safe in a corner. A conversation piece.

"I found out the hard way Lucy is familiar with handguns," I told him, putting a hand on the safe.

"She didn't shoot you? That'd be the hard way."

Good one, Ed. "No, she conned me, then outshot me." I gave it a moment, then said, "Not to bring up what might be an unpleasant topic, but you're aware that we were buried in the trunk of a Cadillac in the desert and left for dead, aren't you?"

His face got serious. "I am."

"And she got shot. Nicked, actually."

"That too."

"Got any comment about any of that, now that we're down here?"

"Not sure what to say, except I'm damn glad the bullet only grazed her and that you two got out of that car. I might like to hear the full story about that car deal sometime, but not now, not yet. Maybe in another year or two."

"Anything else? As a father? Here's your chance to let 'er rip if you're so inclined."

He looked me in the eye. "I appreciate that, but I've got nothing to let rip. Lucy is her own person. Has been for a long time. And I'd trust her intuition over mine any day of the week. She's in love with you. She didn't say as much, but she didn't have to. I know my girl. And I know what you do for a living. I see you in the news all the time. So I hope she remains safe and happy. I think that's about all any father can hope for. Birds leave the nest, then they're on their own." He took a sip of his drink. "Got a gun safe at your place in Reno, Mort?"

"No. But I've been thinking I should get one."

"I'll have one delivered. For Lucy. For you too, obviously, but we'll call it Lucy's. You okay with that?"

"Sure. But I can afford a safe."

"The one I have in mind is kinda pricy. It'll be a gift. For Lucy. I know she's got her own apartment, but I don't think a gun safe is appropriate in a place like that. Will your floor take a big safe? A thousand-pounder? Be pretty unusual if it wouldn't, but it seems as if I oughta ask."

"If it doesn't, I'll check the basement, see if the safe ended up down there, or if it made it all the way to the water table. But the floor took me okay when Jeri picked me up and slammed me down onto a sparring mat. Twice."

"Jeri?"

"Jeri DiFrazzia. Former boss, former fiancée. She weighed a hundred thirty-two pounds at the time. Took first in her weight class in the women's power lifting nationals last year."

He grinned. "Girl put you down hard, huh?"

"She cheated. She used judo."

Ed laughed. "I heard you and Lucy are taking judo. How's that going?"

"Real fine. I'm sore after every lesson. On the other hand, after a lesson Lucy touches the soles of her feet to the top of her head while she's in a handstand. You can't do that, can you?"

"Christ no. She got those octopus genes from her mother then took it to a whole different level." He paused, then said, "So you were engaged a while back?" He watched me as he took another sip of bourbon.

"Yes. Jeri was terrific, an absolutely wonderful person. She was murdered a little after Senator Reinhart went missing last year. Presidential candidate. You probably heard about him."

"I did, yes. You get into some pretty dangerous stuff."

"Not intentionally."

"Still. Lucy ended up buried alive. And you."

"Again, not intentionally. Look, if any of that is meant to imply that Lucy and I shouldn't continue to see each other, now would be the time—"

"No. Oh, *no*, Mort. No implication at all. I want what Lucy wants, that's all. Like I said, she's her own person. And it speaks well of you that you can tell me that that gal you knew, Jeri, was a wonderful person. Means you can say the same about Lucy."

"She's incredible. 'Incredible' doesn't do her justice."

"So you get it. Get her, I mean."

"I do."

"Just . . . try to keep her safe, if you can."

"Will do."

"Her wanting to do private investigation. That never would have occurred to me. But, you know, it suits her somehow. She's been happier these last few months than I've seen her in years."

"Good to know." I waved a hand at the room, indicating it and the rest of the house. "This is a surprise. She never hinted at anything like this."

"She wouldn't. Not if she's serious about you, and there's no doubt about that. None at all."

"As long as it's just the two of us and the walls, mind if I ask where all this came from? If you do mind, then I never asked and I have no curiosity at all."

He smiled. "Mostly from patents. Half a dozen of them. You might say I'm an inventor. Which is simplistic, but more or less accurate."

"Patents?"

"The main one, the real cash cow, is over twenty years old. I came up with a better way to join pipe in offshore oil drilling. Stronger, faster, less chance of a blowout. It's used all over the world now." He gave me a long look. "There's something I want to tell you, feel I need to tell you, but if Luce ever finds out she would kill us both, which would defeat the purpose, so it's got to stay between the two of us."

"Which might mean you shouldn't tell me."

"Your saying that means I should, because I can trust you, and because it's something you ought to know, considering how Lucy feels about you. She uses very little of our money, Val's and mine. Lucy wouldn't tell you this, but she's worth about twelve million. I kick in another million every year or so."

I blinked. Huh.

"I mean, it's hers if and when she wants it, or any part of it for any reason. It's in all three of our names—hers, mine, and Val's. But so far . . . Lucy is her own person, and I respect that more than I can say, since I grew up poor and I've seen what can happen to people when life is handed to them on a silver platter. A lot of them turn out worthless and stupid, like movie stars who think they're God's gift. Lucy didn't go that route. In the past eight or nine years she's taken some godawful menial jobs and lived within whatever means that's given her. She's one of the strongest people I know. Maybe the strongest. A lot stronger than me, I have to say."

"And one of the luckiest, Ed."

He grinned. "You've run into that, have you?"

"Head-on."

He shook his head. "I don't understand it, that business about four planets lined up, but I wouldn't play poker with her if I were you."

"Got that, but lately roulette seems to be her thing."

"Roulette, huh? Casino roulette? Casinos are touchy about winners. They've got no sense of humor when it comes to their money walking out the door."

"Uh-huh. But she knows how to work it. Like you wouldn't believe. She'd go viral on YouTube. So far, money hasn't been an issue. In fact, we can afford a gun safe, and it's a good idea."

"We'll make it a gift. Early Christmas present if that's what it takes. And I want her to have this, too." He hit a six-digit code on a keypad on the safe, a light turned green, and he opened the safe. Big safe. It wasn't nearly full, and it had two rifles that gun haters would call assault rifles even though there's no such thing since you can be assaulted by someone wielding a flyswatter and no one calls them assault flyswatters. But that's neither here nor there. The safe also held three hunting rifles with scopes, a .22 rifle, scoped, a shotgun, and six or eight handguns. Ed got out a Ruger .22 SR22 automatic with a black polymer frame, popped out the magazine, worked the slide, and handed me the weapon, empty.

"Magazine holds ten rounds," he said. "Very little recoil. For self-defense I'd recommend hyper-velocity bullets." He got three boxes of CCI Velocitor rounds, gave them to me. "Plink and practice with the basic stuff, but have her load up with this if the two of you might get into a . . . situation." He hesitated, then said, "I'm not really a gun freak, Mort, but defending yourself is just plain smart and this doggone world's getting more and more dangerous, year after year."

"So I've noticed." I didn't mention my recent knife fights. And I didn't think a gun would have solved the problem in that crowd in Wildcat the other night. Guns and crowds don't mix. But knife fights might make Ed nervous, and I'd had my fill of them, or so I hoped—so I kept that to myself. I handed the gun back to Ed and he slapped the magazine back into it.

Carrying the booty, we took the elevator back up, got off at the living room, didn't take it all the way to the penthouse.

"Guns," Lucy said, eyes bright. Not every girl lights up at the sight of weaponry, but mine does.

"All yours, hon," Ed said, handing it to her.

She popped the magazine, worked the slide, released it and put the magazine back in, sighted the gun at a gondolier on an oil painting of Venice. "Adjustable sights. Very cool."

"And cool ammo," I said, showing her the Velocitors.

She kissed her father on the cheek. "Thanks. To carry it, I'll have to get qualified with it."

"Do that, soon. Just be safe, hon."

"Always."

"Now," Ed said, "isn't it about time we got something to eat? I know I'm hungry. How about Saison? Or Jardiniere?"

"Uh-uh," Lucy said. "How about pizza? We can walk down to Two Guy's. No valet parking, no big production."

Ed scratched behind an ear. "Words of wisdom."

So we walked the six blocks to Two Guy's Pizza. Got two medium pizzas—a basic pepperoni and cheese, and one loaded with the works, including anchovies.

The high point of the meal was when Lucy said, "Mort rode in the WNBR this year. In March."

I sighed. World Naked Bike Ride.

Val gave me an amused look. "*Did* you?"

"I was talked into it." And it looked like I was never going to hear the end of it—riding around San Francisco on a bicycle wearing nothing but a little red body paint. Holiday, of course, rode stark naked at the time with a bit of paint on her back that read *4 Jeri*. She was still on forty thousand Facebook sites.

"Someone twisted your arm, did they?" Val wasn't going to quickly turn loose of something that delicious. This was great, the conversation rolling around to me touring the city in the buff. Ed was smiling, looking down at the table, so I was on my own.

Lucy said, "His boss, mine too now, has a poster on her office wall of Mort standing beside his bicycle. It's very cool."

"A poster," Val said. "How interesting."

"Laminated," Lucy said.

I held up a slice of pizza. "This pizza isn't half bad. And it's within walking distance of the house, too. You're lucky."

All three of them laughed. What a family. We were sitting at wooden tables with bench seats in a room that got noisier with an influx of kids in soccer outfits as we sat there. Just your basic, normal neighborhood adults in for a sit-down, no sign that three of them, in total, were worth a little over three hundred forty million dollars and the fourth one was worth, in total, about a hundred sixty thousand.

Three hundred forty million.

Ho-ly shit.

* * *

Seven twenty p.m., headed east toward Oakland on the Bay Bridge, we passed through the tunnel on Yerba Buena Island and Lucy said, "Whatever you say, please don't make it about money."

"They're just normal folks, kiddo. Don't sweat it."

"You don't care?"

"Hell yes. Given any say in the matter, I'd prefer my girl to come from nice, normal, sane, pizza-lovin' folks. And you do."

She stared at me, then said, "Omigod. I love you so, so, so, so much."

CHAPTER SIXTEEN

LUCY WAS WRAPPED around me like an eel. I thought she was asleep, then she jerked and cried, "Oh, oh, oh, *oh*!"

"And I wasn't even touching any volatile parts," I said. "I am a god."

"Yes, you are. But . . . anagrams, anagrams, *anagrams*!"

"Anagrams?"

"That's what *I* said."

"Multiple times, too. If your needle's stuck I can bump the player to get you back on track."

"How very retro, but, *anagrams*, Mort. Soranden was into that, so get up."

"Get up? We just got to bed. Well, forty minutes ago. And, hey, look, it's one twenty in the morning and really dark out. I mean, *freakin'* dark out, like nighttime already."

"Up," she said, tossing the covers off us. In the dim light she said, "Oh. You are. But I meant like putting your feet on the floor."

"So this other way ain't happening, is that correct?"

"It did happen, not that long ago either, so forget it, Zeus. I want another look at that address book." She lofted herself out of bed, not something I was capable of right then.

"Zeus," I said. "Never forget you called me that. Oh, and you look mighty good naked and tousled, Sugar Plum."

"Up."

So I got up, donned a bathrobe and slippers, as did Lucy, and we trooped downstairs to the office—and, like I told her, it was still dark out. Lucy got Soranden's doodle sheet and we sat side by side on a hunter green couch with a fancy-ass hyper-modern light hanging over us on a chrome fixture that might have to go to Goodwill since it didn't look the least bit noir and being hard-boiled and cynical I was all about noir.

"Anagrams," I said, stifling a yawn, trying to get my retinas to fire up.

"Right. Look at this. Arnold Anderson. I was sort of semi-drowsing half-asleep when it sort of hit me—"

"That's a lot of 'sort ofs,' kiddo."

"Be quiet. It hit me that Arnold is an anagram of Ronald. So maybe—"

"Anderson is an anagram of Soranden."

"Exactly. Which it *is*. And that means Arnold Anderson is Ronald Soranden. There is no Arnold Anderson—well, there might be a few thousand of 'em in the United States, but not—you know what I mean. Which must mean these numbers after Anderson's name are code for something, not phone numbers."

"Like bank accounts."

She kissed me. "Exactly. Like bank accounts."

"Good work. I never would've thought of anagrams even though they were like two-by-fours."

"Two-by-fours?"

"Lumber—used to get the attention of mules."

She gave me a doubtful look. "Right, sure. So, how does it work? I mean, I've had bank accounts but I've never given much thought to what all those numbers mean."

"A bank account has a routing number that identifies the bank, and a person's personal account number in that bank. In combination, those two numbers get the job done so you can pay rent and mortgage and buy Fritos."

"Okay. So what about these?" She indicated the numbers following Anderson's name.

"Routing numbers are nine digits long," I said.

She frowned, put her finger on 115-242-1803. "This one has ten digits."

"Maybe it's the personal account number."

"Which would make 288-101-0134 the routing number, but that has ten digits too. And it has an extension."

"The extension might be window dressing. Misdirection."

That got me another kiss. "Let's go with that," she said. "I get the feeling misdirection is Soranden's thing."

"First, let's check the area codes. Make sure it makes sense that these aren't phone numbers."

"Ma did that already."

"Double-check before you floor it, kiddo."

"Was that like a race car metaphorical-similarity thing?"

"Your English is pretty marginal at"—I glanced at a clock on the wall—"one forty-two in the wee frickin' hours."

"As if I care." She got up and turned on a computer. After it booted, she said, "Give me an area code."

"Try 115."

She Googled 115. "Wow, talk about your sucky English. It says, 'The 115 area code appears to be a invalid.'" She scrolled down. "Another entry says it might be in the United Kingdom."

"I think we'll go with 'a invalid.'"

She made a face. "Who on earth writes this fertilizer?"

"Number-one qualification to write ads and internet stuff is not to have made it past the eighth grade."

"I believe it. The difference between *it's* and *its* is college level English. Okay, what's that other area code?"

"288."

She typed it in. "Same thing. It doesn't exist."

"So these numbers are likely to be coded accounts. Now we can floor it."

She plopped down beside me. "Groovy. He liked puzzles. Let's figure it out."

"If this first number is routing, it has one too many digits. Which might mean one of the digits is camouflage."

"Could be the first number. Or the last. How do we check routing numbers?"

I found the URL for a directory of routing numbers that Ma had given me, among a zillion other things. Lucy got us into the site, then entered 115242180 after stripping off the last number.

"No such bank," she said.

"Dump the first number. That'd make it 152421803."

After a moment she said, "Still nothing."

Then we went through it, omitting one number each time, and still came up empty.

"Well, poop," said my assistant. "Maybe it's not a routing number. Maybe it's the account number and the second one is the routing number."

So we tried that and came up dry again.

"Well, poop," said someone whose cussing was apparently limited to palindromes. "But, then, look at these other names." She ran a finger down the list, stopped on Donna Del Sarron. She studied it for a moment. "That's him again."

"Ah. He's a cross-dresser," I said. "Why am I not surprised? The Toad always did seem a little off."

She made a rude noise.

I shrugged. "Hey, if some guy calls himself Donna, I think tutus, ballet slippers, and expensive hormone therapy."

That got me another rude noise. She continued down the list. "Darren Sandolon. There he is again."

"And," I said, trying to preempt her, "Ian Norse Danlord."

"Nope. Can't be. That one has an 'i' in it."

"Soranden's middle name is Isaac."

"Really?"

"Yeah. Middle name, not like Isaac Newton."

She hit me. "You are *so* weird sometimes, but I love you anyway." She went through Ian's name, checking off letters. "Okay, you're right. That's him, but with his middle initial included. And," she went on, "that 'i' means he's also Lara Rose Donndin."

"Lara Rose. Lovely name for a man in a tutu. A lot of these names look bogus. I'll bet Becky Sue is camouflage, meant to hide the name Donndin. Sneaky, using that last name twice, but I always thought of him as a sneaky so-and-so."

"Uh-huh. He blackmailed Volker for a hundred thousand dollars, so sneaky fits. And larcenous." She got a highlighter and drew a bright pink line through Arnold Anderson, Donna Del Sarron, Darren Sandolon, Ian Norse Danlord, and Lara Rose Donndin. Then she looked at the list. "I think we got him. Well, about half got him, because the numbers still don't work."

"Half is better than nothing," I said. "Good job. You got us partway there. Now how about we go back to bed, give it a rest, hit it fresh in the morning?"

"Anagrams," she said softly.

I offered her a hand and pulled her off the couch. When we were on our feet, I opened her bathrobe and mine, gave her a full-body hug designed to get her mind off anagrams.

"Wow," she whispered. "You're kinda manly, Cowboy."

"You oughta see me rope and ride."

"Rope, huh? Okay, show me that part first."

*   *   *

We blew off Sunday too. Sort of. We phoned Ma, told her about the anagrams. We lifted weights in the home gym, one of the few activities in which I was able to show Lucy up. Then she made me try to touch my toes and do a bunch of other stretches that got me humble again. She bent over so far backward that she touched the back of her head to her butt. I got a video of that. We perused the address book from time to time to figure out the numbers, finally gave it up and went on another ten-mile slow run to Mayberry Park and back. Ate good food. Gave Soranden's sheet another half hour. Read novels and finally fell asleep. Good day, all in all. Except for those damn numbers and me unable to touch my toes without hearing laughter.

*   *   *

Nine forty-five, Monday morning, we were about to head over to Ma's when Reno Lock & Safe phoned. Fifteen minutes later, a van pulled into the driveway and two guys the size of medium-large gorillas got out. One of them came to the front door and rang the bell with a furry index finger.

"Got that safe in the truck," he said. *Paul* was embroidered on his shirt above the pocket. "Where ya want it?"

"Let's have a look at it first, see how big it is."

We went out to the van. Lucy trailed along behind. It was a good-looking safe, powder-black finish. "Nice," I said.

Paul gave me a look. "Nice? It's a Brown 7224, over nine hundred pounds with ballistic armor. Shoot a fifty-caliber bullet at it and all it does is knock off a little paint, doesn't put even a tiny little ding in the armor. So where's it go?"

"Pull the van around back. I'll show you. You get to figure out how to get that monster in the house."

"No sweat, as long as it's on the first floor. Been doin' this a long time."

I showed Paul and the other guy, Judd, a place in a corner of the exercise room. "No sweat," Paul said.

The gorillas muscled it in on a huge hand truck and eased it down without taking out the floor or a wall.

"Best safe made in the U.S.," Paul said. "Temporary code is one-two-three-four-five-six. Here's the instruction manual. You need to come up with your own six-digit code." He punched in 123456 and opened the door.

"What if I forget my code?" I asked. "Can you break into this thing, get my grenades and plutonium out?"

He grinned. "Break in? No way. Not without destroying it. But the serial number is registered with the manufacturer. They got a fifteen-digit code that'll open it, overrides whatever code you put in. There's an eight hundred number you can call if you need to. Anyway, you got to register the safe with them so they know you're you. Read about it in the manual. And don't put the manual in the safe. People sometimes do that and then we have to shoot 'em. Sign here."

He handed me a clipboard, I signed, tried to keep my eyes from bugging out when I saw that the safe cost more than twelve thousand dollars, then he and Judd left.

Lucy looked in the safe. "Groovy. What code should we use?"

"It's your safe, Cupcake. Come up with something you'll remember." I was still reeling from the cost of the thing. I'd seen gun safes in Cabela's for a thousand, good ones for upwards of three. The ballistic hide on this thing must've cost a bundle.

Lucy thought about it for a while. "Landry has six letters. How about the last digit of the number of a letter, its place in the alphabet. Since L is the twelfth letter, last digit would be a two." She worked it out, finally came up with 214485.

"Perfect," I said. "Miss Puzzle Solver."

She was quiet for a minute, working away, then she looked up at me. "Just so you know, M. Angel would be 314752."

"Nothing wrong with your code, kiddo."

"Okay, then. We'll re-code this thing later. Right now, let's go talk to Ma, see what she thinks about Soranden's address book. And remind me to phone Dad this evening to thank him for the safe."

*   *   *

Maude Clary was in her downtown office. Lucy and I went in, and the first thing Lucy did was go to that fuckin' poster Ma had laminated and put on her wall. Two posters, one on top of the other. First was a poster of an old-timey ad for Coca-Cola from the nineteen-twenties: *The Pause That Refreshes.* Swing that out of the way and there I was standing next to a bicycle, stark naked except for a little red body paint covering parts I'd wanted covered, and not a whole lot of paint at that. Holiday had done the artwork in March when we'd ridden in the WNBR in San Francisco. Seventeen hundred people riding around naked in public. I'd gone along with it in honor and memory of Jeri who had wanted to do it, and it was also a celebration of my being back from Borroloola, Australia.

So, of course, Lucy swung the Coke ad out of the way.

"I love this picture," she said. "It's so *you*, Mort."

"It's a mood piece," Ma said. "Whenever I need a laugh. I also show it to clients if they want to know if I can get photos of a cheating spouse."

Aw, shit, no.

"Tell me you're kidding or I'll shoot you," I said.

"Can't do that, stud. Got a gun on you?"

"Not right this minute."

"Then I'd like to see what you think you're gonna shoot me with. Right this minute."

Aw, shit. And, of course, Lucy doubled over with laughter.

"Glad you two are enjoying yourselves so much," I said. "And how about hiding that fucking poster so we can act like adults around here?"

That got more girlish laughter. But we finally got past the poster and put Soranden's phony address sheet in front of Ma, pointed out the anagrams of his name.

"Two of these are women," Ma said.

"Good eye, Ma. He liked pink tutus and white tights. And, I think, tiaras."

She stared at me. "I'll ignore that, boyo. Okay, let's take it slow. You think this guy you called 'The Toad' goes into a bank and opens up accounts as Donna Sarron and Lara Rose Donndin. What's he wearing? And if you tell me a tutu and a tiara you're fired. But, a dress? A wig and a padded bra? Talking in a chirpy falsetto? How about a five-o'clock shadow? Some guys could pull it off, but this Soranden dipwad doesn't sound like he could make it fly even if he went to a mall and got a makeover."

"Well, poop," Lucy said. "Didn't think of that."

"That's *if*," Ma went on, "Donna actually *has* an account. And this other anagrammed-up broad, Lara Rose."

"What would be the point of coming up with anagrams and not using them?" I asked.

"Who knows? I'm just coming up with ifs."

Lucy tapped the sheet. "He's got two sisters, Alice Ann and Esther. Esther has the same last name: Soranden. And she's local, lives thirty miles away in Carson City. What if she opened the accounts using fake IDs?"

"An *accomplice*." Ma smiled. "Accomplices tend not to be a good idea when you're a criminal, but she's family so I like it. I particularly like it that she's still alive, doesn't live far way, so we can track her down and put eyes on her."

"And," I said, "according to Russ, she never married. She appears to have been close to her brother since she's a named beneficiary on his bank accounts here in Reno. Which means he trusts her."

"Trusts her how?" Lucy said.

"Not to kill him, sweetheart. So back to the money—it'd be a good idea to spread it around, thin it out. And I doubt that Volker was the first pigeon Soranden hit. No telling how much he's managed to squirrel away."

"Pigeon," Lucy said. "Nice."

Ma smiled. "We need to get a look at that dame."

"Dame," I whispered to Lucy. "Terrific use of mid-thirties noir vernacular—like pigeon. You pickin' up on approved lingo here? It'll be on the final exam when you get your PI license."

"Yup. Got that 'dipwad' thing nailed down too."

"You two," Ma said. "So, okay, Soranden uses his name to come up with anagrams for two women and three men. And the numbers are probably bank account numbers, that about where we're at?"

"Real close," I agreed. "But Lucy and I didn't get anywhere with the numbers last night so we're still not a hundred percent about that." I told Ma what we'd done, how we'd struck out with routing numbers.

"Huh," Ma grunted. "Sneaky fucker. But they're right here. These numbers mean something." She stared at the sheet a while longer. "Lookit all these extensions. Like businesses. Nobody I know knows so many businesses with so many extensions."

"They might just be camouflage," I said.

"Possible. If so, I think he overdid it."

We gave it another five minutes, then I said, "There's four real people here: Esther, Alice Ann, John George, and Kate. And five anagrams for Soranden. Which leaves eight bogus names and this Triple-A Cal number, which was out of service when we phoned it. No extension on the Triple-A number. Or on the 'real' people either. All of which are just observations."

"But we're getting familiar with this sheet," Ma said. "You never know what'll jump out at you and turn out to be useful."

I said, "Soranden's ex, Debbie Combs, didn't make the list. Russell said she lives in Minneapolis now."

"Extensions on the anagram names are always three digits," Lucy said. "The other extensions are anywhere from one to four digits but none of them have three digits."

Ma nodded. "So it's likely the extensions on the anagram names mean something." She looked at Lucy and me. "You two keep workin' on it. I will too. Something'll pop. Right now, how 'bout we go down to Carson and see if we can get a look at Esther, who"—she peered at the sheet—"lives on Penrose Drive, which we can Google on the way down."

"I could use a nap first," I said.

"Later, Cowboy," Lucy murmured.

"Oh, for hell's sake, you two," Ma said. "Let's go."

* * *

We drove to Carson City in what I call the Chariot of Fire, Ma's '63 Cadillac Eldorado. She says it's vintage, I say antique and on its last legs, so to speak. It has soft springs and good shocks, a combination that gives it an eerie floating glide and makes driving hazardous above fifty miles an hour.

Ma asked me to chauffeur. "Take it up to fifty-five," she said. "Blow the carbon out of it."

"Yes, ma'am." Not sure about blowing the carbon out of it, but I got all eight cylinders to fire up, which was something of a coup.

Penrose Drive was basic fifties housing, one-story houses with what looked like two and three bedrooms. Esther's place was sky blue with white trim, well-kept behind a low Cyclone fence, roses starting to give up their color as fall deepened. We parked in front of the house next door and looked at an angle at Esther's digs. The two-car garage door was up and a new Ford Explorer was parked outside in the driveway. "Looks like she's home, Ma," I said. "Whatcha want to do?"

"First thing—get me a smoke."

"Mort and I can get out and walk around if you do," Lucy said. "Sorry, Ma. I can't do smoke."

"Second," Ma said without missing a beat, "we can't just sit here. Someone'll call the cops. So one of us has to go knock, see if she's home, get eyes on her if she is."

"Draw straws?" I asked. "Or rock, paper, scissors?"

"She'd probably make you in a heartbeat, even if you wore a wig and your old duffer's clothes, which you're not. The guy who found her brother's skull? Nope, I'll go. She doesn't know me from Jane Fonda. Pop the trunk on this buggy, boyo."

"Nice alliteration, Ma."

"Pop it."

She got out, lifted the trunk, got something out, banged the lid back down. She came to the window and held out a bunch of *Watchtower* pamphlets. "I picked up a handful from a couple of Jehovah's Witnesses who came around. Figured these'd come in handy someday."

"Go save her soul, Ma," I said.

"Yeah, I'll do that." She clipped a button to the front of her shirt that read GIVE GOD A CHANCE, stuffed a black box in her pocket, then toddled off to a gate in the fence. She opened it, went through, and Lucy and I watched as she walked to the front door and rang the bell.

Moments later it opened. We could see a woman standing in the doorway—unless it was another cross-dressing Soranden. Ma spoke to her for about half a minute, then went inside. Not the usual reaction to a Jehovah's Witness drive-by.

"What if Esther's a Witness?" Lucy asked.

"Then we might hear shots. Let's hope Ma can fake it, and that Esther isn't a Witness, or another Dahmer." Jeffrey Dahmer being a former cannibal of some renown.

"Little bit dark there, Mort."

"Gotcha. Think Esther would know Ma from Jane Fonda?"

"We could go ask."

"Okay, I'll be quiet. Unless shots are fired."

We waited.

Five minutes later, Ma came out. She reached the sidewalk and ambled away from us. I gave her a minute, then took the Caddy up the street fifty yards past her, stopped at the curb. She opened the front passenger door and got in.

"She guilty as sin, Ma?" I asked.

"Remains to be seen. But the good news is, she and I look quite a bit alike. Good news for us, not for her."

"C'mon, Ma," I said.

"Just tellin' it like it is."

"And why would that be good news for us?"

"Because if she's Donna and Lara Rose, and if they've got bogus accounts, and if all the pieces fall into place, maybe I can go into banks as her and unload an account or two, get some of Volker's money back."

"That's a lot of ifs, Ma. And illegal as hell, in case that didn't occur to you."

"Life is full of ifs. Like *if* I don't get a smoke pretty soon, I might go postal, so how 'bout you find us a place where I can get out and light up?"

"I'm on it. We can discuss those other ifs later."

I took her to a McDonald's, parked in their lot. Ma got out and lit up a Camel. She walked in circles, trailing smoke, then had me pop the trunk again. She got something else out, then got back in the car. "Okay, let's check the video," she said.

She took off the button she'd attached to her shirt. She held it up. "Video camera. Lens looks out of the 'O' in God." She got a small black box out of her pocket. "Wireless recorder. Thirty-two gigs." Then she held up an iPad. "*Voila.*"

She turned on the recorder, set it to transmit, fired up the iPad, and we watched an unsteady video as Ma walked to the house, rang the bell, and Esther answered.

Esther looked about Ma's age, an inch taller, roughly the same weight. Her hair was gray, an inch off her shoulders. They could've been sisters.

Ma gave her a pretty good Jehovah's Witness spiel, which didn't go over very well. Esther was about to close the door in Ma's face when Ma asked, pious and sincere, if she could use the bathroom because she was about to have an accident. That got her inside. She cooled the Jehovah talk and recorded the interior of the living room, a glance into the kitchen, got a good look down a hallway before going into the bathroom. Nothing special in the bathroom, but she got a good recording of herself washing her hands, came out, and kept the camera on Esther to catch as much of her mannerisms as possible. She thanked her profusely, tried one more time to leave a *Watchtower* with her, struck out when Esther gave her a cool, disinterested, get-outta-here look, then she asked Esther if that Ford Explorer got decent gas mileage, got a "what's-it-to-ya" look, then got out of there.

CHAPTER SEVENTEEN

"GOOD WORK, MA," I said, "but you didn't ask her if she was keeping any of Soranden's blackmail money for him."

Ma guffawed. "Didn't fit the narrative, boyo. But she's got nice stuff in there. I'd say her house has been painted in the last year or two, and it's fixed up real good inside. And she's got that almost-new Ford Explorer."

"So . . . money?"

"Some. For sure. But we don't know what her situation is, what income she's got. She might be on Social Security, have a bunch of retirement money of her own."

"Bet Warley could find out," Lucy said.

Ma turned to her. "You're right." She looked at me. "You got your old pal Sullivan on speed dial, right?"

I guffawed. "As if."

Ma smiled. Using one of her investigator's programs, she found Warley's private number on her iPad and read it off to me. "Call him."

"Think that's a good idea, Ma?"

"Yup. If he balks, I'll sink his canoe."

Cool. Now I had two reasons to call. I put his number in, got him on the horn on the third ring.

"Warl, it's me."

"Who?"

"Your fellow IRS thug."

Silence. Then, "Narrow it down."

"It's Mortimer."

"Hey, Mort. Had me goin' there. We should get together for a drink and talk about old times, huh?"

"Maybe not. I've got a job for you, since you're the head racketeer now in Northern Nevada." Doesn't hurt to stroke that fragile, needy little ego, and "racketeer" would put a glow in his heart. "I need you to run down a tax return for me, get me some information."

Silence. Then: "You know I can't do that, Mort. You're not in the . . . the profession anymore."

"Not even for an old pal, huh?"

"Not even. I mean, you know how it is."

Ma drew a line across her throat.

"Okay, Warl. Catch you later." I ended the call. "What's up, Ma?"

"You got that new burner phone with you?"

"Right here." I got it out of a pocket, held it up.

"Gimme it." She took it, found "Will" in the contact list, punched a few buttons, and motioned us for quiet. "Yeah, Willie, it's Maude. Yeah, I know, I got it from Mort. It's just the three of us on this thing. I need a favor." Pause. "Well, what do you *think*, since I'm on this burner talkin' to your burner?" She gave me a wink. "No names, but the man out west here—the guy you gave the top job, if you'll remember—initials WS if that helps—needs a push to get me some info regarding that job you want us to look into, so I'd appreciate it if you'd give him a call and get his mind right." Short pause. "Three minutes or he's fired? Hell, *no*, I don't want him fired. What good would he be in the future if you did *that*?" Longer pause. "Okay, that's good. Tell him to call Mort." Pause. "Nope, he'll know who. He's got the number, and no, it's not *this* number for chrissake."

She ended the call and we waited.

Two minutes twelve seconds later, my regular cell phone rang.

"Yo," I said.

"Is that you, Mort?"

"Mr. Angel, yeah. What can I do for you, Warl?"

"Well, uh, what can I do for *you*? Sorry about that little mix-up a few minutes ago. I spilled coffee on my desk."

"No problem. What I need are tax returns, say two years' worth, for an Esther Soranden, lives in Carson City."

"Soranden? That, that's, you don't mean Soranden's *sister*, do you?"

"The very same."

"Aw, jeez, Mort. What're you gettin' me into?"

"Mr. Angel. You can thank me later."

"Huh? Thank you? What the hell for?"

"Think about it. Think about who asked you to help me out and what that might mean in terms of career enhancement."

"I don't get it."

"That doesn't surprise me. Allow me to spell it out. Think in terms of the fellow who called you and how his request might make him more likely to overlook any future egregious stupidity on your part and therefore less likely to fire you. *Warl*."

Silence. Then: "Oh, yeah."

Ball of fire, that Warley. Peter Principle says the guy would be maxed out trying to run a hot dog stand and there he was, top IRS goon in Northern Nevada. What a world.

"So, what'd you want to know, Mortimer?"

"Print off her entire tax return for this year and last. I'll be in to pick them up in about an hour."

"Ah, jeez, don't . . . don't come in here. I'll meet you at the Burger King down the street. In an hour."

He hung up.

"Like candy from a baby," Ma said. "This is why we got people in our pockets. Okay, boyo, take us back to Reno."

* * *

Warley was in his usual cheap blue suit and tie, sitting at a table with a drink in front of him, sweating. Also in front of him was a manila envelope. He looked around as I came in. In East Germany in the sixties he wouldn't have lasted forty seconds.

"Jesus, Mortimer. You got to Munson?" he whispered.

"Don't know how you come up with stuff like that, Warl, but you oughta try to control it. Is that my package?"

"Yes, it's—"

"Yeah, thanks. If I need anything more, I'll let you know. You should get back to busting piggy banks." I left.

We drove to Ma's office, went in, opened the envelope and dumped out Esther's returns. Lucy and I sat on Ma's couch and went through last year's return. Ma took this year's.

Didn't take long.

"Her income last year was eighteen thousand, four hundred twenty-four," I said. "Social Security and a dollar fifteen cents annual interest from a bank paying something like point zero six percent. Probably started getting Social Security the year before. She was sixty-six during this return."

"Now she's sixty-seven," Ma said. "Eight years older than her brother who, by the way, isn't gettin' any older. For income, all I've got here is what you've got—Social Security, pathetic little speck of interest that might let her upgrade to a happy meal every third year. Interest on her mortgage was sixty-one hundred bucks, so she's probably paying some bank around eight or nine grand a year for the place."

"That doesn't leave much to live on," Lucy said. "Wonder what her payments are on that Explorer since it's pretty new. Of course, she could've paid the whole thing right up front."

"I'm starting to get an inkling of hidden income," Ma said. "What do you think, Mort?"

"I think the word 'inkling' is underutilized." At her look, I said, "*Also*, if the IRS saw what we've seen and Soranden wasn't there to protect her, they might be all over it."

"Might?"

"It would have to be a slow day, although they would most likely back-burner it and go after her in December, try to upend her world right before Christmas. They like to do that. But it's not as if she has millions, so we—the IRS—wouldn't expect to come up with a nice juicy tax cheat we could clap in irons and stuff into a rat-infested dungeon."

"Juicy," my assistant said. "And rat-infested. Wow."

"So," Ma said, "we've gotta break down that address book of Soranden's and get those account numbers, see if Esther's got access to money the IRS doesn't know about."

"Uh-huh," I said. "Blackmail loot. It's his address book and he's a puzzle freak, so it's likely he came up with the anagrams, not Esther. Nice guy, though, sharing the proceeds of criminal activity with his elderly sister like that."

"Esther would need fake IDs to open accounts, wouldn't she?" Lucy asked.

Ma nodded. "Absolutely. Not that hard to do if you've got the money and know where to go to get good paper."

I still had my Stephen Brewer ID, credit cards, and a bunch of wallet stuffers from a trip Ma and I had taken to Paris, a trip that had to be kept forever secret.

Lucy had mentioned that she has a real ID and two fakes. I would have to ask her about that later.

"Not much we can do now except figure out Soranden's address book," Ma said. "But here's something. While you two were out fooling around yesterday, I checked out 'anagrams' on Google and came up with some good stuff. Get this. An anagram for 'the presidential cigar' is 'a cheap girl inserted it.'"

"Oh, no," Lucy said.

"Oh, *yes*," Ma replied. "Also: 'it replaces a dire thing.'"

"Wow."

"An anagram for 'Ronald Wilson Reagan' is 'insane Anglo warlord.' So, had enough?"

"Yep," I said. "But good goin', Ma. You're the best. Now where do we go from here? I feel like we're slogging through quicksand."

"The key is this thing," she said, tapping the address book with a pudgy finger. "If we didn't have this, we'd be nowhere. Like the FBI," she added.

* * *

If the FBI had come up with anything, Munson would have heard about it and let Ma know. That was the deal. And if the FBI had put anyone in handcuffs, it would've been shouted from the rooftops. Or ballyhooed, 'cause they do that then expect raises. None of which had happened, so they weren't any further along with it than we were. I wondered if they'd found the anagrams and were starting to piece any of that together. Anagrams might classify as fun and fun was as foreign to the FBI as honesty is to your average U.S. senator, either party, so I thought not.

Lucy and I went back to my place. We read the manual for the safe and she changed the entry code from 123456 to 214485. Then she stared at the safe for a few seconds and said, "If we use M. Angel, we get 314752."

"And that would be better, why?"

"All the digits are different."

"Not sure that matters, kiddo, but do what you think best."

"Anyway, I like your name."

"Mangel?"

She made a face at me, then changed the code to 314752. "Also, because it's in your house," she said.

Okay with me either way.

"Let's go to a gun range," she said. "I want to get used to this little guy." She held up the SR22 autoloader her father had given her.

So we did. At Reno Guns & Range we paid the $15 fees, donned hearing and eye protection, and Lucy put three hundred basic .22 long rifle rounds through the sturdy little Ruger and a hundred of the hyper-velocity Velocitor rounds. After sighting it in, she was looking pretty deadly out to twenty-five yards. I put three hundred rounds of .357 through my Ruger revolver.

"I'm gettin' a feel for it," she said when we were finished. "Another thousand rounds and then I'll go for a concealed carry permit with it."

Back home it was gun-cleaning time. Out with Hoppe's 9, patches, gun oil. All of this was fun, and necessary when you're a world-class gumshoe, but it didn't get us one bit closer to Volker's missing hundred thousand dollars, though as a former IRS agent with residual goonlike memories that still gave me nightmares, I was aware that Volker had cheated on his taxes and therefore wasn't exactly an innocent party in all of this.

Which, as luck would have it, is about the time Ma gave me and Lucy a call and told us to get back over to her office.

* * *

"What's up, Ma?" I asked. I walked over to the sideboard and touched the bullet hole Isaac Biggs had put there when he'd come hunting for Ma because she'd fingered him sixteen years earlier and he'd ended up in prison.

"Check this out," Ma said, waving a hand at the computer monitor on her desk.

Ads for Title Nine clothing, Kraft Mayo, hot dates, and all kinds of "trending" crap filled up the right-hand side. Pictures and text occupied the left.

"You better point it out," I said. "That looks like the kind of social media manure I don't go near without gloves and a ten-foot non-conducting pole."

"It's manure, but sometimes useful. This's Kimmi Volker's Facebook page. Scroll down forever through the kind of trivial crap that makes you wonder if this country will still be here in twenty years and you finally get to this."

It was a point-and-shoot picture of her father, Mike, and her brother, Derek, in front of a fake old-time trading post out in the desert, scorched dry hills in the background.

"Yup," I said. "Nice picture of the boys."

"Read the caption," Ma said.

Lucy and I got closer. The caption read, "Dad and Derek at a stupid torist place in Arizona, July 2. Shoot me now."

"Arizona," Lucy said. "Where you find harvester ants."

Ma nodded. "Exactly."

"Useful if you have a skull that needs cleaning," I put in. "Nice spelling on tourist, too. She could get a job writing stuff on the internet for small-business owners."

"But the point is . . . *Arizona*," Ma said. "The Volkers were down there this summer."

"Puts Mike Volker back in my sights," I said. "Bet he and his wee tykes caught sight of one of those giant anthills. Maybe he did more than give Soranden a hundred grand. Maybe he didn't want Soranden coming back for more, which blackmailers tend to do, so he took out a onetime insurance policy."

"Possible," Ma said. "Mostly I think this gives us a reason to keep an eye on him. And Esther, who we might not have picked up on if Lucy hadn't come up with those anagrams with women's names."

I looked at Lucy. "This would be a good time to say, 'Aw shucks, it weren't nuthin.'"

"Aw shucks, it weren't nuthin'," she said.

Ma shook her head. "You two. Okay, we need to get eyes back on Volker. And another good look at Esther wouldn't hurt because I've got an idea about that."

"How about Luce and I take Volker?" I said.

Ma pursed her lips. "I think Lucy should go with me. If Esther goes into a store or something, Lucy can follow her but I can't since she's seen me."

"How much time we gonna give this?" I asked. "A day or two or three?"

"Not sure. But I have the feeling we're one step closer to whoever killed Soranden, and if we get there before the FBI, we get Willie Munson's twenty-five-thousand-dollar bonus. That's worth putting in some time and effort."

* * *

None of the Volkers had seen Ma's brown Cadillac, and Esther Soranden hadn't seen Lucy's Mustang, so I sat in the Caddy watching the Volker residence and Ma and Lucy watched Esther's place. We put in the time and effort—and came up dry.

Six thirty p.m., back at Ma's. "That's PI work," she said. "Get used to it. We'll switch cars and give it another try tomorrow."

"How about dinner at the Goose and a nightcap or two in the Green Room?" I suggested.

Ma nodded. "Suits me. I could use a hot toddy."

I gave her a look. "A hot toddy?"

"That's right, boyo."

"And me," Lucy said. "Except probably not a toddy since I don't know what that is."

We ended up at the Silver Lode Steak House in the Golden Goose. Ma and I had steaks, Lucy had a Caesar salad, and at the bar in the Green Room O'Roarke whipped up hot toddies, which turned out to be whiskey in hot water with honey, herbs, and spices. Lucy had one too, but with rum instead of whiskey, and light on the rum.

"You haven't made national news in a week," O'Roarke said, shoving a Pete's Wicked Ale my way. "Not running out of gas, are you, Spitfire?"

"Not hardly. Stick around."

We settled in with our drinks. Ma and Lucy chatted, and I quickly lost track of the conversation. I starting thinking about this entire Soranden-Volker deal, still not exactly sure what we were doing in it, what we hoped to accomplish.

Find Soranden's killer? The chance of that was remote at best, even if it was worth twenty-five grand.

Get Volker all or some of his money back? Same odds, if he even deserved to get his money back considering that he had cheated on taxes. Guess I still had that gene in me that doesn't approve of larceny.

My mind ping-ponged around, neurons playing toss and fetch with trivia. I should have the oil changed in the Toyota. It was about due. And Lucy was driving a six-year-old Mustang. Bought it used when she was worth twelve million bucks. Living within the means of what her job brought in. Maybe she and I could stake out Esther's tomorrow, but that would make it hard for us to get to Rufus's dojo on time, so we might have to go in shifts if we were going to keep tabs on Esther. I didn't remember the code to the gun safe, but I knew how to re-create it using the name Mangel. M was the thirteenth letter of the alphabet, so the first number of the safe's code was 3. And so on.

Trivia.

Lucy had used my name for the code because all six digits were different. And . . . and . . .

Epiphany.

Insight.

A light went on. Maybe.

Digits were a key. Digits were *the* key. Maybe the Pete's had helped. If so, then beer is grossly underrated.

Soranden's address sheet needed a decoding key, and Lucy had changed the code to the gun safe to all different digits, and we'd been staring at that address sheet for hours. In my mind's eye I saw the number after AAA Cal, top of the sheet. All the digits were different. The odds of a random ten-digit number or phone number having all different digits seemed pretty remote.

"Got it," I said.

And, of course, the womenfolk kept chatting because "got it" might've been a burp or acid reflux, and if not a burp it still might not be important, coming from me, so I took Lucy by the shoulders and gave her a kiss to stop her mouth, which didn't work, but it sure changed what her mouth was doing.

"Wow," she said after ten seconds of that. "Not that I'm complaining, but what was *that* for?"

"I gave myself a gift for maybe breaking Soranden's code. His address sheet."

"Coolarama. But ... really? And only *maybe*?"

"I think so. It's nothing like a hundred percent yet. Either of you have that address sheet with you?"

"I do." Ma got a folded copy out of her purse.

I sat between them with the sheet on the bar in front of me. "I think this Triple-A Cal number is a key," I said. "It's not like the rest of the stuff, and all the digits are different." I looked at Lucy. "Like that code you put into the gun safe."

"Okay. Groovy. So how do you think it works?"

"I haven't gotten that far yet."

"Groovy redux. But if you're right, let's figure it out."

We stared at it. AAA Cal's number was 9163824750.

"It's got all ten digits," Ma said.

"That's what *I* just said," I told her. "In case that got by you with the assistance of that hot toddy."

"Bank routing numbers have *nine* digits," she said with a faint alcohol-enhanced snarl. "This number has ten."

"So one of the digits must be bogus," Lucy put in. "And the most likely one is that zero on the end."

"Which," Ma said, "would mean the key is 916382475. Now, how do we use it?"

"It has to unscramble the routing numbers," I said. "Maybe it means, take the ninth digit, then the first digit, then the sixth digit, and so on. Which means Lucy's idea that that final zero is bogus makes sense because there is no zeroth digit."

"Try it on Arnold Anderson's number," Lucy suggested. "Leave off that three on the end."

"Dropping the three gives us 115242180," Ma said. She wrote it on a paper napkin, and the possible key: 916382475. "Okay, the ninth number is zero, the first number is a one . . ." She went through it, came up with 012581214. She got out her iPad and put the number into a website that identified routing numbers. "No such routing number, no such bank," she said.

She deleted the first digit in Anderson's first number, tried again. Still no such bank.

We thought a while longer. Finally, Lucy said, "Maybe that leading nine in the key means something else. Maybe the first number of that coded routing number goes into the ninth place. The second number of the key means the second number of the routing number goes into the first place, and so on."

It took longer to get that straight, but we finally came up with 122105841 for a routing number. Ma put it into her iPad and . . . it came up Parkway Bank of Arizona.

"Son of a gun," Ma said. "Arizona. I think we got him."

"Do I get a bonus for that?" I asked.

*　*　*

Twenty minutes later, we had four more banks, all with offices or branches within ten miles of downtown Phoenix: Mutual of Omaha, Torrey Pines Bank, Metro Phoenix Bank, Parkway Bank of Arizona, and Sunwest Federal Credit Union.

"The guy likes Arizona," Ma said.

"Probably because of those ants," I said. "I hear they clear the mind."

"Ohmigod," Lucy said. "You are *terrible*. But," she added, "I would still marry you in a heartbeat. Well . . . in two hours or less after you ask as long as there's a chapel nearby. Which there is in Reno. Just sayin'."

"Glad we got that cleared up," Ma said. "Not that I haven't heard it before. But we just made a huge leap forward, so, let's think about our next step."

"On hot toddies and beer?" I said. "No telling what we'll come up with."

"What *I'm* coming up with," Lucy said, "is that Volker and his brood were in Arizona this summer. And all those banks are in Arizona. And those ants came from Arizona."

Ma said, "I wonder if Volker was dumb enough to open a bunch of bogus accounts with his kids in tow."

"Might be too much booze in that hot toddy, Ma," I said. "If the accounts were opened by our two favorite Sorandens, not only does that leave Volker entirely out of it, it puts Esther in Arizona at some point, going around with fake IDs. Or Ronald Soranden in drag. We found those banks using his address sheet, which isn't an address sheet but a way to hide account numbers. It has nothing to do with Volker—*if* his story is true, which I think it is because I believe his sister, Marta."

"Well, shit." Ma gave an accusing look at the drink in front of her. "I got those two mixed up. I need sleep. But what's with all this Arizona stuff if there's no connection between Volker and Soranden? Volker's not gonna give Soranden a hundred Gs then get involved in Soranden's accounts in Arizona."

"It might just be coincidence," I said.

"I hate coincidences."

"Which doesn't mean they don't exist. Both Kennedy and Lincoln were shot in the head on a Friday and their successors were both named Johnson. Unless, of course, that was the plan."

Ma stared at me.

"How about we puzzle it out in the morning?" Lucy said. "I don't think this hot toddy is helping me much. And Mort's beer has him totally loopy, talkin' about assassinations."

So we rolled up the day and got out of there.

CHAPTER EIGHTEEN

SOMETIMES WHEN I'M asleep, this happens to me:

Jeri is in dire trouble and it's up to me to save her. I have to get to her. I'm beyond desperate. She's a quarter mile away and I'm running but not getting there. Things get in the way. I run into dead ends and have to backtrack. I lose my way. Paths circle around and force me to go in the wrong direction. I run for half an hour and she's still a quarter mile away. Time is running out. I yell for her to hang on, I'm coming, Jeri, I'm trying, I'm trying, *hang on*—

"It's okay," Lucy said. "It's okay, Mort, it's okay, it's okay, I'm here."

I woke up in a sweat. Lucy was half on top of me, holding my face, trying to use her elbows to pin my arms down. "It was just a dream, Mort. Just a dream."

I sank back in the bed. It wasn't just a dream. It was me, once again unable to save Jeri from Julia Reinhart, unable to save the person I'd loved so much. Every three or four weeks I had a dream like this, running futilely, getting nowhere while Jeri cries out for me to save her.

"Just a dream," Lucy whispered. "That's all. Hold me."

I did. I clung to her and she held me, warming me from head to toe. It wasn't sex, it was pure connection, contact, telling me I wasn't alone in the world. Everyone needs that.

Everyone. Including Lucy.

She needed me. I hugged her closer. Her breath came in a gentle warm rhythm against my neck.

"I love you," I whispered. First time ever. It tumbled out of me because it had to. At last.

She snuggled closer, as if that were possible. "Ohmigod, I have waited so long to hear that. I love you so, so much, Mort." She gave that a moment, then said, "But please sleep now. Just sleep, darling. I don't want this to get tangled up with words. I just want to be with you, like this."

Darling.

I was forty-two. She was thirty-one but looked eighteen. Maybe it was genetics and maybe it was because she was born when four planets were lined up and none of them was Mars. How would I know, since I know so little?

But, no words. For a few minutes I ran my fingers over her body, hands gliding slowly from her rear to her shoulders, back and forth, aware of the vast improbability of her being here with me, a crusty old IRS agent—okay, ex—who'd left Uncle Sam's thuggery and struck gold.

I was in love. Again.

We were in love.

We slept.

* * *

"Where're you going?" Lucy asked.

I was dressed, seven twenty in the morning, not my usual time to head out and conquer the world.

"Gotta go talk to a couple of people, kiddo."

"Alone?"

"Yeah, sorry. Don't worry, though."

"Is it about last night?"

"Yes. But not to worry, okay?"

She looked into my eyes. "Okay. See you."

That kind of trust doesn't grow on trees. You can spend your whole life with someone and not find it.

I drove over to Holiday's apartment. She was finishing up her final year as a civil engineering student. I knocked on her door and a moment later she opened it and greeted me with a smile that illuminated the world.

"Mort!"

She gave me a hug, unaware or unconcerned that she was in a T-shirt and panties, that the T-shirt was stretched as tight as a slingshot about to take down a charging rhino. I'd forgotten how those hugs felt, but I was also immune. Sort of.

She drew me inside, then told me to wait while she put on a robe and did something with her hair.

I looked around the apartment. I'd been there a few times since the time she and I had concocted an alibi for me for that night last October when Jeri was murdered north of Gerlach. It looked the same. Still tidy, still . . . familiar.

Holiday came out, smiling. "So, what brings you by?"

"Got a request."

"Lucky you. I'm honoring all requests this morning."

Nothing to do but dive into it. "I need to tell Lucy about that night, that alibi. And about Paris, but I can keep you out of the Paris part of it."

She sat on the edge of a chair. "You two are getting serious then, aren't you?"

"Very."

"Good for you. You need that." She looked at me for a moment. "But I get it. You can't get more serious until you tell her about Julia and Paris, right?"

"Right."

"You trust her?"

"With my life, Sarah." Her real name was Sarah. Holiday was her name when she was feeling frisky, which she wasn't at the moment, and never would again with me.

"I trust you," she said. "So I trust her too."

"I've also got to get Ma's okay."

"Go ahead and tell Lucy, Mort. It was rough, but I think she'll be okay with it." Holiday and Lucy had met earlier that summer, after that Jonnie Xenon thing down south.

"Thank you."

She stood up and gave me a kiss. A goodbye kiss. It lasted a while, ten seconds, fifteen. It brought back memories I found I was reluctant to let go. But let go I did.

"Goodbye, Sarah," I said.

"Friends forever, Mort. I'll never forget you."

Then I went out the door, not sure that I would ever see her again.

* * *

Seven fifty-five a.m. Ma was in her office when I went in.

"Early bird," she said. "You come up with something on Volker or Soranden? Or this Arizona thing?" She looked past me. "Where's Lucy?"

"At home. Gotta ask you something, Ma."

Her eyes flattened. "Sounds serious."

"It is." I looked into her eyes. "I have to tell Lucy about Paris. What we did."

She was silent for a moment. "That *is* serious."

"Yes, it is."

"But I'm not an idiot, so you don't have to tell me why." Her eyes bored into mine. "Tell her. All of it."

"You sure?"

"I don't sound sure?"

"Well, you do, in fact."

"Because I am. Lucy is tough as an anvil. You're sandstone but she's pure diamond. Now get out of here. I don't want to see your face again until she knows."

So I got out of there and went back home to Lucy.

* * *

"Well, look at you two," Ma said when Lucy and I walked into her office. "You're glowing. Is it that hot out? It's October and only nine forty in the morning."

Lucy held up a piece of paper.

"What've you got there, hon?" Ma asked.

"Marriage license. Turns out I gotta have it before anyone asks me to marry him. It's good for a year. I need it so we can get hitched in two hours if he asks. I thought we could just go in and, *pow*, done, but we had to have this first."

Ma beamed. "Good for you." She looked at me, then stood up and gave me a hug—first time ever. "You've got a brain in there. I might have to keep you around a while longer."

"A ringing endorsement for sure, Ma."

"This mean you two're officially engaged?"

I said, "It's possible that we were engaged thirty minutes after she took my order for fried chicken in McGinty's Diner. In Tonopah. That's when she first said she'd marry me if I asked."

"At McGinty's I only said probably," Lucy said. "But forty minutes after that in your car I would have. If you'd asked."

Maude looked at Lucy. "Marriage license. Which means he told you. All the way up to and including Paris?"

"All of it." A tear rolled down Lucy's cheek. She swiped at it. "I didn't know. Really, I never *dreamed*..."

"It's over and done, Lucy," Ma said.

"Over and done is redundant, Ma," Lucy said in a voice that had gone liquid with tears.

Ma gave her a hug. "We had to do it."

"I know. Mort explained it. He wouldn't be the man I love if he'd let Julia get away with it. I know that means down deep I'm a really bad person, but I don't care. If he loves me like he loved Jeri, then I am so, so lucky."

I turned away and looked out a window before they saw the shine in my eyes. Too late. Lucy spun me around and kissed a salty tear off my cheek before I could get to it. "You can cry. Means you're my kinda guy."

"Destroys my Mike Hammer image though."

"Which you never had, in case you didn't know."

Ma gave us a syrupy smile.

"How 'bout you jump in here and break up this maudlin stuff, Ma," I said.

"Why? I'm a sucker for this kinda thing."

Well, shit. If I didn't do something quick, this was going to turn into a Fred Astaire–Audrey Hepburn moment and someone was going to break into song. In this situation Sam Spade would pull a gun, but I didn't think that would fly. Mike Hammer would say something crude and maybe throw someone out a window.

"Where are we with Soranden?" I asked. Gruffly.

Lucy kissed me. "Who, sweetheart?"

Well, shit again.

"Soranden. Volker. Harvester ants. Skulls. Commissioner Munson of the IRS. Warley, also of the IRS. FBI. Blackmail. Arizona. Any of that ring a bell?"

Lucy grinned at Ma. "He's like really something when he gets like totally wound up, isn't he?" She kissed me again, then said, "Okay, Soranden. Where were we with that last night?"

Ma said, "We were thinking about doing some surveillance. But now I'm not so sure about that. Now that we've got banks and account numbers to work with."

"Remember how we got Julia and Leland Bye to panic and scurry around, Ma?" I said. "It broke that case wide open. How about we do something like that?"

She gave that some thought. "If we give Esther a jolt, she might unload those accounts, take off with the money, end up in Argentina. So, no jolting Esther. We need to keep that quiet until we move on it, *if* we move on it."

"How about giving Volker a poke?"

"Him, maybe. Not about money, but we might hit him with an anonymous hint that suggests he did away with Soranden. If he did, that could get us twenty-five grand—*if* we found proof, none of which is very likely."

"So . . . stir up Volker?"

"I think so. But not yet. Let's work on those accounts we came up with. Which I've been doing this morning while you two were off getting licensed and whatnot."

"Whatnot, Ma," Lucy said. "I like that."

"What'd you find?" I asked Ma.

"All five of those accounts are active. Here's the rundown on each one, just the totals as of this morning." She picked up a sheet of paper and read it off to us.

"Arnold Anderson, Parkway Bank, $149,883.

"Ian Danlord, Metro Phoenix Bank, $208,455.

"Darren Sandolon, Sunwest Credit Union, $167,917.

"Donna Sarron, Mutual of Omaha branch on Forty-Eighth Street in Phoenix, $158,209.

"And Lara Rose Donndin, Torrey Pines Bank, $186,122."

I took the sheet from her. "Pretty good chunks of change, but none of these amounts are obviously criminal."

"Except for the phony names," Lucy said.

"Okay, that. Those two were hiding this plunder under false names, which, according to the IRS, *is* illegal."

"Plunder," Lucy said. "That's good."

"There's more," Ma said. "I just gave you the totals. If you look at how the money went in, it looks even more sneaky. None of the deposits were greater than eight thousand dollars."

"Ten thousand and above gets reported to the IRS," I said.

Ma nodded. "They were keeping it under the radar. And it's been going on since about a year after Soranden became head of the IRS in Reno. It's been coming in sporadically, a few times a year, probably soon after each blackmail payoff."

"Was there a flurry of new deposits after Soranden took Volker for that hundred grand?" I asked.

Ma picked up a wad of papers and thumbed through them. "Volker said Soranden blackmailed him around the second week of June. He rounded up the money and gave it to Soranden a few weeks later. June twenty-ninth, Esther flew off to Phoenix on Southwest. She flew using her own name. I got into the flight manifests. It usually takes quite a while to go through hundreds of flights, but it didn't take long since those accounts had me zeroed in on flights to Phoenix.

"The next day, thirtieth of June, Lara Rose went into each of the banks where Arnold, Darren, and Ian had accounts and deposited $7,500 into each of them. She's listed as the secondary on those accounts. She also put $7,500 into her own account at Torrey Pines. Switching to Donna Del Sarron, she put $7,500 into that account. All deposits were in cash and the time stamps are about half an hour to an hour apart, give or take, as she drove around Phoenix. *And* I got this: the Lara Rose ID is an Arizona driver's license with an address the same as the business address of one Nathan R. Frasier, attorney at law. I checked him out. He exists. He's got an office in Sun City, about fifteen miles from the middle of Phoenix. Odds are he gets Lara Rose's mail and forwards it as needed. Which, by the way, isn't against the law."

"Wow," Lucy said. "You're good."

Ma smiled. "None of this is admissible in a court of law. It was completely illegal to get some of this information, and I had nothing to do with it."

"Understood," I said. "We've been there before. So where do we go from here?"

"Hold on. I ain't done yet. Esther stayed at a Travelodge in Phoenix for three days, probably to let things cool down, then she went around to all those banks and deposited another $7,500 into each one. In cash again."

"Under the radar," I said. "She packed away $75,000."

"And that's all," Ma said. "She flew back the next day, so there's $25,000 unaccounted for."

"She might've put it in a safe deposit box," Lucy said.

"Possible," Ma replied. "Even likely, but we'll never know unless . . ."

"Unless, what, Ma?" I asked, but I had an idea what she would say, and I had a bad feeling about it.

"Unless we go have a look, boyo."

CHAPTER NINETEEN

A LOOK.

That also sounded illegal, but Esther wasn't the only one who knew how to skulk around under the radar. Ma and I had flown to Paris as Mr. and Mrs. Stephen T. Brewer. We still had those IDs and the credit cards and other wallet crud to match.

"Just a look, Ma?" I asked.

"Depends on what we find. If I find a safe deposit box full of cash, I might get Volker his money back."

Which, technically, would be stealing. We didn't know for certain where that money had come from, though we were about ninety-nine percent sure.

I turned to Lucy. "Might be time for full disclosure, kiddo. You said something the other day about having three IDs, two of them fake. Let's hear it."

She shrugged. "No big deal. It was my dad's idea. He got them for me. Driver's licenses, credit cards, a few other things. One license is in my name, but it says I'm twenty-two. I use it if it looks like someone might hassle me about not looking my age. You've seen the other one. It says I'm Britany Taggart and I'm twenty-three."

"Your father got them for you?"

"Uh-huh. He's sort of . . . cautious. About his name and because of having quite a bit of money. The Taggart ID cost a lot, but it's not like he noticed that or cared."

He wouldn't notice if it cost him a hundred thousand. Not when he had over three hundred million bucks floating around.

"That's good for travel," Ma said. "Car rental and motels. But to go into banks, I've gotta have an Arizona driver's license in the name of Lara Rose Donndin. Wouldn't hurt to have a Visa or MasterCard in her name, either, with my picture on it. Not an active card, just one that looks real."

"Alone?" I said. "You're thinking of going into those banks solo?"

"Got to. Lara Rose traveled alone. I think she went into the banks alone. And what would be the point of you going along? The less any of us are seen, the better."

"Okay," I said. "That might work to check those accounts, but you said you want a look in her safe deposit boxes, if she has any. For that you need keys, which you don't have. And you have to sign to get in. You don't know what her signature looks like. How're you gonna pull all that off?"

She smiled. "Give a sly old broad some credit, boyo."

Lucy put an arm around my waist and pulled me closer. "That's probably a good idea . . . boyo."

"We better get moving on this," Ma said. "And fast. When Soranden's skull turned up, Esther probably got nervous about the money. But she would also be leery about travel—drawing attention to herself when the FBI started nosing around, talking to everyone who knew him. Her being his sister, they would be all over her with questions. But once she figures she's in the clear, I have the feeling that dame is gonna be out of Nevada and maybe out of the country like she was on fire."

* * *

First step: Ma wanted another look at Esther, how she wore her hair, how she walked, what kind of clothes she preferred.

"We're about the same height and age. I might have a few pounds on her, but not a lot. Lara hasn't gotten into the accounts in the past three months so it's not likely she's well known at the banks, but I'd like to do this right."

We got that look after just two and a half hours of rotating surveillance half a block up the street from Esther's house. My Toyota took the spot for an hour, then Ma's Caddy, then back to the Toyota. It looked and felt like a Chinese fire drill. Finally, Esther went out and got her nails done, hit a Walmart, a grocery store, and went through the drive-through of a bank, which made me nervous, then went home. Lucy and I took turns in Walmart videoing Esther as she wandered around shopping. We got her walk, front and back, hair, clothes, the works, including the kind of glasses she wore.

First thing Ma did when we got back to Reno was buy a wig, same color and style of Esther's hair, and some low-power readers that looked like Esther's. Then she had me take a picture of her against a plain blue background and another one with her hair different against a light green background. She emailed the photos to Doc Saladin in Albuquerque, telling him she needed an Arizona driver's license for a Lara Rose Donndin, and that it would be a duplicate license since one already existed. She gave him the license number and all the rest of Lara's data, which she got off the DMV site. And, she wanted a Visa or MasterCard in the name of Lara Rose Donndin. *And*, she also wanted all of that for Donna Del Sarron, and she wanted all of it *tout de suite*—and if he didn't know what that meant, she said she needed it no later than day after tomorrow. I figured that little dig meant she and Doc were pretty good friends, possibly drinking buddies. She told him to overnight the licenses and cards to her office, not to her home. The total cost, Doc told her, would be $8,000, which he said was a bargain since she was such a good customer.

"Eight thousand bucks," Ma said to Lucy and me. "This better be worth it."

She got on a genealogy website and had a good look at the Soranden family tree, closed it out after a few minutes.

By then it was three fifty p.m. I'd phoned Rufus about noon and told him Lucy and I would be late. He told me that was okay, but that we would pay for it when we did show up.

Which we did.

Man, what a workout. I could barely stand when we were through. Even Lucy looked a bit wobbly.

I think Rufus was still pissed about that knife takedown I'd given Ramon. First, he had me try to hit his hand while he held a rubber knife on me, same way Ramon held it. Just hit his hand, nothing else. First eighty or a hundred tries, I couldn't do it, but I finally managed to slap his knife hand one time in five. Then he had me run through the takedown two hundred times while he threatened me with that knife. The first hundred or so times he killed me with it. Then I faked a grab and slapped his face with my left hand, not hard but it surprised the hell out of him. And I got in a good fake kick to his knee.

He gave me a cobra's smile. "That wouldn't work in a real fight, dude. We were working on a routine and you broke it. In a fight, there ain't no routine."

"Got you anyway."

Which proved that my mouth isn't connected to my brain, because that's when the entire workout really went south. Lucy got it too, for which she blamed me later. But it was a workout that could save our lives—repetition, building muscle memory, working on timing and speed. Lucy worked mostly on punches and kicks, didn't get any Rufus slaps.

Back in her Mustang, I said, "I'm not sure I can drive. Don't think I can walk home either. And crawling that far is out of the question, so if you've got any suggestions, now's the time."

Her eyes were closed. "We might die right here."

"Possible. Not much of a suggestion though. Want to call an Uber?"

"They've got Uber hearses? When'd that happen?"

And so on.

But we finally made it back home. Too bad the bedroom was upstairs. We solved that by removing each other's clothes on the first floor to keep from having to haul extra weight up a flight.

Lucy looked at me. "Wow," she said before we attempted that long, long climb. "You must be super extra tired."

"Quiet, girl. Don't make me hurt you."

"Seriously? You have enough energy left to hurt me?"

"I can wait 'til day after tomorrow, sneak up on you when your back is turned."

"No problem. By then you will have forgotten."

"Touché. Let's go up. You first."

After getting clean, we collapsed into bed and slept as if dead for three hours. It was after eight by the time we regained consciousness, or what would have to serve as consciousness.

"Hungry," Lucy said.

"That was an incomplete sentence, Sunshine."

She snarled at me. I escaped by crawling out of bed.

"Stretchies," Lucy said, moving slower than usual.

"You gotta be kidding."

"I've got to, after what we did. If not, I'll tighten up like a bunch of banjo strings."

So, stretchies. Took her a while to get loose, but then she went into her octopus routine, sans handstands. Side-to-side and fore-and-aft splits. Laid on her stomach and touched the soles of both feet to the back of her head. Finally stood up and bent over backward and touched the top of her head to her butt. Watching her, I let out a sympathetic groan. By then I was able to touch my legs mid-shin, which was as loose as I was going to get.

Before we went out to find a restaurant, Lucy had to help me get dressed, which was embarrassing.

So, Great Gumshoe, tell me what you learned.

Do not, ever, slap Rufus again.

Got it.

CHAPTER TWENTY

WE USED FAKE IDs to rent cars for the trip to Arizona. Even using those IDs, we didn't want to travel by air. The cameras in airports these days must number in the thousands.

Ma got a standard white Chevy Impala at Avis, and I rented a dark blue Taurus at Budget. We stayed in Vegas the first day out and made it to Phoenix the following day. Lucy drove Ma's Chevy much of the time, probably so she and Ma could talk about me—okay, I know the world does not revolve around me, but I know those two gals. At times Ma rode with me. We went over what she was going to do in Phoenix, how she was going to approach the banks, and, of course, we talked about Lucy.

"I know you got the license, but if for any reason you don't marry that girl, I'll fire you then kill you," she said.

"Glad we got that cleared up."

We rolled into Phoenix at three forty p.m., the thirteenth of October, a Saturday. The temperature was a balmy ninety-six degrees, sun blazing.

"Nice," Lucy said when we pulled up at a Super 8 motel on East van Buren Street downtown and got out. The place was orange-pink stucco trying to look like adobe. Spanish tile roof, free parking, all the dry heat you could use.

Lucy and I got a room with a single king bed as Mr. and Mrs. Stephen Brewer, same name I'd used to rent the car. Ma got a room with two queen beds, one more than she needed. She registered using an ID I hadn't heard about, a bit more of Doc Saladin's magic. She got the room as Ann Goode, wanted to keep the Lara Donndin ID out of it except for use at the banks.

In the room, Lucy bounced on the bed, which I decided is what women do. My women, anyway.

"Why do you bounce on the beds?" I asked. "You did that at the Midnight Rider Motel too."

"Make sure they're strong enough," she said.

I gave her a look.

"Hey, I'm young and in love, and I've recovered from that workout Rufus gave us, so if you're not prepared you better tell me right now."

"I'm good."

"Okay, then." She gave the bed one more hearty bounce. "This thing is good to go."

* * *

The rest of Saturday and all day Sunday was spent doing basic recon work, checking out the locations of the various banks, and that one credit union that I didn't think we'd go after since it was Darren Sandolon's. Going after banks that had accounts in male names seemed iffy. Lara Rose had put money in those accounts in the past, but getting money back out might result in a different level of scrutiny. Also, it was unlikely that Lara could get into Darren's safe deposit box if he had one. I would hate to see Ma marched out of a bank in handcuffs. She agreed with that. First we would go after Lara's and Donna's accounts, see if we could get

Volker's hundred grand that way. The fewer places we hit, the better.

We traveled the interstate through Phoenix, all the major arteries near the banks, especially around Torrey Pines Bank and the Mutual of Omaha branch on Forty-Eighth Street.

Our plan: I would drive in circles around the block for ten minutes. If Ma wasn't out, Lucy would take over and circle for another ten. Then I would go again. We would go clockwise to stay close to the sidewalks. When Ma came out, she would walk around the block counterclockwise. When she saw one of us, we would stop and she would get in, fast, and off we'd go.

That was the plan for outside. Inside, it was all up to Ma. She would get a burner phone going and keep it going the entire time. She wouldn't talk to me, but it would be ready within two seconds if she needed me. I was hoping she wouldn't need a fast getaway, nothing resembling a '30s Bonnie and Clyde outing with bullets flying, sirens, roadblocks, the whole nine yards.

"No gun play, Ma," I told her.

"I'll try to keep it to a minimum."

* * *

Monday morning at ten, I dropped Ma off a block from Torrey Pines bank where Lara Rose had an account. I started to circle the block while Ma ambled back to the bank and . . . this is Ma's story. Let her tell it.

* * *

Yeah, I was nervous, but who was gonna seriously hassle a dingy forgetful old broad if they weren't real damn sure I wasn't who I said I was? I was ready to make a hell of a fuss if I needed to, get people thinking lawsuits if they gave me a hard time. I had a lawyer, Nathan Frasier, Esq., somewhere in Sun City who I didn't know from Adam, but they wouldn't know that. Bringing up a lawyer's name was last resort. I was counting on tolerance and sympathy to carry the day. It should help that my right hand was wrapped in an Ace bandage.

Mort drove me to the bank. I was worried he might throw up before we got there, the big wuss, all the "be carefuls" he hammered into me on the way. Last thing he said was, "If it goes bad, get out fast and run. They might think twice before tackling you on the sidewalk." Typical Mort comment. He let me off on a corner out of sight of the bank and started circling the block.

I walked back toward the bank carrying a quilted cotton purse the size of a Samsonite suitcase. It had knitting needles sticking out and two inches of knitting on one of the needles. I can knit and purl, but don't ask me to cable knit. With my hand wrapped in a bandage, any knitting I did was going to be slow and clumsy and bump up the sympathy level.

The Lara Rose wig made me gag when I looked in a mirror, but it fit well enough and looked natural. I wore an old dress and the running shoes I'd been using to walk around Reno the past month. Last thing I was gonna do was run, all this extra weight on me bouncing all over, but I could walk fast enough if it came to that. Anyway, old broads running attract attention.

I pushed into the bank like I owned the place, took a look around, located the safe deposit area, nothing unusual there—a low, imitation-walnut door, well-lit open vault beyond. Maybe I would get that far, maybe not, but I wanted to get a look in her safe deposit box before trying to unload an account.

I got in line for a teller, one person ahead of me, took the time to gaze mildly around, check the layout of the place, see the glassed-in cubicles where they kept the managers. It was quiet, just the usual subdued burble of banking conversation.

Finally, it was my turn. The teller was a girl about twenty-three, pretty, gave me a regulation teller smile, so I smiled back and said, "I need to get into my safe deposit box, hon, but I . . . well, I lost my key. Actually, I think I accidently threw it out. I looked all over for it, but it's gone, so I imagine I'll need to talk to a manager."

Her name was Ginny. Her smile never faltered. "I'll have to get Mr. Zimmerman to help you. If you want to have a seat in the waiting area, I'll send him over as soon as he's available."

"Of course, dear. Thank you so much."

This was good. A little wait would prove that I wasn't in a hurry, and it would add to the theater. I took a sofa that faced a coffee table loaded with magazines, hauled out my knitting, and went to work, not doing too well with the bandaged right hand. Grandma, knitting a sweater or little blankie for one of her wee darlings.

I stuck a faint smile on my face and knit two, purl one, knit two, purl one, and kept it up for about two minutes before a natty fellow in a gray suit and powder blue tie came up with the same pasted-on smile that Ginny had given me. He was in his thirties, which was perfect. I was old enough to be his mother.

"Hi, there," he said. "I'm Andy Zimmerman. I understand you have a little safe deposit problem, Mrs. . . . ."

"Donndin. Lara Rose, but I've always preferred Rose."

"Rose it is then. I was told you lost your key."

I gave him abject and embarrassed. "Oh, I'm so, so stupid. I didn't really *lose* it. I threw it out. It was the silliest thing. I must be getting senile."

"Oh, no, no . . . uh . . ."

He didn't know where to go with that senile comment. I had two choices: keep on with the story and be a dotty old dame he'd like to satisfy and get rid of, or let him ask questions, give him answers, and see how it went that way.

But I sensed that he had better things to do than deal with me, so I elected to go with dotty but nice, and mildly annoying. If I held him up, he'd want to get this moving right along. So, on with the story while I fussed with my knitting, wound up the yarn and stuffed it back in my purse. "I burned my hand. On the handle of a pot. I was heating soup and managed to dump it all into a kitchen drawer—you know, that drawer everyone has that holds all the junk you can't bring yourself to toss out, like old rubber bands and pens and such."

He murmured that he did know. Glanced surreptitiously at a clock on the wall. Good.

"It was just the biggest mess! A drawer *full* of hot soup, so I, well, I dumped it out, into the garbage. It was just old junk I didn't know what to do with anyway. That was about a month ago. This morning when I found I needed to get into my box here, I realized I must have thrown out the key with all the rest of it." I gave him a wretched look. "I feel so stupid. I know this is going to cause all kinds of trouble, but I really do need to—to get something out of that box." I put a little break in my voice and darn near squeezed out a tear.

"No, no, it's okay, Mrs. uh, Donndin . . . Rose. We can drill it out and get your box open."

I gave him a rueful half-smile. "Of course I'll pay whatever it costs. All of this is my fault, all my fault."

He was relieved about my willingness to pay but tried not to show it. He led me back to his cubicle. "These things happen, Rose. Every year we have to drill out a box or two."

"Oh, bless your heart. I'm getting to be such an old klutz." I held up the bandaged hand. "Like this. I fell getting out of bed. I think it's just a sprain. Grace, my neighbor, wrapped it for me. I'm getting to be so . . . so much *trouble* to everyone." I put a faint note of anguish into that.

"Really, Rose, this isn't any trouble. But it will take a little while. We'll have to get a locksmith in here to drill the box."

"Oh, I *am* trouble. This is terrible. I'm *so* sorry." I let out a heavy sigh.

"Don't give it another thought. I'll call that locksmith right away. But, first, I suppose I should see some sort of picture ID, like a driver's license or a passport."

"Yes, of course." I dug in the purse, came up with Lara's driver's license. "I've also got a Visa card with my picture on it if that would help."

"No need, Rose. This'll do just fine."

"I hate to be a bother, but I, I haven't eaten yet today. I saw a restaurant down the street. If you could tell me about how long it will take to open that box, I could go get a bite to eat, if that's all right." And get out of his hair, I didn't say, but I knew that would suit him just fine.

"Of course. You do that. We'll have the box open in about an hour, maybe a little less."

"Oh, bless you." An old embarrassed broad couldn't come up with too many bless yous.

"Do you know your box number, Rose?"

I knew the number but appeared to give it some thought. "Well, I'm not sure. Maybe two eighty-six? Or, one sixty-six?" I looked down at my shoes. "No, that can't be right. One sixty-six is my old address, when I used to live in Kansas City. My, that was years ago. Years! I lived on Jarboe Street, near the park."

"That's okay, Rose. We'll look it up."

"No, wait. I think it's—maybe it's two twenty-six. Or two thirty-six. One of those sounds right."

He put Rose's name into a computer and looked it up. He smiled. "It's that first one. Two twenty-six."

I gave him a relieved look and a smile. "I don't know how I ever remembered that."

"I'll call that locksmith, Rose. If you're back in an hour, I'm sure we'll be able to get you into that box."

"Oh, I would never fit," I said.

He gave me a startled look.

"Sorry, dear," I said. "I just couldn't resist. You look a lot like my oldest boy, Danny." I patted him on the shoulder, then slowly shuffled my way to the front door and out.

Mort and Lucy sat with me in a coffee shop. No one was within twenty feet of us. We had a view of the bank at an angle across the street. Fifteen minutes later, a locksmith's van pulled into a side street and around to the rear of the bank.

"That's a good sign," Lucy said.

"No cops," Mort said in a nervous whisper. "If we see a cop nosing around that bank, or more than one tight-assed guy in a cheap suit, you don't go back in."

"Relax," I told him. "We're almost there."

"Just remember this is bank robbery."

I put a hand on his arm. "If you need Pepto-Bismol, boyo, I saw a CVS pharmacy down the street."

"Ha, ha, Ma," he said.

I gave it the full hour then walked back to the bank. Andy was in his cubicle, but he saw me when I came in. He got up and hurried toward me.

"Got it," he said. "It's open."

"Oh, bless you."

"If you'll sign in, we'll get that box for you."

"Please tell me what it cost to get it open. I want to pay. It was my foolishness that caused all of this."

"Well, the usual charge for drilling a box is a hundred forty dollars, but in this case, I suppose we can get by with, say, fifty or sixty—"

"Oh, heavens no. I wouldn't dream of it. This was all my fault. If it costs a hundred forty, then that's what I'll pay." I gave him a look. "I do have quite a lot of money here, you know."

He did know. I could tell that he'd checked the account and probably been surprised to find that Rose had over a hundred eighty thousand dollars in savings. I might be a bit dotty, but I wasn't poor. "Even so," he said. "I—I'll let you know. For now, I'll turn you over to Miss Nichols, Amy, in the safe deposit area. I'll let her know you're here."

I went over, didn't have to wait ten seconds before Amy was there. "You're the one whose box we had drilled, ma'am?" she said, smiling.

"Yes. This has been so embarrassing."

"Don't be. I've never seen it done before. I had to be there to watch. Bank policy. It was actually kind of exciting."

It would be exciting. Amy was about twenty years old.

"Well, I'm glad some good came of it," I said. "So, I need to sign in now, don't I, dear?"

"Right here, if you would." She slid a card across the desk toward me, previous signatures covered by a blank sheet.

I took the pen she offered, held it in my bandaged hand, gave it an awkward flip that sent it skittering off the edge of the desk to the floor. I accidently bumped the cover sheet when she bent down to pick up the pen. That gave me a quick peek at the most recent signature. Esther signed it Lara Donndin, no Rose, no initial. Small, a bit cramped, no flourishes, tilted backward a little. After a two-second look I slid the blank sheet back over Lara's signature.

"I'm so sorry," I said. "I've gotten so clumsy lately."

"No worries," Amy said, sitting up again. She handed me the pen.

I produced a slow, awkward signature with the bandaged hand, small, no flourishes, tilted backward, then offered Amy a faint smile. "It's been one of those weeks," I said with a sigh.

Amy barely glanced at the signature. She didn't bat an eye, clearly didn't want to embarrass the old lady, which wouldn't be PC and was probably against bank rules in any case. She tucked the card back in a wooden file box, then stood up. "All set. If you'll come this way, ma'am."

She buzzed me through the waist-high door, and I followed her into the safe deposit vault. Number 226 was still in its slot, but it had had a bad day.

"Oh, my," I said when I saw it. "*I* did that?" A fine, dotty comment. I'd been at breakfast when the box was drilled so, no, I hadn't done it.

"It's okay. Do you want to pull it out, or shall I?"

"Would you mind? With this silly hand of mine . . ."

"Of course." She zipped it out and held it across her chest. "Would you like a private room?"

"I suppose I should. My feet are tired. I'd like to sit to go through it."

"No problem at all."

She showed me to a small room, set the box on a table, shut the door behind her as she went out.

I opened it.

Cash.

Bundles of bills held together by paper bands. The bands were plain white paper, obviously handmade, with the amount printed in ink in Esther's handwriting. I thumbed a bundle. All hundreds. The figure *10,000* was written on the paper, but I was only going to get one shot at this so I had to be sure. A quick count told me it really was ten thousand dollars. I pulled out all the bundles. Some were fifties. A few were twenties. No loose bills. I pressed on the stacks and checked their thickness against the stack I'd counted. All were the same, so it was likely that each contained a hundred bills.

I needed a quick total. This bank had rolled over for me. No telling what I would run into at the Mutual of Omaha branch if I had to go there, so I needed to know how close I'd gotten to a hundred grand. A hundred grand and quite a bit more, actually. We might be doing this pro bono for Volker, but I wasn't about to rob a bank just for the fun of it.

Six bundles of hundreds, six of fifties, three of twenties. In all, I'd gotten my hands on ninety-six thousand dollars.

That might be a reasonable amount to return to Volker. It would certainly ease his pain. But I'd shelled out eight grand to Doc for the IDs and this trip would cost another grand, easy, and none of that paid us for our time. So . . . raiding Lara Donndin's safe deposit box was bank robbery of one kind. Why not go for another?

The box also held papers and certificates, none of which interested me since there was nothing I could do with them. Lara did have three Royal Canadian Mint .9999 one-ounce gold bars tucked into the back of the box. They were pretty, but not quite four thousand dollars' worth, not enough to end this. I took one as a souvenir of my first and last bank robbery, left the rest, then exited the room with the cash and a gold bar tucked into my purse.

Soranden's name had been turned into five anagrams and those bogus names had been in his possession along with bank account numbers, in code. I took all of that to be sufficient proof that this money hadn't been obtained by legal means. We knew one rightful owner, Michael Volker, though the IRS would argue the point. The others, and there had to be others, had very likely disappeared into the mists of extortion. It was possible the FBI could locate them, but I didn't know how to do that without setting the IRS dogs on Volker, and Volker was the client. It would also set those same dogs on the former extortionees and it wasn't likely they would thank me if I blew the whistle on Soranden's scam and put them back in the IRS's sights, with the attendant back taxes, interest, and fines.

Amy was waiting for me at the safe deposit desk. I ambled over with the box held awkwardly under an arm, my purse slung over a shoulder. "What, uh, do you do with this? There are still things inside I need to keep safe."

"I asked Mr. Zimmerman about that. The box is okay. It's the lock they had to drill. We'll put the box in a new slot, assign you a new number, and give you the keys for it."

I gave her a relieved look. "Well, that doesn't sound too difficult."

Amy gave me box number 193. Lara's papers and the two gold bars got tucked away, and Amy handed me the keys. I had to sign a new card with the new number. All of this would come as an unpleasant surprise to Esther the next time she came down to open Lara Rose's box. I would like to be a fly on the wall when Lara discovered she no longer had box 226, and especially when she opened 193, if she got that far.

"Bless you," I said to Amy. "And you," I said to Andy. He had come over to ensure that the transition had gone smoothly. "I was so worried about this, but you made it all so easy. This is *such* a nice bank."

"Not a problem," Andy murmured.

"Now I need to withdraw a bit from savings," I said. "I'll just get back in line to see a teller about that."

"No need," Andy said. "Amy can help you right here at this end window."

As I'd hoped. Another "bless you" might be tiresome so I said, "Thank you. You've both been very kind."

At the window, Amy asked me for my passbook.

"Oh, my. I, I was so upset I didn't think to bring it. But you can look up my account on the computer, can't you?" I gave her my driver's license and got out a card with my account number on it. I also spelled *Donndin* for her because I was a fussy old woman, a bit scatterbrained but trying to be helpful. "I've been able to trace my ancestry back nine generations," I said proudly. "Donndin is Irish, you know."

She didn't know and neither did I, but she smiled and typed my name into the computer, came up with an amount that caused her eyes to widen ever so slightly.

"If I remember correctly," I said, giving her what would amount to another subtle form of identification, "I've got a little over a hundred eighty-six thousand in the account."

"That's right. One eighty-six, one twenty-two. And, uh, it says here I'm supposed to ask for a code word in order to make any withdrawals." She gave me an expectant look.

This was the iffiest part of this deal, but Ronald and Esther were brother and sister and would use the same code word, most likely their mother's maiden name. If not, I might have to fake a fainting spell or heart attack.

"Connor," I said. "Last two letters are O-R, not E-R."

Amy smiled. "Okay, now what can I get you?"

I blessed that genealogy website, then said, "I need three cashier's checks, each of them for eight thousand, if that's okay. Made out to me. And if I could get a fourth one for a hundred forty dollars made out to the bank here to pay for the box you had to break into."

"No problem. I have to get Mr. Zimmerman's signature for those larger amounts. I'll just be a minute." She locked her cash drawer, then went off to Andy's cubicle.

Good. Andy would be helpful, wanting to keep me happy, but also to get me on my way.

Which is what happened. Amy came back, whipped out the three cashier's checks for Lara Rose Donndin, one to the bank, and ten minutes later I was on my way, with a little finger wave to Andy who was at his desk with a customer. He gave me a nod and a smile, and I was out the door.

Walking counterclockwise around the block, I pulled out the burner phone and said, "I'm out, boyo, where are you?"

"Lucy's got this rotation. Keep walking. She'll be along in less than a minute."

Lucy rounded the corner, headed my way. She stopped the Impala in the middle of the street and I hopped in. Didn't take six seconds and no one was behind her at the time, so as bank robberies go, it was letter perfect. I felt I'd earned that gold bar. And a gin and tonic, but that would have to wait.

"Anyone coming after you?" Lucy asked.

"Nope. We can head back home right away." Mort was still on the phone. "We're out," I told him. "We'll see you where we said we would. You can end the call now."

"Gotcha, Ma."

Forty-five minutes later, we were out of Phoenix at a café in a town called Buckeye, ordering food, and the keys to the new safe deposit box were in a ditch at the side of a two-lane road, twenty-some miles from Torrey Pines Bank.

"How'd you do, Ma?" Mort whispered even though no one was within twenty feet of us.

"Hornswoggled 'em," I said.

CHAPTER TWENTY-ONE

I GAVE HER a look. "Hornswoggled, Ma?"

"You need to pick up on the lingo," Lucy told me. "I have a grandfather who said that a lot when he was talking politics with either one of my uncles. He got it from *his* grandfather."

"Doesn't sound PI noir, though. It sounds rocking chair. I doubt Hammer or Spade ever used it." I turned to Ma. "How did you do in *dollars,* which is what we were after."

"Got a total of a hundred twenty grand. And this." She slid a gold bar to me across the table. "I'm keepin' it as a souvenir."

"Groovy," I said, beating Lucy to her favorite word. I slid the bar back to Ma. She was a brick. Count on her to rob a bank of a hundred twenty thousand dollars and a gold bar and make it look easy. It was unlikely that Esther would report the theft. Folks don't generally report their stolen money when it's stolen. Only a guess on my part.

From Buckeye we caravanned west on I-10 to Blythe, then north on U.S. 95 to Vegas where we stayed the night at the Bellagio. We got two rooms, no suites. Lucy was cooling it with roulette and her luck, nor did we need the money.

We got back to Reno the next day at four twenty p.m., returned the cars to their respective agencies. Ma took a taxi downtown to

Harrah's Casino, then another one to the house she shared with two women about her age. Lucy and I took a cab to the Golden Goose and walked home from there.

"It's official," Lucy said when we were inside, up in the bedroom.

"What's official?"

"We're bank robbers."

"Technically, we're only getaway drivers, doll. Wheelmen, to be precise. Ma's the moll in this family."

Lucy wrapped me up in a hot kiss, then said, "Doll and moll. How nineteen thirties. How 'bout we get frisky?"

"We could do that."

She arched an eyebrow. "Could?"

"I misspoke. Here, allow me to help you outta that shirt. It needs washing anyway. Not wearing a bra, are you? I wouldn't want to embarrass you when I whip this off you, kiddo."

"A bra? Like do I ever?"

She almost never did, and she wasn't then, and she wasn't embarrassed when the shirt got whipped off and flung across the room where it landed on a bedside lamp.

* * *

My heart rate was still above a hundred and Lucy was flat on her back, eyes closed, when my cell phone rang.

"You should get that," she breathed.

"It's way over there on the nightstand, sweetheart."

"Which is on your side of the bed and only three feet from you."

"Closer to four. I tried, but my arm fell short. I know what you're gonna say about that, but you're wrong."

"So now what?" she asked.

"Dunno. If I could actually get to the phone I might call 911 to get someone over here with a crash cart and maybe one of those epinephrine injections like you see on TV."

"It *was* kinda aerobic this time, wasn't it?"

"Yes it was. You look slender and very feminine and even break-able with hard use, but that's only an illu—"

"You gonna get that phone, Mort?"

I rolled to my right, managed to get the phone on its fourth and final ring, right before it went to voice mail. "Yo," I said.

"Huh. You out jogging again, Mort?"

"Hell of a guess, Ma."

"Luce with you?"

"Right here, yup."

"You two eaten yet?"

"We don't eat on the run. We sit down to eat like proper folks."

"Well, how 'bout we meet at the Goose, grab a bite, then go powwow in the Green Room? Say, in an hour?"

"Powwow, Ma? Like we did last year?"

"Got to figure out where to go from here. Mostly how to deal with a client and bits of paper."

"We'll be there." I hung up.

Lucy propped her head on an elbow. "Powwow?"

"It's Ma's word. At the Goose. Now if you'll get out of bed and haul me out, help me get on my feet, maybe even dress me like you did a few days ago, we might make it. If not, then Ma's gonna be pissed, and I'll tell her it's all your fault."

* * *

Of course, "bits of paper" was ninety-six thousand dollars in cash and three cashier's checks, currently stashed in a gun safe with ballistic cladding. It did present a problem. Ma solved part of it right away while we were at a table in the Green Room, not lined up at the bar. O'Roarke didn't need to hear any of this since it would make him an unpaid accomplice.

Speaking of accomplices, a new girl was tending bar with O'Roarke. Traci Ellis. He was teaching her the ropes. She was twenty-five, slender, very pretty, very blond, and she gave me a big smile with perfect teeth. This can't be good, I thought. Ever since I became a PI, girls had been flocking to me like pigeons to a statue. But I already had a one-in-a-million girl, and she had a marriage license that was burning a hole in her pocket. In spite of that, I felt Traci nudging up against that nameless PI essence that pulled in hot babes like iron filings to a magnet. If she was going to stick around and be part of the Green Room's ambience—like O'Roarke only better—she and Lucy might end up having a little chat. And Lucy, Ma, and I would have to find out if Traci could be trusted with conversational snippets that tended toward the pseudo-legal. If not, we wouldn't be sitting at the bar as often as we had in the past. Again, not good. Traci would, of course, enhance the ambience in ways O'Roarke never had, but I hoped her being there didn't mean he was going to leave. I would have to ask him what the story was.

Nine fifteen p.m. Lucy in a short black skirt and a skintight tank top molded to her as if painted on—some sort of filmy emerald green material. Me in gray slacks and an off-white Guayabera shirt. Ma in black pants and a no-nonsense brown shirt. We'd eaten at Lucero's, an Italian restaurant at the Goose. Time for a nightcap. Pete's for me, a Virgin Mary for Lucy, double G and T for Ma.

"I'm takin' twenty grand off the top," Ma said. "In cash. Expenses and PI work. I'm not runnin' a charity here. Cashier's checks are made out to Lara Donndin, so I'm not through with that ID yet. Got to get that money to Volker somehow."

"Open a joint account in Lara's and Volker's names," Lucy said. "The checks are in Lara's name so she endorses them and Volker deposits them, alone, days or weeks apart to keep it from the IRS. That way you're out of it, not even on a surveillance camera at the time the money is deposited. Lara vanishes into thin air forever, and it's all on Volker. And Lara should be in a good disguise the day the account is opened."

Ma turned to me. "If you don't let this absolutely lovely, intelligent creature make an honest man out of you—the sooner the better—you're fired."

"The pressure's on," I said.

Lucy took my hand. "No, it's not. It's if and when you say, not before."

"Which only reinforces my opinion," Ma said. "You let her get away, you're a moron. And unemployed."

"No argument there, Ma."

Lucy squeezed my hand. "*Que sera sera*. Okay, back to it." She looked at Ma. "What bank would you use?"

Ma thought about that for a minute. Finally, she said, "Big anonymous bank right here in Reno. Like you said, Volker will have to feed the money in one check at a time, spaced a week or more apart. In fact, I'll force him to do that by giving him the checks one at a time. If he's not happy with that arrangement, we'll use him to chum sharks off the coast."

"Shark chum," I said. "Nice."

Ma zippoed a Camel, blew a cloud of smoke away from me and Lucy. "It'll take Volker a while to pack a hundred grand away. But I think we'll hold off on giving him the money for a while. I'm still not a hundred percent about him yet."

"Cryptic," I said.

Ma took another hit of carcinogens. "The thing is, boyo, *some-one* killed Soranden. Volker might be just what he appears to be. And Marta, who I haven't met, so I'm going on what you and Lucy have told me about her. Nice lady in a wheelchair. But Volker and Soranden's sister both went to Arizona. That might not have been a coincidence, but maybe it was. Arizona's a big state. It borders Nevada. For tourist attractions it's got the Grand Canyon and giant freaking ants. People go there, coincidence or not. But I don't want to hand over a hundred grand to Volker if he's not legit, so I'd like to be sure."

"How do we do that?"

"Only thing I can think of. Follow him a while longer, see what he does. See if anything looks fishy. We made enough on this deal to give it another few days."

"My butt's already tired, thinking about sitting in front of Volker's house eight or ten or twelve more hours."

Ma blew another toxic cloud. "I've got sort of a view of your butt in my office. Odds are it'll handle it."

Lucy snickered.

"Whose side are you on here, Cupcake?" I asked her.

"The side of the angels. Always."

"The side of the angels, right."

"Which is what Disraeli said about Darwin's theory, but the expression is in wider usage now."

I stared at her. She smiled at me. Ma chuckled.

The thought of staking out Volker's house had little appeal. It wasn't a good neighborhood for it. Too rich. Would Russ fix things for me if I was rousted by another cop?

I said, "Can we do anything to get Volker to tip his hand—if there's anything to tip? Last year we got Julia and Leland Bye to run around when Jeri hit Bye between the eyes with a two-by-four—figuratively speaking on that lumber reference."

We gave that some thought—after I told Lucy how Jeri had gone into Leland Bye's office and rattled his cage. She'd gone in unannounced and asked him if he knew that his dead sister was the registered owner of a certain Mercedes SUV. She didn't tell him the SUV was being used in a murder-enhanced blackmail scheme, but he knew that since he was in on it. Just the mention of that SUV lit a red-hot fire under Julia and Leland. It also got Leland killed, but that's another story.

Finally, I said, "Maybe Volker didn't kill Soranden, but he might have an idea who did, or he might have hired someone to do it. Probably not, since hits are expensive. He had a motive though, even if killing The Toad wouldn't get his money back. Lots of possibilities, so giving him a jolt might be a good idea, see if anything falls out of that tree."

So we thought about that.

Lucy said, "If he *did* kill Soranden, then he did that thing with the skull, which means he'd probably be touchy if anyone mentioned Arizona and ants. Or if anyone made any slight hint that he might've dropped a skull in a car."

"That Arizona thing might be enough," Ma said. "It seems out of character for him to have put that skull in your car—or Mort's car, if he thought it was Mort's. Why would he do that?"

"To confuse the Soranden investigation?" I offered. "Don't forget, I'm a nationally recognized figure—like Bing Crosby back in the day. I would've been on Volker's radar for sure."

Ma snorted. "Bing, right. But the investigation was stalled. The FBI wasn't getting anywhere. All Soranden's skull did, showing up like that, was give the FBI a boost, get them running around again. If Volker had anything to do with Soranden's murder, he had nothing to gain by that, so I don't see him putting that skull in Lucy's car."

So we thought about that. And Bing.

I raised my index finger. Traci came bouncing over and I ordered a sarsaparilla to get her on board with my favorite nonalcoholic beverage. Bounced over. My, my. She might've been hoping for a bigger tip. Ma got another double G and T. Lucy was good with her weak Mary.

We continued to think.

Traci arrived, gave Ma her double then set the sarsaparilla in front of me. "One sarsaparilla for Magnum P.I."

Lucy bumped my shoulder. "Magnum. How'd she know?"

"*P.I.*," I said to her. "You left that part out, kiddo."

Traci smiled and left.

Lucy said, "Okay, then. Arizona. What if someone whose voice Volker doesn't know calls him up and says, 'Harvester ants are found in Arizona.' Just that, nothing else. If it didn't mean anything to him, he probably wouldn't do anything. But if it did, who knows what he might do?"

"That's a thought," Ma said.

We sat there a while, thinking.

Finally, Ma said, "Lucy's idea sounds as good as any. We give Volker a shove, see what happens."

"Who's gonna give him that shove?" I asked.

"Not me," Lucy said. "He's heard my voice. A lot. Not you or Ma, either."

We thought about that, then I said, "We'll get Russ to do it. That'll make his day."

Lucy smiled. "I want to listen in when you tell him."

* * *

Of course, Russ was thrilled with the idea. Not that he knew what the idea was when he hustled over to the Green Room to get briefed on the project. I gave him the bulk of the briefing since he was in my pocket and we were pals. And I bought him a beer, his usual, Bud Heavy, to loosen him up and make him pliable.

"What the fuck for?" he said. "I'm supposed to phone some guy and say, 'Harvester ants are found in Arizona'? What's *that* all about?"

Neither loose nor pliable.

"Drink up," I said.

"Again, I ask, what the fuck for?"

"Tryin' to surprise some guy," I said.

"The FBI determined it was harvester ants that cleaned out Soranden's skull."

"Huh." I gave him bland. "I didn't know that."

"Like hell you didn't. Suddenly we're up to our necks in harvester ants? What the fuck, Mort."

"Language," Lucy said.

Russ looked contrite. "Sorry."

"Kidding," she said. "You can say 'fuck' if I can. I just don't use it as often or in the same context."

Russ smiled. Or grimaced. Hard to tell with Russ, but I think Lucy put him off his game. It might've been the outfit she was wearing since it had those no-bra bumps. He turned to me. "Who is this guy you want to surprise?"

"It's a surprise," I said.

Russ shook his head. "Jesus. Gimme your phone. I'll do it just so I can get the hell outta here."

"Not right now, Russ. We've got to get set up. It has to be timed just right."

"We? Who's we? Get set up how?"

"You really want to know?"

Give the guy credit; he gave that some thought then finally said, "No. Don't tell me."

"Better that way," Ma said. "Gives you deniability like they do in Washington. Keeping people out of certain loops is called professional courtesy."

"Jesus. Okay, when?"

"I'll let you know," I told him. "Soon, though. Most likely tomorrow sometime. You should buy a burner phone and give me the number so I can let you know when to call. Pick one up at Walmart on the way home tonight so you can get it charged up. I'll reimburse you since RPD pay isn't enough for both that and a mortgage. You can use the burner to call this guy. In fact, it might not hurt to keep it on you 'til the minutes run out in case I need more police work done on the sly."

"Sonofabitch. This is police work?"

"You're police, it's work, so, yup, kinda. We could call it that if the FBI ever gets wind of it. Hope not, though. I wouldn't show 'em your burner and, you know, brag about it."

"*Son*ofabitch."

CHAPTER TWENTY-TWO

RUSS DRAINED HIS Heavy and left. We stayed.

Bartender-in-training Traci Ellis stopped by our table and asked if we wanted anything right then, said she was about to go on break. We were good. When she left, I strolled over to the bar and asked O'Roarke what was up with the new girl, not that I minded a new face in the place since, I told him, his mug with its red Yosemite Sam moustache and squinty eyes wasn't a tenth as photogenic.

"Ella's leaving," he said, ignoring the editorializing.

Ella Glover. She'd been there almost three years.

"Sorry to hear it," I said.

"Don't be. She's getting married to a guy who just got out of law school and passed the bar."

"Sorry to hear it—that part about law school. She deserves better."

"You should tell her that, see what she does to you. When were you last in intensive care?"

"I might pass on that. What's the story with this new girl, Traci?"

"Story?"

"Ah, circumlocution. Means there *is* a story."

He sighed. "Hands off, Spitfire."

"Got my hands full already, so no problem. But if I didn't have my hands full . . ."

"It would still be hands off. Traci is my niece. My sister's kid."

"Nepotism, cool. Does she call you Uncle Patrick? But a *niece*? Then why would it be hands off? I'm a nice guy."

"Nice being an indefinite relative term. Thing is, you're a dangerous guy to be around. You find bodies and people try to kill you and people around you. And she's only twenty-five and you're a crusty old fart with scars and bullet wounds."

"Got me there." I grabbed some peanuts from a bowl on the bar and tossed them in my mouth. "Though a lot of women find the scars sexy, and the bullet wounds have healed."

"That's because they really are the weaker sex."

"You've got a death wish. Didn't know that about you." I grabbed a few more peanuts. "Sometimes Lucy, Ma, and I come in to discuss things. How would Traci be if she caught snippets of iffy conversation?"

"Iffy? That what you call them?"

"Sounds better than conspiratorial."

"Dunno. You could fill her in on whatever you're cooking up with that detective, Fairchild, see how that goes."

"You think I'm cooking up something with Fairchild?"

"You, Lucy, Maude. He comes in, the four of you put your heads together, he leaves looking like he swallowed a roach."

"What kind of a roach? A bug or a doobie?"

He didn't get a chance to elucidate because Traci returned and grinned at me. "How're you doin', Sarsaparilla?"

"Jest fine, little lady."

"Uncle Pat says he got food services to order an entire case of sarsaparilla just for you."

I smiled at O'Roarke. "Okay if I call you Uncle Pat too?"

"Depends on how attached you are to those incisors."

"Touchy."

Traci laughed. Then she put a hand on my arm. She must have had it in a microwave because it sizzled. "I'll be here Monday and Tuesday evenings after this training, which I don't need. And I'll be on the ten to six-thirty shift during the day, Wednesday to Friday."

I lifted an eyebrow at Uncle Pat.

He said, "Lucy's watching. If you're contemplating suicide, you could juggle chainsaws. Or just pour gasoline on yourself and light up a Havana, but not in here."

I knocked twice on the bar and went back to Lucy and Ma.

"What's *her* story?" Lucy asked.

"She's Patrick's niece."

"That's like a backstory. What's the *real* story?"

"Real story is she's replacing Ella, and even if she's a hot kid—I only say that because I notice things like that even when they're irrelevant—she doesn't hold a candle to you, and you're the one with the marriage license, so you two can be friends if you want since that's in your easygoing, non-jealous nature."

"Then we could talk about you. Cool."

"There's that, sure. But I'd want transcripts."

Lucy gave me a big wet kiss that tasted of Virgin Mary, the drink, not the other one, which I wouldn't recognize anyway, and said, "Okay, Cowboy. Sorry I sparked off like that."

"You might spark off later tonight, Sugar Plum."

"We should leave now."

* * *

Here's how we set it up:

Wednesday. Lucy and I were in her Mustang half a block west of the office of Joss & Volker. We had an angle where we could see Volker's BMW in a parking lot. I wanted to get eyes on him here. His neighborhood felt too exposed. Ma was waiting in her fifty-six-year-old Cadillac at the corner of Kietzke Lane. Fifty-six. She was in the first grade when it rolled off the line in Detroit. I pointed that out to her last year and she'd given me a trucker's response that ended with "boyo." Volker came out at 5:25 p.m. and got into his car.

"He's out, Ma," I said into a burner phone.

She burnered back, "Gotcha."

Four words total. Heady stuff if the NSA was listening in. Black helicopters could arrive at any minute.

Volker rolled out of the lot and headed east, away from us and toward Ma. I let her know, then followed him.

"Call Volker now or when he gets home?" Lucy asked.

"Home," I said. "If the call makes him go somewhere other than wherever he's going now, we would never know. If he gets home and then leaves right after Russ shakes his tree, we might glom onto something interesting."

"Glom. Cool."

I'd told Russ to stand by, keep his new burner handy. We waited until we were sure Volker was headed home, then Lucy called Russ. "Soon, sweetie. I'll let you know." She ended the call.

My head whipped around. "Sweetie? Since when?"

"He likes it. And, hey look, Volker is turning right."

"Ma's on him. What's with that 'Sweetie' thing?"

"I think it puts him back in high school. Girl like me calls him Sweetie, he's all over it. You think guys in their forties have grown up, but they haven't."

"I'm in my forties, kiddo."

"Wow, do I ever rest my case."

Okay, no argument. I remembered the new bartender, Traci, her hand sizzling on my arm. Grow up? How? What for? What's the upside?

Ma fell back and Lucy and I took over, keeping a hundred yards or more back. Finally, Volker made it home. He pulled into his driveway next to the beater Honda, hit the remote, raised the garage door, and drove in. The garage door rolled down.

Lucy got Russ on the burner. "Phone him in two minutes. You know what to say." She ended the call.

Three minutes later, Russ called back. "Done. And I wish I knew why I did that."

"No you don't," Lucy said, then hung up.

We waited. To save time, if it became necessary, I had Ma active on a different burner system. I could see her Caddy at a curb a hundred fifty yards north of us. No chatter on our burners. We let our phones chew up a few silent minutes.

One minute.

Three. Five. Eight.

Nothing.

Then Kimmi came out, got into her junker Honda, backed out and took off, fast.

"Follow her?" Lucy asked.

Tough call. But Ma was still on Volker and Kimmi was in a hurry, so why not see what the brat was up to? If anything. It might be a true emergency; she might've run out of meth. Okay, now I *know* I'll have to talk fast at the Pearly Gates.

We gave Ma a heads-up, then split. Lucy and I stayed well back, keeping Kimmi in sight. We went north on surface streets, which made it harder due to traffic lights. I had to move up on her so she couldn't leave me at a red light.

Which she did anyway as she blew through a yellow light. Perfect timing.

"Well, poop," Lucy said as Kimmi's car dwindled off in the distance. "Now what?"

Quick decision. We were on Virginia Street. Lots of lights that might slow Kimmi down. I thought I knew where she was going, so I went left on Plumb Lane and raced up to Arlington. Arlington was free of traffic lights as far as California Avenue. I went through that light on green, crossed the river to First Street, turned right, east on First, and there was Kimmi's Honda, coming in our direction. We'd beaten her there by no more than ten seconds.

"Wow," Lucy said. "You rock."

"Me boulder."

She whipped a smile on me, then said, "Hey, look, there's a place at the curb."

I just made it. Parked before Kimmi found a place around the corner on Ralston. She returned a minute later and went in the front door of the Truckee River Apartments.

"Room 307," I said.

"Interesting," Lucy said. "You know this how?"

"Did I not mention that Mira is occasionally in 304? Thought I did."

"Yeah, I guess. But you left out Kimmi's place."

"I doubt it's hers since she lives with Daddy. It's probably Dooley's. And the number wasn't important until now. Also, his name might not be Dooley. It might be George Orwell."

"Who, sadly, is deceased. Why might this guy be Georgie, and how'd he end up here?"

I told her about the name on the mailbox.

Lucy said, "Maybe he's into English Lit."

"Which is even less likely than Orwell still living there. Or maybe George used to live there when he was writing *1984*, and no one's gotten around to changing the name yet because people are always busy as little bees, no time for minor tasks."

"You're so logical. Now what?"

Good question. We were back in hazardous territory. Not good. Dooley or Ramon could be around, though I'd never seen Ramon in or around the place, didn't know if he lived there or in a penthouse somewhere paid for with drug money. It had been almost two weeks since I'd knocked him out in Wildcat the night Ma was there. Two weeks. It was likely he was up and around again, though his right arm wouldn't be good in a knife fight for another year or so, if that. If ever, I hoped.

And Mira could be in the building. I still didn't have much of a handle on her.

But we couldn't see anything sitting out there in the car so this gumshoe thing was stalled on the tracks.

"Sit tight," I told Lucy. I got the driver's door open an inch before she said, "Why? Where're you going?"

"Gonna have a look or a listen at 307."

"Without me? No way."

"Way." I used teen-speak since she looked eighteen. I gave her a hard look then got out of the car.

She opened her door, popped out, and glared at me over the roof of the car.

I returned the glare. "Back inside, kiddo."

"See," she said, "that's where you're wrong, because you and I are in this together and I'm not about to let you go into that building and traipse around by yourself."

"See," I said. "That's where *you're* wrong, because you are *not* going into that building and I *am* going to traipse around in that building by myself, so get back in the car."

"Time's wasting, Cowboy. Kimmi could read Tolstoy's *War and Peace* and write a term paper by the time you get me back in this car if you try to set one foot inside that place without me."

"Kimmi couldn't read the first chapter of *War and Peace* in six years on a desert island. And a term paper? *Hah.*"

Lucy just glared at me.

Well, shit. We'd come this far. I wanted to know if it was just coincidence that Kimmi had taken off minutes after Russ's cryptic call to Volker. So, one more try.

"How about I tie you up, Sugar Plum?"

"Don't you 'Sugar Plum' me, bozo."

Bozo? This had gotten serious.

So, disguises. We didn't have much, but we'd tossed wigs in the back seat before leaving to stake out Volker's office. Mine was over-the-ears and gray. Hers was shoulder-length, curly, and blond. And we had guns in the trunk.

"Wig up, girl," I said. "And arm up."

"Groovy. We're going in? Check out Orwell? Maybe hear an old typewriter clacking away?"

"If I had rope to tie you up, no. But I don't, so yeah, we'll go in. Armed to the teeth. Put your gun in your purse. Keep it ready. And that's last, last, last resort—but if we happen to run into Ramon . . ."

"Blast away, since we'll be armed to the teeth."

I gave her an IRS stare.

"Kidding," she said. "Unless he pulls out a shotgun."

Wigged and armed, we crossed the street. Rufus's voice whispered in my ear that this wasn't the all-time smartest move I'd ever made as a private eye. But it wasn't the worst, either. I'd done a lot of really dumb things since I left the IRS. Worst move was when I climbed moose-like through a window with Jeri into an old mansion on Virginia Street around midnight and ended up in a cold basement with two psycho women hell-bent on killing us.

The front door was locked. Glass. I cupped my hands to cut the glare and looked inside.

Empty lobby, no one in sight. "Maybe we'll cancel this," I said.

"Excuse me," came a voice from behind me. A young girl, no more than fifteen, eased past me, trying not to touch the old guy who probably had cooties, and opened the door with a key.

Fifteen's a good age. Old enough to have a key, not enough life experience to have much of a clue or to challenge an adult. I caught the door before it shut, and Lucy and I were in. The girl glanced at a mailbox as she went by, then trotted up the stairs.

We waited a minute, checked out Orwell's mailbox, didn't see royalty checks piling up through the narrow viewing slot, then we hiked up the stairwell to the third floor.

"Ever read *Animal Farm*?" Lucy asked.

"Hush."

I peeked through the window in the fire door. No one in the hallway, so we went in, walked cautiously down to room 307. I listened at the door. No television murmur. No voices. Nothing. Lucy shrugged her lips and shook her head at me.

Now what?

Knock on the door? What for? What would I say? "Howdy there, kiddo. We were just in the neighborhood"? Not an option. In fact, I didn't see much of anything we could do. So, stymied.

But in fact, I'd been stymied from the time Kimmi had gone into the apartments. I'd hoped to hear voices, and even then, I didn't know what I would do. This gumshoe shtick wasn't always what it was cracked up to be.

At the end of the hallway, I heard Spade chuckle. Yeah, right. As if he could do better.

Six ten p.m. Here we were in the hallway, looking lost, or like we were casing the joint. People who got off work at six would be arriving soon. Those who actually had jobs.

Lucy tilted her head, gave me a "now what" look.

I wondered if Mira was around. If so, maybe we could hide out at her place and keep tabs on 307 for a while.

I backtracked to 304, rapped quietly on the door as Lucy stood off to one side. The peephole went dark. Seconds later the door opened wide and there was Robin, all four foot ten of her, barefoot, topless, nipples the size of Binkies—which made sense considering their function. All she had on was a scarlet thong the size of a MasterCard.

"Oops," I said. "Didn't mean to interrupt anything."

"Hey, you." She smiled like we were old buds. "I don't like to wear a bunch of clothing when I'm here alone."

"And you whip the door open for strangers, too."

"Which you're not. We've already met." She stood hipshot, one hand on the door frame, inviting, an attitude that suggested we were buds with benefits and that she'd been expecting me. "Wow, you're still really big," she said. "C'mon in."

She hadn't seen Lucy, out of sight to my left. By the look on Robin's face when Lucy appeared and stood beside me, Lucy was that three's-a-crowd, fifth wheel you hear so much about when people go around mixing metaphors.

"Who the hell are you?" Robin said.

"Mata Hari," Lucy replied.

"That's a weird name, and you need to leave. Right now."

"Bye," I said.

"Not *you*." Robin grabbed my wrist, then shot a daggered look at Lucy. "You."

"More giant tits," Lucy said to me. "Naked, too. Isn't that special?"

"I told you, Sugar Plum, this particular career attracts them like nobody's business. I've got no control over it."

Robin's gaze bounced between us. "What career?"

"How about you deal with it?" Lucy said. "I would just say the wrong thing. Well, things—plural. I'll be outside." She took a step into the hallway and pulled the door shut behind her.

Robin stared at the door. "Sugar Plum? Where'd you get that? She's like boiled turnips." She still had a grip on my wrist. Then she smiled at me. "You came back. Cool." Another glance at the door. "What'd you bring *her* for? Like for a three-way? I guess I might go for that."

I got control of my wrist again. I would have to tell Lucy about that turnips comment. Boiled, too. She would like that. I might mention the three-way, too, see how that went over. "Mira been around lately?" I asked.

"Mira?" Robin made a face. "Don't tell me you like 'em skinny as a rail?" She shot another look at the door. "Like her. All bones and gristly."

I would have to tell Lucy about that, too. I'd never noticed that she was like gristly boiled turnips.

"Well, gotta run," I said. I got the door open a few inches, then said, "It's been nice. Seeing you, I mean."

I had to say it, couldn't help it.

I got out of there. Lucy was in the hallway, grinning, trying to smother a laugh.

"Ohmigod," she breathed. "Been nice *seein'* you?"

"Guffaw later. Now's not a good time."

Another giggle, then: "You weren't in there very long. Did your eyes fill up that fast?"

"We'll talk outside."

"Okay, then. *Now* what?"

The fire door at the end of the hallway opened, and in came Dooley. Still six-one. Still a hundred fifty-five pounds. Still had long greasy hair, looking like he'd been paroled a few days ago.

I spun Lucy around and we headed for the fire door at the other end of the hallway at a fast walk.

"Hey, you," Dooley called out. "You two."

We kept going.

Footsteps behind us, coming at a medium jog. Shit. Might have to pull a gun here.

I turned around. "Yeah? What can I do for you?"

"Haven't seen you around here before, dude. Or you." He tried to look behind me at Lucy. "You lookin' for someone?"

He didn't recognize me. I hoped. Only time he might have seen me was in Wildcat the first night I was there. I'd worn a blond wig then, glasses with black rims. No glasses now, and the wig was gray. I'd tried to stay behind him that night, didn't think he'd noticed me since he was intent on buying drugs to further enhance a towering intellect. But here he was, hassling me and Lucy, so what did I know?

"I don't see a badge," I said. "You *are* the hall monitor, aren't you? I thought that went out in the fifties."

He stared at me. "Huh?" Then: "Who're you, man?"

"Lord Greystoke."

"Me Mata Hari," Lucy said, syntax jumping all over that Greystoke-Tarzan reference. What a girl. "What's yours?" she asked.

He stared at her, surprised me when he said, "Mike."

"Mike *Hammer*?" I said. "Wow. It's nice to meet you after all this time. I saw Spade a couple of weeks ago, but it looked as if he was tailing someone, couldn't stop to chat."

"Hammer? Spade? Who're they?"

Lucy giggled. I pushed her farther behind me, then pointed at Dooley's ears. "Hey, nice gauges, Mike."

That threw him. Probably the first time anyone told him his gauged ears were nice. He could've taken out the black onyx rings and stuck a banana through the holes in his earlobes, kept them there for lunch. Sarcasm was probably lost on this guy, but worth a try, so I added, "Makes you look quite dashing."

"Dashing?" he said. "What the fuck? Like running?"

I smiled. "A person whose literary ability is challenged by *Incredible Hulk* comics might think so. Hundred-yard dash and all that. So what's your mom think about your gauges?"

His eyes narrowed. "What the fuck's it to you, dude?"

"Limited vocab," Lucy said. "You're not getting through." I put a hand behind my back and waved her off.

"Not a thing," I said. "Holes in your lobes you could drive a Harley through give you an enchanting look." A faint snicker came from behind me. "But I think gauging is the kind of self-mutilation fad that will run its course and die, like that Middle-Ages thing where you pluck out your own eyes if you happen to see something disagreeable. Which, if you think about it, was pretty cool and really got the point across. Darwin might explain it like this: What will you do when your gauges give would-be employers the impression you have the intelligence of a bucket of sand crabs?" As if they didn't now.

He looked like he wanted to jump me. Maybe I was going to get more use out of my judo lessons. But Rufus had warned me that you can't tell how dangerous a person is by the way they look. Skinny whipcord guy might come at me like a chainsaw so it was time to leave to keep Lucy from shooting him. I knew she would have her hand on that gun in her purse.

"Anyway, we've gotta run, but it was nice meeting you." I stuck out my hand.

That took him by surprise. He stared at my hand.

I shrugged. "Men shake hands. Of course, if you'd rather curtsy, go ahead. I won't tell."

"Hey, *screw* you, dude."

"If you're not up to it, that's okay. I understand." I kept my hand out, kept my eyes locked on his.

He went for it. Took my hand and gave it his all. Which, I have to say, wasn't much.

So it was testosterone time. I gave his hand a four-second Borroloola squeeze. I'd lifted a sixteen-pound iron bar up three feet about half a million times down under in Australia between November and March last year. I hadn't let my grip get weaker since then. Four seconds is a long time. Dooley's hand folded up like an aluminum can. His face went white and a little squeal of pain chirped out of his throat. His eyes rolled up in his head and he sank almost to his knees.

"Oops," I said. "Sorry 'bout that. Got a little carried away."

I pushed Lucy toward the end of the hallway as I backed away from Dooley. Lucy and I went through the fire door and down the stairs, quickly. I made a lot of noise as we went.

At the second-floor landing I held her up, listened for a moment, then motioned for us to go back up, quietly. I peered through the window in the third-floor fire door. Dooley was just opening the door to room 307. He went in and was gone.

"Stay back," I said to Lucy. I opened the fire door and went soundlessly down the hallway. Lucy, of course, was right behind me. What a great assistant.

I listened at the door to 307, heard voices, couldn't make out any words. Lucy looked at me, shook her head.

Well, shit. Gumshoes-in-training strike out.

We listened another half minute, then gave up, went back down the stairs.

"I take it that was Dooley?" Lucy said as we reached the second-floor landing and started down to the ground floor. First chance she'd had to ask.

"Uh-huh. Or George Orwell. Take your pick."

"I'm not thinking Orwell. Where do you think he's from? Carson State Prison? Folsom? Maybe Lovelock?"

Lovelock Correctional Center. Where O.J. had hung out for years after that ill-considered robbery and kidnapping deal down in Vegas. Some people get a Hail Mary second chance and still run their Lamborghini off a cliff. Not much you can do about it if it's in your DNA.

We hurried across the street toward her Mustang, then I put an arm around her waist and got us walking east along the river toward Virginia Street.

"Where're we going?" Lucy asked.

"Their window faces the street. Dooley might be watching. I don't want him to see us get into a car, get any sort of a handle on us. He buys drugs from Ramon and Ramon likes knife fights. Or used to. These are not nice people."

"We should go to the firing range, blast away. I want to get that concealed carry permit for the gun Dad gave me."

"Which gun is currently and illegally in your purse?"

"Yup."

So we left the Mustang at the curb, circled around, walked home, then drove to Reno Guns & Range in the Toyota and got rid of extra adrenaline after our moment with Dooley by blasting away at human-silhouette targets. Lucy drew dumb-ass gauged ears on them with a Sharpie and went for head shots.

What a girl.

* * *

Ma had called earlier when we were shredding targets at the firing range. I'd told her about Kimmi and Dooley, didn't mention Robin or Robin's Binkies, didn't see any point in that, told her about Dooley in the hallway, voices at the door, that Lucy and I hadn't learned anything new by following Kimmi. Ma had had nothing interesting to report at that time either.

She called a second time as we were getting dressed, about to head over to the Green Room for hot toddies. "Volker stayed put so I'm outta here. I'm thinking he's clean."

"We're headed over to the Green Room, Ma. Want to join us?"

"Hell, yes. I need a drink."

"Really? Just one?"

She hung up. I get that a lot, not sure why.

It was dark when Lucy and I left the house. A half-moon was high overhead, no clouds. The night was cool, temperature into the sixties as I locked the front door.

My back was turned when I heard a strange crackling noise and Lucy let out a little cry. I whipped around and something hit me between the eyes and I went down.

Out.

CHAPTER TWENTY-THREE

I REGAINED CONSCIOUSNESS with a headache and a possible concussion, which is how I do it when someone tries to take my head off with a sap or a length of pipe. Lights flickered across my vision. Couldn't make sense of them. Finally, I realized I was seeing double. Maybe triple. Hard to tell. Fuckin' concussions were going to be the death of me yet. If I had one, it would be the fourth in two years. In my sixteen years with the IRS, I never got a concussion even if I deserved a few. Maybe this career move was to blame?

About then I became aware that I was in a car. What car? Going where?

I blinked, trying to corral the multiple images. No go, but blinking made my left eye hurt. A lot. I tried to rub my eye but discovered I couldn't lift my hands.

Sonofabitch, I had another plastic tie around my wrists. I'd had to cut one off last year by rubbing it on the sheet metal of a burned-out travel trailer.

"My uncle's," someone said.

I realized that I'd been hearing voices for a minute or two but hadn't processed anything that was being said.

"I still don't like it," said another voice. "We should take 'em out in the desert and do 'em there." Both voices were male.

"I already got this planned. The place is old, wood siding, wood everything inside. It'll go up fast. Won't be anything left of him." Ramon's voice.

"Yeah, but, dude—your uncle's place? That points a finger at you. Which points at me, kinda. I don't like that." Dooley.

One voice came from in front of me. The other was beside me to my left. It was still night. I couldn't see much except dim shadows and doubled lights smearing across my vision.

"Places burn down all the time," Ramon said.

"Not by arson. And your *uncle's* cabin?"

"It's just a summer place. It's old. And insured. It's way up in the forest, so it better be."

"You don't know?"

"How would I? Like I'd ask him, right? Hey, Uncle Wes, is this place insured? Anyway, he's seventy years old and I haven't seen him in two years. It's not like we're close."

"I still think this is fucked, man."

"I *told* you, I got this all worked out. That's why I got that cordless and those screws. I had sheets of plywood delivered up there a week ago. I used cash, gave 'em a fake name." Ramon paused, then said, "I've been thinking about this, waiting for it. I want him *alive* when we do it—in a room tied to a chair, place sealed up tight. Fucker's gonna go screaming in a ball of fire."

I was in the back seat, door to my right. I tested my wrists, discovered my arms were on opposite sides of a seat belt around my waist. The plastic tie holding my wrists completed a loop. The shoulder strap was keeping me upright. If I opened the door and jumped out, the seat belt would drag me alongside the car unless the plastic tie gave way. With my luck, it wouldn't.

I looked to my left. Oncoming headlights revealed Dooley beside me, Lucy on the other side of him. Her eyes were open. She was conscious, silent. Kimmi was driving, so Ramon had to be in the passenger seat up front.

I tested my legs, found them tied at the ankles using rope instead of a plastic tie, which might mean they were thinking of making me walk somewhere. I hoped so. If they freed my legs I might try to kick one or both of them to death. Odds are I'd end up taking a bullet, but that sounded a lot better than what Ramon had in store for me.

I blinked, squinted, and up ahead I saw the gaudy lights of Boomtown, a big hotel-casino seven or eight miles west of the city for people who don't care for Reno's ambience and traffic. We were on Interstate 80, headed west.

"So where the hell is this place?" Dooley asked.

"Off Dog Valley Road," Ramon replied. "Nearest house is miles away. You can't see it from the cabin."

Dog Valley. Northwest of Reno. I'd been up there a time or two when a crazy friend was doing a fifty-mile ultramarathon up over Peavine Mountain. It was mostly wilderness, dirt roads maintained by the Forest Service. Access in the winter would be by snowmobile or snow cat.

We weren't in Kimmi's Honda. Best guess, it was a Ford or Chevy, big sedan, big engine, at least ten years old. It had lost that new-car smell. Now the odor was either Dooley or Ramon, and a hint of marijuana, burgers, unwashed socks, and beer.

Ramon gave Kimmi directions. At Boomtown we got off the interstate, went past the hotel-casino, then took a back road into Verdi, right turn in the middle of town, across a bridge, then onto a dirt road that went up into empty black hills.

Headlights picked out sagebrush, rocks, scattered trees. We went around a switchback, trees becoming more dense as we went higher, moon faintly illuminating the thickening forest.

Ramon was probably in no condition to knock anyone out, fight, handle a two-by-four, but he was clearly in charge. Dooley was muscle, not brains. I could thank him for the concussion, if I had one.

At the house, Lucy had made a sound of pain or surprise, then I'd gone down. I wondered if Kimmi had taken Lucy down. If so, how? One-on-one, I figured Lucy could beat the crap out of Kimmi. I'd heard a faint crackling sound. Best guess, Kimmi had used a stun gun on her. If I got my hands on a stun gun, I would fry these guys until they turned into cabbages.

We went four or five miles into the hills, then Ramon told Kimmi to turn left off Dog Valley Road onto a bumpy dirt road.

"Christ, this washboard son of a bitch got a name?" Dooley asked. He didn't sound happy.

"Three Butte Trail," Ramon replied.

"Weird fuckin' name."

"It's a Forest Service road most of the way to Wes's cabin. It forks off half a mile from the cabin and dead-ends two or three miles higher up."

"Yeah, great. It still sucks."

The trail went south along the side of the hill. It climbed, not steeply, but steadily. We reached a switchback and headed back north, still climbing. Another half mile, past a granite cliff eighty or a hundred feet high, then another mile on a smoother dirt section. Kimmi took the car up to fifty. We reached another switchback, went back south again, still climbing.

"Where the hell *is* this place?" Dooley's voice had a whine in it like an eight-year-old kid.

"Relax," Ramon said. Nothing else.

Relax? Not me. I was twisting my wrists in the dark, trying to lever them apart, break the plastic tie. Not having any luck. But if they were going to get me out of the car, they would have to cut the tie. Or cut the seat belt, which didn't seem likely.

We traveled another half mile, came to another switchback, tight one, went level for a while then sloped down a quarter mile to another switchback, finally ended up at a decrepit-looking cabin surrounded by pine trees, dark, single-story with a metal roof. A covered porch faced east and an empty woodshed stood off to one side.

Kimmi pulled up close to the cabin and cut the engine.

"Leave the lights on," Ramon said. "Get those two outta the car. If that guy's still out, drag his ass out on the ground."

He opened the passenger door with his left hand. The dome light came on and he got out. His right side was still in a body cast. He had a coat on, right sleeve empty and flapping.

Kimmi got out and opened the rear door, driver's side. "Get out, bitch."

"How about you make me, Chicklet?" Lucy said.

There was a brief scuffle, then Dooley braced himself and shoved Lucy out, clambered out after her. Her hands were held behind her with a plastic tie. Dooley punched her in the face and Lucy went down, flat on her back.

I saw red. I wanted to kill him. Get this plastic shit off my wrists and I'd break every bone in his body. Every single bone, including the hammer, stirrup, and anvil in both his ears.

Lucy sat up, didn't make a sound. She was a dark shape in the night, tough as a railroad spike. Give her an opening and she'd rip these guys to pieces like a wildcat.

Dooley came around, opened the door to my right, looked in at me. "He's awake."

Ramon said, "Outta the way." He pushed Dooley aside then crouched at the open door and stared at me. His left hand held a black automatic with a four-inch barrel. Didn't look comfortable in his left hand, but it looked nasty. "Dooley's gonna cut that tie on your wrists," he said evenly. "I'll have this gun at that girl's head. If you want to see brains all over, just try something." He backed away. Kimmi brought Lucy around to my side of the car, kept her well out of reach. Ramon put the muzzle of the gun against Lucy's head.

"Okay," he said to Dooley. "Cut 'im loose."

Dooley opened a wicked-looking knife and stuck it under the plastic tie, ripped upward. My wrists came free. He shut the knife, hauled me out on the ground, and kicked me in the ribs with the toe of a boot. Okay, that hurt.

"No!" Ramon said sharply. "I want him awake. I want him to *feel* it when he's on fire, not some broken fuckin' ribs."

"Fucker about broke my hand," Dooley said to Ramon by way of explanation. "I owed him one."

"Fuck your hand. It ain't broke. Look what he did to me. Get a tie on his wrists, then untie his feet and stand him up."

"Want his hands in front or back?" Dooley asked.

"In *back,* dude. What the hell you think? Jesus."

Dooley rolled me over, yanked my hands behind me, got another tie around my wrists, pulled it tight, then freed my feet. Ramon kept his gun against Lucy's head. "Stand up," he said to me. "Try anything and she's dead."

Awkwardly, I got to my feet. My head still hurt, but my vision had mostly settled down.

The headlights revealed plywood sheets leaning against the side of the cabin. The place was more shack than cabin, built without logs. Single story, basic two-by-four construction, six hundred square feet, if that. Its outside walls were horizontal planks of weathered wood that hadn't seen paint in twenty years. If they were going to set the place on fire, it would go up fast.

I looked over at Lucy. She was staring at me, terrified. Her nose was bleeding. I tried to offer up a smile but knew it didn't take.

Finally, Ramon had a chance to get a good look around. He stopped and stared, looking east. "Fuck."

"What?" Dooley said.

Ramon pointed. "That. Out there."

Dooley looked out at Verdi, six or seven miles away, lights sparkling in the bowl of the valley where the Truckee River cut through. Interstate 80 was a ribbon of lights snaking between low hills. He made a disgusted sound. "Man, you light this place up, it'll be reported by two hundred people. We'll be up to our asses in police and firefighters."

Ramon was silent for a while, thinking. "Means we'll have to get outta here fast after we get it going," he said at last. "Not too fast though. I want to hear this sucker scream."

"Let's just take 'em out in the desert. Like I *said*. He can scream there."

Ramon didn't respond. Finally, he said, "No. We're here. I got this all set up. I want to seriously light this fucker up. Once we get it going, we'll go back down to Dog Valley Road, then up into the hills. We can go all the way to Truckee. Police and firefighters won't come in that way."

He got a flashlight out of the car. "Cut those lights," he said to Dooley. "Bring those two along. Grab a few plastic ties too, we'll need 'em."

Dooley cut the headlights. The night avalanched in on us. Dark. It took a moment for my eyes to acclimate enough to see a faint moon glow over the valley to the east, Verdi, the city glow of

Reno beyond that. The top six or eight stories of the Golden Goose Casino were visible above low black hills.

Ramon hit the switch on the flashlight. The car was an old Dodge Charger with dings and scrapes, a bent front bumper, rust damage. Ramon headed for the cabin. Kimmi followed, pushing Lucy ahead of her.

Dooley grabbed my left arm and forced me to trail along. Against the moonlit sky, I saw a power line arcing downhill into the trees. Ramon felt under the porch and came up with a key. He climbed two steps to the porch and opened the front door, flashlight swinging around, then a light came on and we were in a small living room with a basic kitchen to one side. The room was furnished in Goodwill—a sofa with tufts of stuffing visible through torn upholstery, a pine dining table with flaking varnish, three mismatched wooden chairs around it, an old wood stove that looked antique but might get the job done on a chilly night. A pair of old oval rugs were laid over a dusty wood plank floor. The walls were panels of fake knotty pine. All in all, the place was a tinderbox, ready to go up.

A tremor went through me. I hoped Lucy wasn't going to be included in this, but she was here so it was likely we were both about to be burned alive.

Ramon opened a door in the far wall, went into a room, turned on another light. "Bring 'em in here."

It was a bedroom, fourteen by twenty feet with a bathroom to the left. Two doors, one to the living room, the other to the bathroom, and two windows, one in the back wall, one on a side wall that would look out on the car parked outside. The walls had faded into a shade of mold green. Standard drywall, not the knotty pine of the other room. Queen-size bed with a sag in the middle, no headboard. D-Con in the corners for the mice. There was an old dresser with a mirror on the wall above it, a wooden chair that might have come from a forties library, worn rug on the floor, cheap light fixture full of dead bugs in the ceiling. All five of us gathered in the room. Kimmi stared around silently, chewing her gum in an expressionless, bovine way.

"Get another chair," Ramon said to Dooley. Dooley left. Ramon aimed the gun at my face and smiled. "We gonna have us some fun now." The gun looked unnatural in his left hand, but he only had to pull the trigger.

Dooley returned with a sturdy, paint-spattered oak chair.

"Put it over there with the other one." Ramon wagged the gun at the other chair in the room.

They sat Lucy in one chair, me in the other. Ramon was in charge. He gave orders and Dooley carried them out. With only one arm, Ramon couldn't do much. He told Dooley to strap my ankles to the legs of the chair and tie a rope around my waist and around the back of the chair.

Dooley strapped my ankles. As he tied the rope around my waist, I scooted forward a little. When he was done, I could slide back half an inch and the rope would be slightly loose. I didn't know if I would be able to use that, but anything was better than nothing.

Dooley put a tie around one of Lucy's ankles and around a leg of her chair. He pulled it tight. Ramon came closer. "Just that one leg," he said to Dooley. "She's goin' with us."

He crouched in front of me. "I'm gonna burn you up, dude, not her. No way I'm passing up pussy that sweet."

I bounced in my chair, trying to rip loose and kill him, not that it did any good.

He laughed, still in a crouch. He looked at Lucy. "You're somethin' else, girl. I'm gonna make you last a while, maybe a couple of days."

He was still in front of me. Lucy was flexible and tough. Ramon should've strapped both her legs. She whipped a leg up and kicked him in the face. Too bad she was wearing running shoes. He went over with a grunt, then screamed curses. Dooley charged over and punched Lucy in the face. He pulled his fist back to hit her again.

"*No!*" Ramon barked, still on the floor. "I don't want her hurt, you dumb-ass." He sat up and stared at her, keeping out of reach. He held his nose. "After I'm done with you, bitch, that'll cost you. More than you can imagine."

Lucy didn't answer. Dooley had hit her in the mouth. She had blood on her teeth, dribbling over her chin. Her eyes looked wild, savage. I looked at Kimmi. She stared back, then produced a little shrug with her lips. Nothing else moved. Her eyes were like worm holes in rotten wood.

Ramon staggered to his feet. Having learned a lesson, he had Dooley tie Lucy in the chair, rope around her waist same as me, then he ordered Dooley to haul the furniture out of the room. It didn't amount to much. Spavined queen bed, dresser, battered night table, a canted coat rack. It all got piled in the living room. Ramon dragged the rug out.

The room was empty except for the mirror on the wall and the chairs Lucy and I were tied to. Ramon kept the gun on us as Dooley hauled in sheets of plywood. Kimmi got a chair from the other room and sat facing us, six feet away, out of reach of Lucy's lethal feet. Dooley began to cover windows, using a drill-driver to screw plywood sheets to the window frames.

"Christ, this is gonna take a while," he said, again with the whine in his voice. "We really need to do this, man? He's tied to a chair. He ain't goin' nowhere."

"I thought about it," Ramon replied. "I dreamed about this. I want him in a box, no way out." He looked at me. "My parents died in a house fire when I was nineteen. Down in San Berdoo. By then I was gone, living in Reno. I heard 'em screaming. My dad made it out a window even though he'd been tied up. Later I thought the rope must've burned through before the fire really got him. Learned something that night. It took him a few hours to die, which was pretty cool, even better than what I'd hoped for. Police said it was arson." His eyes glowed with the memory. "They never did find out who did it."

"You didn't get along with your folks," I said.

"Not much." Then he smiled. "Not much, man, but if I got caught, it was worth it just to hear the two of 'em screaming in there, just like you're gonna do pretty soon. Then my dad came out that window. Surprised the shit outta me. He came out like a torch, set fire to an acre of weeds out back. But there ain't gonna be no window for you, dude. No door either. Just this empty box sealed up tight and fire crawling up your legs."

CHAPTER TWENTY-FOUR

"Don't," Lucy said.

Ramon lifted his eyebrows at her. "Don't what?"

"Do it to me, not him."

"No way, girl. You're the best-looking piece I've seen in a long fuckin' time."

"I won't be. I'll rip your heart out."

"Spread-eagled and naked? That I've gotta see." He looked over at Dooley. "How're you doing?"

"About got this one done. Eight screws on a side like you said. That's . . . like twenty of 'em. It's takin' a while."

Lucy snickered softly. "Genius."

"Do that other window the same. Then cover the bathroom door. We need to get movin' here."

"Goin' fast as I can," Dooley said. He set a plywood sheet against the second window and went to work.

Ramon went over to supervise. In her chair, Kimmi was hugging herself. She looked chilled in a thin shirt showing a fair amount of pale breast, pants that ended at mid-calf, flip-flops, toenails painted black, same as her fingernails. Lovely.

"What's *your* story?" I asked her.

She stared at me. "What story?"

"You're sixteen and into drugs, lowlifes, murder. Must be a story there. Dropped on your head when you were young?"

"Fuck you."

"An intellectual response for sure. But seriously, kiddo, what do you want out of life? Lethal injection? That's boring, all you do is pass out, but they don't do firing squads or the electric chair these days. They might hang you, so there's that. You'd probably have to ask, though."

"Fuck you, asshole. You don't know shit."

"Educate me. You and these two killed that guy Soranden, didn't you?"

"So what if we did?"

"So there's a story there. Why him?"

For a moment she was silent. Then, "Daddy was gonna buy me a new Jetta. He tole me, promised me, then that guy stole a bunch of Dad's money, and all I got was that cruddy old piece of shit Honda."

"Seriously? People are dying because you didn't get the *car* you wanted?"

"Hey, he *promised*! Then he said he couldn't because that guy stole like a hundred thousand dollars from him."

"He told you that?"

"No. I heard him and stupid Marta talking about it."

"Anyway, it was just a car."

Her eyes boiled over. "It's a fuckin' piece of shit *Honda*!" she screamed. "I wanted a *Jetta*!"

I looked over at Lucy. She rolled her eyes at me, then gave me the bleakest look I've ever seen.

The room went silent, except for Dooley putting in screws. Ramon looked over at me and smiled, nodded his head at Kimmi, and raised his eyebrows a quarter inch.

"Okay," I said to Kimmi. "You got a lousy car so naturally people had to die. I totally understand that. Lots of people would kill for a Jetta. How did you get to that IRS guy, Soranden?"

"Get to him?"

"Capture him, kill him."

"I didn't. How would I do that? I got Dooley and Ramon to do it."

"They do what you tell 'em to do?"

She shrugged.

"You must be a good lay," Lucy said.

"Better'n you, bitch."

"Don't think so."

Kimmi started to get out of her chair.

"Keep the hell away from her," Ramon said sharply.

Kimmi sat back down. "You should burn up too," she said to Lucy.

I didn't want her thinking that way, or Ramon, not that I knew what he had in mind for Lucy once he was through with her, not something I wanted to think about. I said, "This whole thing with the ants and putting his skull in our car. Whose idea was that?"

Ramon drifted over. "Mine. You've been in the news for a year or two, finding dead people. Now they'll find you. You'll look like a briquette. They'll identify you by your teeth."

As I'd thought. There was a downside to this famous PI bit. I'd felt it last summer when Reinhart's hand was FedEx'd to me for much the same reason—weird, insane deaths following me around like the churning wake of an ocean liner.

"Wish I could've kept that skull," Ramon said. "Thing was ugly but so cool. I had it on an entertainment center. Then some bimbo I had over picked it up and asked if it was real. I told her no, but I don't think she believed me so I figured I better get rid of it. It's illegal to own a skull. I mean a human skull. I followed you and hot tits to that casino that night and dropped it into your car. Like a kind of joke."

"Ha, ha," Lucy said. "So funny."

Ramon smiled. "It was, kinda. And I knew it would end up on TV so we could see what happened. Didn't know it would turn out like this, though—you two up here, famous dipshit PI about to go up in flames. That'll make the news too. I'll TiVo it and play it back whenever I need a laugh."

I looked over at precious Kimmi. "What got you going this evening? Your father gets a phone call, you rush out. How'd that work out?"

"You oughta know. You're the one who phoned him."

"Actually, I didn't."

She didn't believe me. "I was right there. I answered the phone. It was for Dad. He listened, then hung up, said some guy said something about harvester ants and Arizona. He thought it was just a weird joke, but I knew it had to be you and that you must've figured things out, sort of anyway. So I told Dooley and he told Ramon. Ramon said we had to get rid of you."

Shook the tree. Kimmi fell out.

"You thought you were so smart," she went on. "That day you came over and talked to my dad, got him all upset. I put a recorder under an afghan on the back of the couch and heard everything you said, accusing him of stealing thirteen thousand dollars, maybe getting the police involved. When you left, he was totally freaked. He and Marta had a big talk after. I listened to that too."

Dooley finished putting up the second sheet of plywood. He started on the door to the bathroom.

"You listen in on adults' conversations?" I said to Kimmi.

She shrugged, didn't say anything.

"Ants?" I said. "That was really something."

She smiled. Not a nice smile. I didn't think anyone would ask her to the prom with a smile like that. "That IRS guy was dead," she said. "Dooley wanted to put him in the river or take him into the desert and dump him, but then I remembered those ants we saw in Arizona on vacation. Some guy down there told us those ants were super vicious and always hungry and to keep away from them. Said they could eat a coyote in like a day. I mentioned it to Ramon and he thought it would be way cool to watch 'em strip out a person's head. We had to take out his eyes so the ants could get in easier, then it took them like only four or five hours to totally clean him out."

I shuddered. They took out his eyes. She'd said it like she had gone to a 7-Eleven and bought gum. She had even less soul in there than Ramon. She was a perfectly amoral creature.

"His head," I said. "What about the rest of him?"

She looked at Ramon. He gave her a little nod, so she said, "We left it off the highway in a kind of gully. In three of those big garbage bags."

Three bags. They'd cut him up. Putrid child. "Where?"

She shrugged. "Just some place. I don't remember where." Then Ramon said, "We dumped him in the hills south of Fallon on the way to Arizona. Before we got to Schurz."

I looked at Precious. "Which one of you winners cut off his head?"

"Who cares?"

"Just wondering which one of you falls asleep at night with that treasured memory rolling around in their brain."

Another shrug. "I did some. Dooley did the backbone neck part, it was so tough. The guy was creepy, like staring at us until Ramon said we should take out his eyes."

"Done," Dooley said. He stepped back from the bathroom door and grabbed an edge of the plywood sheet, braced himself and pulled on it, hard. "No one's goin' through that." He looked at me and grinned. "Especially not tied to a chair."

"Good work," I said, then I looked at Kimmi. "None of this would've happened if you'd gotten your Jetta?"

She stared at me without expression. "Jesus. You just go on and on. Like my dad and his creepy asshole sister."

She wasn't much of a conversationalist. A talk with Hitler might've gone pretty much the same, all I, I, I, and me, me, me, except Adolf might've clicked his heels a few times since he had that fetish.

Ramon said something to Dooley. Dooley grabbed Lucy's chair, tilted it back and dragged her out the door, left her facing the bedroom. Then he dragged me into the center of the room on the chair's back legs. Tilted like that, I saw that he'd strapped my ankles to the lower part of the chair's legs, below the cross bracing that strengthened the chair's legs. *Below* it. I couldn't believe it. Given his stupidity and Ramon's inability to do the work, I might have a chance to get out of this. Slim, but maybe. As a kid, Dooley was probably too busy torturing small animals to work puzzles. With all four legs of the chair on the floor, the straps might look secure to your basic lowlife dimwit, something to do with gauged ears holding black onyx rings, which implied an IQ somewhere south of eighty. Farther south than I'd given him credit for earlier.

He left me in the middle of the room facing the door. And Lucy. She gave me a terrified look as Dooley and Ramon exited the bedroom. Dooley set the last sheet of plywood against the door frame and began to drive screws into the plywood, but not yet into the frame.

After he'd readied half a dozen screws, he slid the plywood sheet off to one side. "Get the diesel," Ramon said.

Dooley left, returned half a minute later with a plastic one-gallon container. "Check this out," Ramon said to Kimmi. "This is so cool." He motioned her back into the bedroom. She came in like a sheep, expectant little smile curling her lips, and when she was inside he lifted the gun, aimed it at her face.

"Hey, that's not fun—"

He pulled the trigger, blew out the back of her head.

My ears rang. The smell of gunpowder filled the room. Dooley stuck his head in the room and grinned. Kimmi was sprawled on the floor, blood and brains covering the wall behind her. Ramon said, "I shoulda done that sooner. Never met a bitch half that dumb. Motor mouth would've bragged about this to a bunch of her friends. Now, not so much."

He turned to Dooley. "Get some of that under his chair. Not too much. I don't want him to burn up too fast. Pour a little on his shoes, too. Then douse the girl real good and make a trail out the door."

Dooley opened the can, sloshed diesel under my chair and around my feet, ankles. A pungent odor wafted up. Cold liquid crept into my shoes, soaking my socks.

Aw, shit, no.

"That's enough," Ramon said. "I want it to take a while."

Dooley poured diesel on Kimmi then backed out the door, leaving a dark glistening trail on the floorboards that included my feet. Lucy bucked in her chair, screaming, "No, no, no! Oh, don't, please *don't!*"

Ramon stopped at the door and looked back at me. "Enjoy the ride, fucker." Then he turned out the light, shut the door, and in the other room Dooley drove half a dozen screws through the ply-wood and into the door frame.

I was left in absolute darkness.

*   *   *

Lucy's screams got weaker as they took her outside and put her in the car. The smell of diesel was nauseating, permeating the room. I sat in the dark, heart pounding, anticipating fire. I couldn't see a thing, but I had to get free of that chair, fast. First thing, I had to tip it over backward. I bent forward then threw my weight back as I shoved with my toes, tipping the chair over. I tucked my chin into my chest to keep from banging my head against the floor. I heard them come back, then the only sound was that of Dooley driving the rest of the screws through the plywood into the door frame. Ramon wanted me in a box and he thought he was getting it. Which shows how dumb drug dealers can be. You wouldn't want one as a contractor on your house. It'd be a mistake to hire one to build a birdhouse.

Ramon knew drugs, supply and demand. He also had more than the average homeowner's knowledge about knives, not that it had served him well, but what he knew about the real world wouldn't fill a thimble. He looked at the room with its windows and doors covered and saw a box. He was a modern-day savage, not a carpenter.

And speaking of boxes, we were at the end of a dead-end road in the mountains, no way out except to backtrack down a bunch of switchbacks. I was thinking about that, too.

Freeing my legs took longer than I thought it would. On my back in the chair, I slid my left leg down, taking the plastic tie with it, but it snagged, held, slid half an inch, snagged again. It took a full minute to slide it off the end of the chair leg.

I worked on the other leg, felt as if I almost had it when the sound of screws being driven into wood ended.

A moment of silence followed.

Muffled voices. Insane laughter.

Then a scratching sound, a faint *whoosh*, and a golden line of fire came under the door and traveled toward me, not as fast as if it were gasoline, but fast enough.

CHAPTER TWENTY-FIVE

I USED MY elbows, knees, and shifting weight to roll to my right, chair clattering across the floor, away from the puddle of diesel where I'd been sitting. I was six feet away when the pool ignited. Eighteen-inch flames boiled up, hot, bright, and smelly, throwing off oily black smoke. Moments later, Kimmi went up.

My rolling had left disconnected drops of fuel on the floor so they didn't ignite. Nor did my feet, for which I was more than a little thankful. I was still tied to the chair, on my back on the floor. I worked on my right leg. If Ramon was in the other room, he would expect screams, so I screamed as if I were on fire. I didn't know if they'd already left, but I gave them a show just in case. It might slow Ramon down. They had several miles of dirt road with switchbacks ahead of them. I felt a clock ticking. I had to hurry. If Ramon killed Lucy, my life would truly be over. Jeri, then Lucy? I wouldn't be able to live with that.

My right leg came free. Awkwardly I staggered to my feet, straddling the chair, still shrieking. I couldn't hear anything in the other room but I hoped they were still there. The rope around my waist bound me to the chair, but it was loose. I jumped, bounced, shimmied, finally got it to slide up and off the back of the chair.

Then I was on my feet, mobile. The rope dropped off my waist to the floor. I kicked it away.

My wrists were still held behind my back with a plastic tie. I tried but couldn't break it. I had no choice about how to free myself, no time to think, I had to *move*. Flames flickered on the trail of burning diesel that had come beneath the door. I dropped to the floor with my back to four-inch flames and held my wrists in the fire.

I screamed, this time for real. Holy fuck it hurt. I'd never felt anything like it. I tried to look behind me but couldn't see what I was doing. I smelled burning flesh. The pain was unreal, but I had to do this. For Lucy. For a chance to save her, however unlikely that might be.

I pulled on the tie, tried to keep it in the flames. It parted abruptly and my wrists whipped out of the fire. I rolled, got to my feet, coughed in the thick oily smoke that was filling the room from the ceiling down to four or five feet from the floor. The roar of the fire drowned out all hope of hearing the car's engine, but Ramon would probably get out fast now that I was no longer yelling and the flames would be visible from Verdi or the interstate.

I dropped to the floor near the plywood sheet Dooley had put over the back window. I kicked the wall. I was motivated, and my foot went through it like it was nothing. As I'd thought, it was crumbly drywall. Ramon had seen a solid, impenetrable barrier because he didn't know shit. I saw it as a flimsy coating over two-by-fours. I tore more drywall out, grabbed fiberglass insulation, flung it into the room. The frame of the house was two-by-fours on sixteen-inch centers. I kicked between the studs and felt that old outside plank siding give way.

Black smoke boiled around me. The heat was building, fire giving off a lusty roar. I hammered at the siding with a foot, felt it splinter, nails pulling through old wood. I pounded out a hole big enough to crawl through, felt something sharp rip at my face as I scooted through feet-first, then I was out.

* * *

Lucy.

I came out at the back of the house. I ran around to the side where they'd parked the car. Headlights were visible up through the trees. The Charger was through the first switchback, headed back this way, climbing fast.

I ran.

Across the yard and straight downhill into the trees. Ramon and Dooley had two miles of switchbacking dirt road to traverse before it would pass below the house. How far below the house? A quarter mile? Half? I didn't know, but it was my only hope of cutting them off.

Cutting them off how?

I didn't know, but I ran all out, breakneck speed down the side of the mountain. It was steep, with dead branches littering the ground, rocks underfoot. A steeplechase in the dark, down a hillside of tricky moonlit shadows.

I ran toward the lights of Verdi. Fell. Got up. Fell again. An unseen branch sliced into my left cheek. I barely felt it. I had to get to Lucy. Which meant I had to stop the car.

How?

A log across the road. Or a rock big enough to take out the engine, oil pan, transmission, something in the drive train. Only thing I could think of, and all of that was moot if I didn't reach the road below the house before the Charger went by.

I ran. Couldn't see the headlights, couldn't hear the engine. I fell again and my ribs slammed into a rock. I felt one go. I got up.

Suddenly each breath was a knife in my side, but I had to go, run, *sprint*, ignore the pain, get down that fucking mountainside, and now I saw a flicker of headlights off to my left, maybe half a mile away. The car was past that tight northern switchback and coming fast.

No time, no time, and I raced downhill and then the land in front of me looked weird, *wrong*, and I damn near ran right off that cliff I'd seen as we were coming up. I was eighty feet above the road, car racing toward me, no way to get down to the road in time. I looked around wildly in the dark, saw a rock, tried to lift it, couldn't, move, Mort, *move*, and I heard that big engine, car doing sixty miles an hour, and I found another rock, big sonofabitch, at least a hundred fifty pounds, but this was for Lucy goddamnit and I got it up and over to the edge of the cliff, the road down below, and I lofted it over the side, praying that it would land in the middle of the road, gut the car's engine, blow transmission parts all over, rip out the differential. It hit a jutting rock and fell spinning into space. The glare of headlights on the road below revealed a tumbling black silhouette and then it was all about Lucky Lucy and her four lucky planets because that beautiful sonofabitching hunk of rock hit the hood of the car and blew right through the windshield on the driver's side, tore through the car, came flying out the back window a tenth of a second later in a shower of glittering ruby glass in the taillights as the car shot by.

The Charger jerked right, wheels up on an embankment by the cliff, slowed as it traveled another hundred yards then it went off the road to the left, crashed through trees, came to rest with a crunch of metal against something solid. Its headlights went out, but the taillights were twin bloody eyes in the night.

I had to get down there.

I moved away from the cliff edge and went south along the hill-side, past granite outcroppings, loose rubble, finally worked my way down to the road.

No sound. Nothing.

I jogged over to the car not knowing what I would find. The Charger was still upright. Its front end was crumpled against a granite monolith the size of a Greyhound bus.

"Lucy," I yelled. "Luce!"

No answer. Ramon or Dooley might still be conscious, still dangerous, so I opened the driver's-side door in front first, ready to kill anyone I found, Ramon or Dooley, surprised when the dome light came on. Dooley wasn't going to be a problem because there was nothing but a bloody stump on his shoulders where the rock had ripped off two-thirds of his head. Guy had a concussion that made mine look like nothing.

A glance at the passenger side and there was Ramon with a shard of mirrored glass sticking out of his left eye. His head was turned and he would've been looking right at me, if he could see past that sliver of glass.

"Help." His voice was a breathy sigh. "Help me."

Lucy.

I opened the back door, driver's side. Lucy was on the back seat, facedown, both seat belts wrapped around her like snakes, hands behind her back, plastic ties around her wrists and ankles and around the belts. She was gagged. They'd arranged her for safe transport, out of sight of the police.

Lucky Lucy. That rock had blown through the car over the top of her, never touched her as it went by.

Carefully, I got the gag off her. "Don't move. You've got glass all over you."

"Ohmigod, you're okay," she said, already crying. "How did you . . . how . . ."

"In a minute," I said. "Ramon's hurt but not dead. I don't want him to pull a gun on us."

"*Kill him*, Mort."

"Don't move. I won't be long."

I went around to the other side of the car, opened the door cautiously in case Ramon was ready to go with that automatic. He wasn't. I grabbed his hair, pulled his head back. The sliver of mirror poking out of his eye was an inch wide, no telling how deep. It looked almost like the blade of a knife, which was well deserved and poetic.

"Hurts," he whispered. "Help me." The impact had broken his body cast. That would hurt too. His left hand scrabbled against his thigh as if searching for something. A seat belt held him in place. I grabbed his left wrist to keep him from finding his gun and pulling it, then I searched him, not gently I have to admit. I found a Kimber Super Carry still wedged between his legs where he'd kept it ready, probably for police if they'd been stopped. It figured that the drug dealer would have a gun worth over sixteen hundred dollars. I tossed the gun outside the car.

I wanted to shove that sliver of mirror deeper into his eye, down into his thinking jelly, then give it a few twists to put his lights out forever. I'd played God once. Could I do it again?

Maybe, but not yet.

I needed a knife. Ramon was the knife fighter, but Dooley had cut the plastic tie around my wrists when we'd arrived at the cabin, so he had a knife too. I searched Ramon again, ignoring his feeble cries as I went through his pockets. No knife, so I went around the car to Dooley. About the time I found a knife in a front pocket of his jeans, my wrists started screaming. I'd been too keyed up, too full of adrenaline, to feel the burns, but they were bad. With Ramon and Dooley out of it, the pain came on abruptly and it was almost more than I could stand.

With tears in my eyes I got the knife open and cut the ties holding Lucy in the back seat. She scrambled out and held me so tight I could barely breathe. My busted rib didn't help. She was blubbering so hard I thought she might drown.

She was banged up, not seriously hurt, and alive. I couldn't have asked for more.

"How?" she said when she could finally speak again. "How on *earth* did you do this?"

In my peripheral vision I saw the blown-out rear window of the Charger. "Gumshoe Rock," I said.

Couldn't help it.

CHAPTER TWENTY-SIX

ACCORDING TO O'ROARKE, the new girl, Traci Ellis, was about to be turned loose in the Green Room, on her own, ready to fly solo. She was a real pip. Not only beautiful, but after I'd hit up O'Roarke for a few measly free drink coupons for having solved the Soranden murder, made national news again, and sustained injuries worse than anything he'd ever endured, and *then* been refused coupons because of my tendency to play havoc with the Green Room's bottom line, Traci slid a big stack of coupons my way when O'Roarke's back was turned. I got a friendly wink, too. Trouble was, she was also one of those cleavage-rich girls, not shy, able to circumvent the female bartender dress code by two buttons' worth—just enough that I thought the place would fill up with a bunch of drooling poli-sci grad students who didn't see much coed thumbing of dress codes in the classroom as October approached November. With their honking laughter and nightly salt-tequila-lime contests, grad students would ruin the place, so I thought those buttons needed buttoning up.

"Nice view?" said my young assistant.

"A view is a view," I said. "You look because that's what eyes do, the scenery is interesting but transitory and irrelevant, so you turn away and, hey, right about then someone suggests a shower, orders

up a boob rub, and that irrelevant view moseys off into the past
and doesn't matter in the least because you've got your hands full
and busy with the real thing."

"Cool," she said. "Okay, fill your eyes."

Then Ma came in wearing navy pants, a hot pink shirt, and
bright green jogging shoes. I smiled. Until, that is, Munson and
Warley came in behind her like ducklings waddling after mama—
IRS Commissioner Munson and Northern Nevada's IRS chief
Warley Sullivan, both of whom had been compromised by Ma
and me and were therefore in our pockets. I stared at them, then
at Ma. "Shit, Ma. Seriously? You brought in upper management
IRS? The ambience of this place just fell below a single star."

"For twenty-five grand, boyo, who cares?"

* * *

But that was ten days after a caravan of paramedics, police cars, and
fire trucks had come roaring up Dog Valley Road in the dark in
search of fire, took a left up Three Butte Trail—thank God for trian-
gulation, trigonometry, and GPS—and ended up coming our way.

First, we heard sirens, then headlights flickered in the tops of
distant trees, then red and blue flashing lights appeared.

Lucy and I stood on the road. I had opened the Charger's trunk
and found plastic ties, put one around Ramon's neck and around
the headrest of the seat to make sure he stayed put, didn't come
after us like a grade-B movie psycho. Insurance, though that glass
sliver buried in his eye was likely to slow him down quite a bit. I
know it would me.

The rock had shattered the rearview mirror as it ripped through
the car and Ramon had stopped a shard. Nice. There was a God
after all. I'd never seriously doubted it, but now I had proof.

First vehicle up the road was a fire department paramedic van, which made sense because saving lives is always the first priority. The next vehicle, half a mile behind, was a lumbering fire tanker trying to haul eighteen hundred gallons of water up the mountainside. A police car was next, then another tanker, then a bevy of police cars and a trio of news vans.

We stopped the paramedics and convinced them that no one at the fire was in need of their services, but we were. The van pulled as far off the road as it could, and the tankers were able to squeeze by. Following the tankers and police cars, news crews went up and filmed the fire, missed the first hour or two of the real story, God love 'em. Of course, they made up for it later using yellow journalistic principles taught in universities.

The driver of the paramedic van was a woman of thirty, Heather, outdoorsy and damn good-looking. Riding shotgun was a tall, angular guy in his mid-twenties, Rick.

They got out. Lucy pulled me over to them and said, "He's burned real bad. Do something fast, please."

These guys were good. It may have helped that we didn't mention Ramon until my wrists were coated in Water Jel and Cool Blaze burn dressings, and I had a bandage on the gouge in my cheek where a branch in the dark had tried to end up in my mouth, and Lucy had a cold pack on the side of her face, and I'd whined about my broken rib, and they'd told me that wrapping it was actually a big no-no and here's three ibuprofen and don't play rugby for a day or two, ha, ha. Great roadside humor. And now we'd better load you two up and get you to the hospital for MRIs and patching and such.

About then it seemed as if telling them about Ramon's little problem over there in the Charger where taillights were still aglow in the dark was the right thing to do—at which point Lucy's and my complaints got second billing and Ramon got a ride to the hospital in what was slated to be *our* paramedic van because, in spite of all our pains and whining, we weren't critical. Heather ordered up a replacement for us and I was given a cold pack for my ribs, ten minutes on, ten minutes off, and don't worry, an ambulance will be here in twenty minutes, give or take. Oh, and try to take deep breaths as soon as you can so you don't get pneumonia. Bye.

So, shit, we stood around chatting with six or eight cops who got a look at the Charger and the granite cliff and what was left of Dooley's head, gathering fodder for the war stories they tell at briefings and during shift changes. And I still had a bit of diesel fuel in my shoes. I mentioned it, but all it got was a laugh. One cop asked if I wanted a light. Cops are a riot. I took off my shoes and socks and rubbed powdery dirt on my feet.

Our ambulance missed the turn and got lost up Dog Valley Road and had to backtrack six miles, so of course Russ Fairchild showed up before we left because the name Mortimer Angel was being bandied about by various emergency services on various radio frequencies.

"What the *hell*, Mort," he said, leading Lucy and me away from our latest band of admirers.

"Solved another one for you, Russ," I said.

His head jerked around. "Which one?"

He hadn't heard that part. Well, it was early times.

"The Soranden murder."

"Aw, shit, no. Really?"

"And another one, higher up in the hills."

His eyes jittered. "Who?"

"Sixteen-year-old girl going on forty-six. Kimmi. She got two lowlifes to kill Soranden because she wanted a new Jetta and all she got was a beat-up old Honda Civic. That, by the way, is just between you, me, and Lucy. I'll explain later."

His jaw sagged. No words followed.

"*And* I killed one of the lowlifes with a rock. His name is Dooley. He's over there in a Dodge Charger. Not much head left, but he's still got fingerprints you can play around with."

He stared at me. "You killed some guy with a *rock?*"

"Not just any rock, Russ. A big-ass rock. Oh, and I kicked out a wall and escaped from a burning building."

Lucy put an arm around my waist. "He's like a superhero or something, but he lost his cape in the dark. And he's barefoot and a bit stinky because he had diesel in his shoes."

His eyes bugged out.

About then the ambulance pulled up. Two guys got out. One of them said, "Where's the awesome-lookin' chick and some old guy they said was pretty banged up?"

Awesome-looking chick and "some old guy." Everyone in the vicinity of Lucy plays second fiddle. Man, I hate that.

* * *

We ended up at Renown Medical Center. I got my feet washed and rubbed with some kind of cream, and an MRI, and they checked me for a concussion, fourth one in two years. I was informed that it wasn't much of a concussion by a woman doctor with gray hair and the kind of smile they learn in med school. Sort of a baby concussion, she said, but I had a lump on my forehead which warranted a five-second look and a shrug and a cold pack that I had to hold in place myself.

My rib got a "tsk, tsk" and a second shrug, which is often the treatment for a cracked or broken rib. My gouged cheek got cleaned up, five stitches, ointment, a bandage.

All of that was out-patient stuff, but my burns got me into a minor burn unit overnight. Nice. I think when you kill someone and you're damn near murdered, you've earned a little downtime in a hospital with hot and cold running nurses. I've learned to enjoy hospital stays. Not even in a Las Vegas casino suite does anyone offer to change your bedpan at four in the morning.

But this was observation and bandage changing, not a lot of bedrest with catheters and drains, no bedpan needed, so at two fifty a.m. I was awake and on my feet, and Lucy and I went down one floor in an empty elevator to the general surgery floor where Ramon Surry had a private room and a good-sized cop planted in a chair outside to keep him safe.

"Can't go in there," the cop said, getting up and standing in our way.

"I'm the one who put him there."

"Then you deserve a medal, but you still can't go in. Wish you could, though. You did a good job on the son of a bitch. I heard he killed some high school girl."

"Among other things, but hold on," I said, pointing to a cell phone on the cop's belt. "Can I borrow that for a minute? And what's your number?"

I called Russ who was, as always, happy to hear from me in the cold dark hours after midnight. He then called the cop in front of us, Pete Wells, who smiled and came in with Lucy and me to have a peek at Ramon. Surry was strapped in bed with a terrific patch over his left eye that covered half his head, arm and shoulder cast immobilizing his right arm, handcuff holding his left hand to the raised side rail of the bed. It looked like it would be a bitch if he had to scratch his nose. I've had itches as bad as gunshot wounds.

"Hi there, bud," I said. "We were in the neighborhood, saw the light on, and thought we'd drop by, say howdy."

"Fuck you," he said in a post-anesthetic rasp.

"You look a little worse for wear, dude. Maybe knife fights and arson-murder aren't your thing. You should see a counselor about different career options and training opportunities."

He was still slightly groggy, but he was still Ramon Surry, extreme lowlife. "Fuck you." His right eye blazed with hatred.

"How articulate," Lucy said. "Beautiful sentiment, really. He might be able to read poetry or Hallmark on YouTube—*if* he doesn't end up on Death Row."

Surry's right eye swiveled, locked on her.

"Hey, cool patch," I said. "Makes you look like a pirate. Girls really go for that—just look at Johnny Depp—though the girls in prison go by the names Earl and Bubba. Can I get you anything? Enema, a bigger catheter, designer handcuffs? How about a balloon with a smiley face on it? Those're nice."

"Fuck you, man."

I stood over him. "Like you said up at the cabin, 'Enjoy the ride.' Oh, and because we're eyewitnesses, we'll probably meet again. At the trial. We'll be with the prosecution. In the state of Nevada, it's against the law to blow a person's head off. You'd think they'd teach that in school, at least give it a mention, but they didn't in high school when I was there."

I turned to go, then Ramon whispered hoarsely, "How? We were gone. We were home free. How'd you do it?"

I turned back, forming a response, then Lucy stood beside me, smiled at him, and said, "Gumshoe Rock. *Dude.*"

Stole my line.

* * *

Twelve hours later, Ramon died. So, no trial, and he'd had no chance to talk to the FBI, which was probably just as well. A four-inch length of glass shard in the eye is an iffy thing and brains are complicated. Four inches, wow. At least two and a half inches of that went into the jelly. No telling what damage it had done. He was lying peacefully in bed, not what he deserved, then he flatlined and headed for the Pearly Gates, not that he would get in when he rang the doorbell.

I didn't grieve. When someone tries to burn you alive and threatens to rape and kill your woman, "Good riddance" is not an unreasonable response.

* * *

Three days after that, Ma informed Mike Volker and Marta that Clary Investigations had rounded up seventy-six thousand dollars in cash and three cashier's checks totaling twenty-four thousand dollars. But she was going to hang onto all of it until FBI agents weren't running around like roaches in a tenement. So far, they'd uncovered no motive for Soranden's murder. I had Russ under control, so that business about the Jetta was out of it. I told a couple of FBI guys that Dooley and Ramon had admitted to killing Soranden, cutting off his head and using ants to clean out his skull, but they hadn't said why they'd done all that.

And why had they kidnapped me and Lucy?

I shrugged. How would I know? They didn't tell us why. Who knows how guys like that think? They dropped Soranden's skull in my car. I'm famous. Start with that. Bring in a Quantico psychologist.

They had no idea how Kimmi was involved. A Jetta is hard to explain so I didn't try. Seriously, who would believe it except Volkswagen salesmen, and even that's a stretch. A *Jetta*? The feds were calling it a thrill killing, but that would change in a heartbeat if they got a whiff of Soranden's blackmail schemes. They were still digging, so that could still come out.

Kimmi was an obvious link to Volker, but Volker wasn't an obvious link to Soranden or to his murder so we were looking good there. Kimmi was simply a puzzle. A girl that age had the FBI flummoxed. They found no motive for her to be involved in kidnapping and murder other than her ill-considered association with Ramon and Dooley, and we—Clary Investigations, that is—didn't tell Mike or Marta that an "old piece-of-shit Honda" had set Kimmi off, or that she'd even *been* set off, so they came across as clueless and desolate, which, of course, they were, and that was much better than the truth.

The FBI concentrated on Ramon and Dooley because they both had police records, histories of violence. Ramon had been in the hospital twice recently for injuries sustained in Wildcat so they had that, but no idea who had put him there. I wouldn't be going back anytime soon even though they had Pete's Wicked Ale and the music was starting to grow on me. The FBI went through Dooley's place, Truckee River Apartments, and found Robin in room 304 who didn't know anything, and they spoke to Mira, a more or less homeless girl who "circulated" in the building. They also found that Volker had been audited that year by Soranden's gang, but the IRS had audited over four hundred others in Northern Nevada and Mike's audit had come up clean. A bit of coincidence, but not compelling. Even so, this was not a good time for him to suddenly come up with a hundred thousand dollars, so Ma said she'd hang onto the money for a while.

She told him she'd picked out three banks. He would have to be patient. She was going to wait until at least December or January before he and Lara Rose Donndin opened joint accounts in those banks for a hundred dollars. At that time, she would start giving him endorsed checks and cash, not enough to get the IRS involved. To stash the money safely would take a while. If there was the slightest hint that the FBI was nosing around Kimmi, still looking for a motive other than a dumb kid running around with killers, Volker would have to wait—as long as it took. Ma didn't tell him she was going to get FBI updates from Willie Munson regarding Soranden's murder, but that was the plan. If you had someone in your pocket, you used it, and the more you used it, the deeper they went in.

Volker might eventually get his money back and get away with everything he'd done. But Internal Revenue was a "service" like Schwarzenegger was a terminator, so . . . maybe not.

Time would tell.

* * *

Both Munson and Warley in the Green Room? The place might never be the same.

Okay, Traci Ellis helped. A lot. And O'Roarke, if the truth be known, but I would never tell him that.

"Whatcha drinkin', Mort?" Warley asked.

Before I could answer, Lucy said, "His name is Mr. Angel and he's drinking sarsaparilla, what's it to ya?"

"Thanks, hon," I said.

"De nada."

"I believe we have a bit of business to transact," said Slick Willie Munson. "Perhaps we should adjourn to a table. That is, after I order up a drink." He gave Traci an appreciative look that lingered topside. "Might I have a glass of sherry, miss?"

"*Might* you? Does that mean I can say no?"

O'Roarke sidled over. "Traci, sweetheart. That is not how we speak to our paying customers."

She love-tapped the side of his face and blew him a kiss. "Okey-dokey, ducky."

"Wow," Lucy stage whispered.

Man, what had happened in the ten or twelve days since I'd been in the place? Personal interactions had gone sideways.

O'Roarke gave me a cast-iron squint. "Don't say it."

"Say what? Nothing comes to mind except she's your niece and you're forty-six, she's twenty-five, so that 'ducky' comment and the air kiss will require some thought. But don't worry, I'll get back to you on that."

"She's my niece's roommate, not my niece. I told you that to make sure your hands stay off her since by all accounts that's what your hands tend to do around beautiful women."

"Hey!" Lucy said. "That hands business ended two minutes after he met me and I said I'd marry him."

"Huh?" O'Roarke grunted. "You two're married?"

"Workin' on it," Lucy said. "Paperwork's all done. All he needs to do now is ask and we'll be hitched in under two hours."

I looked at Traci. "What happened to 'Uncle Pat'?"

She shrugged as she gave Munson his sherry. "He told me to say that. The big silly." She gave O'Roarke a quick kiss.

"Wow," Lucy said again.

"Okay, how 'bout you, hon?" Traci said to Warley, which might've been the first time in his life he'd been called "hon" by anyone, including senile grandmothers and great-aunts.

"How about me what?" Warley asked.

She rolled her eyes. "What're you drinking?"

"Oh, I'll take a . . . a screwdriver. Uh, virgin."

She stared at him, then looked over at O'Roarke. "Can't I? Ple-e-e-ease."

"Okay," he said, "go for it," and Traci doubled over behind the bar and whooped with laughter, came up with tears in her eyes and hiccups. "Ohmigod. A virgin screwdriver." She sloshed orange juice into a glass and slid it across the bar. "I sure hope you've got a designated driver, Sport, 'cause I made it a double."

"A double? Hey, thanks."

Never say the IRS doesn't have its sophisticates.

Lucy tried to control her snickers, didn't get them all, then the five of us crowded around a table for four, out of earshot of the bar.

"You brought company, Ma," I said. "Good job."

"Had to. I was about out the door when these two showed up."

"Groovy," Lucy said. She looked at Munson. "Where are your bodyguards, Renner and Bledsoe? Haven't seen them for ages. We really miss those guys."

He smiled. "Outside. They don't need to hear this. Or you," he said to Warley. "But since you're already involved, let's get you involved even further."

"Not sure I like that," Warley said, at which point I upped my estimate of his Stanford-Binet by five points.

Munson gave him the hairy eyeball. "You're head of the IRS in Northern Nevada. Do you want to remain in that capacity or go work a drive-thru at Burger King?"

"Well, yeah. No."

"Then keep this under your hat and maybe you can keep your pension." Munson turned to Ma. "I'm not certain this was worth it, but a deal's a deal and you beat the pants off the FBI and we haven't lost any more agents since that one in Toledo." He handed her a check for twenty-five thousand dollars.

She looked at it, smiled, then fanned herself with it. "Now I can pay that damn phone bill."

"You could've given her that before coming over here and putting a wrench into the feng shui in this place," I said. Which might have been uncharitable and slightly unpolitic, but Munson and Warley still weren't on my Christmas list.

"I needed a break from D.C.," Munson said. "And I haven't heard how you found those two who killed Soranden. I want the 'rest of the story,' as Paul Harvey would say—*if* he were still with us. Newspapers never get it right. Television is worse."

He turned to Warley. "You didn't hear *any* of what you're about to hear. If I find out you did, your pension will bottom out like the *Titanic,* but I want you in this up to your eyeballs, so stick around." He looked at me. "Okay, let's hear it."

Munson didn't believe what he saw on TV? I might have underestimated him. Our country's alphabet media is staffed by fiction writers. Stalin would've been jealous, but Cronkite was undoubtedly spinning in his grave. So I told Munson and Warley how it went down, which took a while with pauses and real-time editing to keep Volker, Jettas, blackmail, and bank robberies out of it. It took long enough that we went through a few more drinks and even Warley ended up glassy-eyed when I told Traci to hit his OJ with vodka. So, of course, he ended up deeper in our pockets, which might be useful in the future.

Finally, I turned to Ma. "Do I get a bonus for the burns, and for removing two-thirds of Dooley's head?"

"I gave you a bonus for that already," Lucy said before Ma could answer. "Six days ago."

"Oh, right. You got a bit rambunctious. Took me two days to recover from that."

"From what?" Warley asked.

Ma and Lucy rolled their eyes. Lot of that going on around good old Warley.

"Don't tell him," I said to Lucy. "He would be forced to kill himself."

"Yeah? What's the downside?"

Everyone laughed except Warley because he was born without a soul. Or a sense of humor, though he does chuckle when elderly widows owe back taxes with interest and penalties.

CHAPTER TWENTY-SEVEN

OCTOBER THIRTIETH, TWO weeks after I'd broken out of the burning cabin, stopped Ramon and Dooley with that rock off the cliff and saved Lucy, she and I went back up Dog Valley Road and turned left onto Three Butte Trail. Not wanting to damage anything of value, we took my Toyota.

"How will we find it?" Lucy asked. "Everything looks so different in the daytime."

"It won't be far from that cliff."

"Oh, right."

"And I think it weighs more than you."

"Groovy."

We went around a switchback and came back north, still gaining elevation. Half a mile later, Lucy pointed ahead.

"Is that the cliff?"

"I'm pretty sure there was only one."

I stopped the car in the middle of the trail just south of the cliff and we got out. All was quiet, not like the insane activity of that mid-October night. Three Butte Trail was four miles to the ashy remains of an old cabin. Or we could take a fork in the trail and go another few miles on the forest service road until it dead-ended.

"You didn't see what happened to it?" Lucy asked.

"Nope. I was distracted. I only saw what it did. But the car would've given it a pretty good hit, knocked it in this direction. It wasn't there that night, so it probably rolled off the road."

We climbed down a three-foot embankment then hunted around in low, wild shrubbery beneath tall pines. Farther to the south, the trail of broken undergrowth made by the Charger was still visible. The Charger itself had been removed. And, of course, Dooley.

"Is this it?" Lucy asked, crouching by a granite rock that was about half boulder.

"Hell, no. No way I could lift that."

"Yeah? Then what's this on it?"

I got down beside her. Bits of glass were embedded in the granite. And a dark stain.

"Glass," I said. "And blood."

"This is it, then."

"Sonofabitch. I lifted that?"

"Must have. Now do it again. That's what we came for."

I got my hands under it, couldn't get it off the ground. Lucy tried to help, but it was too heavy, too awkward.

"Now what?" she asked.

* * *

"Now what" consisted of leaving the rock where it was, no choice, driving back to Reno, considering several options, then ringing the bell at Rufus Booth's house, the dojo entrance.

"Not here for a workout, are you?" he said when he saw me. "Those ribs'll take another week or two to heal right."

"I need some help, if you've got time. Out past Verdi, up in the hills."

He lifted an eyebrow when I told him what we needed.

"Let's go. This I gotta see."

So the three of us went back, and between Rufus and me, we got that big son of a bitch in the back of the Toyota, got it back to my house in Reno, and weighed it.

Lucy read the scale. "Ohmigod. It went all the way around and a bit. Like three hundred and twenty pounds." She looked up at me. "And you lifted it with a cracked rib."

Then she burst into tears.

* * *

It took both Rufus and me some major grunting to get that beautiful boulder on top of the gun safe where it sits to this day, still embedded with glass, still stained, still beautiful.

Our Gumshoe Rock.

The End, except . . .

PS:

Lucy and I were married on the sixth of November. I asked, she screamed, and as she'd planned, we were hitched within two hours. Got 'er done at Golden Bells Wedding Chapel on Fourth Street. Ma was matron of honor, and Day, Officer Day of all people, the Behemoth, who had saved my life earlier that year, was best man because he was at the police station and Russ couldn't be located on such short notice and Lucy wasn't about to wait and go past that two-hour deadline she'd promised me a dozen times in the past four months. Her parents understood but suggested that a second ceremony with a bit of the traditional hoopla would be in order after we returned from the honeymoon, which was a thirty-six-day cruise that began in Hawaii and went to

Tahiti, Pago Pago, Fiji, New Zealand, Australia, Singapore, and ended with four days in Hong Kong.

Her parents paid for it.

No one tried to kill us.

Best damn month of my life.